HUMBUG

David McIlroy

Amber Hill

ALSO BY DAVID MCILROY

The Book of Uland (Young Adult):

The Soulburn Talisman
Empress of Nymm

Horror (Adult):

The Substitute

***

For Mum and Dad.

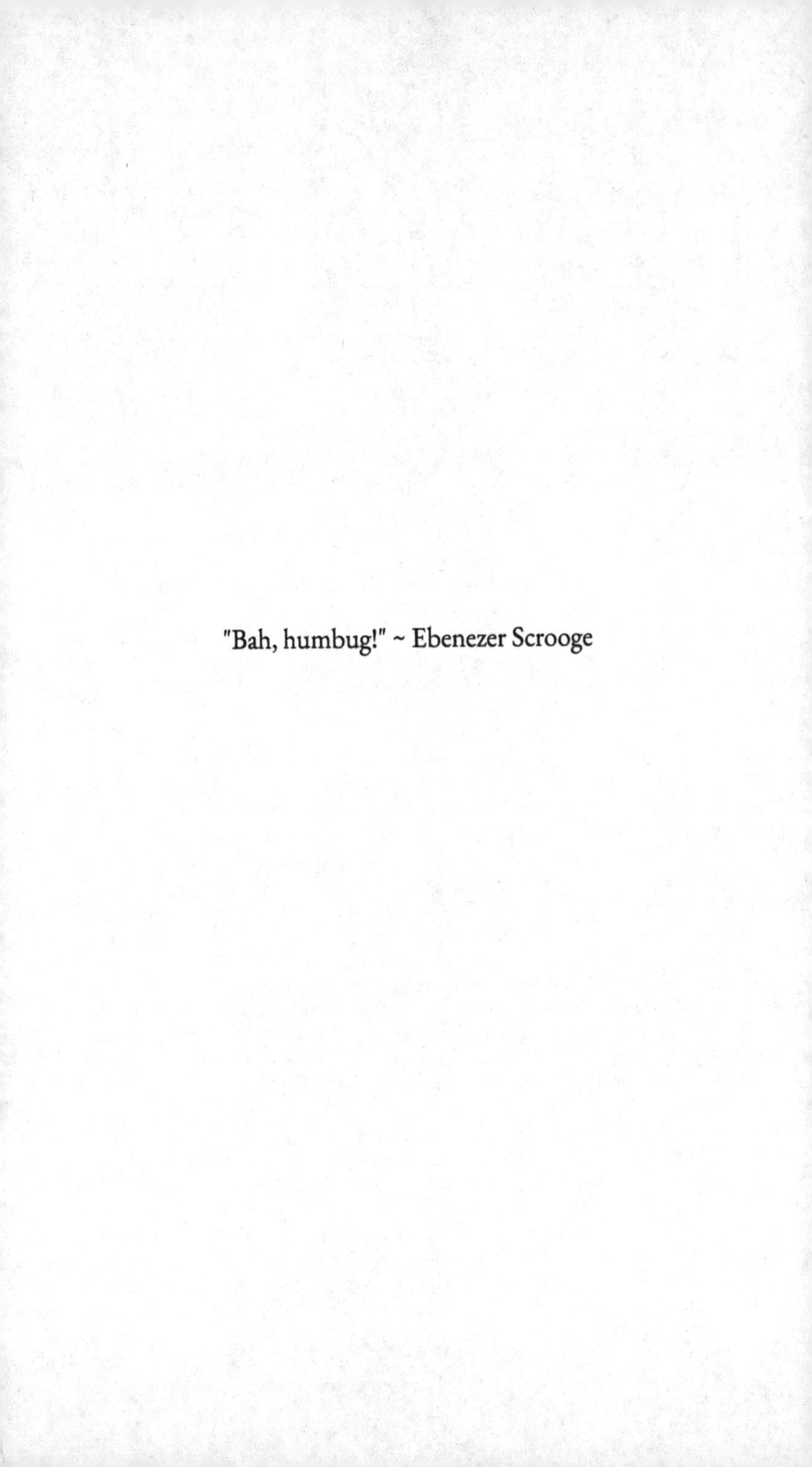

"Bah, humbug!" ~ Ebenezer Scrooge

Part 1: Movie House

House
NATELI HOME

ONE

The credits rolled. Next to Taryn, Jeremy eased back into his seat and said, "The guy out there's lost somebody."

She stretched. "What?"

"The guy in the lobby," said Jeremy. "He's looking for someone called Mary. He asked me if I'd seen her. I think it's his wife."

"Were they the old couple behind us?" said Ash, already on her phone. "Geez, they were annoying. They actually shushed me."

"Well, you *were* talking," Taryn pointed out.

"Yeah, but still. There was *literally* no-one else here."

Taryn grinned, watching Ash scowl in the glow from her screen. Her blue eyes caught the light as they navigated her social feeds. Everything in Ash's life happened *literally*.

"What happened at the end?" said Jeremy.

"If you'd stayed, you'd know," Taryn replied.

"I had to pee."

"For like the third time since it started. Do you have diabetes, Jer?"

"Funny." He pushed his glasses up his nose. "Think there'll be a post-credits scene?"

Ash scowled again on Taryn's right. "It's a horror movie, dumbass. There *are* no post-credits scenes in horror movies."

"Some might have them," Jeremy said.

Taryn watched cast names flash up on the screen as the movie score blared. Jeremy pulled his phone out, too.

"The lights haven't come up," he said. "There *must* be another scene."

"There won't be," said Ash.

"Why haven't the lights come on?" said Taryn, frowning.

She'd been to enough movies to know that by now cinema staff should have brought up the wall and ceiling lights, nudging the audience out of the auditorium so they could clean it before the next showing. House lights only stayed down for movies with post-credits scenes, but as Ash pointed out -

"See?" said the other girl, holding up the Wikipedia page for the movie. "There's nothing at the end."

"Then let's go," said Jeremy, standing again.

Taryn did the same. Next to her, Ash's seat flipped up as she rose. She brushed popcorn kernels off her lap.

"How do I always get so much on me?" she complained. "This skirt is *new*."

In the intermittent light from the credits, Taryn followed Jeremy towards the aisle. She glanced up the auditorium at the rows of empty seats. Apart from the older couple near the back, they'd been the only members of the audience.

"This place is weird when it's empty," muttered Ash, scrolling on her phone as she walked.

Even for a matinee, Taryn agreed.

They descended the steps to floor level, turned the corner past the empty trash bin, and headed for the auditorium exit. Ash stumbled in the dark and swore, but still didn't take her eyes off her phone.

Jeremy pushed open the auditorium double doors and they walked out into the movie theater lobby, blinking in the suddenly-changed light.

"I'll be right back," said Taryn.

"Where're you going?" Ash said, not looking up.

"Bathroom."

"Be quick," said Jeremy, "I'm hungry. Hey, where is everyone?"

Taryn Meyer heard the question as she walked away but didn't register it - she hadn't realized how badly she needed to pee until they stepped out into the lobby, and the situation suddenly felt urgent.

She hurried towards the bathrooms; as she went, the soles of her All Stars squeaked on the floor and she wondered vaguely how she could hear them so clearly. She passed new release posters on the left (*how was Tom Cruise* still *doing those Mission Impossible movies?*) strung with gold and silver tinsel, and doors to the other auditoriums on the right. The screening titles and showtimes displayed in digital red lettering above each entrance. All but one of the screens were active.

The women's bathrooms were at the far end of the lobby in a gaudy, fuschia-painted corner just beyond the doors to Screen Six. There was a yellow "Caution: cleaning in progress" sign standing next to the entrance. Taryn's sneakers squeaked louder as she approached.

I hate peeing when they're being cleaned, she thought, rounding the corner.

But other than a bucket of sudsy gray water next to the hand dryers and a sodden-headed mop lying on the tiled floor, the bathrooms were empty, and she had her pick of the cubicles. As she came out, she lifted the mop and propped it against the wall next to the bucket. She assumed the cleaner would be back for it shortly, wherever they'd gone.

She went to the sink to wash her hands, glancing at herself in the mirror. The ceiling lights in the bathroom were harsh, intensifying the blue in her eyes and throwing every spot and blemish on her face into sharp relief. She'd been engaged in a constant battle with her skin for most of high school, and right now, it was winning the war. To make matters worse, her shoulder-length, tawny-colored hair looked pretty greasy after spending the afternoon under her pom-pom hat, which she'd jammed in Jeremy's baggy coat pocket during the movie.

Should've just stuck a bag over my head instead, she thought. She dried her hands and ruffled her hair out, then left the bathroom.

As soon as she came back into the lobby and saw Ash, she knew something was wrong.

Ash Buckley had been in her year group since kindergarten but they hadn't become real friends until Eighth Grade: they'd been in the locker room after gym class and Becky Wright had asked Taryn if she planned on growing boobs someday, and Ash had asked Becky if she planned on being "a pussy-ugly, buck-toothed pony whore" her entire life, which landed her in detention for a week and gained her a new best friend.

Right now, Ash was tugging on her lower lip - a sure sign she was worried about something.

"What's wrong?" said Taryn.

Ash turned to face her, blinking purple eyelids. She was a few inches shorter than Taryn and had to tilt her head up slightly to meet her gaze.

"There's no-one here."

"Huh?"

"In the whole place. There's no-one else here."

Taryn looked past Ash, squinting down the lobby. Its red walls, illuminated with a soft glow from mounted uplighters, usually gave the movie theater a warm, familiar feel that she liked, and the Christmas fairy lights fixed to the pillars and ceiling only added to that vibe, but right now all the additional festivity only emphasized how quiet and empty the place was. The brightly-lit concession stand halfway down the lobby was unmanned, as far as she could see, and there was no-one at the ticket booth. The Christmas tree positioned opposite the main entrance was a twinkling sentinel in the stillness.

Eerie, Taryn thought, and said, "Where's Jeremy?"

"That guy came back when you went to pee," said Ash. "You know, the one who was looking for his wife? He was, like, really upset, and Jeremy said he'd help him check for her. Did you see anyone in the bathroom?"

"No," said Taryn, thinking about the mop lying on the floor. "It was just me."

"This is weird," Ash said. She looked at her phone, still in her hand. "I've lost signal, too. That literally *never* happens anymore."

At that moment, the door to Screen Five opened and Jeremy emerged, followed by a man in a red-checked shirt and dark slacks. He had gray-white hair and a thick beard of matching color, and he gripped a navy Harrington jacket in one white-knuckled hand. His face was lined with age and worry. Taryn guessed he might be in his late forties, like her dad.

"...just don't understand," he was saying anxiously. "I mean, where've they all gone? Where's *she* gone?"

Jeremy shook his head and said he didn't know for what might have been the dozenth time, and then the man saw them. He came over immediately, staring imploringly at Taryn.

"You were in the bathrooms, right?" he said. "Was she in there? Was *anyone* in there? I mean, I've already checked myself, but there was no-one..."

He trailed off as she shook her head. Taryn thought his face might crumple in on itself. He turned away, his head bowed.

"There's no-one in there," Jeremy said, thumbing behind him. "Or in Screen Six. I checked. All three on this end, empty."

"What about the others?" said Taryn, watching the bearded man pace away from them.

"Same. Mr Bloom... um, Spencer... said he's already checked them, more than once. And the men's toilets. Nothing."

"This is so *weird*," Ash repeated. "Major gloomo depresso."

"Yeah," agreed Jeremy, adjusting his glasses again.

Jeremy Lewis had always had poor eyesight, for as long as Taryn could remember anyway. He'd worn glasses since Elementary School, which was about the time she'd met him, and he was forever repositioning them on the bridge of his nose. His family were town blow-ins from Philadelphia; his father had come for work, intending to move them on before Jer and his sister Katie reached High School, and they'd never left. Taryn liked Jeremy because he was an unashamed dork like her, and she was of the opinion that there weren't enough dorks in the world these days.

"What do you think happened to her?" Taryn said, watching Jeremy watch Spencer, who was across the lobby with his phone to his ear.

"I really don't know," said Jeremy. "He said she went to the bathroom during the movie and didn't come back. He told me he didn't notice the time at first, and when he did it was almost over and she'd been gone for half an hour..."

Across the lobby, Spencer looked at his phone screen and said "Bastard!", and slapped the wall with the flat of his hand.

"... and he hasn't got phone signal, either."

Taryn pulled out her phone. "Me neither."

"I had it during the movie," said Ash. "Maybe there's signal in there."

She went to the door of Screen Four, grabbed the handle, and hesitated. Taryn knew what she was thinking: it was dark in there, even with the movie credits rolling. Ash looked towards her and Taryn shook her head. "Go yourself," she said.

Ash scowled, pulled open the door and went inside. Spencer Bloom slapped the wall again and walked away, heading for the concession stand.

"Should we just leave?" said Taryn. Something was beginning to niggle at the back of her mind, growing more insistent by the second. "I mean, what's the point in staying? The movie's over. We'd leave anyway, right?"

"Right." Jeremy took out his phone, looked at the screen, put it away again. "The next bus should be here in about ten minutes. Once Ash - "

The Screen Four door opened and Ash reappeared. Taryn could tell she'd hurried out of there. The other girl shook her head: *no signal*.

"Ok, let's just go," said Jeremy. "We can wait at the bus stop."

"Good idea," said Taryn.

"What about him?" Ash said, gesturing towards the concession stand. Spencer stood in front of it, looking from the glass-topped counter to the stairs on the right of it, which led to the second floor and three more auditoriums.

"He'll be alright," said Jeremy. "He's an adult."

He started in the direction of the doors and they followed. The main entrance to the movie theater was around the corner, opposite the concession stand and the Christmas tree, which was beginning to feel out of place now in the empty lobby.

As they neared it, Taryn saw Spencer bend over the concession counter, searching behind it for his missing wife. His shirt rode up at the back and she got an eyeful of the top of his buttcrack poking out of his boxer shorts. She looked away quickly and her eyes fell on the podium opposite the entrance, where a cinema employee would scan your ticket and say "Screen Two, that way" or "Screen Eight, right up the stairs", as if you couldn't read the damn signs yourself.

She knew from experience that the podium was always manned, even during showings, just in case someone tried sneaking in for a freebie. There was no-one behind it now, but there *was* a cup of coffee on it. And it was still steaming.

The feeling at the back of her head niggled again, stronger now. She reached back and touched it.

"What the hell?" Ash exclaimed.

Taryn came around the corner and stopped. Ash and Jeremy were just ahead of her, facing the glass entrance doors. On their left, the ticket booth sat vacant.

At least two feet of snow was piled up against the movie theater entrance.

"Where did *that* come from?" Taryn said.

"It was snowing when we got here, right?" said Jeremy.

"Yeah, but barely," Ash said. "There wasn't even any on the ground."

Taryn thought back. When they'd stepped off the bus a few hours ago, there'd been light snowfall over the parking lot outside the movie theater and the mall, dusting the asphalt. There hadn't even been enough to hold a footprint.

"There's, like, a day's worth of snow out there," said Ash, "and it's still coming down."

"It's pretty heavy, too," Jeremy observed.

Ash walked towards the doors and they followed. Outside, beyond the glass, the world was shrouded in flurrying white; they couldn't see the parking lot or the gas station on the far side of it. As Ash stepped onto the rubber sensor mat at the entrance, Taryn braced herself for an icy blast when the doors slid open and snow spilled into the lobby.

But the doors remained shut.

Ash walked right up to them and put her palms on the glass, then drew back quickly. "Holy shit, that's cold!"

Taryn touched the glass too, and also pulled her hand away. It was freezing. Thick, fluffy snowflakes battered noiselessly against the other side of it before tumbling down to join their comrades piled along the bottom. She couldn't make out the vehicles in the parking lot.

"Why aren't they opening?" Ash said.

"I can't see anything out there," said Taryn, squinting.

"Why won't they open?" Ash repeated, panic lacing her voice now. "Are they frozen?" She gripped the inner edges of the doors and tried prying them apart. They didn't budge.

"That's an insane amount of snow," Jeremy said, peering through the glass.

"Why won't they open?" Ash yelled suddenly, causing Taryn to jump. She pounded the glass with her fist, knocking some built-up snow loose. "Why won't they *shitting-well open*?"

"Ash! Stop it," Taryn said, grabbing her friend's arm.

Ash jerked it free and stepped back from the door, breathing hard. Her cheeks were flushed red.

"I don't like this," she said. "I just *don't*. Ho-lee shit, I just want to go home now."

"I know."

"It feels like we're trapped in here. We're - "

"But we aren't, though," Taryn said quickly, taking Ash's arm again. "It's just that the doors are stuck, but we'll get them open. Or there'll be another way out, ok? You need to chill."

Ash looked at her. Taryn saw the fear in her eyes, making them huge.

She'll see it in mine, too.

"Maybe they're broken," suggested Jeremy.

"Ho-lee - "

"Jer!" Taryn snapped.

He glanced their way, saw Ash's face, and shrugged sheepishly. "It's either that or someone's locked them. But why, when we're still in here? Did they forget about us?"

Taryn looked at the empty ticket booth adjacent to the automatic entrance doors. Overhead lights were still on inside, and even from their side of the glass, she could tell the computer monitors were active.

"They didn't forget," she said, her eyes on the digital clock above the ticket clerk's seat. "It's not even four in the afternoon. They're just not here."

"Well *some*body must be," said Ash, turning on the spot. "Isn't there, like, a security guard or something?"

"He'd be over there, right?" said Jeremy, pointing at the podium with the steaming mug.

"Maybe he's checking the rest of the building," Taryn said. "Maybe he's upstairs?"

"Maybe we should break the glass," Ash said, eyeing the fire extinguisher next to the doors.

"Don't bother trying."

Ash yelped. Spencer had reappeared right behind them. The man's face was drawn and haggard.

"There's no shutter, so the glass must be reinforced," he said. "If you threw something heavy at those doors, it'd most likely bounce back and break your face. I saw it happen once. We need someone to open them, or we find another way out.

"If, that is, we even *want* to go out there."

———

Spencer saw the kids' eyes widen at that. On some obscene level, and under very different circumstances, it might have been a little funny.

"What do you mean?" said the taller girl, the one who'd been in the bathroom.

"Why wouldn't we want to go out there?" asked the black boy with the glasses.

Spencer sighed. "I don't know. Maybe I'm overreacting. I probably am..."

"Why can't we go outside?" the shorter girl said earnestly. Her voice was whiny and Spencer thought, *Where the hell are you, Mary?*

"Well, let's think about this for a second," he said, looking at the polished floor rather than the kids. *They can't be more than fifteen years old.* "As I recall, this movie theater was pretty busy when my wife and I arrived earlier. Obviously, the film we saw wasn't so popular, but there are nine screens in this place and almost all of them were running something this afternoon. Some of the auditoriums have more seats than others, but let's say they each have a one hundred-person capacity on average, and even if each was only fifty percent full today, that'd still be almost five hundred people in this movie theater for matinee showings. Maybe less. Probably less. But either way, a lot more people than are standing in this lobby right now."

He looked up and the kids were nodding.

"So the question is, where's everyone gone? And why are we the only people still here?"

The girls looked at each other, but the boy - Jeremy, was it? - held his gaze. "What do you think happened?" he asked in a low voice, "and why would it stop us going outside?"

Spencer Bloom sighed again. He suddenly felt very tired, and the panic he'd been suppressing was beginning to bubble inside him. He had to stay in control now, for Mary's sake - he wouldn't find her if he got himself in a flap.

"Like I said, I don't really know. But I've checked every screen on the ground floor of this theater and they're all empty with movies still rolling, so something made those people get up and leave. Or, they just disappeared."

He saw the shorter girl's face grow paler, a shock of white beneath her jet black hair. She tugged at her lower lip.

"I haven't checked upstairs yet," he added, "but I suspect we'll find the same thing: empty seats, discarded coats, half-full boxes of popcorn. I even found a phone resting on the toilet roll dispenser in the men's bathroom."

"There was a mop on the floor in the women's," said the taller girl, her blue eyes huge. "It was like someone had just dropped it and walked away."

"Ho-lee shit," muttered the shorter girl.

Spencer finished his thought: "I'm concerned about what's outside because, like in this movie house, I didn't see anyone out there. It's snowing heavily, yes - and where the hell did all *that* come from so suddenly? - but there should still be folks walking about out there, going to their cars, going to the mall. Everyone who was inside this building has to have gone *some*where. But if they've all just disappeared, maybe they were... I don't know..."

"Taken?" said Jeremy. The girls stared at him.

"Maybe," said Spencer.

"Taken by what?" the taller girl said.

"Aliens?" the dark-haired girl cried, slapping her palms to her face.

"I was thinking more like terrorists," Spencer replied. He looked at the navy jacket in his hand for a moment, then started to pull it on. "People with guns, herding everyone outside. Or, they were ushered out by staff because of something dangerous inside the building."

"So there's a *bomb* in here?" the dark-haired girl moaned.

"Stop it, Ash," said the taller girl. "There's no bomb."

"How do you know?" said Jeremy.

"Well, if there was a bomb, or if there were terrorists, wouldn't there be police? Or soldiers? There'd be *some*one, any-way."

Spencer nodded, adjusting the jacket collar. "Good point."

"Maybe it was a chemical attack," said Jeremy carefully. "Some gas or toxin in the air. It might have made everyone go crazy, and..."

"...and they ran outside into the snow?" finished Ash. "*That* makes sense."

"More sense than aliens, dumbass," replied Jeremy.

"Aliens are real!"

"Ok, ok," said Spencer, holding up his hands. "Let's assume it wasn't terrorists or aliens, for now. But we don't know what's out there. Personally, I don't like the fact that the doors are locked, or that much snow's fallen in less than two hours. That alone is weird enough. My priority right now is finding Mary, my wife. She went to the bathroom during the movie we were all watching and didn't come back, so whatever happened to everyone else must have happened to her." He swallowed. "We'll just have to hope and pray - "

"We'll check upstairs," Jeremy cut in. "We'll help you find her."

"I'm not going up there," said Ash, looking past the Christmas tree towards the staircase.

"Fine," said Jeremy, annoyed. "Taryn and I will go. You stay here and keep a lookout for aliens."

"Screw you, four-eyes."

"We'll *all* go," said Taryn, the taller girl. "We can check the screens faster that way."

Spencer nodded again, scratching his beard. "Ok, if you're sure. I'll stay here, just in case someone comes back. Be quick. And if you find anyone, holler."

"Will do."

Jeremy and Taryn made for the stairs. Ash hesitated for a second, then scurried after them. Spencer watched them cross the lobby past the Christmas tree and start up the staircase. Their footfalls echoed up the walls, and then they were gone.

He turned back to the entrance and put both hands on his head.

"Mary, where are you?" he breathed.

Two

"I don't like this," said Ash. She grabbed absently for Taryn's arm as they ascended the stairs. "This shit is scary."

"Only because you keep saying it is," said Taryn.

"You're not scared?"

"Kinda. But not as much as you." Taryn was glad Ash didn't have a good view of her face then - she'd have known the truth if she had.

They turned the bend in the stairs, passing more movie posters strung with tinsel, and went up the remaining steps to the second floor. Jeremy led the way; Taryn followed, trailing Ash with her.

The second floor of the movie theater was just as empty as the downstairs lobby. A cardboard cutout from yet another Santa movie had been positioned next to the stairs, facing the three auditoriums on this level. On the far side of the area was another, smaller concession cart and a seating zone with tables and chairs.

"No-one here either," observed Ash. "Let's go."

"Wait, we have to check," said Jeremy. "Look above the doors - all of these screenings are still going."

Taryn saw he was right. The digital displays above each set of auditorium doors showed the title and start time of the movie playing inside. All three had started less than an hour ago.

"Let's take one each," Jeremy said. "We'll just have a quick look inside and then meet back here, alright?"

"Alright," said Taryn.

"Not alright," said Ash. "This is really starting to freak me out, you guys. I don't want to go in there alone, in the dark - "

"It won't be dark, there'll be a movie playing," said Jeremy. "Look, you take Screen Seven, right there. It's an animated Christmas movie, how scary can that be? Taryn can check Eight and I'll take Nine. We'll meet back here in a couple of minutes. Let's go."

With that, Jeremy strode towards the third set of auditorium doors.

"Tar..." Ash started.

"Just go, you baby," said Taryn, pushing Ash towards Screen Seven. She started to protest, then uttered an over-the-top sigh of exasperation and stomped towards the doors. Taryn waited until she'd gone inside before pulling open the doors of Screen Eight.

She went through the inner doors and was immediately hit with a wall of light and sound. The theater often showed older Christmas movies during the holidays, the kind of classics cinema-goers continued to flock to year after year. As Taryn made her way up the slanted aisle towards the screen, John McClane flicked on his lighter in the elevator air duct and muttered something about going out to the coast, and she grinned.

She came around the bottom of the aisle and scanned the auditorium. In the shifting light from the screen, she saw dozens of rows of plush red seats stretching upwards to the back wall; above the last row, the projector fired images through a square hole to the screen opposite. The theater was still old enough to have a projection booth, although the process was now entirely automated and digital.

And of course, the auditorium was empty.

For a moment, Taryn remained next to the bottom row and just stared. It was something she'd never seen before - an entire movie auditorium, completely empty, with the screened movie midway through its run. The strangeness of it struck her then and she shivered. Behind her, long-haired German terrorists were zeroing in on John McClane, who was still hiding in the air duct.

She started up the aisle steps, peering down each row. There were plastic Coca-Cola and Pepsi containers in the cup holders, half-empty buckets of popcorn on the floor (some upright, some tipped over and spilling their contents), even jackets and scarves still draped over neighboring seats. She saw a lady's handbag at the far end of the middle row with the clasp wide open.

What happened here? she thought. *Where* is *everyone?*

The terrorists were shooting now; the auditorium filled with noise and flashing lights.

She came to the top row and looked up at the opening to the projection room on the back wall. From this close, she could hear the faint whir of the machine on the other side, churning out the movie on a timed cycle. But it was still possible there was someone in that room, right? Just because the projector -

A hand closed around her elbow and she screamed.

"What the shit!" Ash cried, stepping back.

"Ash!" Taryn gasped, turning to her. "The hell are you doing in here? You scared the crap out of me!"

"*You* scared *me* screaming like that, you psychopath."

Taryn put a hand to her chest; her heart was hammering under her sweater.

"Did you check the other screen?"

"Yeah," said Ash, waving a hand towards the empty seats. "It's like this. No-one's inside."

"You're sure?"

"Yes, I'm *sure*," Ash said, glowering at her in the flickering light. "I didn't hang around long. It's creepy as hell in there, with the cartoon playing and no-one watching it. And all the stuff people left behind as well. I could have stolen a few phones if I'd wanted to. But I didn't."

"How noble of you, princess."

Ash gave her the finger. Taryn looked past her at the screen, where John McClane had just narrowly avoided discovery by the terrorists. She knew he'd be out of the air duct by the next scene.

"Let's get out of here," she said.

"Fine by me," Ash replied, glancing at the screen. "What movie is this, anyway? Is it new?"

"You've *got* to be kidding me."

They descended the steps and left the auditorium.

Jeremy was over at the seating area when they came out, inspecting a blue Slush Puppie container. He held it up as they approached.

"Still cold," he said. "Whoever was drinking this hasn't been gone long."

"The red ones are better," Ash informed them.

"Your screen empty too?" asked Taryn.

"Yup." He set the cup down, wiping his fingers on his jeans. "Lots of left-behind stuff, just like the others. No sign of Spencer's wife, though."

"Would you know her if you saw her?"

He frowned. "Well, no, but... Ash, what're you doing?"

Taryn followed his gaze. Ash was behind the concession cart in the corner, rummaging around. She came up with a popcorn box in her hands, grinning.

"That's stealing," Taryn said with put-on disapproval.

"So? D'you think all those people who've been abducted by aliens care?"

"It's not aliens," Jeremy muttered. He walked towards the windows overlooking the parking lot below.

"Is it still warm?" asked Taryn, drifting towards Ash.

"Sure is. But get your own, fatty."

Taryn did, helping herself to a handful directly from the heated container behind the cart. She stuffed it in her mouth and Ash giggled. Taryn joined in, spraying popcorn.

"Jeremy, come get some," Ash called through a mouthful, "before Taryn eats it all."

"Hang on," he said. He was by the window now, staring out at the whirling snow.

"There's candy too, Jer," Taryn managed, spraying more popcorn. "They have Milk Duds and Twizzlers, and -"

"Hey," Jeremy said suddenly, palms to the glass. "Hey!"

"What is it?" said Ash, another handful of popcorn halfway to her mouth.

"There's someone out there."

"What?" Taryn said.

"In the parking lot." Jeremy jabbed the glass with his finger. "Down there, in the snow. They're going towards the mall. Look!"

Taryn and Ash dropped their popcorn and hurried over, slaloming between the tables and chairs. Jeremy was still pointing out the window.

"Look," he said again.

They looked. Outside, thick flakes of snow continued to swirl in the air, making it difficult to see much of anything. But Taryn spotted what Jeremy was pointing at right away.

A figure in green crossed the parking lot, heading towards the mall on the right. Everything else beyond the glass was blanketed in white, so it wasn't difficult to make them out as they went, drifting between snow-covered cars, leaving a trail of already-disappearing footprints in their wake.

"Who is that?" said Ash, her face against the glass.

"Is it... a kid?" asked Taryn.

The figure reached the end of the parking lot and started towards the mall entrance. The building loomed over them, huge and brightly illuminated in the rapidly fading afternoon light. Taryn couldn't see anyone else out there, but -

They all jerked away from the glass as someone yelled downstairs. Ash let out a yelp of her own.

"What was that?" she gasped.

"It sounded like Spencer," said Jeremy. "Quick!"

He wheeled away from the windows and darted in the direction of the stairs. Taryn and Ash followed, tripping over each other in their haste to keep up and not be left alone on the second floor of the movie theater.

As they came to the top of the stairs and started down, there was another shout from below. Ash grabbed at Taryn's arm, almost causing her to overbalance. She managed to steady herself just in time with the handrail.

"Watch it, Ash!" she snapped.

"I'm sorry," replied the other girl. "Don't leave me!"

"No-one's leaving anyone."

They came around the bend in the stairs. Jeremy was a few paces ahead of them, taking the steps two at a time. He reached the lobby first and disappeared from view for a second, and for whatever reason, in that moment Taryn felt an electric surge of panic. Jeremy was the same age as her - a month younger, in fact - but he also represented fifty percent of the people she actually knew inside the building and she didn't like losing sight of him, even briefly.

She and Ash reached the lobby and saw Jeremy heading towards the Christmas tree, his footsteps *thwacking* on the floor. He started to go around it, then skidded to a stop. They drew up alongside him, panting, and saw what he was looking at.

Spencer Bloom was bent double next to the security podium, leaning on it with one hand. His other hand was pressed to the back of his head and his face was bright red. He groaned, long and low, and Taryn thought he might faint.

"Sir, I am *so* sorry."

The young man standing next to Spencer wore a black polo shirt and matching baseball cap emblazoned with the words *The Movie House* in yellow text. He was tall and gawky with greasy dark hair down to his shoulders. His left foot was in a plaster cast and he was leaning on a crutch - a second crutch was on the floor by his feet.

"I didn't mean to hit you," he said, stretching his free hand towards Spencer like he was a warm fireplace on a winter's night.

"You didn't *mean* to hit me?" Spencer exclaimed, straightening up. "What the hell were you trying to do then, give me a surprise head massage with that damn crutch?"

"No, sir, not a massage," said the cinema employee. "That's not... my job here..."

"Of course it isn't, you idiot!" Spencer took his hand away from his head and looked at his palm, perhaps expecting to see blood there. "Shit, I thought my skull had caved in."

"Are you alright?" said Taryn.

The cinema employee, who hadn't noticed them before she spoke, let out a little cry of surprise and visibly jumped. His right hand was already up and balled into a fist.

"Who are you?" he demanded, looking wide-eyed from one of them to the other.

"Who are *you*?" Ash replied.

"Um, I *work* here." His tone instantly shifted from apologetic to indignant. He pointed at the yellow logo on his shirt, just to emphasize the point - a name tag pinned above it read *Lincoln*. "I'm the concession stand *assistant manager*."

"Whoop-dee-fuckin-doo," said Ash.

"Enough," snapped Spencer, rubbing his head again. "You said you work here..." He read the name tag, "...Lincoln?"

"Yes. Lincoln Ward."

"And you've been working here today?"

"Since before lunch, sir," said Lincoln, nodding.

"Then, Lincoln, would you mind telling us where in the sweet-shitting world everyone else is right now?"

Lincoln, greasy-haired assistant manager of *The Movie House* concession stand, looked around, and realization slowly dawned on his face.

"Oh..."

"You're damn right, 'oh'," said Spencer.

"There's no-one here."

Jeremy caught Taryn's eye and smirked. Spencer sighed.

"No, there isn't," he said wearily. "Everyone other than myself and the three amigos here are gone, including my wife. Unless...?"

Jeremy shook his head. "They're all empty, just like down here."

"Perfect."

"What's empty?" said Lincoln, frowning. "What do you mean, everyone's gone."

Jeremy handed Lincoln back his other crutch and they spent the next few minutes explaining to him, as best they could, what the situation was, though there really wasn't much to say when it came down to it, beyond "everyone's gone except us and we don't know why" (that was Ash's interpretation, and the others couldn't argue with it). By the time they were done, Lincoln's dull confusion had begun to dissolve into a simmering panic that manifested itself in an incessant tapping of his uninjured right foot on the smooth floor of the lobby. Taryn wondered how he was even doing it without leaning on his left one.

"Ok," he said. *Tap tap tap.* "So... what you're telling me... so what you're saying is..." *Tap tap tap tap.* "Everyone who was here... the staff and, and... everyone..."

"They're all gone," Ash repeated, with an air of boredom.

"It's just us," added Taryn.

"Ok. Ok..."

"Lincoln," said Spencer, grabbing one of his bony shoulders. Lincoln stared at him, his eyebrows working to find the appropriate expression. "I can't find my wife. She was here, in this movie theater, and now she isn't. Almost everyone who was here now *isn't*. I'm really worried, and I'm sure these kids are as well. Can you do anything to help us, son?"

Lincoln continued to stare for a moment until Spencer let go of his shoulder. Then his face brightened.

"Have you tried calling the cops?" he asked hopefully.

"We can't," said Jeremy, "there's no signal, or internet connection. None of us have it, right?"

The others, including Spencer, nodded.

"What about the landline?" said Lincoln Ward, tapping his foot again.

"What landline?" Spencer said.

"You know, the one in the office."

"What's a land line?" Ash asked.

"Lincoln, that's great!" Spencer exclaimed. Lincoln beamed. "A landline should work, even if our cells don't. Can you show me where the office is?"

"Sure," Lincoln said, "it's back this way. And you guys can call me Linc."

Ash snorted. "*Linc?* What kinda dumbass name - " Taryn dug her in the ribs with her elbow. "Hey! What'd you do that for?"

"Take me to the office please, Linc," said Spencer quickly.

"Ok, follow me," Lincoln said. He turned on his good heel and started working his way towards the concession stand, swinging awkwardly on his crutches. Spencer hurried after him, calling back, "You three stay by the door in case someone comes. And don't try breaking the glass."

Taryn watched Lincoln take Spencer through an unmarked door next to the concession stand, and then they were alone again.

"What now?" said Jeremy, looking towards the entrance doors again. The lower half of the glass was now completely frosted over.

"Guess we wait," Taryn said.

"I want to go home," said Ash.

Me too, Taryn thought.

Spencer knew the kid was high the moment he opened his mouth.

He'd been waiting in the movie theater lobby for the three teenagers, muttering to himself about Mary, when Lincoln had come around the Christmas tree; he'd started to turn, said something like "Hey, you", and then the kid had clocked him on the back of the head with one of his aluminum crutches and he'd almost gone down, right then and there. He was glad Mary hadn't been there to see that, at least.

Sure, the kid seemed appalled once he realized what he'd done (*how had he managed to hit him so damn hard without falling over himself?*), but that didn't do much for the lump already forming on Spencer's skull. And when the rambling apology started spilling out of the boy's mouth, he'd known something wasn't right. Everything else he said after that point, and the way in which he reacted to the other kids, only confirmed it. *High as a kite.*

He followed Lincoln through the unmarked door and down a narrow hallway that must have run parallel to Screen Three on the right of it. There were two doors on the left-hand wall: the first was marked 'Staff Toilet' and the second 'Office'. Lincoln went to the second door and pushed it open with his shoulder.

"It's in here," he said.

Spencer followed him inside. The office was actually more of an employee lounge, featuring a faded two-seater couch, a small table with four chairs tucked in under it, and an untidy kitchenette in the far corner. There was, however, a desk to the right of the door, and on the desk next to a very old-looking computer was a cream-colored landline phone.

"Can I get you anything?" ask Lincoln, going across to the kitchenette. "We have coffee."

"Why don't you make yourself a cup?" said Spencer. He motioned towards the phone. "May I?"

"Oh, sure."

Lincoln did indeed head towards the coffee maker. Spencer put his hand on the phone receiver, thought *Please, Lord*, and lifted it from the cradle. He put it to his ear.

There was a dial tone.

A cool wave of relief rushed through him and he punched in 9-1-1. Across the room, Lincoln balanced himself against the kitchenette counter and poured tar-like coffee into a ceramic mug printed with the words 'I wish this was beer'. As the call rang through, Spencer noticed a screen mounted in the corner opposite the desk displaying four images from other parts of the theater - on the bottom left quarter, he could see the kids by the main entrance.

"Is that monitor recorded?" he asked.

"Huh?"

He pointed at the screen; Lincoln followed his finger, clutching the coffee mug in one hand.

"Oh, um... I think so?"

The phone was still ringing. Spencer thought: *No-one's going to pick up*. His stomach began to sink.

"Can you play it back," he said, "on this computer?"

"Maybe?"

Maybe? Fucking stoner -

"Nine-one-one," a woman's voice said in his ear. "What's your emergency?"

"Hi," Spencer replied, and immediately, his mind went blank. What was he supposed to say now? What exactly *was* his emergency? A missing person?

He stared at Lincoln by the kitchenette, slurping coffee from his mug; the kid had managed to get his phone out and was frowning at the screen, no doubt wondering why he had no service.

"Sir?"

"Yes, I'm here. Sorry." Spencer looked down at the desk and saw the corner of a *Sports Illustrated* sticking out from under a half-completed staff schedule. "My emergency is... I'm, uh, locked inside *The Movie House* theater, at the *Outlet Complex*."

"What do you mean, sir?" the dispatcher asked. "How exactly are you locked inside?"

"The, um, the doors are locked," Spencer said. *I sound like an idiot.* "Someone's locked the doors and we can't get out."

"Who - "

"Hang on, that's not why I'm calling. I mean, it's not... I'm calling because my wife's missing. *Everyone* in the movie theater is missing."

There was a pause on the other end of the line. Spencer watched Lincoln scroll on his phone, the coffee in his hand forgotten.

"Sir," said the dispatcher, slower now. "I need to clarify this. Are you inside the movie theater right now?"

"Yes."

"And you're locked inside?"

"Yes."

"And you're saying everyone else is gone?"

"Almost everyone. There're three kids here, and the manager's assistant."

"Assistant manager," Lincoln corrected, without looking up.

"So there's a member of staff there?"

"Yes, but - "

"Is he with you now?"

"Yes, he is, but I don't think he'll be much help."

"Why's that, sir?"

Spencer watched as Lincoln shoved the phone back in his pocket, shaking his head. He looked into his mug and seemed surprised to find coffee there.

"He's a little incapacitated."

"Sir, do you require medical assistance?"

Spencer sighed, running a hand down his face. "No. Well, maybe. Yes. I need the police, first and foremost. Like I said, my wife is missing. Everyone is missing."

"Ok, sir, we'll send someone right away. And you're inside the movie theater at the *Outlet Complex*, just off the highway?"

"Yes," said Spencer. He glanced at the monitor on the wall; the kids were over by the entrance doors now. "Please hurry."

"Of course, sir. Can I take your name?"

"Spencer Bloom. My wife's name is Mary."

"Thank you, sir."

"Tell the officers they might have to find another way in," he added, "because of the snow."

Another pause on the line. "Snow?"

"Yeah. It's really coming down here, like a blizzard. We're snowed in."

He looked at the monitor again and frowned. *What're they doing?*

"Sir," said the dispatcher. There was an edge to her voice now, an uncertainty. "Can I clarify once more that you're calling from *The Movie House* theater at the *Outlet Complex*?"

"That's right."

She hesitated. "Sir, there's no snow in that area today."

Spencer stared at the desk again. He read the names on the schedule: Mandy, Gareth, Jen, Timothy. They were probably all kids, like Lincoln.

"What d'you mean?"

"We're just a few miles away from your location," the dispatcher said, "and I'm looking at a weather report, too. There's no snowfall in your area today."

Spencer swallowed - his mouth had gone dry. "I... don't think that's accurate."

"I'm looking at the weather report right now, sir."

Absently shifting papers across the littered desk, he croaked, "But you'll still send someone?" His eyes fell on a sheet with the words 'Emergency Evacuation Protocol' printed at the top - it'd been tugged halfway out of a tattered red binder covered in doodles.

"Yes, officers will be on the way shortly, Mr Bloom."

"What the hell?" Lincoln said.

Spencer looked up at him, and then at the monitor.

"Oh shit," he said.

He dropped the receiver back in the cradle.

THREE

Taryn swiped through her apps again. None of them seemed to be working, whether they required an internet connection or not - her phone had become a useless chunk of plastic. Still, it was worth checking, just in case.

She closed the last of the apps to preserve battery, paused briefly on the homescreen image of their family dog Rex, then put the phone back in her pocket.

"Nothing?" said Jeremy.

"Nothing," she replied. "Nada."

"Same here," he said, also putting his phone away. "Hope Spencer and Linc are doing better with that landline."

"*Linc*," Ash scoffed again.

Taryn allowed her gaze to drift from the unmarked door next to the concession stand to the Christmas tree in the center of the lobby (it was fake and sparsely decorated), across the plexiglass screen of the ticket booth, and finally to the automatic entrance doors. She watched snow flurry silently against the glass and thought of home, where it'd be warm and safe. She willed herself to be there right now: she wouldn't care if her younger brother Neal bugged her, picking fights over nothing, just to get her attention; she wouldn't care how her parents punished her for bunking off school that day to go see a trashy horror movie with her friends (*hadn't* that *been a great idea in the end?*). She just wanted to get out of the building before that lingering feeling of wrongness at the back of her mind grew any stronger.

What was she so afraid of, anyway?

"Are you *sure* we can't just smash it?" said Ash, joining her by the doors. Taryn hadn't realized she'd been moving steadily closer to the glass - she was just a foot away from it now and her face reflected back at her, distorted by the lobby lights.

"You heard what Spencer said," replied Jeremy, looking anxiously towards the staff door.

"Yeah, but who *is* Spencer anyway?" Ash said. "He's just some random guy we met, like, fifteen minutes ago. For all we know, he could've locked the doors himself."

"That doesn't make any sense," said Taryn.

Ash and Jeremy sounded far away to her. She leaned closer to the glass, squinting out through the falling snow. She could just make out cars in the parking lot, white mounds in the fading afternoon light; beyond the lot, the *Outlet Complex* gas station was barely visible. The lights were still on inside it.

"Why not?" said Ash. "It *does* make sense, actually. Think about it. He goes out during the movie, bumps off his wife, hides the body, and locks the doors. Then he pretends we're all trapped inside together. Soon, he'll start picking us off, one by one. Bet he's already got Linc back there."

"So where's everyone else, genius?" asked Taryn, still staring through the glass.

Weren't there people in the gas station when we got here?

"Duh - he killed them all too." Ash grinned impishly. "Jeremy's next. It's always the one with the glasses who's next."

"Not because I'm black?" Jeremy said.

"Too clichéd. This isn't the eighties, yunno."

Jeremy rolled his eyes. Ash snickered.

"Where did that person go?" Taryn said, almost to herself. "You know, the one we saw from upstairs. Did they go into the mall?"

"Seemed that way," Jeremy said. "Looks like the place is still up and running, too. All the lights are on."

Taryn pressed her face to the glass, straining to see the front of the mall building. It was just beyond her line of sight, but she could see where fallen snow in the parking lot off to the right was colored by artificial light from the mall's bright exterior. She also noticed the streetlights lining the parking lot hadn't come on yet.

"Bet everyone's in the mall," said Ash, tugging her lower lip. "Bet they're just sitting around the food court, all nice and warm, eating ice-cream and fries, waiting for the snow to stop. And we're just standing around here like dicks."

"We can't get *out*, Ash," Jeremy said.

"Um, hello? Doesn't this place have, like, emergency exits?"

"Oh, right," said Jeremy slowly, "why didn't I think - "

Taryn screamed.

The man had come out of nowhere. Her face had still been pressed to the glass when his bloodied hands slammed into it. She met his eyes, wild and crazed, and staggered backwards.

Ash turned at the sound of his hands hitting the glass, saw him, and started screaming too.

"What the hell?" Jeremy cried.

Taryn took another step back. Her left heel caught on her right foot and she sat down hard, smacking her tailbone on the floor. She barely felt it.

The man outside the doors swept snow off the glass, smearing trails of blood on it instead. He stared in at them, open-mouthed. Falling snow gathered on his head and shoulders.

"Taryn," Ash spluttered, "who is that? Who *is that?*"

The bloody-handed man looked directly at Ash, who moaned and stepped further back from the doors. Taryn remained on the floor. Jeremy was somewhere behind them.

Then the man started speaking - yelling, really - and Taryn's blood ran cold.

"Help me!" he cried. His nose was squashed against the glass; Taryn saw snot dribbling from his nostrils. "HELP ME!"

"Taryn," Ash whimpered.

Jeremy appeared between them. Taryn felt his hands close on her arm. She grabbed at him and he hauled her to her feet.

Outside, the man with bloody hands gawked at them. His bulging eyes shifted from Ash to Jeremy, and settled on Taryn.

Not me, the voice in her head protested. *Stop looking at me.*

"Please," the man said. "Please, help me. Let me in!"

He wore gray coveralls, which Taryn now noticed were also stained red with blood in places. His hair was dark and frizzy and thick with snowflakes.

"Let me in," he said again. When none of them moved, his face contorted with desperate panic and he thumped the glass with his fist. "Let me in! Open the doors!"

"What do we do?" said Taryn. The question came out in a low mumble.

"I don't know," Jeremy replied, shakily adjusting his glasses.

"We should leave," said Ash.

"And go where?"

"Anywhere!"

The man hammered the glass with both fists, yelling at them to open the doors. Spittle and mucus sprayed out of him.

"We should get Spencer," said Ash, already starting to turn away.

Suddenly, the man stopped pounding the doors. He twisted round and stared towards the parking lot. He was tensed under the coveralls, like he was readying himself to flee. Taryn could see he was a big guy, well over two hundred pounds. She wondered how he hadn't at least cracked the glass when he slammed into it.

What's he looking at?

"Come on," Ash said, clutching at Taryn's sleeve. "Let's - "

The man spun round again and pressed himself to the glass with a muffled *thump*. Taryn read the fear on his face, the undiluted panic in his eyes.

"Please," he said, insistent but no longer yelling. "Please open the doors."

Taryn swallowed. "We can't," she called back.

Ash dug her nails into her arm. "What're you doing? Don't *talk* to him."

"Why not? Ow!" Taryn jerked her arm away. "He can't get in, can he?"

"Yeah, but still. I know you. If you figured out how to open the doors, you'd be stupid enough to do it."

The bloody-handed man watched their exchange. Taryn wasn't sure how well he could hear them, but he wasn't talking anymore. There were tears in his eyes now.

He's terrified.

"Jer, what do we do?" she said.

Jeremy's mouth opened and closed, fish-like. "I, um... I'm not sure..."

"We're not opening the doors," Ash said. "We're *not*. Don't even think about it, you idiots."

"Ash, shut the hell up," Jeremy snapped.

She did, but flushed with anger.

"Jer, I think he's hurt," said Taryn. "He's got blood on him."

"Might not be his blood," Jeremy said.

"Ho-lee shit," Ash muttered, turning away.

"Who is he?" Taryn said. "Do you think he works here?"

"Gas station," said Jeremy, pointing.

A logo on the left breast of the man's coveralls read *Outlet Fuel Depot*. He saw Jeremy pointing and began nodding furiously.

"Yeah, yeah," he said quickly, "I work right over there. At the gas station. Please, kids - open the fuckin' doors!"

Taryn took a step towards him and called, "Are you hurt?"

The gas station employee frowned. She pointed at his hands, still flat to the freezing glass. "The blood," she said.

He followed her gaze, then shook his head slowly. "Not mine."

"Ok, that's it," Ash cried, throwing up her hands. "Forget it! Where's Spencer?"

Taryn ignored Ash and took another step closer to the doors. Jeremy was by her side.

"Whose?" she said to the man on the other side of the glass.

"Tar..." Ash started.

"Whose blood?" Taryn said, more forceful this time. "Whose blood is that?"

The man hesitated, deliberating. His eyes darted from side to side. Taryn moved closer, close enough to see him grinding his teeth.

"It's... it's, um..." Then, without warning, he cried, "Just open the fuckin' doors, kid! Open them! You gotta let me inside, right now. Come on, please!"

Taryn looked at Jeremy. He shrugged.

The guy saw it and exploded.

"YOU LITTLE COCKSUCKERS!" he screamed. "OPEN THIS FUCKIN' DOOR RIGHT NOW! I SWEAR I'll FUCKIN' SMASH IT IF I HAVE TO, YOU STUPID LITTLE SHITS! OPEN THE - "

He abruptly broke off and pulled back from the glass; he turned to face the parking lot, staring at something through the whirling snow.

Taryn heard him say "Fuck" before he bolted out of view and disappeared.

Silence.

After a moment, Jeremy exhaled and said, "What the hell was that?"

"Where'd he go?" said Ash, moving closer to the doors for the first time since the guy appeared. The glass was still smeared with blood - snowflakes landed on it and stuck.

Taryn felt her knees start to give way. She staggered sideways and grabbed the edge of the ticket booth counter. Her heartbeat pounded in her ears.

"Are you ok?" said Jeremy, coming towards her. He was just as shaken as she was - she didn't have to be his best friend to see that.

"Yeah," she replied, pushing her hair back. "Just... scary, you know?"

"Yeah," he agreed.

"Told you we shouldn't have opened the doors," said Ash.

Jeremy rounded on her and she flinched back, but before he could speak, the door next to the concession stand burst open behind them and Spencer ran into the lobby, followed by Lincoln, who was almost knocked off balance by the door as it swung closed again.

"What happened?" Spencer cried, puffing over to them. "Who was that at the door?"

"How did you know?" said Taryn.

"There's a screen in the office. Who..."

He caught sight of the blood on the glass and trailed off.

"Wow," said Lincoln.

"Are any of you hurt?" Spencer asked tonelessly.

"No, we're fine," replied Jeremy.

"The hell we are!" cried Ash. "Did you *see* that nutjob out there? He could've killed us! He definitely killed someone else, anyway. And Taryn wanted to let him in!"

"No I didn't!" Taryn shot back. "I just... wasn't sure what to do."

"He had blood all over his hands," Jeremy told Spencer. "He said it wasn't his."

"Wow," Lincoln said again.

"Maybe we should have helped him," Jeremy said, glancing at Taryn. "Maybe he was hurt or something. But we weren't really sure if it was... safe."

"It's ok, you did the right thing," said Spencer, still looking past them at the bloody smears on the glass. "The police are on their way now, they can deal with him when they arrive. Besides, the doors are locked - we can't open them."

"Sure we can."

They all looked at Lincoln. He stared back bemusedly. "What?"

"We can *open* them?" Taryn said.

"Yeah, right there." Using his crutch, he pointed at a small gray panel on the wall to the left of the doors. "There's an emergency release button, in case the power goes out. But we've never had to use it before."

Spencer sighed, exasperated.

"We could also go out of one of the emergency exits," Lincoln added.

"I *told* you so!" exclaimed Ash. "Why does no-one ever *listen* to me?"

"It's because you yell everything," said Jeremy.

"I do not!" she yelled.

Spencer put a hand to his forehead. "Kids, please shut up. Just for a second." He closed his eyes, thinking, *Mary, I wish you were here right now*. "Linc, those emergency exits - can they be opened from the outside?"

"Huh?"

"Could someone open them from the outside? And come into the building?"

"Oh. Um, I don't think so." Linc scratched the back of his head, tipping his baseball cap to one side, almost hitting Taryn with his crutch. "I always prop the staff exit open with a brick or something when I go for a smoke out back."

"Is that where you were earlier, when all this happened?" Jeremy asked.

Spencer looked at the kid and thought, *Good question*.

"Yeah. Well, I mean, I was out back for my break - I usually take it outside when every screen's rolling and the concession stand's gone quiet - and I thought I'd light one up. There was plenty of time, you know? Mandy was on duty when I left. She knows what to do, even though she's new. Anyway, I lit one up and, you know, had a smoke. And when I came back in, there was no-one in the office, and I couldn't find Mandy. And then I came into the lobby and you were there - "

He indicated Spencer, who said, "And you hit me over the head."

"Oh yeah, I did. Sorry."

"You didn't notice the snow?" said Taryn.

Lincoln frowned. "Huh. Guess I didn't."

"But it *was* snowing by the time you came back inside?" Jeremy said.

The assistant manager considered the question for a moment. "Yes."

"But not when you went out? Or not much, at least?"

Another long pause. "No."

"I'm troubled by this," said Spencer. He told them about his telephone exchange with the dispatcher, about how there didn't seem to be snowfall anywhere nearby. Jeremy shook his head as he relayed the story - the action made him look far older than Spencer assumed he was. "Something very strange is going on here today, folks. I can only hope Mary didn't get caught up in it, and she's somewhere safe right now."

No-one spoke for several moments. Ash tugged at her lip; Lincoln started tapping his foot on the floor again.

"So what should we do now?" Taryn asked finally. "Just stay here?"

Spencer nodded. "I think so. The police are coming. Best to be here when they arrive."

"What about the guy?" Ash said. "What if he comes back?"

"Even if he does, he can't get inside, according to Mr Ward here. Right?"

Lincoln nodded. "Right."

"So it's safest to stay put for now."

"What about the mall?" said Jeremy. "We saw someone going towards it when we were on the second floor."

"You what?" said Spencer, a little sharply. "What did they look like?"

"It was hard to tell with all the snow," Taryn said. "I think they were wearing a green coat or something. We didn't get a good look, really."

Spencer felt his shoulders slump. *Not Mary.*

"If that person - whoever they were - went to the mall, maybe we should too?" suggested Jeremy. "Maybe that's where everyone went. It might be safer there. There could be security guards there, too. And phone signal."

"I *said* this already," Ash muttered.

Spencer studied the boy. "How old are you, son?"

"Fifteen."

"We all are," added Taryn.

"Fifteen," Spencer repeated. "You're wise beyond your years. I know a lot of adults who'd be hysterical by now in the same situation."

Jeremy Lewis ducked his head, but Spencer saw the beam on his face.

"Should we vote on it?" asked Taryn, arms wrapped around her body.

"We can," said Spencer, "but, um..."

"You'll just overrule us," Taryn finished with a sigh, "because you're the adult here."

"Hey, I'm *also* an adult," Lincoln protested.

"Yeah, and you're *stoned*," said Ash.

A snort of laughter escaped from Spencer before he could stop it - the look of stunned indignation on Lincoln's face had been too much. He shook it off, ashamed. *I shouldn't laugh when Mary's missing*, he thought. Taryn was grinning at him and he avoided her eye.

"Let's vote then," he said. "This is still America, after all. Who votes we go to the mall?"

Jeremy raised his hand. After a second, Taryn did too.

"And who votes we stay here?"

He raised his own hand. Lincoln followed suit, and after a moment's hesitation, Ash did the same.

"Ashley," Taryn said, disapprovingly.

"I don't want to go out there," Ash said. "If you wanna make snow angels with scary bloody-hands man, be my guest."

"I guess that settles it," said Spencer. "We'll stay where we are, for now at least. The cops will be here soon, and then we'll find my wife and get you kids home." He frowned. "Come to think of it, why're you here so early in the day? School's not finished for the holidays yet, is it?"

The kids glanced furtively at each other.

"We took the day off," Jeremy admitted.

"We would've just been watching movies in class, anyway," added Taryn.

"It was Taryn's idea," said Ash.

"It was *not*!" Taryn exclaimed. "*You* wanted to skip it, I just went along with you."

"If I jumped off a bridge, would you do it too?"

"I'd be the one pushing you, princess. Besides, it was Jeremy's idea to go to the movies, not mine."

"Hey, don't blame me - "

Somewhere in the movie theater, a door slammed shut.

"What the shit was that?" Ash yelped, springing to Taryn's side.

Spencer wheeled in the direction of the sound. His eyes darted across the lobby, scanning for movement. Jeremy took a step towards where the sound had come from, down at the Screen One end, and Taryn grabbed his arm.

"Don't," she said firmly.

"Kids," said Spencer, keeping his voice measured. "You definitely didn't see anyone else inside the building, did you?"

Taryn met his gaze and shook her head. Her eyes were flooded with fright.

Spencer turned to his left. "Linc."

"Yeah?" murmured the assistant manager, suddenly sobered. Like the others, he was staring down the now-silent lobby, rooted to the spot.

"The emergency exits can't be opened from the outside, right?"

"Yeah, that's right."

"Is there any other way into the building?"

Lincoln hesitated, then shook his head. "No."

Spencer's heart thumped rhythmically in his chest. He didn't want to ask the next question, because he thought he might already know the answer. "And when you propped open the staff exit to go outside earlier, did you close it properly afterwards?"

Lincoln looked at him. "I... I think so."

"Are you sure?"

A long pause. "Um... no."

"Oh SHIT!" cried Ash, hanging off Taryn's arm. "We're all gonna get eaten by fucking ALIENS!"

"This is bad," said Jeremy.

Spencer turned a full three-sixty where he stood, squinting up both ends of the theater lobby, flipping over the possibilities in his mind as fast as he could.

The door was blown open by the wind.

Another movie-goer, like themselves, had been left behind and was wandering through the building, searching for their loved ones.

The cops had responded remarkably quickly and were looking for them.

The man with the blood-stained hands had gotten inside.

And lastly, filtering maddeningly through them all: *What if it's Mary?*

"What should we do?" asked Taryn, watching him turn like a spinning top.

Of course, they're all looking to me now.

"I think we should leave," said Jeremy, pushing his glasses up his nose.

"No way!" Ash replied. "We can't go out there."

"What if it's the guy?" Taryn said.

"I know, but..." Ash dropped her gaze to the floor; Spencer could see she was on the verge of tears.

"Maybe going to the mall isn't such a bad idea," said Lincoln, already drifting towards the entrance doors.

"Maybe not," said Spencer.

Just then, another door slammed and they all jumped. Spencer felt his heart leap into his throat.

"Ok, let's get the hell out of here," he said quickly.

They went to the doors, unconsciously clumping together. On the other side, the snow had piled up to almost waist-height. The blood was an upturned smile on the glass, bright red against the white beyond it.

"Hurry up, Linc," said Jeremy, pointing at the gray panel above the fire extinguisher.

"What? Oh, yeah. Hang on."

Lincoln stepped up to the panel and leaned against the wall, jingling a set of keys from his pocket. He began fumbling through them, muttering to himself. The wind whistled along the length of the building outside.

"Linc..." said Jeremy.

"Almost got it."

"Linc, hurry the hell up!" whined Ash, dragging Taryn closer to the glass.

"Stop rushing me!" Linc snapped. Then: "Ah! Got it."

He jammed a tiny key into the lock on the panel and twisted it. The panel swung open, revealing a red handlebar lever inside. Instructions had been taped to the inside of the panel door on now-yellowed paper.

Lincoln grabbed the lever and cranked it down. There was a muffled *thunk* sound and the sliding doors parted, but only by a couple of inches. Snow tumbled inside and dropped to the floor around Ash's boots.

"Why're they not opening right?" she said, releasing Taryn's arm.

"The snow's compacted against them," said Spencer. "It's pinning them in place - they would have opened all the way otherwise. Come on."

He stepped forward and took hold of one of the doors. The metal was freezing against his skin. Ash and Taryn grabbed the other one.

"Ready?" he said. They nodded. "Ok - one, two, three."

He heaved on his door and they did the same. The doors resisted for a second or two, then scraped open. They all pulled until a gap of at least two feet had appeared, then let go. Snow blew through the space, eager to fill the lobby. The doors stayed put.

"Alright," said Spencer, zipping up his jacket. The others did the same, tugging their outer layers tighter around them. Linc rubbed his bare arms, clacking his crutches together. "It's going to be real cold out there so we have to move quickly. Straight across to the mall and inside, ok? Don't stop for any reason, even if you see the police. Or someone you know."

He added the last part for himself as much as for them. They all nodded.

They're all looking to me now, he thought again, and for whatever reason, the acknowledgment of it emboldened him.

"Jeremy," he said, "is that extinguisher heavy?"

Jeremy turned, following Spencer's gaze towards the red can in the corner. He lifted it off the hook; it was one of the smaller ones, about the size of a large soda bottle.

"It's not heavy," said the boy.

He handed it to Spencer, who tested the weight. It was light enough to carry easily, but hard enough to knock out an attacker, if it came down to it. Just having it in his hands made him feel a little easier.

"What's that for?" said Ash.

Spencer knocked on the metal casing with his knuckles. "Just a precaution."

The girl frowned, then seemed to understand.

"Ok," Spencer said, "I'll go first. Everyone stick close, and don't stop until we're inside the mall. Let's go."

Taking a deep breath, he stepped through the gap.

FOUR

Taryn's feet sank deeper into freshly-fallen snow with every step; her All Stars were already soaked through. Why hadn't she worn boots that morning?

Because it wasn't snowing at all when I left home, she thought. *And it was barely snowing here when we arrived.*

Behind her, Jeremy stumbled and grabbed onto Ash for balance.

"Hey! Watch it," she cried, almost falling herself.

"Sorry," replied Jeremy. "It's deeper than it looks."

"Just keep moving," Spencer called back, his voice almost lost in the wind and whipping snowflakes.

They were halfway between the movie theater and the mall, tramping along the edge of what had once been the parking lot. Every car in the lot was now mostly buried in white; here and there, flashes of metal and glass were still visible, but there was no getting any of those vehicles out while the snow continued to fall.

Spencer led the line, clutching the little fire extinguisher in his hands like a shiny red club. Taryn wondered if he'd ever hit someone before, with anything. He was a big enough guy, but there was an academic, almost teacher-ish air to him that suggested he may not be much use in a straight fight. At least she knew that Lincoln - who made slow progress at the back of the line on his crutches and plaster-encased foot - could hit someone if he had to, though that someone had been Spencer, and he'd suckered him from behind with a metal stick.

We *might have to protect* them, she thought.

Jeremy stumbled again, and this time Ash was out of reach. He stuck out his hands to stop himself and his arms disappeared up to the elbows.

"You ok?" Taryn called.

"Yeah," Jeremy said. His glasses dangled by one leg from his ear.

"You oughta watch your step, man," Lincoln advised, looking on as Jeremy hauled himself up. He was trying, and failing, to keep his injured foot out of the snow.

"Yeah, thanks."

"Wait here a second," Spencer called, and abruptly walked off into the parking lot.

"Hey!" Taryn cried. "Where're you going?"

He didn't reply. Seconds later, he disappeared between the snow mounds.

"Well, that's just great," said Ash, hugging herself. "He did exactly what he told us not to do. *Just* like an adult. Now what?"

"Guess we wait," Taryn said, sweeping her eyes across the parking lot.

When Ash had suggested ditching school for the day - and it *had* been her idea, no matter what she said - Taryn had agreed without much thought. Even Jeremy, who'd never missed a day of school in his life, hadn't resisted too much. It was three days before Christmas and their teachers had all but given up trying to make them work. No-one would take particular interest in their absence from a school day filled with movie-watching and half-hearted personal study sessions. They wouldn't be the only ones skipping, and if (or, more likely, *when*) they were caught out, there were only so many punishment options available so close to the festive break, when there were more important things going on: Taryn's parents were set to host Christmas dinner for the whole family this year and they'd need her help, so she couldn't be confined to her room in the days preceding it. And after all, it'd be Christmas - parents couldn't ground their kids over the holidays, right?

She'd waited until homeroom and her two morning classes were done, and then slipped away with Ash and Jeremy during break. The bus from Rockmount took around thirty minutes to reach the *Outlet Complex* (there'd been hardly anyone on it) and it'd been plain sailing from there. No-one had clocked their absence from school, not even their classmates - by midday, the students and teachers of Rockmount High would be lost in a fog of apathy while Will Ferrell skipped around New York City in yellow tights and a pointed hat on the classroom TV screen.

The complex had been busy when they stepped off the bus, which wasn't unusual for the time of year: it was a late nineties build composed of a gas station, a nine-screen cinema, and a two-tiered shopping mall boasting thirty stores and eating places, ready to serve the good people of Illinois passing by on the highway; the gas station, movie theater and mall bordered the outdoor parking lot on three sides, with a turnoff road running along the far end that filtered vehicles in and out of the complex, and mothers and fathers were making the most of their child-free daytime hours to grab last-minute presents - on December twenty-fifth, these would be passed off as gifts from the North Pole, delivered with a smile by the jolly man in red. The outdoor parking lot was at least half full as Taryn, Ash and Jeremy passed; a digital sign at the complex entrance assured arriving shoppers that there was no need to panic, the underground lot still had dozens of free spaces, please veer left to enter and have a nice day.

Jeremy had been eager to head straight to the theater for the earlier showing of the R-rated *Jingle Hell Rock* ("it's got seventeen percent on Rotten Tomatoes, we *have* to see it!" he'd exclaimed earlier that week - Jeremy was weird that way when it came to movies), but Ash had wanted a milkshake first, so that's what had happened. They'd made their way to *Shakey Bakey* in the food court, dosed up on sugar, watched with amusement as desperate parents rushed from store to store in search of *that* elusive toy in their kid's letter to Santa, and then headed back outside to the movie theater. There'd been a little fluttering of snow by then, but not enough to get excited about. Taryn hadn't even bothered putting her hat back on.

And now, as she scanned the mounds of snow in the parking lot that'd formerly been cars, she could still hardly believe what was happening.

"Does anyone see him?" Ash said. Her black hair was dusted with snow - she'd forgotten to pull her hood up.

"Who? The old dude?" Lincoln replied.

"His name's Spencer," said Taryn, "and yeah, him. But if you see a guy with blood all over his hands, point him out too."

"Gotcha," said Lincoln.

"It's freezing out here," Ash said, rocking from foot to foot. "Can we just go inside?"

"We shouldn't leave without him," said Jeremy.

"Why not? He left us, didn't he?"

Jeremy didn't respond. He had a hand above his eyes, shielding them from the last remaining shafts of sunlight. Taryn noticed for the first time since leaving the movie theater that it was almost dark, and an icy shiver trickled down her spine. She looked across at the mall, brightly lit against the navy sky beyond.

There'll be people in there. Security guards. More adults.

"Was that car there earlier?" Jeremy said.

She followed his gaze towards the gas station. Even with its internal lights on, it was barely visible in the snow. She couldn't see the car Jeremy was referring to.

"It's under the canopy," he said, as if reading her thoughts. "An SUV, I think. I don't remember it being there when we came out of the movie."

"Maybe it's the police," said Ash.

"In an SUV?"

"Hey, there's the old dude," said Lincoln.

Spencer had appeared from between the snow-impounded cars, trudging towards them. He shook his head as he approached, muttering to himself.

"What is it?" Taryn called through the wind.

"My car," he said, stepping back onto the sidewalk. "It's still there. Mary had the keys and she hasn't taken it. I hoped it'd be gone."

"You don't have your own set?" asked Jeremy.

"Not with me, no. We never need both, we're usually together." Spencer used his free hand to shake snow out of his hair, rougher than was necessary. "Even if I'd had them, I don't think I could've gotten the car out. She's packed in on all sides."

"Sucks," said Jeremy.

"Sucks indeed. Anyway, let's get out of this snow before we all freeze. It'll be warm inside the mall, at least."

"I have a car," said Lincoln.

They all looked at him, standing there in his polo shirt with snow piling on the brim of his baseball cap, shivering.

"You have a car?" said Spencer. "Here?"

"Didn't your *mom* drive you to work?" Ash added.

"No, assface," Lincoln replied, glaring at her. "I drove here myself. I *can* drive, you know. I'm almost twenty-four."

"*And* you're the concession stand assistant manager."

"Yeah. Wait, what - "

"You have a car, and you drove it here today?" said Spencer, "with a broken foot?"

"Yeah," Lincoln said sheepishly. "I, um... needed to be here. My boss said so. And it's not a bad break, really. Don't tell anyone."

"Who would we tell?" Ash said.

"Where's the car?" asked Taryn.

"Round back." Lincoln thumbed towards the movie theater and almost lost his balance. "We're not supposed to park there but the boss said I could, on account of my foot. Think it's the least he could do since he made me come in today."

Ash opened her mouth again but Spencer cut her off with, "You've got a car, that's all we need to know. If we need to leave here, we can. I can drive if necessary. You have your keys, right Linc?"

Lincoln thought about it, patted his pocket, and nodded.

"Good. Then come on."

Spencer started towards the mall again, holding the fire extinguisher by the operating levers on top. Taryn imagined its metal body must be freezing by now. She followed, throwing a quick glance back at the movie theater, where a warm glow spilled out from the lobby onto the compacted snow at the building entrance. There should be people in that lobby right now, buying tickets, waiting in line for candy and popcorn;

there should be kids, tugging on their parents' hands, buzzing with excitement. But the theater remained silent and unmoving in the late December twilight.

Where is *everyone?* she thought again. This time, the thought was followed by another voice, which came unbidden from some dark recess in her mind, and whispered, *they're all dead.*

Taryn hugged herself and hurried after the others.

The weather seemed to somehow worsen in the brief period it took them to walk the perimeter of the parking lot, and by the time they reached the mall entrance, the wind had risen from a low whine to a high-pitched howl, whipping snow into their faces. Ash walked with her arms crossed over her mouth and nose, cursing incomprehensibly against her sleeves.

Spencer stopped suddenly a few yards from the main doors and Jeremy blundered into him from behind.

"Sorry," he called over the wind.

"What's wrong?" said Taryn, looking left and right, half-expecting to see the man with bloody hands appear through the blizzarding white.

Spencer pointed at the ground. "Look."

Taryn squinted, not quite sure what she was supposed to see. Like the front exterior of *The Movie House*, the mall was brightly illuminated and inviting; colorful posters encased in glass paneling announced clothing discount sales, late store opening hours for Christmas shoppers, a new triple-stacked burger at *The Hunger Buster* in the food court, and a last chance to meet ol' Saint Nick and his elfen helpers at Santa's Grotto. A handful of sad-looking Christmas trees still remained stacked in a mesh bin to the right ("Half-price! Grab a festive bargain now!") and the lights on a kids' coin-operated rocket ride to the left continued to blink.

Both the trees and the ride were dusted with snow, as were the outdoor trash cans and benches, but none were covered as much as Taryn might have expected. In fact, most of the area directly in front of the mall entrance doors had largely escaped the bulk of the snowfall, whereas the exterior walls beyond it now supported ever-growing drifts. She looked up at the glass canopy above them - it was heavy with snow and she understood - and when she dropped her gaze to the thin layer of snow on the ground again, she saw what Spencer was pointing at.

There were footprints, dozens of them.

And they all led into the mall.

"I think we may have found our missing people," Spencer said. Taryn heard the faint note of hope in his voice.

"There're so many," said Ash, staring at the ground.

"Did *everyone* go in?" Jeremy said. He turned, looking back towards the movie theater, and then across to the gas station. "It looks like they came from all directions."

"I don't get it," said Taryn, frowning. She could see small footprints among those of the adults. "Why didn't they just stay where they were?"

"Um, can we go inside now?" said Lincoln, still shivering.

"Yes, please," Ash added, in a rare moment of agreement.

Like the movie theater, the mall entrance featured glass sliding doors below a rolled-up shutter; *un*like the movie theater, these doors slid apart easily as they approached. Warm, thermostat-controlled air gusted out at them and Ash sighed with relief, spreading her arms wide.

"Don't let your guard down," said Spencer, taking the lead again. "We still don't know what's going on here."

They walked inside (Lincoln caught his injured foot on the threshold and almost went down), leaving the cold behind. Taryn's fingertips began to prickle as her blood started to warm again. The doors slid closed with a *swoosh*.

"It's so quiet," Jeremy commented after a few seconds. "I've never heard this place so quiet before."

"Keep your eyes open," Spencer said, still clutching the fire extinguisher.

Taryn listened. Jeremy was right - the mall, normally humming with activity, was almost entirely silent. The only sounds she could hear as they walked along the entrance corridor were their footfalls on the tile floor and the low hum of the AC. Earlier, when they'd come for milkshakes before the movie, the ceiling-mounted speakers had been belting out corny Christmas songs to get shoppers in the festive spirit (and to get them to part with more of their holiday cash) - now, they'd gone quiet, though Taryn imagined she could hear a very faint crackle of static as they passed beneath them.

Up ahead, the corridor branched right at a pair of wall-embedded ATMs and then turned immediately left again, opening into the main concourse of the mall. Taryn strained, but still couldn't hear anything above the clapping of their footsteps. No voices. No people.

Ash skidded, almost overbalancing. "Shit, the floor's wet!"

"Melted snow, from the others who came this way," said Spencer. Taryn caught a waver of tension in his voice now. "Watch your step. The last thing we need is you falling and breaking your ankle."

"That's not the last thing we need," Ash said. They turned right, to where a line of vending machines welcomed shoppers into the mall proper; Taryn saw a woman's handbag lying on the floor next to one of them. "The last thing we need is for that guy with the bloody hands to come back, that's what. *That's* the last thing we need. Then we'd be right in the shit. If that psycho appeared..."

They turned left into the concourse and she trailed off.

None of them spoke.

The *Outlet Complex Mall* was essentially one long unit housing thirty different stores split over two levels. A double set of escalators to the left of the concourse entrance ferried shoppers between each floor; a staircase and elevator at the far end also provided access to the second floor, as well as to the underground parking lot beneath the main building.

The bottom level of the mall mostly featured stores selling clothing, shoes, jewelry, beauty products, gifts and souvenirs; the upper level was for electrical goods, specialized items (Taryn and Jeremy were particularly fond of *Larry's* comic book store) and the food court. Whatever you needed, the mall at the *Outlet Complex* more than likely had it - if they didn't, you best keep on rollin'.

Normally the mall concourse was a bustling hive of activity, even on quieter weekdays, but in the run-up to Christmas, the place was positively zoo-like: red-faced mothers dragged screaming, red-faced toddlers away from toy stores, audibly vowing to never bring them anywhere again; fathers who'd left their gift-buying until the last minute (as usual) hurried about in a daze, searching in vain for the things their wives had been hinting about all year; teenagers slunk from store to store in packs, snickering and posturing and intimidating the few older folks who'd unwisely decided to shop so close to the holidays. Everyone was in a rush, everyone was in someone else's way, and almost everyone just wanted to get the hell out of there as fast as possible.

That's what the mall was normally like three days before Christmas.

Right now, it was completely empty.

"What... the actual... fuck," whispered Ash, staring wide-eyed across the expanse of the concourse ahead of them.

Taryn stared too, but her eyes were drawn to one thing in particular.

Halfway down the ground floor of the concourse was an enormous knee-level fountain, the bottom of which was littered with pennies and nickels from years of wishing passers-by. It was where a boy first held Taryn's hand on her first real date, a date that ended less than an hour later after he made a fumbling attempt to squeeze her butt in front of his friends; he hadn't been granted a second date, so naturally, he told everyone she was a lesbian. Taryn had been more selective about boys after that.

Just beyond the fountain was the thing that caught her eye. It was something she'd walked right past earlier on the way to the food court and hadn't even noticed. Back then, she hadn't taken the time to notice very much.

It was a small building composed of cardboard sections made to look like lumber, with a fake chimney and fake painted windows on either side of a red door hung with a festive wreath. There was fake snow on the roof and more on the path leading to the door. Instead of trees, the garden featured giant candy canes, and the whole area was bordered by a white picket fence strung with fairy lights. A sign propped on a stand next to the little garden gate read 'Santa's Grotto', and in that moment Taryn realized why she hadn't noticed it before - at the time, it had been surrounded on all sides by children and their parents, waiting their turn.

"Taryn."

She blinked. *How long had she been staring at it?*

Ash nudged her again. "Hey."

Taryn broke away and looked at her friend's upturned face. "You ok?"

"Yeah," Taryn said. "I just... there's something..."

Just then, the trash bin Lincoln had been leaning against toppled over with a crash, spilling its contents across the floor. Spencer jumped and dropped the fire extinguisher, which clanged at his feet. The abrupt sounds shattered the silence and echoed around the concourse. Ash let out a brief shriek of surprise, right in Taryn's ear. She winced.

"Dammit, Linc," snapped Spencer, flustered. "Are you trying to give me a heart attack?"

"Sorry guys," Lincoln mumbled.

Spencer sighed, then turned back to the concourse and put his hands on his hips. He looked like a man surveying a lawn he was about to mow. After a few seconds, he said, "Well, it looks like this place is empty, too."

"It can't be," said Jeremy. "All those footprints out there - where'd they all go?"

"Beats me," Spencer replied, now stroking his beard.

"Beats me, too," Lincoln chimed in, eager to participate after startling everyone.

"There's gotta be *someone* here," Ash said. "This place is huge."

"We should search it," suggested Taryn.

"You first," said Ash.

"No, she's right," said Jeremy. "We need to check it out. Those people have to be here somewhere, right? And your wife" - he gestured to Spencer - "could be here, too. We should try to find her."

Spencer nodded, still stroking his beard. Taryn could see that his jaw was set beneath it. She also realized they were all speaking in low voices now, as if afraid to disturb the settling silence again.

"Ok, but let's walk the length of it first," Spencer said. He pointed towards the elevators and stairwell at the other end of the concourse. "We'll go as far as there, see what we can see, and then we can decide what to do next. Keep your eyes open and watch your step."

"He means you, trash-tipper," Ash said to Lincoln, who made a face back at her.

They started forward, moving shoulder-to-shoulder. Spencer left the fire extinguisher behind, apparently deciding he no longer needed it.

All the lights were still on in the concourse, as well as in the stores that lined it on both sides. The store doors were all propped open, too, ready to receive customers. Brightly-colored Christmas trees with stacks of fake wrapped presents beneath them stood sentry next to pillars supporting the second floor balcony on either side; the pillars themselves had gold-white fairy lights running up and down them, and artificial garlands had been woven between the posts of the balcony railing above. In fact, almost every surface within the mall had a Christmas decoration pinned or tied onto it. Nothing about the scene was suggestive of anything planned or premeditated, and certainly not of anything sinister. The mall had simply been abandoned.

Taryn was glad to have Jeremy and Ash on either side of her. Jeremy was smart and sensible, and Ash would be the first to scream at the slightest hint of trouble. She desperately wanted to grab hold of their hands, but refrained in the presence of these two relative strangers.

Strangers, she thought. *We're alone in this massive building with two strangers - what a weird situation.*

And why does it feel like someone was just here, moments before we arrived?

Their footfalls weren't quite as loud now - they were all taking more care with their steps. The wet rubber soles of Lincoln's crutches squeaked on the floor each time he swung his body forward. Outside, wind whistled around the walls and across the roof of the mall, causing the building to groan.

It knows we're here, Taryn thought, and quickly shook it away. She spotted a child's backpack resting on a bench. There was snow on it.

"Did you hear that?" Ash whispered.

"What, the wind?" Taryn said.

"No, not that..."

"I hear it too," said Jeremy.

They all listened. At first, Taryn wasn't sure what they were talking about. And then she did hear it, and the hair on the back of her neck stood up.

Music. Christmas music.

"Where's that coming from?" Lincoln said.

They kept going, and the music steadily grew clearer. Taryn looked into the stores as they passed, trying to pinpoint the source, but they were all silent. She caught a glimpse of two stuffed shopping bags in a boutique clothing place, discarded by the counter. Every store was empty.

"This is uber creepy," said Ash.

"Geez," muttered Jeremy. He stooped down and came up with a child's doll. It had bright orange hair and rosy cheek circles stitched to its fabric face. He held it up to Taryn and Ash.

"Get that fucking thing away from me," said Ash. Jeremy tossed it aside.

"The music's getting louder," Taryn noted.

"It is," Spencer agreed, scanning the area. They were just a few yards from the fountain, almost halfway along the concourse. He looked up towards the second level, which circled the ground floor, overlooking it like a balcony. Above both levels, the roof came to a point that ran along the center of the concourse; skylight windows set into the ceiling were caked with snow. "I wonder where it's coming from."

"Shouldn't the police be here by now?" said Jeremy, glancing back the way they'd come.

"It hasn't been that long," said Spencer, "and if that blizzard gets any worse, they might struggle to get into the complex. We're safer inside. We can wait."

"Hey," said Lincoln, "there's snow on me."

"What?"

"Yeah - look."

Lincoln held out one of his skinny arms. Taryn saw there was indeed snow on it. As she watched, a few more flakes settled onto the black shoulder of his polo shirt.

"Where's that coming from?" she said.

They all looked up at the ceiling, searching. Then Jeremy pointed. "There."

"What's that?" Ash said.

Taryn squinted - one of the ceiling lights was going right in her eye - but she was just able to make out what Jeremy had spotted. There was a hole in the ceiling between two of the skylights on the left side of the roof point, not too far away from where they now stood. Snowflakes drifted through it and floated down into the concourse. As they watched, a gust of wind *whooshed* past outside and sent a little clump of snow tumbling off the ragged edge of the hole.

"Wonder what did that," Jeremy said.

"Whatever it was, it must have hit the roof with some force to punch straight through like that," replied Spencer.

"Maybe it was, like, a rocket, or something," said Ash. "Maybe that's why everyone left."

"A rocket?" Jeremy repeated incredulously. "So where is it now?"

"Oh, I don't know, Jer. Maybe it flew up your ass, along with the stick."

"Shut up, guys," said Taryn, annoyed and embarrassed. Spencer and Lincoln were staring at them. *We're acting like little children.* "You're not helping."

"Wasn't trying," muttered Ash.

"It probably wasn't a rocket," said Spencer, and Taryn was surprised to see the beginnings of a grin at the corner of his mouth. "But whatever it was, it doesn't seem to be here now. Maybe part of the roof just gave way because of the snow. This place is falling apart, after all."

"That's comforting," said Ash.

"Has anyone tried their phones lately?" asked Jeremy.

"Oh, of course!" said Spencer, reaching into his pocket.

The others did the same, except for Taryn. She hadn't fully registered Jeremy's question because she'd spotted something up ahead. Something on the other side of the fountain.

"Shit, I still don't have any service," said Ash. "What the hell's going on today... Tar, what're you doing?"

"Hang on," she replied.

She hadn't realized she was walking. She was already at the fountain and going around it.

"Taryn?" said Jeremy.

The water feature in the center of the fountain was switched off. Snowflakes from the hole in the ceiling floated down and settled into the water, disappearing instantly. The Christmas music continued to grow louder as Taryn came around the rim of the fountain. She was dimly aware the others were following her.

"Taryn, what is it?" Jeremy called.

She came round to the far side of the fountain and stopped. She stared at the thing on the rim, frowning. Her brain wasn't quite able to compute what she saw.

Ash came up beside her. "Taryn, what're you... HOLY FUCK ME!"

Taryn jumped, startled back to consciousness by Ash's shriek. She gasped and clapped a hand to her mouth.

"Oh, wow," Lincoln said, joining them. He leaned towards the rim of the fountain on his crutches, peering down at the red thing lying there. "Is that real?"

"Is that an *ear*?" Jeremy exclaimed.

"That's a motherfucking ear," Ash wheezed. She turned away and bent double, holding her stomach.

Spencer stared down at it. His hand went involuntarily to his beard.

"Why is there an ear there?" said Taryn, muffled behind her hand.

"Where's the rest of him?" Lincoln said, reaching for it.

"Don't touch it!" cried Spencer. Lincoln withdrew his hand. "Nobody touch it."

"Wasn't planning to," said Jeremy.

Taryn felt her knees begin to shudder. She stared at the ear, not quite believing what her eyes were showing her. It lay in a small pool of congealed blood like a little fleshy boat.

"Do you think it was... the guy?" Jeremy said, adjusting his glasses with a shaky hand. "You know, from the movie theater? Is that why his hands were all covered in blood?"

Ash moaned behind him, still bent over.

"I don't know," said Spencer. His face had gone a shade paler. "But I'm not sure I want to stick around and find out."

"Me neither," said Taryn.

"I think we should go," Jeremy said. "Back outside. Anywhere."

"Yes," said Spencer. He abruptly began looking around again, as though he'd just heard something. "Back outside. We can go to the gas station if we have to."

"The hell are we waiting for?" Ash managed.

As one, they retreated back around the fountain in the direction of the main entrance. Taryn heard the Christmas music swell briefly, then die down.

Echoes from their footsteps seemed louder than before. They hurried back down the concourse without speaking. Spencer, older and in worse shape than the rest of them, was panting by the time they reached the toppled trash bin.

Taryn could feel her heart pounding in her chest. She was scared now. Really scared. It wasn't hard to tell that the others were, too. Even Ash had fallen silent.

That was an ear, she thought. *A person's ear. Just lying there.* And then: *someone cut it off.*

Her stomach churned. She pressed a hand to her midriff.

"When we get outside," Spencer said, breathing hard, "we'll go straight to the gas station. Not the movie theater. There might be another landline there. The police should be here soon, but we can call them again. Just keep your heads down and stay close, it could be bad out there now."

Leaving the concourse they turned right, passing the vending machines. Again, Taryn noticed the woman's handbag on the floor.

They turned left into the entrance corridor, and one after another, slowed to a stop.

"Umm..." said Ash.

Taryn stared.

The shutter was down.

"Was that there when we came in?" said Lincoln.

"No, it wasn't," Spencer replied quietly.

"Shit," breathed Jeremy.

Taryn gazed down the corridor at the shutter. It was one of those mesh grill types, so they could see through to the snow-blanketed parking lot outside. Thick white flakes swept through the gaps and battered the glass of the sliding doors.

Even from distance, they could see the heavy-duty padlock clamping the shutter to the floor.

"Who?" Taryn heard herself say in a small voice. "Who... who locked it?"

"I don't know," said Spencer. "But they're in here with us."

Part II: Mall

FIVE

"D id you see that?"

"See what?"

"*That*. In the sky."

Adam bent low over the steering wheel and peered upwards.

"I don't see anything."

On his right, Olivia sighed and folded her arms. "Well, it's gone now."

"What was it?" said Adam.

"I don't know."

"Was it a bird?"

"No."

"Was it a plane?"

"Shut up, Adam."

He grinned. He could tell she was glaring at him.

"Seriously, what was it?"

"I said I don't know. Some sort of streak, like lightning. Only straight."

"Could've been a meteor?" he suggested.

"Meteor*ite*," she corrected prissily. "Meteors don't survive the atmosphere. Meteorites do."

"Ok, so at least we can agree it definitely wasn't a meteor, then."

"Adam." She closed her eyes and put a hand to her forehead, which signaled it was time for him to stop.

He glanced up at the rearview mirror. "What do you think, Em? Was that a meteorite in the sky just now?"

From her booster chair in the back seat, Emma Price met his gaze and said, "Yeah."

"Yeah? It was?"

"Yeah."

"Do you know what a meteorite is, girl?"

Emma looked out the car window. "Yeah."

Adam grinned again. Next to him, Olivia shifted in her seat.

"Don't call her 'girl' like that," she said.

"Why? She *is* a girl."

"It's demeaning. Like you're talking down to her."

Adam opened his mouth, and with some effort, closed it again.

Olivia had been in a bad mood all day, pretty much since they left Madison. She'd already been quieter than usual when they pulled out of the drive that morning, hardly responding to any smalltalk he fired her way, and by the time they crossed the Wisconsin-Illinois state line, she was downright irritable. She'd cheered up a little when they stopped for an early lunch at that roadside diner south of Bloomington, but that respite hadn't lasted long, especially when Em started complaining she felt sick and Adam had to take the journey a little easier, delaying their eventual arrival in St Louis even more.

He wasn't surprised when she asked if they could "skip" Rockmount a few miles back, and he'd chosen not to argue.

There was no point. Besides, his parents hadn't lived there in years and the place no longer held much sentimental value for him. He hadn't called that pokey little country town home himself since he'd left for college at eighteen.

In the back, Em said, "Mommy, I need to pee."

Olivia twisted round in her seat. "Can you hold it, baby? We're not too far away now."

Adam saw Em squirm in the rear view mirror. He knew what the answer would be.

"No, need to pee now."

Olivia sighed and turned back.

"Is there a gas station or something round here?"

"We passed one a while back," he replied. "But there might be another one coming up soon."

"You know she can't hold it for long."

"I know, Liv."

"And we're on the highway, so she can't go beside the road again."

"Affirmative."

Olivia sighed again, becoming exasperated now.

Adam ignored it for the moment, keeping his eyes on the road. There'd be a gas station soon. They'd get Em sorted, and maybe grab themselves a snack while they were there. He glanced at the fuel gauge - they were ok in that regard, but if the gas was cheap at the next station, maybe -

"Mommy," said Em.

"Adam," said Olivia.

"I know, I know. I'm looking for somewhere."

Now he was starting to get annoyed, too. This always happened during the holidays, didn't it? Every year in the run-up, they talked about how it'd be different this time, about how they wouldn't bicker about every little thing, but it was always the same. They both thought - especially him - that when Em came along it would get easier, but it hadn't. Her presence had changed things, for sure, but it hadn't made things easier. Just different. Hard in different ways.

Breaking news: having kids doesn't solve all your problems, folks. Spread the word.

"Mommy," Em said again, a little more insistent now. At three-and-a-half years old, she already sounded a little like her mother. "Mom-*mee*."

"It's ok, baby," Olivia called into the rear view mirror. "Just hold it a little longer, alright?"

"I *can't*."

"You can, sweetie. You've done it before." Next to him, Olivia lowered her voice. "Find somewhere, Adam."

"I'm trying, Liv." He pressed his foot down harder on the accelerator. "I can't just... hey, wait. Look!"

An arrow-shaped sign flashed by on the right - it read 'The Outlet Complex, 1 mile'.

"The *Outlet*, of course," Adam said, lightly slapping his forehead. "I forgot that place was round here. There're restrooms in the mall."

"You hear that, Em?" Olivia called cheerily. "There're toilets just up ahead, ok?"

"Ok."

"You hold it 'til then and I'll get you a treat, alright?"

"Alright," Em repeated, brightening at that.

Olivia's tone dropped again. "Hurry, Adam."

"I'm hurrying, honey," he replied, watching for the exit.

Neither of them noticed the first snowflake light on the top corner of the windshield. It was gone in an instant.

When Adam had agreed to bypass Rockmount earlier that day, Olivia had been relieved, and not so secretly, either. She'd long since given up pretending to like the place. Adam had taken her there twice before, and on both occasions she hadn't enjoyed the experience. Rockmount, Illinois, was one of those little backwater towns where everyone knew everyone else, like one big, weird family, and if someone showed up who you *didn't* know, well, that just wouldn't do, would it? Strangers were liable to get stared at in Rockmount, even if they were dating, engaged or married to former residents of the town.

She knew Adam wasn't especially fond of it either now that his parents had moved out of state, but she suspected that if they'd stopped off there, even for a short time, someone would have stumbled across him while moseying down the street and one of those "Hey, you remember such-and-such?" type conversations would have begun, and their brief stop off would have turned into an hour-long nostalgia session about nothing in particular. Olivia was born and raised in Milwaukee - small-town smalltalk made her uncomfortable, and it'd frustrated her to see Adam slip back into that mold each time they were there. He was better than that.

She glanced up from the news report on her phone (another group of skiers had died during an avalanche on the French Alps) and noticed Adam was grinding his teeth again. He always did that when he was nervous. She found many of her husband's quirks endearing, or had at least learned to tolerate them, but the teeth grinding thing really creamed her corn. She went back to her phone and said, "Stop grinding your teeth, hon."

He grunted in reply. She couldn't tell if he'd stopped or not.

Adam Price, with his wavy chestnut hair and turquoise eyes, was the kind of guy everyone liked. Whether you ran into him in Rockmount or Madison or St Louis, or wherever you might be in the continental United States, you'd be mighty glad you did; he was a funny, charming extrovert who rarely forgot a name

Hey, you remember such-and-such?

I sure do - isn't she married to such-and-such?

and could make you feel like he was your best pal in the whole damn world with an easy flash of his pearly whites and a quick slap on the shoulder. Olivia loved that about him, mostly because she knew for a fact that *she* was his best pal and had been since they first met back in college; girls had been falling over themselves to get him (and he knew it), but in the end he'd chosen her, the one woman who didn't immediately roll out the red carpet the moment he opened his charisma-filled mouth. She knew he was funny, but she made him work for her laughter; she knew he was smart and ambitious and would one day be rich, but she didn't allow herself to be bowled over by it. It drove him nuts that she wasn't easily impressed and he ran himself into the floor chasing her, and when she finally let him catch her, the payoff was sweeter than either of them ever expected.

She knew Adam's choosing her had royally pissed off the gaggle of college girls sniffing after him, and not just because she hadn't joined their transparent, sycophantic hunting party. She was smarter than them, and she was more independent, but most pertinent of all was what she *wasn't*, and that was white. In their eyes, Adam Price was the ideal trophy boyfriend and future trophy husband, a man who'd please their wealthy fathers with their "traditional" views on who their daughters should and shouldn't mix with, and he'd overlooked them all in favor of the reserved, bookish girl with Mumbai-born parents. There'd been a few bitter sophomores at Northwestern that year, yes sir.

Adam wasn't the sort to hang about, either. They'd gotten engaged towards the end of their senior year, married two years after that, and had Emma four years later; they each had stable, well-paying jobs in their respective fields (she was in biotech and it was industrial engineering for him), felt settled in Wisconsin (Adam had been keen to stay in Illinois, but she'd won out in the end), and still loved each other as much as they had when they first met. If you bumped into the Price family in the street, you'd be forgiven for thinking everything was A-ok.

But something had been niggling at Olivia recently, some ugly worm that'd buried itself deep inside her, and she knew it was eating at Adam too. Em's arrival had done little to placate it, nor had the hours and hours of couples therapy they'd forced themselves to sit through. In truth, it often didn't feel like a *big* thing, and sometimes it didn't feel like it was there at all. But when they were tired or stressed, or Em was acting up, or either of them had had a bad day at work, the thing reared its head and reminded them that it was, in fact, very much still there.

Today was one of those days. Olivia had been mad at Adam since that morning (in truth, she'd been mad at him since long before then) when he'd rushed her out the door. He was anxious to get going as soon as possible, just in case there was traffic or the weather turned, and then his parents would get anxious too, and she was "making them late *yet again*", wasn't she? That was when the fight had started, hours ago, simmering carefully below the surface where Em couldn't see. Olivia hated that, how Adam was so easygoing and infectiously jovial with everyone else and reserved that nit-picky, pedantic side of his personality just for her. No-one else ever saw it, and no-one else believed her when -

"What the hell?" Adam said.

"Adam!" she snapped, throwing a glare at him. *Why did he always swear in front of Em? Didn't he know by now that she picked up on that sort've thing?*

He didn't see the glare. He wasn't looking at her.

"Adam? What is it?"

Then she followed his gaze and she saw, and she almost swore herself.

"It just came out of nowhere," Adam said.

Snow. Thick, white, swirling snow. They were driving into a blizzard.

Adam bumped the wipers up a notch; they whipped across the windshield but the snow fell faster than they could clear it.

"What happened?" said Olivia, peering out at it. "Where are we? Have we gone the wrong way?"

"Well, a snowstorm wasn't on the map, if that's what you mean."

She ignored it. "Do you know where we are?"

He leaned nearer the windshield; in the back, Em declared, "Snow!"

"I came off the highway and it just started. Like I said, it came out of nowhere. There was a little flurry and then boom - this."

"Mommy, snow!" Em said, pointing out her window.

"Yeah, sweetie, and lots of it," Olivia replied. "Isn't it pretty?"

"Pretty," Em agreed. "Can we make a snowman?"

"Maybe." *At least she's not talking about peeing, for now.* "Adam, where's this mall?"

"It should be right around here," he said, still leaning towards the windshield. She didn't like how he was doing that, like he couldn't see the road properly. As a matter of fact, she couldn't even see the road anymore herself. There was nothing ahead of them but white, with more white falling on it.

"Adam..."

"Relax, Liv-baby. We must nearly be there, unless the damn place has moved or... wait, there it is! You see it?"

She squinted through the falling snow and battling wipers. At first, she wasn't sure what Adam was seeing. But then it appeared, a collection of huge dark shapes looming out of the blizzard to the left of the road, barely visible in the snowfall. They passed a sign, lit from below, which read *Welcome to the Outlet Complex*. An arrow directed them to bear right, and Adam flicked on his blinker.

"We'll be inside in no time," he announced cheerily, easing onto the turnoff.

"Just take it slow," said Olivia, watching the Volvo eat up the snow-covered turnoff lane, too fast for her liking. She noticed there were no tire tracks ahead of them. "This place is definitely open, right?"

"Just a few days before Christmas? Gotta be."

Even so, she heard a trace of doubt creep into his voice and the Volvo slowed slightly.

The turnoff lane fed them towards a large parking lot lined with unlit streetlights. The lot itself was full of cars, and almost all of them were buried in snow. Off to the right was a long, windowless building emblazoned with *The Movie House* in glowing neon yellow lettering; the glass entrance area below the sign was also lit up, though it was almost impossible to see inside from so far away.

"Wow," Adam said softly. "It's bigger than I remember."

Up ahead, the one-way road circling the parking lot passed a gas station on the left, positioned across from the movie theater. It, too, was lit up and appeared to be open, but Olivia couldn't see any activity in the forecourt. Still, at least it was *open*.

Then she saw the mall itself, directly ahead of them. It was enormous, stretching across their view, with the last glimmers of navy-purple twilight framing its bulk. Like the movie theater, most of the front of the building was windowless brick partially disguised behind sidewalk-potted trees and illuminated with dual rows of blue lighting near the top and bottom of the wall; an all-glass section featuring the words *The Outlet Mall* in glowing white-blue lettering ran down the middle of the facade to double entrance doors, all bright and welcoming in the December chill. Drifts of snow were already piled against the front of the building - only the entrance area, shielded by a canopy, wasn't completely covered in white.

"Where is everyone?" said Olivia.

"Mommy, look at the snow!" Em said happily.

"Let's stop here," Adam said.

He turned off onto the gas station forecourt, slowing to a crawl. The Volvo was handling the snow pretty well so far, but Olivia knew that one misjudgement could see them sliding into a fuel pump, and wouldn't that be a great way to kick off the holidays?

Her phone was still in her hand, forgotten for the last few minutes. She unlocked the screen and immediately saw she had no signal. Not just service, or a data connection. No signal of any kind.

What the hell?

"Adam," she said, flicking through her apps just to make sure. "There's no signal here."

"What?" he replied absently, easing to a stop beneath the forecourt canopy. An old brown sedan sat empty by the pump to their left, nearest the store doors.

"My phone," she said. "I can't get signal."

Adam shifted into park, then lifted his phone from the holder below the radio. She watched him swipe through his screen. A frown furrowed his brow.

"Huh," he said.

"No signal?"

"None."

"Why is that? Because of the snow? Does that happen?"

"I've no idea." He ran his fingers through his hair. "Well, there'll be WiFi in the mall, we're probably just out of range here. Anyway, that's not why we stopped in the first place - "

"Mommy," said Em.

"That's why," said Adam.

Olivia looked past him towards the gas station store. "Are there restrooms in there?"

"There might be. The ones in the mall are probably better though. Especially for Em."

"Yeah, I don't like the idea of going in there."

"Alright, your majesty," Adam said, smirking. "Let me check if they have any, first."

He switched off the engine and unbuckled his belt. Olivia watched him, suddenly anxious and unsure of why she should be.

It slipped out: "Be careful."

He looked at her and his smirk widened, but there was no unkindness in it. He reached across and squeezed her knee.

"You don't have to worry." Then, to Em: "Take care of Mommy, ok?"

"Ok, Daddy."

Adam opened his door and a blast of cold air swept into the car. Olivia heard him swear under his breath. She shivered and automatically reached back for Em, but then Adam was outside, his boots crunching in the thin layer of snow on the forecourt, and he slammed the door closed again.

"Mommy, can we play in the snow?" Em asked.

"Maybe in a little while, baby," Olivia replied, craning her neck to watch Adam. She saw him tug his jacket tighter as he strode towards the gas station store.

"Please, Mommy."

Olivia unbuckled her seatbelt and turned to face her daughter. She took both of Em's little hands in one of her own. They weren't as warm as she'd have liked.

She needs her mittens.

"If we have time to play, baby, we will." She watched Em watching the snow fall a few feet away beyond the cover of the canopy, and her heart swelled.

Em, with her taupe brown curls and big hazel eyes, all cozied up in her favorite pink sweater and light-up sneakers; Em, already so patient and sweet, who loved the outdoors and animals, and the taste of honeycomb in anything, no matter what it was. Olivia squeezed Em's hands. *Maybe we'll get some honeycomb ice-cream in St Louis tomorrow.*

"Are you cold, sweetie?" she asked.

"No. I need to pee."

"I know, we'll get you to a bathroom very soon. Daddy's just checking this place first."

"Ok."

Olivia looked back at the store. The brown sedan partially blocked her view of it, but she caught a glimpse of Adam leaning over the counter.

What's he doing?

"Mom."

"One second, sweetie."

In the gas station store, Adam moved away from the counter, out of sight.

"Mommy."

"Hang on, Em."

"Mommy, there's a man."

Olivia turned sharply. "What?"

Em put her finger to the glass. "There's a man."

"Where?"

"Out there. He's got red gloves on."

Olivia peered through the snow towards the parking lot. Her heart, swollen with love for her daughter moments before, was now tight and thumping. She couldn't see anything.

"Where is he, sweetie? Where is the man?"

Em lowered her hand. "Don't know. He's gone."

Olivia continued to stare at the snow mounds in the parking lot, but she saw no movement. No red gloves, no color of any kind. On the far side of the lot, warm light spilled from the glass entrance of the movie theater like a beacon.

Suddenly, the driver's side door opened and Olivia jumped. Em saw it and giggled.

Adam stooped his head inside and said, "Howdy, ladies."

"You scared me, Adam," Olivia said. *Wasn't her heart racing now?*

"Sorry, hon. I'm like a ninja in the snow." He winked at Em and she giggled again. "There's a bathroom inside."

"Is it clean?" Olivia said.

"About as clean as a gas station bathroom can be."

Olivia's nose wrinkled involuntarily. Adam rolled his eyes. "Hon, come on..."

"Maybe we should wait to use the ones in the mall."

Adam looked past her. "Em, can you hold it?"

"Nuh-uh."

"Ok, then let's go. Everybody out."

Still screwing up her nose, Olivia opened her door and swung a leg out. Instantly, the December chill bit right through her jeans and into her skin.

"Holy shit, it's cold," she gasped.

"What, hon?" Adam called.

"Nothing. Come help me."

She opened the rear passenger door as Adam came around to her side, and between them, they got Em bundled up in her blue wool beanie and mittens. She protested when her coat came out, but only for a moment or two - as soon as Adam lifted her from the car, the sight of the snow (*so* much *snow*, Olivia thought) mollified her into silence.

"You got her?" Olivia said, tucking Em's beanie around her little ears.

"Sure do," Adam replied. "You coming?"

"I'm not staying here by myself."

Adam hoisted Em onto his right arm and started towards the gas station store. Olivia locked the car, threw another nervous glance towards the parking lot, and hurried after them.

A man with red gloves on? Who the hell was that, and where is he now?

Her boots skidded on the forecourt as she followed Adam and Em. Only a little snow had managed to settle under the canopy, but it was enough to hold Adam's footprints in sharp relief. There were no tire tracks behind the sedan and no footprints around the driver's side door. As they passed it, Olivia glanced through the rear window and saw a double-barrelled shotgun in the back seat, half-concealed under a sleeping bag. She shook her head and walked on.

Adam shouldered the gas station door open and held it there. Olivia slipped by him, hands tucked under her armpits.

"It's freezing out there," she said.

"Yup. Not much warmer in here, either."

Olivia scanned the interior of the store and frowned. "Adam..."

"I know," he said. "Something weird's going on."

The store was empty. There was no-one behind the counter on the left, no-one perusing the aisles to the right. No-one was in line to pay for gas, or a pack of cigarettes, or a can of Red Bull. And yet, all the lights were on, and Billy Joel continued crooning *Just The Way You Are* through the corner-mounted speakers, unperturbed by the lack of audience.

"Well, I guess this tracks with what's going on out there," Olivia said, motioning behind her. "No-one in the parking lot, no-one going in or out of the mall, that I've seen anyway. What do you think's happening here?"

"I really don't know," Adam said. He lowered Em to the floor; her sneakers flashed as her soles touched the tiles. "There's no-one at the counter - clearly - but whoever *was* there left their phone behind. And all the pumps are on, so anyone could just waltz in and fill 'er up."

"Maybe the staff are on a break?"

"And all the customers, too?"

"Daddy," said Em, tugging on Adam's hand.

"I'll take her," he said, tipping his tall frame to the right so Em could lead him. "You keep an eye out, ok?"

"For what?" said Olivia.

"Who knows? More meteorites, maybe?"

He grinned and followed Em towards the rear of the store. A sign on the door in the back corner read 'Public Restroom: Please request access from staff'. Olivia looked from it to the counter, and back to Adam again - he held up a set of keys in his left hand and jingled them.

That's what he was grabbing from behind the counter.

"Be quick," she called.

Adam and Em disappeared into the restroom. Olivia heard the lock click over Billy Joel, who'd now moved on to a rousing rendition of *Piano Man*. Her father had liked that one, hadn't he?

She turned on the spot, surveying the interior of the store. It looked just like the hundreds of other gas station stores she'd been inside over the years: chaotically-arranged aisles displayed everything from USB chargers and novelty air fresheners to canned peas and beef jerky; refrigerators on the far wall stocked bottled water, fruit juice and energy drinks, and a coffee machine in the corner opposite the restrooms hummed invitingly, though Olivia no longer touched the stuff, especially whatever mysterious liquid currently occupied that thing.

Her phone was back in her hand, retrieved from her pocket through muscle memory alone - the act of taking it out had become an unconscious one.

She unlocked her screen (the image of Adam and Em building sand castles on Bradford Beach vanished instantly) and began swiping through her apps, but she still had no signal, no data, no WiFi connection. Nothing.

Maybe inside the mall?

She glanced at it through the storefront window and something caught her eye, a flash of color through the snowfall. Someone in green, near the mall entrance.

Em's voice: *he's got red gloves on*.

She took a step closer to the glass, squinting. There'd definitely been someone there, right? Someone in green, going into the mall? Were they wearing red gloves?

I didn't tell Adam, she thought.

Just then, the toilet flushed in the restroom.

Olivia turned away from the windows. Suddenly and completely, all she wanted to do was get out of the gas station and leave the *Outlet Complex*. She wanted to get back on the highway, out of the snow, and motor on down to St Louis, where Adam's parents would meet them at the door with beaming smiles and mulled wine. They'd sweep Em into their arms and ask how the trip down was, and Olivia would tell them about the snowstorm, about how strange it'd been when they found the gas station empty, and about how Adam had readily agreed to drive them the hell away from there as soon as possible.

The restroom door swung open. Em marched out, once again leading Adam by the hand.

"All done?" Olivia asked both of them.

"I peed everywhere!" Em announced.

Adam nodded gravely. "There wasn't much toilet paper in there, either."

Olivia smiled and took Em's hand, just as she reached for a bag of Skittles on the nearest shelf.

"Adam, I think we should go. Right now."

"Yeah, we will." He set the restroom keys back on the counter.

"Seriously. I don't want to stay here anymore."

"Ok, ok," he said, holding up his hands. "We'll go, right now. Besides, we've done what we came here to do, Little Miss is happy..."

"Please?" asked Em, pointing at the Skittles. Olivia shook her head.

"...and we've got no reason to stay. So let's hit the road."

"Thanks," Olivia said. "Catch, stud."

She tossed him the car keys and led Em to the door. There was a little tug of resistance on her hand (*tantrum incoming*) but she kept Little Miss moving. Adam held the door open for them and they walked back out into the cold.

"I think it's easing up," Adam said, unlocking the car. The Volvo's blinkers flashed.

"A little," replied Olivia, guiding Em across the forecourt. It'd be easier to carry her but she needed to stretch her legs. They still had over a hundred miles to go and she'd likely get cranky fast, especially when she realized they were leaving the snow behind.

The weather people hadn't forecast a white Christmas for St Louis.

Maybe we should toss a few snowballs before leaving, just to keep her happy.

Adam went round the back of the car and opened the door for them. Olivia bent to scoop up Em.

"I can do it," Adam said.

"It's alright, I've got it," she replied, slipping her hands under Em's arms. She lifted her into the car, thinking *Gosh, she's getting heavy* and placed her back in the booster seat.

As she clipped Em in (she was already mumbling about the snow - her big question was coming, wasn't it?), Adam took her by the waist and said, "Everything ok?"

"Yeah, I'm ok," Olivia said. "Actually, there's something. Em thought she saw someone out there, in the parking lot. A man. She said he was wearing red gloves."

"Gloves?"

"That's what she said." Olivia adjusted Em's seatbelt straps. "And then when you were in the bathroom, I thought I saw someone too."

"The man with red gloves?" He'd released her waist and was scanning the parking lot, like an intrepid explorer in the arctic.

"I'm not sure, I think they were in green. I didn't see any red gloves, but there's a lot of snow. Whoever it was went into the mall."

Adam took a step in that direction, shielding his face from the falling snow that made it under the canopy. Olivia made a half-move after him, then turned back to the car.

"I can't see anyone," he said. "There's no-one out there, hon."

"Adam."

"What?"

"The car."

He turned back and looked where she was pointing.

"Oh shit," he said.

Olivia pushed the car door closed.

"Oh *shit*," Adam said again, hands going to his head. "How in the hell did that happen?"

"Adam, don't. Not in front of her."

"But how did this *happen*?"

He stared in disbelief. Both of the Volvo's right-side tires were flat.

Not just flat. *Slashed*.

"Liv," he said, "what happened here? Did you see anyone near the car?"

"No," she replied, shaking her head. Her dark hair spilled over her face and she pushed it aside. "No-one near the car. Just that person over by the mall."

"Was it them?" Adam asked. He could feel his blood starting to boil. *She wasn't watching the car. She was probably on her phone, even though there's no signal. She can't stop herself.* "Do you think it was them, Liv?"

"I... I don't think so. They weren't nearby. I don't know." She shook her head again, cupping her cheeks in her hands. "What do we do, Adam?"

He bit back the anger. "Fuck me, I don't know."

Two tires. We might have been ok with one, but two?

Em banged the window with her little hand. Olivia went to her and said, "It's ok, baby. Just wait a sec, alright?", smiling and nodding. Em banged it again, leaving her palm against the glass.

Adam crouched by the car. He ran his hand over the front tire, tracing the jagged three-inch tear with his fingers. The thing must have gone flat almost instantly.

Fuck me, he thought, *who did this?*

"It's ok, Em," Olivia was saying. He could hear the tremor in her voice, the fear. "We won't be long, sweetie."

Adam straightened up and his knees cracked. *I've been sitting behind that wheel for too long today.* He gripped the back of his neck with one hand and put the other on his hip, looking from tire to tire. What the hell were they going to do about this?

Olivia started to open Em's door.

"What're you doing?" he said sharply.

"She's scared, Adam," Olivia said, looking back at him. Her light brown eyes were wide and swimming with alarm.

"It's too cold for her," he said, and immediately thought *it's too cold for all of us out here*. "Leave her in the car. You get back in, too."

"Why?" Olivia said, closing the door again. "What're you going to do?"

"I need to go get help, don't I?"

"No, Adam." Panic rising in her voice now. "No, stay here with us."

"Liv, I can't just sit here and wait. In case you haven't noticed, we seem to be the only people in this whole damn place. That is, apart from whoever slashed our shitting tires with what must've been a pretty *big fucking knife*."

He saw her lips press tight, a sign she was suppressing tears. She wouldn't cry, though. He knew she'd swallow them down instead.

"I have to go, hon," he said, forcing his tone to soften. "I have to get help. We're stuck here with only one spare tire and no phone signal, and it's still snowing. I need to find someone."

She held his gaze for a moment, reading him. Then she nodded. "Ok. But we're coming too."

"No, Liv - "

"Adam," she said, hard and sharp. That was it - end of debate.

He sighed, looking past her at Em in the back seat. She was
trying to tug her beanie off her head.

"Alright," he said. "Wrap up warm."

Within minutes, they were heading for the mall.

Olivia had suggested going to the movie theater: there were
bound to be people in there, she said, and it didn't seem so far
away. Adam pointed out that crossing the parking lot, which
by now looked like an icy, igloo-covered tundra, would be easier
said than done, especially when they had to carry Em, and the
mall would have security guards. They needed to tell someone
their tires had been slashed - it was no small thing.

She conceded, though he knew the situation was frightening
her more with each passing second. He knew she didn't want
to go to the mall because she'd seen that person in green going
there first. He didn't like that much either, but what other option did they have? They could only stay in the car or gas station
for so long without having to go for help, unless by some miracle
the security personnel in the mall spotted their car and came
outside to investigate. And in hindsight, leaving them behind
in the Volvo while he tramped off in the snow would have been
a remarkably foolish thing to do.

Olivia had bundled Em up in her little purple puffer coat
(she hadn't liked that) and handed her over, then she'd grabbed
their daughter's dinosaur-patterned backpack and checked the
car was locked, and they were on their way.

Adam held up his free arm, trying to keep fast-falling snow out of his face. Em squirmed in the crook of his other arm and he had to keep adjusting her position. She was getting heavy. Next to him, Olivia walked with her head ducked low under the hood of her jacket, Em's backpack slung over one shoulder.

He wanted to reach over and put his arm around her, but the anger and frustration were still there, broiling just below the surface. He knew he wasn't angry with her - not really, anyway - but as the only other adult in his vicinity, she'd take the brunt of it. He wished she'd paid more attention to what was going on outside, but she hadn't been the one who'd slashed the tires. That charming individual was still out there somewhere, armed with a large blade. Adam just wanted to get his family inside and find a security guard with a baton.

Or better yet, a gun.

As they drew near the entrance of the mall, stepping into the pool of light flooding from the entrance, a momentary wave of nostalgia washed over him and he dropped his free arm to look up at *The Outlet Mall* sign glowing high above the doors. A memory came to him then, abrupt and powerfully vivid: Calem Harrett shoving him into a girl he liked - Arabella Rolinson - as they walked up to the entrance; she'd been coming the other way with her friends and Adam never forgot the look of disgust on her face when he stumbled into her, a gawky thirteen-year-old with a retainer stuck to the roof of his mouth. Calem had laughed until snot ran from his nose, even as Adam wailed on him with both fists.

Back then, the mall had been new and exciting, a time before constant internet access and smart phones, when you congregated with friends on the weekend to eat junk food and chase after girls. The complex had been perfect for that, but those days were long gone now.

Olivia saw the footprints first and pointed them out.

"So *that's* where everyone is," Adam said, scanning the ground. There were dozens of them, all coming from different directions, all leading inside. He spotted the coin-operated rocket ride near the doors and turned Em away from it before she noticed.

"It looks like they came from the movie theater, too," said Olivia, looking back that way. "And the gas station."

"There'll be someone inside who can help us," Adam said. He hoped he at least *sounded* confident.

The doors slid apart and they stepped gratefully into the warm blast from the AC. Adam lowered Em to the floor with a grunt and took her hand.

Olivia led the way now, her boots squeaking on the tiles. They were sodden from the snow and probably ruined, but she didn't seem to care. Her gray jeans, Adam noted, were also soaked and clung to her slender calves as she walked - even in the most bizarre and unnerving of circumstances, he still found his wife's legs spectacular.

"Can you hear anything?" Olivia said, pushing back her hood.

"No, nothing," Adam replied, moving as quickly as Em's small strides would allow. "I thought there'd be music, you know?"

"Yeah, or voices. Anything."

They rounded the corner at the ATMs. Up ahead, Adam noticed a woman's purse lying on the floor by the vending machines and thought *that's weird.* Then they turned left onto the concourse entrance and stopped.

A short time later, another group coming from the movie theater would find the interior of the mall just as Adam and Olivia Price did. They would stand in the concourse and listen, just like the Prices were listening now, and they'd hear nothing, and that dead silence would run the blood cold in their veins.

When Olivia spoke again, she couldn't manage more than a whisper.

"Adam, what's going on? Where is everyone?" Even the whisper seemed too loud and she flinched back from it.

Adam didn't reply right away. His brain was struggling to process what his eyes were showing it. The *Outlet Complex* mall, huge and cavernous and ordinarily filled with people, all bustling between stores as they laughed and joked and ate burgers from the food court. That's how he remembered it.

Not like this. This was jarring.

"Adam..."

"I... I'm not sure," he said, looking from the empty benches to the empty second floor balcony overlooking the concourse, down again to the big fountain he remembered so well and the faux-wood cabin that must be a Santa's workshop just beyond it. He turned over the possibilities in his mind like playing cards on a blackjack table.

they've evacuated the building because of
a fire
a shooting, or a terrorist attack
everyone's gone outside through
the emergency exits
the underground parking lot
we just didn't see them, but how's that possible?
maybe it was the person who slashed our tires
they had to evacuate because of him
some guy with a knife

That's what he thought. What he said was, "There's a simple explanation. Has to be."

"But what... Em!"

Olivia darted forward and grabbed Em. Adam had released her hand without realizing and she'd headed straight for the nearest Christmas tree.

"Em!" Olivia cried, snatching her up, "don't *do* that! Stay with us." She was right on the precipice of panic now. She glared at Adam. "You need to be careful."

He nodded, snapping himself out of whatever trance he'd fallen into.

I need to get help.

"I'm going to find a security guard," he said, " or someone who works in this place. I think there's an office somewhere near the back. You two stay here."

"Adam - "

"No," he said firmly, and she stopped. "Stay here, out in the open where I can see you. Trust me, I'm not going far. As soon as I find someone, I'll come straight back, alright?"

Olivia didn't say anything. That was enough.

"Em, take care of Mommy again, ok?" he said.

Em looked up at him with hazel eyes that were bright with innocence. A surge of protective anger flared in Adam's chest and resolved him. *I'll protect my daughter and my wife. I'll keep them both safe. Nothing's happening to them.*

"Stay here," he said again, and started up the concourse in the direction of the elevators and stairwell.

"Be quick," Olivia called after him.

He didn't look back. He kept going, on past the fountain, past the white picket fence surrounding Santa's Grotto.

He kept going, even when he caught a few notes of music drifting out of it.

Olivia watched Adam until he disappeared from her field of vision further down the concourse, then she led Em to the nearest bench. She offered to lift her but Em chose to scramble up by herself, as was often the case these days. Olivia watched, smiling a little, as her girl maneuvered into a sitting position and placed both mittened hands in her lap. She sat down next to her, sliding Em's backpack off her shoulder.

The silence inside the mall pressed in on her. She imagined the huge open space would normally reverberate with voices and footsteps and background music. It wasn't meant for this. The only sounds she could hear (unless her mind was playing tricks on her) were the faint whistling of wind above the ceiling and an occasional creak or knock as the building shifted on its decades-old foundations.

She started to look around and quickly dropped her gaze back to the floor - the place was just too big and too empty. She felt like it was watching them.

Hurry back, Daddy, she thought. And then, hot on its heels: *who the hell slashed our tires back there?*

"Are you warm enough, babe?" she asked, tucking one of Em's curls behind her tiny ear.

"Yeah," Em said. "Where's Daddy gone?"

"He's just getting someone to help with our car."

"Is it broken?"

Olivia smiled again. "Sort of. But we'll get it fixed soon, and then we'll go see Grandma and Grandpa. Sound good?"

"Yeah. Will they have cookies?"

"For you? I'd say so."

Em stared straight ahead. "I like cookies."

"I know you do, sweetie." *Is she ok?* Olivia brushed Em's nose with her fingertip. "Just sit tight for a second. Daddy will be back soon, and then we'll get going."

Get back here soon, Daddy.

Olivia saw Em's eyes go to the Christmas tree again. She was tracing the fairy lights wrapped around it, following them up to the star on top.

"Mommy?" she said.

"Yes, baby?"

"Who's that?"

Olivia looked up to where Em was pointing, at the star on the Christmas tree. She frowned.

"Who're you talking about, swee - "

Movement above the tree on the second floor balcony. A glimpse of green, a scuffling of feet on tiles.

"Holy shit!" Olivia cried - no, yelled - standing. Her voice echoed up and down the concourse.

"Mommy, you swore," said Em.

Olivia stared, horror-struck, at the balcony railing. Had she seen what she thought she'd seen?

"Mommy."

Holy shit.

"Sorry, Em," Olivia said. It came out in a breathless pant. "Sorry for swearing."

Her heart was jackhammering in her chest. She dropped back onto the bench, pulling Em close.

Did I see...?

"Em," she said, tilting her daughter's face towards her own with a shaking hand. "We have to go find your Daddy, ok? We have to go right now."

"Mommy, did you see?"

"Yes, baby, I saw." *Holy hell, I saw.* "Let's go, ok? Come on."

She stood, hauling Em up with her.

Without looking towards the balcony again, Olivia Price hurried breathlessly down the mall concourse with her daughter in her arms.

"So now what do we do?" Ash said.

She stood with her hands on her hips, waiting for him to respond.

I didn't agree to this babysitting role.

"I'm not sure," Spencer replied, looking back down the entrance corridor. The padlock glinted in the light from the ceiling. It was brand new and, as he'd guessed, heavy-duty.

Babysitting three teens and a pothead on crutches when I should be searching for my wife. What did the universe catch me doing to deserve this shit?

The doors had slid open as they approached and ice-cold air blasted straight through the gaps in the shutter, which sat a couple of inches out from the glass. They'd rattled it, kicked it, tried pulling it up. But it was no use - the thing was sealed shut. A futile minute passed before they retreated back beyond the sensor range of the doors and they slid shut again.

"Who the hell locked it?" Ash asked for the fourth or fifth time. "Who? Was it that guy with the blood on his hands? I bet *he* cut off that person's ear."

"Ash, stop talking," said Taryn.

"Can we break the lock?" said Jeremy, using his sleeve to clean snowflakes off his glasses. He'd gotten a good dusting while trying to yank up the shutter, even with the canopy covering the entrance.

"Maybe," Spencer said. "But we'd need something to smash it with."

"Like a hammer?" suggested Lincoln, doing his foot-tapping thing again.

"Possibly," Spencer replied.

"Or bolt-cutters?" said Jeremy.

"Yes, that'd be better. Is there a hardware store in this place? I can't remember."

"Yeah, there is," said Taryn. "I'm not sure what it's called, but we passed it earlier. It's on the second floor, near the food court."

"Shouldn't we try finding, like, *another* way out?" Ash said. "That's gotta be easier than breaking a padlock, right?"

"Guess she's got a point," Jeremy conceded.

Ash crossed her arms and said, "I think *I'm* the only one here using my brain."

"First time for everything."

Spencer, sensing another squabble was about to begin, said, "Let's go back to the main area, I don't like hanging around this dead end. We can plan our next move from there."

"What about the cops?" said Lincoln. "What if we miss them, I mean?"

Oddly perceptive.

"We could watch for them from the coffee place upstairs," suggested Taryn. "It looks out over the parking lot. We'd see them coming."

"If they come at all," added Jeremy.

"They'll come, don't worry," said Spencer, feigning confidence. "Until then, however, we'll need to look after ourselves, and I don't think sticking around this particular one-way street meets that criteria. Come on."

They made their way back to the concourse. Spencer found the kids had taken to bunching around him every time he moved, flocking like chicks after a mother hen, and he didn't like it one bit. Even Lincoln bumbled awkwardly after him, struggling to keep up on his crutches.

Spencer didn't like it because it implied they thought he could protect them, if it came down to it. But of course, he couldn't. He was the last person they should be looking to for protection. He couldn't even protect Mary.

Where the hell is she?

They arrived back in the concourse. He stopped by the escalators and they stopped too.

"Alright," Spencer said, clapping his hands together. Lincoln jumped at the sound, which was louder than it should have been in the empty belly of the mall. "I don't know about you guys, but I'd like to get out of this place as soon as possible - "

"Second that," said Jeremy.

" - so we need to explore more than one avenue simultaneously, if we can, to save time. If we track down a set of bolt cutters, we can get out through the main entrance, but we don't need five people to do that. There may also be another way out, as Ash suggested, so we should check on that as well. Unfortunately, I think this means we have to split up. Temporarily, of course."

"Uh-uh," said Ash, shaking her head. "No way. Weren't we all watching the same movie earlier?"

"What movie?" said Lincoln.

Ash ignored him, holding up her index finger. "The first rule of surviving a horror movie is *don't* split up. If we split, we're toast."

"This isn't a movie, Ash," said Jeremy. "Spencer's right: if we split up, we get the job done faster. Get what we need and get out."

"Divide and conquer," added Taryn.

"Well, I'm not going anywhere by myself," Ash said, hands going to her hips again in that my-word-is-final sort of way.

"That's right, you're not," said Spencer. "You're coming with me."

"What?" said Ash, faltering.

"We're going to find us some bolt-cutters, 'lil lady," Spencer said, in his best wild western drawl. "While these two varmints" - he indicated Taryn and Jeremy - "track down the nearest emergency exit and see if it'll open. Though if things keep going the way they've been so far, I suspect they mightn't have much luck with that one."

Ash looked to Taryn, crestfallen. "But... but - "

"But what about me?" said Lincoln. "Who am I going with?"

"There's a coffee place at the top of this escalator, right?" Spencer said, directing the question at Taryn. The girl nodded. "Then you're going there, Mr Ward. We need someone to keep an eye out in case... when... the police arrive. Can you handle that one?"

Lincoln looked doubtfully at the escalator steps, which weren't moving.

"Um, yeah, I think so," he said. "But it might not be easy getting up there with my foot."

"Sure it will," said Jeremy.

They all watched as he walked to the foot of the escalators and, stooping, pressed a large red button at the base. Immediately, the steps thrummed to life and resumed their endless up and down cycles. Jeremy stood back, pleased. "Thought it might work both ways."

"Ah, the emergency stop button," said Spencer. "Of course."

"Of *course*," repeated Ash, rolling her eyes.

"So you all know what you have to do," Spencer said, as though Ash hadn't spoken. "Jeremy and Taryn, you two take a walk through this level of the mall and see if you can spot any emergency exits. There's got to be at least one leading off the main area. If you see anything suspicious, just yell and we'll come right away. Linc, head up to that coffee place and stay by the windows - same goes for you regards the yelling."

"Got it," said Lincoln. "Yell."

"And as for you, Miss... whatever you said your surname was... you and I are off to check out that hardware store upstairs. I need your keen eyes and ears to cover for my old, tired ones."

Ash shrugged. "If it gets us out of here, fine."

If it gets all of you out of here, fine. I'm not leaving without Mary.

Spencer pushed up his jacket sleeve. "We'll meet back here - right here - at five o'clock. That's about fifteen minutes. Everyone got that?"

They nodded.

"Good. Then let's get to it."

Taryn had known Jeremy since elementary school. They'd first bonded over their mutual love of comic books, then progressed to movies and TV shows *inspired* by comic books; by the time they reached high school their tastes had evolved even further, and they were now neck-deep in a shared passion for horror movies, especially the critically-panned variety. Taryn had watched horror flicks with Jeremy Lewis for years, often late at night in pitch-black rooms, and in all that time she'd never seen him truly scared. Not once.

But as the escalator ushered Ash, Spencer and a wobbly Lincoln towards the second floor of the mall, she saw a look pass over Jeremy's face, and that niggling sensation at the back of her mind became a high whine of alarm.

He was just as scared as she was.

Jeremy turned, caught her staring, and smiled grimly. "You heard Spence - let's get to it."

They started away from the escalators. Immediately, Taryn angled them towards the stores on the right-hand side of the concourse, keeping well clear of the fountain. She didn't need to see that ear again any time soon.

"So, an emergency exit," said Jeremy, keeping his voice low. They could hear the others behind and above them - Ash's voice carried easily in the quietness. "Have you seen one?"

"Probably," Taryn replied, sweeping the concourse. She tried to avoid looking towards the fountain and Santa's Grotto, but the pull was almost unavoidable. "I mean, there should be more than one, right?"

"Yeah."

They passed along the store fronts beneath the second-floor overhang. Taryn trailed a hand along the white pillars as they went by. She found she needed the grounding those little touches provided, as if she might lose her sense of place otherwise and float right off the floor.

"I don't remember where it is," Jeremy said.

"Me neither."

"Even if we find it, there could be another padlock on it. That'd be cool, wouldn't it? Who the hell locked that door, Tar?"

"No idea, Jer." They passed the luxury clothing boutique; a mannequin dressed in a pin-striped pants suit watched them lifelessly. "I just want to leave. That ear on the fountain really freaked me the hell out."

"Same." Suddenly, Jeremy swung to face her. His eyes were wide and her immediate thought was *The guy with blood on his hands is right behind me and he's going for my ear*, but what Jeremy said was: "We're in it now, aren't we Tar? We're in a shitting horror movie, aren't we? This is so messed up. I mean, what the hell's going on? Where is everyone? Who was that guy from the gas station? Who locked the door, and *who owns that fucking ear?*"

"Jer!" she said, grabbing his arm. His voice had risen sharply; in the open space of the mall concourse, it was dangerously loud. "Trust me, I get it. I'm right here with you. So's Ash, and Spencer, and that Lincoln guy. None of us know what's going on. We just have to find a way out, and the sooner the better. Ok?"

Jeremy stared back at her, breathing heavily. *He's on the verge of a panic attack*, Taryn thought. *I've never seen Jeremy have a panic attack before.* "Let's just find the emergency exit, alright? You're good at finding stuff. Just use those high-powered binoculars hanging off your face."

"Screw you," he said, still dancing close to the panic line. But a semblance of a grin touched the edge of his mouth all the same.

Taryn kept hold of his arm until they started moving again. They were almost halfway up the concourse now, still in the shadow of the second floor overhang. Every store they passed - *JeanScene, The Gadget Store, Amy's Scent Shop* - was open, lit, and completely empty. Taryn spotted more abandoned shopping bags and purses, all discarded on the floor when customers had simply left. Or been taken.

Taken? Taken by who, or what?

They were almost level with the fountain in the center of the concourse, her heart rate ticking steadily upwards, when Jeremy said, "There."

She looked to where he was pointing: a sign jutting out from the wall ahead with the word EXIT in bold red lettering.

"Yes!" she exclaimed. "How've I never seen that before?"

"You weren't looking for it," Jeremy replied.

Their pace quickened. Taryn didn't bother glancing into the *American Fashion* store as they passed - she knew by now what she'd see, which was a big bowl of nothing. She realized with only a fleeting glimmer of guilt that, in a way, she didn't actually care where everyone had gone. There was probably a pretty reasonable explanation for it, one they hadn't even considered yet; maybe even the ear had a rational story behind it, if it wasn't just a realistic-looking fake. She just wanted to get out of the mall and go home.

Jeremy reached the exit first. It was a set of double doors with 'Emergency Only' printed across the top. Nothing fancy. Crucially, there was no padlock on them, no chain. The doors appeared unsealed.

Come on, Taryn thought. *Don't be locked, you assholes.*

Jeremy puffed his cheeks and said "Please" to no-one in particular. He grabbed one of the handles and gave it a twist.

The door swung open.

Taryn exhaled with relief. Jeremy issued his thanks to no-one in particular and pushed through the door.

They found themselves in a narrow hallway with two barely-lit ceiling lights, one of which flickered intermittently. The hallway smelled of damp and fust. At the far end of it was a single door with the word EXIT above it.

"No padlock," Jeremy observed.

The inner door swung shut. Taryn followed Jeremy down the hallway, sticking close. She had the distinctly unsettling feeling that someone was right behind her, practically on her heels. Her heart continued its faster-than-usual thumping in her chest, pounding blood past her ears.

There were two other doors in the emergency exit hallway, both set into the left-side wall. One was marked 'Storage' and the other 'Staff Toilet'. The opposite wall, separating the hallway from the neighboring *American Fashion* store, was doorless.

They reached the outer exit, which featured a push bar instead of a handle. Jeremy placed both hands on it.

"Don't let it swing closed behind us," he said, "or we might not be able to get back inside."

"I won't," said Taryn.

Jeremy met her gaze from behind his thick lenses, reading her as he so often did, then pushed against the bar. The door opened (Taryn's heart leapt into her throat) then *clunked* against something and didn't go any further. Cold evening air rushed in through a one-inch gap between the door and the frame.

"What happened?" Taryn said.

Jeremy released the bar and the door swung shut again. He repeated the exercise. The door opened, banged into something, and went no further.

"It's blocked," he said. "There's something on the other side."

"I'll help you."

They leaned into the bar together, straining against the door with everything they could muster, but it didn't budge more than the inch it already had. After a few seconds, they released the bar and stepped back, breathing hard. The door immediately swung shut again.

"Son of a bitch!" Jeremy cried, slamming the sole of his boot against it.

"The others can help us," Taryn said, brushing hair from her face. "We'll get it open."

"We won't," said Jeremy. "Whatever's out there on the other side is heavy. *Really* heavy. Like a car, or something. I think this route's closed."

Sighing in frustration, he turned away. Taryn scanned the door frame on the off chance they'd missed a chain or something.

Who blocked it? she thought.

Jeremy was already halfway down the hallway.

"Hey, wait!" she called, hurrying after him.

He stopped, but not for her.

"What're you doing?" Taryn said as he pulled open the 'Staff Toilet' door.

"What d'you think?" he said. "I haven't peed since before the movie ended. I'll be right back."

"Holy shit, Jer, don't leave me out here!"

"If you want to watch me do my business, come right ahead."

He went inside, deliberately leaving the door open behind him. Taryn called him a dick and slammed it shut.

The bang ricocheted around her. She cast a nervous glance back towards the inner emergency exit door, hugging her arms to her body.

"Hurry up, Jeremy," she whispered.

"What the fuck is *with* this place?" said Ash. "I *still* can't get any signal on my fucking phone."

"Has anyone ever told you that you cuss an awful lot?" said Spencer.

"No. Never." She stuffed her phone back in her pocket with a sigh. "Besides, I've heard you swear plenty, old man."

"Yes, but I'm a miserable old crank who can't find his wife. I have permission."

He suspected Ash would've argued further if he hadn't mentioned Mary. At least she had the sense to reel it in at that.

A miserable old crank who can't find his wife.

Mary Bloom had first graced Spencer with her intoxicating presence in 1992, back when he was finishing up college and she was already a couple of years out of it, working as a staff nurse in the local hospital. Naturally, they'd met right there in that building: Spencer had been out drinking in celebration of his best pal Marty Shanks finally popping the question to his high school sweetheart Alice Pauson, a bookish-type girl from the next town over, when he'd tripped on a curb stone and landed hard on his left arm, popping his shoulder right out of the socket. Marty and the other guys were all pretty far gone at that point and, between gales of laughter, had tried hauling Spencer back to his feet, not realizing they were actually tugging his already-dislocated shoulder further out of the joint. They didn't stop pulling on his arm until the extreme pain caused Spencer to vomit all over Marty's Reeboks and then pass out, and only then did they decide it might be worth taking him to the hospital.

He woke up later that night with Mary in the room. When he asked how he'd gotten to be there, she'd explained how his friends ("Though you should think about getting some new ones if you ask me, Mr Bloom") had half-supported, half-carried him from the car to the reception area and dumped him in a chair before skedaddling. Only Marty had hung around long enough to fill out some forms and he was now asleep himself, sprawled out across three seats in the lobby with his cheek in a puddle of beer-scented drool.

Spencer had been doped up on painkillers at the time, but they hadn't done much to dull his charm, in his mind anyway. He'd told Mary she was the prettiest nurse he'd seen that night and she'd asked if he'd seen any other nurses in the minute since he woke up and he said why no, he hadn't, now that she mentioned it, but he was *sure* she'd eclipse them all anyway, were they to stand shoulder to shoulder at the foot of his bed like they were in a police lineup. That'd made her chuckle (as much *at* him as with him) and it'd been all he needed. He married her less than a year later.

Right now, he'd give anything to be back in that hospital ward with Mary (dislocated shoulder or no), or in their living room watching some classic eighties slasher movie they'd each grown up loving. Hell, he wouldn't even mind being in the office right now, working on the end-of-year accounts for a boss who was fifteen years his junior. Anywhere but here, stuck inside this mall with a bunch of kids, one of whom was a stoner with a broken foot.

Getting Lincoln onto the escalator hadn't been a problem - it was getting him *off* it again at the second floor that'd caused a few issues. Spencer was sure the kid was going to catch his plastered foot on the top and hit the deck, and when he *did* stumble for a second, Spencer had grabbed for his shirt. Fortunately, Ash had been leading the way and Lincoln only succeeded in bumbling into her, causing a string of expletives to explode from her fifteen-year-old mouth.

The coffee place (literally called *The Coffee Place*) was, like everywhere else in the mall, completely empty. Spencer found it to be the eeriest area they'd set foot in so far. Every table featured a reminder that a person - a real, living *person* - had been there only a short time ago: mugs half-full of coffee, sandwich remains on plates, books and newspapers still open. Behind the counter, water dripped from a nozzle on the espresso machine into an overflowing cup, and a laptop on a table near the entrance still displayed a page from someone's partially completed manuscript. Some poor schmuck was trying to write a novel.

Spencer had guided Lincoln to a chair by the huge windows looking out over the parking lot and told him to watch for the cops arriving.

"As soon as you see them - "

"I know, dude, I know," Lincoln had said, rubbing his bare arms, which were still bright pink from the cold. "When I see them, start yelling."

Spencer had looked at him for a moment, then shrugged out of his jacket (doing so still made his left shoulder ache a little - it'd never been the same since 1992) and dropped it in Lincoln's lap.

"Put that on, you idiot," he'd said gruffly. "You'll catch your death in that polo shirt."

Before Lincoln could protest, Spencer had said "Come on, you" to Ash and left the coffee place. She'd hurried after him.

And now, walking past the stores on the second level of the mall, he wished more than ever that he'd just stayed home that afternoon. He and Mary would be by the fire right now, wondering aloud who'd be crazy enough to venture out in this weather. Except, it was only snowing where they were, right? That's what the dispatcher had told him on the phone.

I'm looking at a weather report. There's no snowfall in your area today.

"One thing at a time."

"What?" said Ash.

"Nothing." He hadn't realized he'd actually spoken the words. "Where's this hardware store?"

"Think it's just up here."

They continued along the second floor, he, a man in his early fifties with a substantial paunch and too-high cholesterol, and her, a fifteen-year-old girl wearing purple eyeshadow and Doc Martens that didn't bring her too far beyond the five-foot mark. Spencer looked down at the ground level of the concourse but couldn't see Taryn or Jeremy.

Where'd they disappear off to? he thought. *Have they found an emergency exit already?*

"It's just up here," said Ash.

Spencer could see at least three more stores on their left before the upper level opened out into the food court, which stretched to the rear of the mall. The smell of fried food grew stronger as they neared the court and Spencer felt his stomach rumble. Other than a few handfuls of popcorn during the movie, he hadn't eaten since lunch.

"There, the last one," said Ash pointing. Then, in a puzzled voice: "Why's the shutter half down? And what's that on the floor?"

Spencer squinted. The hardware store shutter was indeed most of the way down, and there was something dark on the tiles by the entrance. As they neared it, he instinctively stuck his arm in front of Ash. "Wait a second."

"Why, what's... oh shit, what is that? Is that *blood?*"

He approached the store. A sign above the entrance read *Big Al's Hardware* and featured a cartoon builder gripping a hammer in one oversized hand. The shutter was down to about three feet off the floor, and the floor itself was splattered with dark, dried blood, which trailed into the store. The lights were off inside.

Of course, Spencer thought, shaking his head. *Of course. The only store we need to get into, and it's like this.*

A low moan escaped Ash's mouth; she was over by the rail, well away from the entrance.

"This is some gnarly shit, Spence," she said.

"It sure is," he agreed, "but we need to get those bolt cutters."

Her response was as he'd expected. "I'm not going in there."

"That's ok," he said, "you can stay here. I'll get them." He took a step towards the entrance and, as he'd expected, she did the same. "You *can* stay here, Ashley."

"Don't call me that," she replied. Her eyes went to the blood on the floor and she exhaled through pursed lips. "Can you even get under there?"

He looked down. "I think so. Don't have much choice, do I?"

Ash stared at the blood - there wasn't much of it, really, but Spencer thought he could smell it now - then at him, then back at the blood. Finally, she drifted forward.

"I'll go first."

"No," he said, but she'd already taken out her phone again. She activated its flashlight and bent down, shining it under the shutter. Her boots remained staunchly beside rather than in the blood puddle.

"I don't see anyone," she said.

"Good."

"I'll find the lights."

"Ok, but be careful. I'll be right behind you. And if you see anything - "

"Yeah I know - yell. Your solution to everything."

Ash took a breath and ducked under the shutter. She was gone.

"Most wonderful time of the year, my ass," Spencer muttered.

Holding the bottom of the shutter for support, he eased himself down to his haunches. His knees went off like starter pistols and he winced. Even in that position, he could still barely get his head low enough to duck under the shutter. He leaned down, shimmying himself through the entrance. Down this low, the pungent tang of congealed blood was nauseating.

He was halfway under the shutter when Ash yelled "Holy shit!" from inside the store and his foot skidded in the puddle. With a cry of surprise and disgust, he went down on his right forearm and his hand slapped square into the blood. It was cold and sticky under his palm.

Cursing, he scrambled the rest of the way under, getting more blood on his knees, and struggled back to his feet. Ash's flashlight swung his way and he shielded his face.

"Oh GROSS, you've got blood on you!"

"Yes, I noticed," he snapped back. "Get that light out of my face."

She turned it away; stars zipped and popped behind his eyes.

"What happened?" he said, wiping his hand on his pants leg. "What did you see?"

"Oh," said Ash, "I thought I saw someone over there in the corner, but it was just a dummy. It looked so *real*!"

Spencer sighed, exasperated and still disgusted. The blood wasn't coming off his hand so well. "It's not the only dummy in here."

Ash turned the flashlight on him. He was about to snap at her again when she said, "There's the light switch, over by the counter."

He started to turn that way but she breezed past him and reached it first. Light flared inside the store and he blinked, raising an arm to cover his eyes. He saw the blood on his sleeve and dropped it again, repulsed.

"Ho-lee shit," said Ash.

"Took the words right outta my mouth," Spencer said, grimacing at the thin trail of blood running from the entrance towards the back of the store. It went straight down the center of the aisles before veering sharply to the right along the back wall, disappearing from view.

"What do you think happened there?" Ash said, switching off her phone flashlight.

"Best not to give that too much thought," he replied. "We'll search this place and get out fast. I just need to do one thing first."

He went to the counter, where a bottle of hand sanitizer gel sat resolutely next to the computer. Some stores still had them there and he was glad to see it. He jammed down the plunger half a dozen times until his right hand contained a golf ball-sized blob of clear gel, then proceeded to scrub the blood off as best he could. The gel quickly became red liquid between his palms; some of it squirted out onto the floor at his feet.

"Really gross," Ash said, turning her nose up.

Spencer grabbed a microfiber cloth from the bargain bin, dried his hands, and tossed the cloth onto the counter.

"I don't know about you," he said, pushing up his blood-stained sleeves, "but I want to get out of here as soon as possible."

"Me too."

"Stay away from wherever that trail ends, ok?"

"Yup. So what're we looking for exactly?"

"Bolt cutters. Something with two handles, probably about a foot long, and a scissor-like metal head. You'll have seen them before, I'm sure."

"Probably not. My dad isn't much of a handyman."

She moved towards one of the central aisles. He took the cue and went to the right-hand wall, opposite the counter.

To fill the silence (and distract them from the disturbing implications of the blood trail running to the back of the store), Spencer asked, "What does your old man do?"

"He works in a bank," Ash said, her voice echoing, "but he's not my real dad. He died when I was, like, six or something."

"Oh. Sorry."

"Don't be, I don't really remember him." He heard her rifling through items on the shelves. "My mom married Rodney, my step-dad, a few years ago. He has kids too, three of 'em."

"Your step-siblings?"

"Yeah, I guess. Is this it?"

He turned to see her hold up a pair of pliers.

"No, they'd be a lot bigger."

"Ok."

He went back to his wall. The store was larger than it appeared from the entrance, and it was packed with tools. This wasn't the snatch-and-grab job he'd expected.

"Do you have any brothers? Or sisters?"

"I have one brother," said Spencer. "He lives up in Canada now."

"Bummer."

Bummer? He smirked at that. Then, suddenly, he knew what the next question would be, and he steeled himself in anticipation.

"And do you guys have any, yunno, kids of your own?"

Spencer pushed aside a row of gardening shears. "No. We don't."

Ash didn't reply. He could hear her flipping through items on hangers, further down the aisle.

He knew what she was probably thinking. It's what everyone thought when he told them he and Mary didn't have kids, despite enjoying a long and happy marriage together. *They're not able. They've tried and they can't do it.*

The truth was, neither of them really wanted children. They liked the idea of it, sure, but they didn't *love* it, at least not enough to really try. They hadn't gone out of their way to avoid having kids, nor had they made any concerted effort to test their potency (or *his* potency, at least). It wasn't that they disliked children, either - they just weren't sure if parenting was something they'd been properly equipped to handle, and if they weren't totally sure, it was best not to pursue it, right?

"I don't know if I'd want kids either," Ash said from the far side of the store.

Spencer paused, one hand on the shaft of a rake. "What?"

"Kids," Ash repeated. "Don't think I want 'em. All that screaming, and the dirty diapers and shit. Screw that noise."

Spencer turned to look in her direction. He couldn't see her over the aisles.

"It's a little early for you to make that call, isn't it?"

"I'm *fifteen*."

"My point exactly. At least wait 'til you're sixteen."

"You serious?"

"No, of course not." He thought he spotted something near the end of the central aisle that might be a bolt-cutter and started towards it. "You've got your whole life ahead of you, madam. Take your time and drink it all in."

"You sound like my teacher."

"Your teacher's a wise man."

"She's a woman." He heard her snicker.

"Well then you should listen to her. Oh, found it."

"The bolt cutter things?"

"No, the meaning of life, right here in this hardware store."

"Screw you, beardy."

He heard her coming over and grinned, lifting the bolt cutters off the hanger. They were good quality and heavy-duty, easily strong enough to break the padlock.

"These'll do it," he said.

"Um, Spencer?"

The abrupt change in her tone made him freeze on the spot. She was somewhere at the back of the store.

"What's wrong?"

"C'mere and look at this."

Gooseflesh started on his arms. He walked to where her voice had come from, the bolt-cutters in one hand.

She was at the back of the store by the paint section. In that moment, standing there in her wool tights and too-large boots with her hands by her sides, she didn't look anywhere near fifteen. She was staring at something off to the right, beyond his line of sight.

"What is it?" he said.

"Just look."

Then he saw the blood trail at her feet, curving away from between the central aisles towards the back corner of the store. There, it ran under a door marked 'Staff Only' into what must be a storage room.

"What d'you think's in there?" Ash said in a faraway voice.

The gooseflesh had reached Spencer's shoulders and was heading for his neck.

"It... it doesn't matter," he said. The fear he heard in his own voice threw him and he took an involuntary step back. "I have the bolt-cutters. We should go."

"Do you think it's Mary?"

His heart contracted in his chest; he stared at her. "What're you talking about?"

The faraway quality in Ash's voice was now manifested on her face. Her eyes had glazed over and her mouth was ajar. She looked like she was sleepwalking.

"Ash, what - "

"Do you think Mary's in there?" she said dreamily. "Do you think it's her blood?"

Spencer felt his hackles go up. Fear bubbled into anger inside him.

"Stop this," he said. "Stop saying these things. It's not Mary."

"It might be."

The blood's still on my sleeve.

"It's not. She's not here."

"I want to see." Ash took a step forward. Her foot squished right into the blood trail. Spencer grabbed her shoulder (wasn't it small in his big clumsy hand?) and twisted her round to face him.

"We have to leave," he said firmly. "Right now. I don't know what's gotten into you, but we can't stay here. We're leaving, and - "

"Mary's blood is tainted, isn't it?"

Spencer goggled at her. His knees wobbled and he almost dropped the bolt-cutters.

"Ash," he said.

Before he could say any more, someone moaned on the other side of the door.

Seven

The bathroom door swung open and Jeremy emerged back into the hallway, wiping his hands on his jeans. "The dryer wasn't working," he explained, following Taryn's gaze.

"What took you so long?" she said.

"I wasn't long at all. It was like two minutes."

"It feels longer when you're alone. This place gives me the heebie jeebies."

They returned to the inner doors. Taryn had a momentary flash of them trapped in the emergency exit hallway, banging in vain on the doors while the others escaped the mall. Fortunately, they opened without a fuss, and they stepped back into the concourse. The door swung shut behind them again.

"So what now?" Jeremy said. "Back to the coffee place and wait for Ash and Spencer?"

"Guess so," Taryn replied, glancing up at the second level. There was no sign of them. "Here's hoping they did better than us, anyway."

"Guarantee Ash finds it first, even if she doesn't know what she's looking for." They started back in the direction of the escalators. "Remember when I lost my compass in Sixth Grade Math, and she found it?"

"By sitting on it."

"Yeah, and she was all like "what the fuck just stabbed me in the ass?" and would've *thrown* it at me if - "

There was movement in the corner of Taryn's eye, just past Jeremy's shoulder. She grabbed his arm again, digging her fingers into his flesh.

"Ow!" Jeremy cried, "what're you doing?"

"Jer, look," Taryn hissed.

"Look at what?"

"Over there."

He followed her gaze across the mall. When he saw what she saw, his arm stiffened beneath her fingers.

The emergency exit was almost directly opposite an enormous toy store called *The Play Emporium*. Like every other store on the ground level, the doors were wide open and the interior was brightly lit. But that wasn't what had caught Taryn's attention.

It was the little girl going into the store. As she walked, lights flashed on her sneakers.

Then she was gone.

"Did you see?" Taryn said softly.

"Yeah," Jeremy replied, staring at her now. "Why're we whispering?"

She stared back. "I don't know."

"Well... should we go get her?"

Taryn thought about it for a moment. "I guess we should."

"Ok, then."

Jeremy started out from under the shadow of the balcony. Taryn's hand slipped off his arm. she'd rather have kept it there, but he was already striding towards *The Play Emporium* in that purposeful Jeremy Lewis way of his.

She hated that.

Going after him, she cast a glance towards where the escalators must be (she couldn't see them past Santa's Grotto) and on up to the second level, where the sign and top half of *The Coffee Place* entrance were visible. If Lincoln was still up there, she couldn't see him from her lowly vantage point.

He's wandered off, hasn't he?

Her eyes continued traveling upwards and came to rest on the mall ceiling. She saw the hole again, clearer this time from her new angle. It was behind them now, a few dozen yards further back. Wind whistled past it as snowflakes danced their way through, floating down into the concourse.

What did that? she wondered afresh.

Jeremy reached *The Play Emporium* entrance first and stopped, peering inside. Taryn came up behind him and thought, absurdly, that he looked like a little boy then. *It's his coat*, she realized. *It's way too big for him. I've never noticed that before.*

"See her?"

"No," Jeremy said, still hovering by the entrance. "She's disappeared. Geez, I forgot how big that store is."

"You still go there?"

"No, I... shut up. Come on, let's look for her."

The Play Emporium was, as a matter of fact, one of the biggest stores in the mall, and for the countless children who were dragged to the *Outlet Complex* each year by their parents, it was a veritable oasis in a desert of adult retail monotony. Aisle upon towering aisle stretched the length of the store, each chockablocked with all manner of toys and games: action figures, dolls, stuffed animals, radio-controlled cars, mini construction vehicles, board games, science sets, building blocks, games consoles, sports equipment, bicycles, go-karts, inflatable swimming pools, arts and crafts, and more. If you were a kid craving a gosh-darn genuine good time, *The Play Emporium* more than likely had what you were looking for.

Taryn had been there plenty of times before with her parents ("But what *would* you like Santa to bring you this year?") and she never strayed far from the arts supplies, but it'd been a while since she crossed that colorful threshold. Once you hit your teens - even your pre-teens - toys cease to be cool and must be reluctantly surrendered to your young siblings. Pickings were slim for Taryn's younger brother Neal, though she'd once caught him playing with her *My Little Pony* collection, which had given her fantastic ammunition for months afterwards. Any time he started bugging her she simply asked if he'd fed his ponies that day, and he'd slink off in a huff.

She missed the little twerp now.

"How do we find her in this place?" Jeremy said, still speaking with an overabundance of caution, as if the contents of the toy store might suddenly spring to life and rush at them.

"Let's just call for her," Taryn said. She took in a breath and Jeremy hissed "No!", waving his hands apprehensively; she let it out again in a puff and said, "Why not?"

"I don't know," Jeremy replied, looking into the store again. "I just... don't think we should. It's too quiet, you know? Someone might hear us."

"Who?"

"Like I said, I don't know. But someone."

They stood that way for a moment, facing the open entrance. The mall creaked and groaned around them.

"This is stupid," Taryn said finally, and walked into the store. Once-purposeful Jeremy Lewis hesitated, then hurried after her.

There was no music playing inside - for some reason, Taryn found that even more unsettling than the silence throughout the rest of the mall. A clown leered down at her from a shelf and she quickly looked away.

"I'll go this way," she said, indicating to the left. "You take that side."

"Ok," said Jeremy. "Shout if you find her."

Taryn angled left, moving past the checkout counter. It ran across the front left side of the store, hidden behind an eye-catching window display. Behind the counter, for what must have been the dozenth time, she spotted a discarded cell phone on the floor.

Dropped right from the owner's hands, she thought.

Glancing back, she saw Jeremy and his big coat disappear behind the aisle on the far right. She turned off the entrance area into the board game section. Rows upon rows of titles stacked the shelves on either side of her, some of which she knew well, others less-so: classics like *Clue*, *Monopoly*, *Ticket to Ride* and *Settlers of Catan* stood out, kindling memories of rain-soaked Fall evenings in the family room when she was in Middle School, trying in vain to explain trading games to her father, who'd only ever played *Yahtzee* and *Connect 4*, and wasn't even good at those; newer titles like *Exploding Kittens* and *Zombies* had become her forte in recent years, when she'd graduated from board game evenings with her family to all-nighters at Ash's house (Ash Buckley was a board game fiend and had about fifty of them packed onto her bedroom shelves).

One thing was for sure, though - a little girl with flashing sneakers wouldn't waste her precious toy store time in the board game section.

Taryn walked swiftly to the end of the aisle. She thought of calling out to Jeremy, but held off. She didn't like that she couldn't hear his footsteps anymore.

She turned right at the end of the board game section, expecting to see another aisle running perpendicular to it, linking up the various sections of the store. But instead, she found herself in what must be the *Lego* department (boxes and boxes of the stuff), and suddenly remembered a crucial fact about *The Play Emporium* they'd forgotten upon entering - it was one of the most disorganized stores in the mall, and always had been.

Brushing aside a tingle of uncertainty, Taryn entered the *Lego* section, then took a left. Up ahead, *Legos* became *Duplos*, and then wooden blocks, and finally chunky plastic stackers for babies and toddlers. No little girl. No Jeremy.

She took a right past the action figures, then another left into arts and crafts. The place just kept going and going. There was no rhyme or reason to how it'd been ordered, no natural connection between each section. It was a maze of color and blinking lights and dusty plastic packaging.

She was halfway up the doll aisle (creepy as hell, weren't they?) when something compelled her to stop. Had she just heard footsteps? She looked back the way she'd come - nothing. The aisle was empty. She strained, listening, trying to pinpoint the source of the sound, but there was nothing. No footsteps.

It was in her head, wasn't it?

I'm losing my mind in this giant toy box maze.

"Jer," she said, and it came out in a weak croak. She cleared her throat and called again, louder this time: "Jeremy. Jeremy!"

His voice sounded miles away. "What? Did you find her?"

"No," Taryn replied. "I - "

A shuffling behind her. Shoes on tiles.

She spun back around, ready to scream. The aisle was empty. *What the hell...?*

Now her heart was really pounding, thumping blood into her skull. Every muscle in her body was tensed, preparing her for flight ("fight" wasn't viable). She was just as she'd been earlier, after they'd discovered the ear, ready to get out of the mall as soon as possible.

But the little girl. They couldn't just leave her behind.

There's something else in here.

"Jer," she called, "where are you?" Her feet were already moving, taking her down the aisle. "Which section?"

There was no response.

She turned another corner into another multicolored aisle. Stuffed animals this time. Lime green dinosaurs craned long necks above her head.

"Jeremy!" she yelled. "Where the hell are you?"

Still, Jeremy didn't answer.

Suddenly, the sensation that she was being followed, that someone was right behind her, mirroring her every step, became overwhelming. It drove shards of ice panic into her chest, flooding her veins with terror, and she started to run.

"Jeremy!" she yelled again, almost screaming it now. She turned another corner, scattering a bundle of purple squid beanies across the floor with a flailing arm. "Jeremy, you asshole! If you're hiding, it's not funny at all. Answer me, right now! Jer - "

She rounded another corner at speed and collided with Jeremy. Her lungs instantly emptied. She staggered backwards with a breathless gasp, overbalanced, and sat down hard on the floor. Her spine jolted painfully and she cried out.

Jeremy had also been knocked backwards but managed to stay on his feet. He stumbled towards her, reaching for her hands.

"What the hell are you doing, Tar?" he said. He'd been winded too and the question came out in one long exhalation.

Still cringing with pain, she grasped his extended hand and allowed him to haul her back to her feet. Her head felt too light on the end of her neck and she grabbed the nearest shelf for support.

"Are you ok?" Jeremy said. "Why were you running?"

Taryn opened her eyes. Jeremy swam back into focus.

"I... I thought..." she said, rubbing her lower back. "I thought I heard someone behind me in the aisle." Then she swung for him with her free hand, catching him on the arm. "Why didn't you *answer* me?"

"What? I didn't hear you... OW! Stop hitting me!"

"I was yelling, you dick! The others could've heard me upstairs."

"I didn't hear you," Jeremy repeated, annoyed now. "It's a big store and I was pretty far away. You're just freaking out, Meyer."

"Of course I'm freaking out," she snapped. "There's something in this place and it was *following* me."

"Bullshit," said Jeremy, but she saw him glance past her shoulder, just for a second.

Taryn sighed, rubbing her eyes. "I'm so tired, Jer."

"Me too."

"Did you see her? The girl?"

"No. I thought I heard something, but - "

"Footsteps?"

He stared at her. "Maybe."

That coat's far too big for him.

"Geez, Jer," she said. "We really are in the shit now."

"That's a bad word."

Taryn screamed. Jeremy threw himself into her arms.

The little girl looked up at them and giggled.

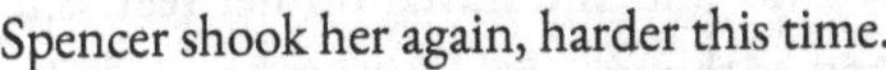

Spencer shook her again, harder this time.

"Ash. Ash!" She stared back at him, *through* him. "Kid, you talk to me right now. Hey!"

She was slumped against the back wall of the store in a half-standing position, mouth open and arms by her sides. Immediately after asking if Mary's blood was tainted (*what the fuck had that been about?*) she'd stopped talking entirely, and her face had gone deathly white. She was still on her feet - just - but Spencer feared she would collapse at any moment. Then what was he supposed to do? Did any of them know CPR? He sure as shit couldn't remember how it was done.

What the hell's wrong with this girl?

"Ash," he said again, cupping her face now. Her cheek was stone cold; one of her pupils was significantly more dilated than the other. Was she having a seizure or something? "Ash, listen to me. Ashley."

Her lips moved in response but he couldn't make out the words. He leaned closer, tilting his ear to her face.

"Say again?"

It was barely audible. "Hum... hum..."

"What?"

"Hum... don't... call me Ashley."

Relief ran through him like warm liquor.

"Ashley," he said again, deliberately. "Why can't I call you Ashley?"

Her eyelids flickered. She started to shake her head, slowly at first.

"Because... because..."

She was coming back. He could feel her shoulders tensing in his hands.

"Because... that's not my *fucking name*."

He took his hands away and she stayed on her feet. She blinked, looking around as though she'd just woken up. Her eyes came to rest on him and she frowned. "What happened?"

"I have no idea," Spencer said. "Are you ok now?"

"I, um... yeah."

"Are you sure? Because you looked - "

"I said I'm fine." She looked towards the store room door. "There's someone in there."

"Sure sounds like it. Here." He scooped the bolt-cutters off the floor and pushed them into her hands. "Get behind me."

"Why? Shitballs, don't open it!"

"I have to see who's in there."

"It's not her," Ash said quickly. Spencer's heart skipped a beat. "It's not. I don't know why I said those things. It... felt like I wasn't - "

Another moan drifted from the other side of the door. Ash moaned in response and slipped behind Spencer, holding the bolt-cutters protectively across her body.

"How do you know it's not her?" Spencer said, his eyes on the door handle.

"I just do," Ash replied in a small voice.

Spencer hesitated, glanced down at the thin blood trail by his feet, then said "Fuck it" and pulled open the door.

The first thing he saw was the boots, sticking out from the right-hand side of the tiny store room. He knew right away they were expensive, or they had been once upon a time. Now they were splattered with dried blood and some other substance he didn't recognize. The boots were in the light; Spencer had to take a step to his left to see the rest of the guy.

He was propped in the corner with his legs splayed in front of him. His left arm was across his chest and he gripped it with his right hand. Spencer could clearly see the guy's shirt sleeve was soaked through under his hand, surely the source of the blood. But there was so much of it on the floor...

The guy was breathing hard, his chest rising and falling sharply. His eyes went to Spencer and then to Ash, who retreated a few steps further back.

"Hey, buddy," the guy said, through gritted teeth. "Can you gimme a hand here?"

The question shook Spencer out of his stupor. "Oh, yes of course. Ash, hold the door a second."

She held it open (the closing arm would have pushed it shut again otherwise) and Spencer moved into the store room, crouching with some discomfort next to their new injured friend. His own bulk blocked most of the light but he could make out enough to see the sweat matting the guy's hair to his forehead.

He's hurt pretty bad.

"What happened to you?" Spencer said, ducking further so the guy could throw his right arm over his shoulder. He kept the left one pinned to his chest, gripping his own collar with bone-white fingers to keep it elevated above his heart.

"Got cut," said the guy.

With considerable effort, Spencer heaved him to his feet. He was tall, which didn't help, but he was able to use the inside wall of the store room for support and slide his way up. His blood-soaked right hand dangled near Spencer's face and he had to force himself not to recoil from it. Horror movie blood was one thing, but the real-life stuff was a whole different story.

Once the guy was back on his feet, Spencer helped him out of the store room. Ash let go of the door and it swung shut behind them. Spencer could see her out of the corner of his eye, watching the guy warily. She was still sheet-white from her own episode just a minute prior.

"Thank you," breathed the guy. He closed his eyes as, presumably, blood rushed from his head back to the lower half of his body. Spencer wondered how much of that blood was now soaked into his clothes, or remained on the store room floor behind them.

"Your arm," Spencer said, "how'd you cut it?"

The guy didn't respond right away. Ash shifted uncomfortably next to them. Right then, the utter absurdity of their situation hit Spencer like a cold, hard slap across the face and he had to swallow down the genuine urge to laugh.

Not the right time, Mr Bloom. And then: *Mary, where in the hell are you?*

"I didn't cut it," said the guy finally. "I mean, I wasn't the one... who did it." He had to push each word out between breaths. "I... was attacked."

Ash caught Spencer's eye and he read exactly what she was thinking - it started with "holy" and ended in "shit".

"Who attacked you?" Spencer asked.

"It was, um... I think I need to sit down."

"That's a good idea," Spencer said, thinking *I can't prop you up for much longer.* "But not here. Ash, how about we get our new friend out of this store?"

"Yeah."

"Can you lead the way?"

"Yeah."

She stepped gingerly over the blood trail and headed for the entrance. Spencer started after her, lugging their bleeding companion with him.

"Thanks, by the way," said the guy, still through gritted teeth. "I don't know how much longer I could've stayed in there."

"Any time," Spencer replied, helping him down the aisle towards the entrance. Ash was already at the shutter, doing her best to slide it further up. "You were lucky we needed something from this store."

"Lucky," the guy repeated, with something that might have been a snort of laughter.

"Oh, I'm Spencer. Spencer Bloom. And she's Ash... something."

"Nice to meet you, Spencer."

"And you are?"

They were almost at the door. Ash had succeeded in raising the shutter another couple of inches.

"I'd love to tell you," said the guy, wincing as Spencer slid out from under his arm. "But that's the thing: I can't remember my own fucking name."

The little girl looked from Taryn to Jeremy with enormous hazel eyes and mumbled her response. Taryn took her little hand gently and asked again; this time, her answer came out clearly.

"Emma. Mommy calls me Em."

"Em," Taryn repeated, smiling. "That's a pretty name. I'm Taryn, and this is Jeremy."

Jeremy waved awkwardly. Em tilted her face up at him again, then dropped her eyes back to Taryn, who was crouched next to her.

"Are your parents here, Em?" Taryn said.

Em looked around. "No."

"Were they here before, in the toy store?"

"No. Just me."

Taryn glanced up at Jeremy. He shrugged.

"Where was the last place you saw them, Em?"

The little girl considered the question for a moment. Her eyes drifted to the toys lining the shelves; Taryn gave her hand a small squeeze to bring her back.

"I don't know," Em said.

"Were they out there?" said Jeremy, pointing towards the concourse. Em followed his finger and nodded.

"They must've already been here," Taryn said to him, "when it happened."

"Yeah."

"So what do we do?"

"I guess... we bring her with us?"

"You *guess*?"

"I'm hungry," Em announced.

"Me too, Em," said Taryn, smiling again. It wasn't a lie, either - she hadn't eaten since lunchtime and her stomach had started rumbling. "Maybe we can get you something to eat upstairs, in the coffee place."

"Or the food court," suggested Jeremy. "Geez, I could go for a burger right now."

Taryn's stomach gurgled louder. "How about it, Em? You wanna come with us, get some food? And then we can help you find your Mom and Dad?"

Em nodded, smiling.

"Alright." Taryn stood up, still holding Em's hand. "Let's go."

She turned to go and felt a tug of resistance.

"What's wrong?"

"I want a toy."

Taryn looked at Jeremy. He sighed and gestured around them. "Take your pick."

"What toy do you want?" Taryn asked.

Em put a finger to her lips, puzzling. Taryn grinned - in her powder blue beanie hat and purple puffer jacket, she looked like a cute, oversized doll.

"This way," Em said, turning the opposite direction from the entrance.

"Umm..." said Jeremy.

"It's ok," Taryn said, allowing Em to lead her. "We'll help you find something. Right, Jer?"

"Sure." He lowered his voice. "But we shouldn't stay much longer."

"Trust me, I don't want to either."

Em led them to the end of the aisle, paused, and went left. Another turn later and they found themselves in the electronic toys section. Em drifted along the row, gazing up in wonder at the battery-powered gadgets laid out on the shelves.

After a minute, Jeremy whispered, "This is so weird. I mean, who owns this kid?"

"Somebody," said Taryn, watching Em take a toy from the lowest shelf.

"Duh," Jeremy muttered. He looked over his shoulder towards where the entrance must be. "We should go."

"We will - just let her get something first. You don't have to be so impatient."

Jeremy sighed. "We sound like we're married."

"You wish, Lewis."

Em dropped the toy she'd been holding and pointed at one of the shelves beyond her reach.

"Can I have that one?" she asked.

Taryn went to the shelf and lifted down the toy Em had selected. It was a little robot cat with a bubble head and light-up eyes. Em received it gratefully, turning it over in her hands.

"Happy now?" said Taryn, tapping her on the head.

"Yes," Em grinned, hugging the toy to her coat. "I like cats."

"Me too. Maybe Santa will bring you a real live one for Christmas."

"Yeah."

"You'd like that, right?"

"Yeah. I saw him."

"Who?"

"Santa."

Taryn frowned, glancing at Jeremy.

"Where? In the mall?"

"Yeah."

"She must mean in the grotto," Jeremy said, "before everyone... left."

"Oh, ok. Is that where you saw Santa, Em? In the little house with the candy canes and stuff?"

"No. Not in the house. Just out there."

Taryn's heart, which had taken a back seat since they'd found Em, began to make its presence felt again.

The footsteps.

"So, you saw Santa? In the mall?"

"Yeah."

"Tar, we should go," Jeremy said uneasily.

"Wait," she said. "Em, where did you see him in the mall?"

"Just out there," Em replied dismissively, focused on the cat now.

"Not in the toy store?"

"No."

"It was just you in here?"

Em sighed, as though they'd worn her patience thin.

"Santa's not in here," she said, looking up at them. "It's just the elf."

EIGHT

Taryn blinked. She hadn't heard her right. "The what?"

"The elf," Em replied, matter-of-factly. She was already looking around her again, her attention broken by the walls of colorful toys.

Taryn glanced up at Jeremy, who mouthed *elf?* and shrugged. Taryn shrugged back, then crouched down next to Em.

"Did you say there's an elf in here?" she asked slowly, watching the little girl's face. She wasn't exactly sure what she was looking for, maybe a flicker of deception. *Can kids this age lie that way?* "Inside the toy store?"

"Mm-hmm," Em nodded, still not meeting her gaze.

"Emma," said Taryn. She took her little arm in her hand; Em looked at her then. "Em, who else is in here?"

"I told you," Em said, leaning close, her hazel eyes huge. "It's the elf. *Ellllf.*"

Something crawled down Taryn's spine. She rocked on her haunches and had to grab Jeremy's shin to stop herself tipping over.

"Tar," said Jeremy in a low voice, "let's go."

"Yes." She straightened up. Her head was swimming. "Let's find the others."

"Elf," said Em again, louder this time. "*Ellllf!*"

"Em, not so loud," Taryn urged. *The footsteps right behind her, she hadn't imagined them.*

"ELLLLF!"

"Hey!" Jeremy hissed, thrusting his face towards Em. "Shut up, ok? We don't *need* this. We'll leave you here."

"Jer..."

He spun away on his heel, biting back a string of angry words. But it had been enough - Em went back to her cat toy in silence.

Taryn's head still felt lighter than it should and she reached for the nearest shelf. Suddenly, *The Play Emporium* seemed enormous. The gaudy menagerie of toys stacked on either side of the aisle became walls of sickening color stretching to the ceiling, towering over them. Anyone else in the store would be well hidden behind those shelves, wouldn't they? Whoever was in here with them

I told you it's the elf

would be able to move around freely without being seen. In fact, whoever it was could easily follow them anywhere in the mall without them knowing. It was a big place with plenty of person-sized, inanimate objects to hide behind. One could comfortably slip out from behind a Christmas tree or even a vending machine and, say, padlock a shutter closed.

Or leave a human ear on the rim of a fountain.

"Em, can you come with us now?" said Taryn, straining to keep her voice level. "Will you come and meet our friends?"

The little girl looked up at her. Taryn thought *She'll be pretty when she's older* and instantly resolved (perhaps without knowing it) to get Emma safely out of the *Outlet Complex* mall and back to her family.

Em responded as though Taryn had spoken directly into her head: "Where's my Mommy?"

"I don't know," Taryn said. "Not far." That could be a lie, of course. She could be dead. "Do you remember where you last saw her, Em?"

"Taryn," Jeremy insisted, "come *on*."

She heard it in his voice then, as she'd heard it before back on the concourse. Back when she thought he might be about to have a panic attack. Jeremy Lewis, who'd never had a panic attack for as long as she'd known him.

"Em, you're coming with us, ok?"

Without waiting for an answer, Taryn took the little girl's hand. Her skin was cool - cold, even - and Taryn wondered why she wasn't wearing gloves or mittens. She turned to follow Jeremy, preparing for a tug on her arm and another cry of "ELF!", but there was none. Em waddled along after her without complaint, clutching the toy cat against her body as her sneakers flashed red blooms across the dimly-lit floor.

"Good girl," said Taryn. The words tasted strange coming from her teenage mouth, which wasn't accustomed to addressing children in such an adult manner. The only child she spoke to on a regular basis was her younger brother, and she'd never called him "good" before (though she often called him a girl). She and Jeremy were barely more than children themselves, and they needed to find adults again as soon as possible. They needed Spencer, the stranger they barely knew who'd become their surrogate guardian for the day. Hell, Taryn wouldn't even turn down Lincoln's help right now either, crippled and stoned though the guy was.

She followed Jeremy as quickly as Em's much-shorter legs would allow, trailing him through the shelf maze towards the store entrance. She had no idea how Jeremy knew where he was going, but she didn't care. Not one bit. The sooner they were out of *The Play Emporium* and back with the others, the better. She never wanted to set foot in this store again, even if it was full of bustling shoppers, conversation and music. Never again.

And the faster she hurried, the more unshakable that creeping sensation of someone following her became, the notion that someone was right on her heels, reaching for her hair with gnarled, skeletal fingers. The urge to look back was almost maddening, but she kept her eyes fixed on Jeremy. She didn't even look down at Em.

They turned into the sports equipment aisle - footballs, basketballs, tennis racquets, hockey sticks, all sized for children - and the front of the store came into view. Taryn saw a chaotically-arranged Christmas display in the store window she hadn't really noticed earlier when they'd first spotted Em. How many kids had been drawn inexorably towards *The Play Emporium* doors throughout December by that display, dragging grumbling parents in their wake? Is that why Em had wandered inside?

Now Taryn did glance down. Em was keeping step by her side, staring ahead without expression, and for the first time Taryn wondered if she might be in some form of shock? After all -

She blundered into Jeremy, who'd stopped at the end of the aisle.

"Hey - "

Without turning, Jeremy reached back and grabbed her arm, hard. *Stop talking*.

Taryn looked past him and saw it. She heard Em inhale next to her and knew what was coming; dropping to her knees, she clapped a hand over the little girl's mouth before she could yell the word again. It came anyway, muffled against Taryn's palm.

She pressed her hand tighter to Em's mouth, wrapping her other arm around her body, pulling her close.

The elf was standing near the store entrance.

Its back was to them and its head was bowed. It had something in its hands, working at it busily.

The elf was real.

Taryn could feel her hand trembling against Em's mouth. She tightened her grip on the little girl's body, pinning it against her own.

It's actually real.

She wrenched her gaze from it and looked at Jeremy. He'd eased down next to her, his eyes bugging out behind his glasses. The three of them were partially hidden behind a barrel of foam softball bats, but the elf would surely see them if it looked directly their way.

Jeremy's finger went to the bridge of his glasses, pushed them partway up his nose, and stayed there, frozen. Jeremy was no good.

With some reluctance, Taryn went back to the elf. She watched it between the softball bat handles, noting that it was shorter than her, maybe around Ash's height. It wore a bright green coat and hat with white fur trim, candy cane leggings, and black boots with curled toes. A black belt was buckled around its waist. Its shoulders jerked spasmodically in line with its hand movements, and even from the far side of the store front, Taryn could hear it whispering to itself in a high, child-like voice.

A cold bead of sweat started at the base of her neck. Warm breath puffed against her index finger from Em's nostrils and she relaxed her grip slightly. Catching Em's eye, she uttered a silent *shush* and shook her head slowly. Em blinked up at her, then nodded.

Taryn turned back to Jeremy. His finger was still on the bridge of his glasses and he wobbled a little on his haunches. He was more exposed in the aisle than she and Em were - the elf would see him first if it glanced over its left shoulder.

What's it doing with its hands? Taryn thought.

She nudged Jeremy with her elbow. His head turned towards her but his eyes stayed on the elf. She nudged him again, harder, and he looked her way. She nodded past him at the shelf, where bright yellow softballs were displayed on plastic holders. Jeremy studied them for a moment, not really comprehending, then shook his head at her. Taryn nodded vigorously back at him, mouthing "Yes!"

At the store entrance, the elf giggled.

Taryn saw sweat on Jeremy's brow now. The store wasn't especially warm, but they were both sweating. Her hand was slick against Em's mouth.

We've got to get out of here, she thought (no, *screamed* the words in her mind), and as if he'd heard it spoken right in his ear, Jeremy reached over and plucked a softball from the shelf.

Taryn leaned close to Em and gently took her hand away from her mouth, cupping her chin instead. She whispered what was to happen next, her voice barely rising above the sound of the girl's breathing. Her heart was now thumping so hard it was becoming painful.

"Em," she whispered, "we're going to run, ok? I'm going to carry you. Nod if you understand."

Em looked down at the toy cat and nodded.

"Don't make a sound, alright?"

She nodded again.

Taryn looked at Jeremy. Something passed between them then, something that never had before, and never would again. It was fleeting and wholly tangible, and then it was gone.

Jeremy stood up.

When Spencer, Ash and their injured friend got back to *The Coffee Place*, Lincoln was fast asleep in his chair by the window. He still had Spencer's jacket draped over him and he was snoring softly.

"Shit, we haven't been gone *that* long," said Ash.

Spencer, who was still supporting the man they'd found in the hardware store and was starting to feel more than a little strain in his shoulders, kicked Lincoln's chair. "Wake up!" he snapped.

Lincoln snorted, then sat bolt upright and uttered a yelp. "What happened?" he said groggily.

"You were supposed to stay awake, but you fell asleep," Ash replied, setting the bolt cutters down by the entrance as she came in, "that's what."

"Oh." Lincoln rubbed his eyes; Spencer's jacket, a once-upon-a-time birthday gift from Mary, slid down to his lap. "Um, sorry guys."

"Sorry doesn't get us the hell out of here," Spencer said. Then, to the man whose arm was slung across his shoulders: "Could we sit you down somewhere?"

"Course."

Spencer eased him down into a wooden chair by one of the tables. Both he and the wounded man winced throughout the move. Ash drifted over to the windows and pressed her face to the glass.

"I can't see anything," she said.

"No cops?" said the man from *Big Al's Hardware*, grimacing as Spencer lifted his arm off his shoulders.

"Nopers. Can't see any lights out there at all now."

During the slow walk from the hardware store to the coffee place, Ash and Spencer had relayed to the wounded man their experience in the movie theater, starting with their discovery that the place was totally deserted, then on to the bloody-handed man at the doors and Spencer's strange phone conversation with the 911 dispatcher, and finally to how they'd come to be locked inside the mall. They told him about Taryn and Jeremy, who were somewhere else in the building searching for an emergency exit, and about their dutiful lookout Lincoln, keeping a watchful eye on the parking lot from the coffee place windows. The only thing they didn't mention was the severed ear on the fountain.

As they'd walked, Spencer had asked the guy how he'd ended up in *Big Al's* store room with a deep slice in his left forearm and received the answer he'd expected.

"I don't remember exactly."

"What *do* you remember?" Ash said.

Spencer was on the verge of rebuking her (*why, when she's not your kid?*) but held off. He, too, was eager for more answers. Anything that might lead to Mary.

The guy frowned, gritting his teeth against the obvious pain in his left arm. His right arm was around Spencer's shoulders, plastering yet more blood onto the older man's shirt. The guy could walk fine but he'd clearly been bleeding steadily for a while, and Spencer didn't want him passing out just yet.

"I honestly can't remember much," he said, staring hard at the tiled floor ahead of them. "I was here to do some shopping, I think... for Christmas. Get some presents... for people."

"Your wife?" suggested Spencer.

"Huh?"

"You're wearing a wedding ring."

The guy looked down at his left hand, as if surprised to find it there against his chest. A platinum wedding band, speckled with blood, glinted on his third finger.

"Oh," he said. "Yeah, I guess... I must have been shopping for her. Yeah, that's why I'm here. I was buying something for my wife."

"And what happened?" Spencer said. "Where is everyone?"

"Geez, that's a good question."

Ash sighed; Spencer shot her a look. The guy didn't seem to hear.

"I remember a little, but not much," he said. "The mall was full, really busy, like you'd expect just before the holidays. Lots of families in buying gifts, parents getting Santa presents for... wait, how old is she?"

"I'm fifteen," Ash said, without looking his way.

"Right. So everything was normal, as it should be. Maybe even busier than usual. I've been here plenty of times since I was a kid and it's always been real popular at Christmas. They have a Santa Claus here and lots of parents bring kids in to meet him - you know, sit on his lap and shit."

Spencer nodded and thought, *hurry the hell up.* The guy's cologne was overpowering this close.

"Something happened earlier, in the afternoon. Must've been while you guys were watching your movie. There was an incident, or something. Everyone had to be evacuated from the building."

"Evacuated where?" said Ash.

"What kind of incident?" said Spencer. His skin had prickled at the word.

"I... I can't remember exactly. Sorry. I must've been hit on the head when I was... attacked."

Spencer bit back the "Who attacked you?" question and said instead, "The incident - what was it? A fire? Terrorists?"

"No fire," the guy said, wincing again. They were almost at the coffee place by then. "Nothing like that. But everyone had to leave right away. They just dropped what they were doing and cleared out."

"But where did they go?" Spencer said.

"And why'd the people in the movie theater come here, too?" added Ash.

"They did?"

"Yeah. There were loads of footprints at the door, going inside."

"Shit, that's weird. Hell if I know why, though." They reached the entrance to *The Coffee Place*, a doorless archway a few yards in from the second floor railing. "What I *do* know is everyone in this place just upped and left, en masse, about an hour ago. Maybe more. I think that's when it was, anyway. Spent most of the time since then bleeding in a back room."

"You said you were attacked?" said Spencer, and then he saw Lincoln asleep in the chair by the coffee place windows and muttered, "Hang on."

Now, as Ash came away from those snow-smattered windows and Lincoln fumbled for his crutches, clearly eager to get out of Spencer's reach, the man with the injured arm answered their earlier question. "I was coming out of the bathroom, the one off the food court. I saw everyone was gone... not much more than a glimpse... and then something came at me with a blade. A knife, like the kind they use in the sandwich place. Fucker got me in the arm before I knocked him over one of the tables. Then I ran. But I must've hit my head somewhere along the way, because the next thing I knew I was in that store room in the hardware place, bleeding all over myself. Could've been in there for hours if you guys hadn't found me."

"You left quite the trail," said Spencer.

"Yeah, *quite*," said Ash. "Quite a whole fucking lot of it."

The guy nodded. Under the brighter lights of the coffee place, Spencer noticed for the first time the sweat running down his forehead and the gray pallidness of his complexion. He turned to Lincoln. "Go see if there's a first aid kit behind the counter. And Ash, get some water, please."

Ash went to the counter and Lincoln hobbled after her. Spencer lowered himself into the chair opposite his new, blood-stained acquaintance and exhaled slowly.

The guy smiled grimly. "Hard day, bud?"

"You could say so," Spencer replied. "My wife's one of the people who's missing."

The smile vanished. "Shit. Sorry about that. What's her name?"

"Mary."

"Mary. You'll find her."

"I intend to."

"I suppose my wife's missing too, except, uh..."

"Except you can't remember her name?"

"Yeah, that."

The guy dropped his blue-green gaze back to the wound on his arm. His tousled brown hair, which looked recently-trimmed, was matted to his scalp. Spencer guessed he was in his early thirties at most.

"Is this it?" Lincoln said from behind the counter. He held up a small red pouch.

"Does it say First Aid on it?" Spencer replied.

Lincoln studied it. Ash came up beside him with a glass of water in her hand and pointed at the pouch. "It says it right there, trash-tipper. Can you even *read*?"

"You're a little turd, you know that?"

"Just bring it over," Spencer said wearily.

"Anyone want a coffee while we're back here?" Ash called, once again chipper now they were well away from the hardware store. "I make a mean chai latte. I can even do the foam pattern thing."

Spencer sighed again. "No, no coffee. Well, maybe in a minute. Just come here!"

Ash snatched the first aid kit from Lincoln's hand and started back around the counter. He maneuvered after her. Spencer watched them approach, watched how easily Ash moved now, lighthearted and teenagery. Was it all an act? A defense mechanism, shunting aside what she'd seen back in *Big Al's Hardware*? The blood trailing across the floor, the bleeding stranger moaning behind the door. It was enough to scar a world-worn adult, never mind a potty-mouthed Zoomer born well after nine-eleven.

And the way she'd been, just before he'd opened the door. She looked like she was about to have a stroke.

Mary's blood is tainted, isn't it?

He shook that off. There was no way she could have known. He'd misheard her.

"Can you roll that sleeve up?" he said, pointing at the guy's arm.

"Yeah, I think... shit!"

"Stuck to your skin?"

"Fucking right it is. Bastard sleeve."

Ash set the water on the table and handed the first aid kit to Spencer. He took it, stole another quick glance at her expression (*was that look still in her eyes, just below the surface?*), and un-zipped it. The guy managed to push his sleeve up to the elbow, taking a thin layer of ragged skin along for the ride. The knife wound was on the outside of his forearm, running down to the back of his hand; it was about six inches long and still oozing dark blood at its widest point. Spencer could clearly see how the wound grew shallower closer to the hand until it became no more than a thin scratch, like an oversized paper cut. If the knife had stayed deeply embedded that far down, it would have nicked several veins and he probably wouldn't have made it.

Spencer swallowed and opened the kit.

"You done this before?" said the guy, grimacing at the wound.

"Well, no," Spencer replied, taking out a bandage roll. "But how hard can it be?"

As it turned out, it was much harder than they'd all imagined. Both Ash and Lincoln turned gray when they got a good look at the laceration under the coffee place lights and Spencer had to order them away from the table. Immediately after this, the guy almost bit through the sleeve of his good arm when Spencer squirted antiseptic gel onto the wound to clean it. And when Lincoln saw the bloodied strip of gauze come away from the cut, he had to lean his face against one of the ice-cold windows and take a series of deep breaths.

At one point, Spencer Bloom genuinely thought he was about to be the only conscious person left in *The Coffee Place*, waiting at an abandoned table in a deserted mall for two teenagers to come rescue him.

But after a couple of painful minutes, it was done. He secured the bandage with some medical tape and it held well enough. It would need to be changed in about an hour or less, of course, but they'd be long gone by then.

"Good as new," Spencer said.

The guy downed the water Ash had brought him and clunked the glass down on the table. "Thank you," he said, scrutinizing the bandage doubtfully. It covered his entire forearm below the elbow and most of his left hand.

"Keep it elevated," said Spencer, "I don't know how to make a sling."

Lincoln started back towards the table. Spencer quickly gathered the bloodied gauze into a bundle (the wound was messier than he'd first thought) and took it over to the condiment station at the end of the counter, stuffing it through the trash hole. He noticed a full takeout cup of coffee next to the hole; an unopened sugar sachet floated in the liquid.

Ash popped up from behind the counter, chewing on a chocolate donut. She caught his look and shrugged. "They'll go to waste," she said, spraying crumbs. "You want one?"

Spencer's stomach growled automatically.

"In a minute," he said. "You're feeling ok now?"

"What d'you mean?"

He hesitated. "Never mind. Come out from behind there."

"Yes, boss."

He pumped anti-bac into his hands, scrubbing them as clean as he could manage. Ash came back around the counter and they returned to the table in the center of the room. Lincoln had seated himself next to the guy and was poking around inside the first aid kit.

"Still no idea what your name is?" Spencer said, standing by the table. The guy looked up, thought about it for a moment, then shook his head. "Fine, then I'm going to call you John, ok? Just until you remember."

"Hey, that's my middle name," said Lincoln brightly.

"Steve," said Spencer quickly. "I'm calling you Steve."

The guy - now Steve - nodded. "Sure, if that makes it easier."

"It does. So, Steve, here's the deal. We've got work to do if we're going to get out of this place. First up, I think we need to grab you some medication to manage your pain, otherwise you might wig out on us once we get outside. Can't have you passing out in the snow. I think there's a drug store somewhere on this floor - "

"There is," said Ash.

" - so we'll go there next, together. We should be able to spot Jeremy and Taryn along the way, too, and if they've found an emergency exit, then great. If not, we'll use the bolt cutters to get out through the main entrance. The police should be here by then, if they aren't already. Either that or the folks from the mall, who you say were evacuated earlier. They can't be too far from here. And if, for whatever reason the cops don't show up, we can borrow another car from the parking lot and drive to the nearest town."

"Rockmount," said Steve. "It's Rockmount."

"Ok, Rockmount it is," Spencer said, spreading his hands. "Either way, I think it's really important we get out of this building as fast as humanly possible."

"What about my car?" said Lincoln. "Yunno, behind the movie theater?"

"Oh yeah, I forgot about that. We'll cross that bridge if we come to it. That is, if there're no cops outside and we can't get another vehicle out of the snow. Then we'll go for your car. I'd rather not go back into the movie theater if we can help it, though."

"The keys are in there," Lincoln said.

If only you hadn't been too stoned to remember when we were in the office earlier.

"A car sounds good to me," said Steve. Spencer noticed he was grinding his teeth, maybe to deal with the pain. "I can't remember if I have one, but I don't have any keys on me anyway. And between this guy's crutches and my light head, we won't get anywhere fast on foot. The elevator's just down there."

"Ok, fine, we can vote on it - "

"I say yay," said Lincoln.

" - when the time comes. We need to grab that medication first."

"And find Taryn and Jeremy," added Ash.

"Yes, that too. But first, I want to know one thing, Steve."

"What's that?" said Steve, gingerly patting his already-reddening bandage.

"I want to know about that," Spencer said, nodding at the wound. "I want to know who it was slashed you with a knife. Because that person's probably still in the mall, and they probably put that padlock on the entrance shutter, and left the ear on the fountain."

"The what on the fountain?"

"Never mind," said Spencer, dismissing it with a wave of his hand. "Just tell us, Steve, as best you can remember - who the hell stabbed you in the food court?"

Steve opened his mouth.

Just then, someone started yelling from the concourse.

NINE

Jeremy had never been great at sports. His father had been a moderately decent basketball player, and he'd always not-so-secretly hoped his only son might one day enjoy some success on the playing field, or on the court, or even in the pool. Anything at all, really, so long as it got Jer out of the house and playing with other kids his own age. *Really* playing, too - nothing that involved a screen, or that Dungeons and Dragons nonsense. Physical activity was key to a young boy's development, according to Christopher Lewis, especially if it involved kicking or throwing or hitting a ball. Those were *real* activities for real, salt of the earth, *American* teenagers.

Unfortunately for Christopher Lewis, his only son had negligible interest in sport and even less desire to take part in it, in any form. To Jeremy, physical activity meant walking home from school rather than taking the bus. He wasn't lazy or unfit, and as with most things in life, he could probably have picked up some sporting ability if he'd really put his mind to it. He just didn't want to, and so he hadn't.

Taryn knew all of this about Jeremy, so when he pulled his arm back to throw the softball, her breath caught in her throat. She'd seen him toss a ball before and knew it was more likely he'd bounce the damn thing off the shelf and smack himself in the face than actually get it across the store. If that happened, there would surely be a commotion in their aisle, and the elf would hear.

But against all the odds afforded by ridiculously poor hand-eye coordination and years of crippling paternal pressure, Jeremy Lewis managed to heave the ball over the top of the shelf; it bounced off the ceiling with a *thud* and came down somewhere at the far side of the store, crashing into something metallic.

At the store entrance, the elf's head jerked towards the sound. Taryn saw a fake pointed ear and a scraggle of dark hair. She saw more than that, much more, and her breath remained trapped in her throat.

Then the elf bounded off towards the far side of the store, disappearing from view. Jeremy grabbed her hand and yanked her to her feet.

"Come on!" he hissed.

Without really knowing what she was doing, Taryn scooped Em up in her arms and followed Jeremy towards *The Play Emporium* entrance. Their cautious jog broke into a run almost immediately and their sneakers slapped on the floor, far too loud. Em twisted in Taryn's arms, trying to see where the ELF had gone.

Taryn didn't look back. She didn't want to see where it was. She didn't want to see that hideous, distorted face swing in their direction and have those bulging, bloodshot eyes lock onto hers.

As they crossed the store threshold, she looked down and saw a splatter of scarlet red blood on the floor where the elf had been standing.

Then they were out in the concourse again. Jeremy was a pace ahead of her, sprinting now, his skinny legs pumping. She thought he was going for the emergency exit and tried to shout, but she was already winded from carrying Em. The little girl squirmed in her arms, still trying to spot the elf.

Oh please oh please don't let it be right behind us

Suddenly, Jeremy veered to the right. Taryn turned after him, almost skidding on the smooth floor.

"Where..." she started, but then she saw where he was heading. The Santa's Grotto was just ahead, a little way up from *The Play Emporium*. If they could get behind it, they'd be out of sight.

Jeremy reached it first, ducking beneath one of the giant inflatable candy canes that leaned over the white picket fence. He got behind the grotto's painted plywood wall, extending a hand for Taryn. She grabbed it gratefully and he hauled her and Em behind with him. They dropped back to their haunches, breathing hard. Taryn couldn't hear anything past the blood pounding in her ears.

She eased Em to the floor and pressed a finger to her lips, shaking her head. Em copied the movement and Taryn smiled at her, so relieved for a second she almost laughed.

Jeremy's hand was on her arm again. He beckoned her towards the corner of the grotto. Holding Em back with one hand, Taryn shifted next to Jeremy and looked.

Her heart skipped a beat.

The elf was at *The Play Emporium* entrance again, facing out into the concourse. It must have gotten there mere seconds after they'd reached the grotto and somehow hadn't spotted them.

As Taryn watched, keenly aware of Jeremy's trembling hand gripping her wrist, the elf's head turned left and right, scanning the wide open area normally occupied by Christmas shoppers carrying bulging bags and toffee nut lattes and cinnamon bear claws, searching for them.

As its face swung in their direction, Taryn heard Jeremy's sharp intake of breath by her ear. It wasn't because it had seen them, though - they were mostly concealed behind the corner of the makeshift building and the gaudy decorations in the garden surrounding it. Jeremy had almost gasped aloud, as Taryn had very nearly done, because he'd gotten a good look at the elf's face for the first time.

It was, Taryn thought, as if there were invisible weights attached to the elf's skin, dragging it down in horrible, loose folds around the rest of its features; the skin itself was corpse-gray and ran red in places, barely clinging to the flesh beneath. Its jaw hung open exposing bone-white teeth, and the corners of its mouth were turned up in a grotesque, frozen leer. Saliva dribbled over its cracked, bleeding lips and ran down onto the shining buttons of its cartoonish-looking green coat. One of its fake plastic ears jutted out at an angle through a wisp of tangled dark hair.

But none of that compared to the eyes.

Back in the store, Taryn had imagined them as being bloodshot, like the eyes of a drunk man might be after a long night on the town, but that wasn't it at all. The elf's eyes weren't just bloodshot.

They were *bleeding*.

Jeremy's fingers dug into Taryn's wrist. He was visibly shaking next to her. She slowly pulled her hand back until the movement forced Jeremy to turn away from the elf and look at her. His eyes were enormous behind his fogged-up glasses.

Clenching her teeth to keep them from chattering, Taryn peered past him.

The elf was still by *The Play Emporium* entrance but it was no longer gazing about the concourse with its horrific red stare. It had something in its hands now and was working at it with the same erratic, fitful motions as before, as though it'd completely forgotten it'd heard them rush out of the store. There was a glint of metal in the midst of those spasmodic hand movements, just for a split second; Taryn squinted, saw what the elf was doing, and drew back behind Jeremy again.

"We have to go," she whispered, and he jumped at the sound. She tried to keep her voice from rising, barely containing the rising terror building deep inside her. "We have to go *right now*."

Jeremy just stared back at her, not reacting to what she was saying. Just like back in the store. He was shutting down again.

Taryn felt a tug on her sleeve. She looked down, saw Em's mouth start to open, and immediately pressed her finger to the little girl's lips, shaking her head furiously. Em's brow furrowed but she stayed silent.

I have to look, Taryn thought wildly, responding to the part of her begging to run screaming for the emergency exit. *I have to know if it's still there.*

She took a breath and leaned past Jeremy again.

Peering between the festive fixtures of the grotto garden, she spotted the elf just as it turned and disappeared back into the toy store, leaving a small puddle of blood where it had stood. It was gone.

"Let's go," she whispered to Jeremy. He stared right through her; she grabbed his chin, not gently. "Jer. Let's go."

Jeremy met her gaze and nodded.

"Straight back to the others, ok?" Taryn said. "And then we..."

She felt the movement behind her and twisted round, too late. Em was already going.

"*No!*" Taryn hissed. She swiped, missed the purple puffer jacket by an inch and overbalanced, toppling onto her side. Em darted to the far corner of the grotto, and then she was gone.

Taryn scrambled to her feet. She grabbed Jeremy's jacket collar and yanked him out of his stupor. "Come on!"

They hadn't made it more than a few yards before Em's happy cry came from further down the concourse and Taryn's blood ran cold in her veins.

"Santa!" Em declared.

"Who's that?" said Ash.

"Is that a kid?" said Lincoln.

Spencer's heart fluttered. It'd sure sounded like a child, and if there *was* a child, that meant there were parents somewhere in the building. And if there were other people here...

Mary.

He hurried across to *The Coffee Place* entrance, sending a chair clattering to the floor with one clumsy swing of his leg. Ash beat him to it, darting nimbly out to the second level balcony, her jet black hair whipping about her head. Behind them at the table, Lincoln groped for his crutches.

"There!" said Ash.

Spencer joined her at the railing and saw: a little girl in a light blue hat and purple coat, running up the concourse towards them. Lights flashed on her sneakers as she approached.

"There's Taryn," Ash said, pointing, "and Jeremy."

The other two kids were passing the fountain now, sprinting after the little girl. She must have been faster than she looked.

"What's she saying?" said Spencer.

Ash had turned away from the railing for a moment. When she came back to Spencer's side, the bolt cutters were in her hand. She frowned. "I think she said... Santa?"

Taryn had almost reached her. She'd catch her in a second.

They look terrified, Spencer thought with some alarm. *What's happened to them?*

"Why's she yelling Santa?" Ash said.

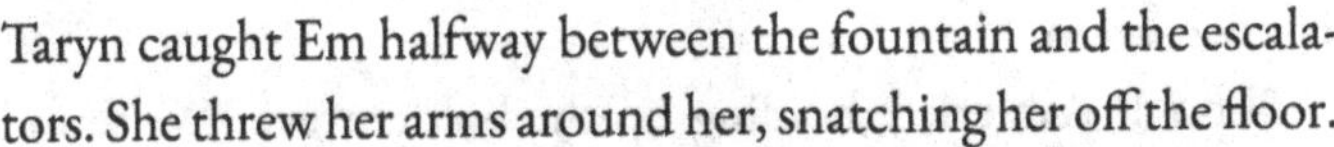

Taryn caught Em halfway between the fountain and the escalators. She threw her arms around her, snatching her off the floor.

"What're you doing?" she cried breathlessly. She knew she was holding her too tightly but she didn't care, not right now. Her heart was pummeling the inside of her chest. "Why did you run?"

"Santa!" Em replied, waving her free hand. The toy cat's head bobbled in the crook of her other arm. "Santa! Santa!"

"What's she talking about?" said Jeremy, puffing up beside them.

The elf. Taryn swung round, expecting to see it charging up the center of the mall towards them, grinning its mad, evil grin. *It'll have heard us.*

"Taryn," said Jeremy.

"Where is it?" she gasped, scanning the motionless concourse. "Is it coming?"

It had a knife. She couldn't see the toy store anymore - the grotto was in the way.

It had a knife in its hands and it was cutting something. Carving it.

A chunk of flesh.

"Taryn," Jeremy said again.

Ash's voice from somewhere above: "Taryn!"

She turned. In her arms, Em whooped with delight.

⁂

"Taryn!" Ash called again. "Jer! Where've you guys been?"

Spencer watched as Taryn turned in their direction; her tawny hair, smooth and tidy when he'd first met her back in the movie theater (*and didn't that feel like a lifetime ago?*), was now a wild tangle. Jeremy's glasses were fogged white with condensation.

"Look!" Ash cried, holding up the bolt cutters. "We found them!"

"Who's the kid?" Spencer said haltingly.

His anti-bacced hands were slippery on the metal railing. He let go of it and looked back into the coffee place. Lincoln was on his feet, making his way towards the entrance. Steve was still seated at the table, staring blankly ahead.

Why isn't he getting up?

Spencer started to turn back towards the railing, and only then did he finally notice what Jeremy and Taryn had already seen, what little Em Price was gleefully yelling about. He'd been coming up the escalator to their left, riding the mechanical staircase to the mall's second level, and somehow they hadn't spotted him. Staring at him now, Spencer couldn't think how. He was huge and red, his bulk filling the full width of the escalator as he stepped off and started towards them without pause, his eyes spewing blood into the once-white mass of his beard, eyes that were now locked on Ash, grinning down at her friends from the railing, oblivious, and well within the swinging arc of the ax Santa Claus brandished in both hands.

Taryn screamed, "Look out!" but it was already too late. The ax rose, its blood-stained head flashing in the light. Ash turned as if in slow motion, gazing up at the enormous man in red, at the weapon raised above his head.

Spencer didn't remember crossing to where Ash stood. It couldn't have taken more than two steps to get there, and in that time the ax seemed to hang in the air, dripping blood, poised and hungry. He didn't remember grabbing Ash by the shoulders, and he didn't remember throwing her to one side. She felt like a rag doll in his big clumsy hands. Spencer didn't remember being heroic because it was perhaps the first time in his life he'd had to be.

Either way, he was in Ash's place when the ax came down, and instead of cleaving her skull in two, it buried itself deep in his chest, all the way up to where the ax head met the handle. At first he wasn't aware of the pain - his brain was slow to respond, made sluggish by the sheer unreality of what was happening to him - and he took in the sensation of a foreign object occupying his chest cavity with a kind of wonder. *There's something there that shouldn't be*, he thought with remarkable lucidity. Then the ax head shifted inside him, severing his aorta like an over-boiled carrot, and that was that for Spencer Bloom.

He hit the floor with the ax still in his chest, briefly pictured Mary's smiling face, and then was gone.

***

Ash didn't see the ax hit Spencer but she heard the sound, and she never forgot it as long as she lived. It was most comparable, she thought later, to a butcher's cleaver thunking into a juicy ribeye and not quite making it all the way through to the chopping board beneath.

Spencer had thrown her into the plastiglass divider separating *The Coffee Place* area from the second floor of the concourse. She bounced off it, somehow kept her footing, and stumbled a few paces away from Spencer and the Santa before falling to the floor. An electric burst of pain shot through her left wrist as she came down on it, and she cried out. For whatever reason, she kept hold of the bolt cutters with her right hand.

Taryn screamed again from the floor below, but there were no words in it this time.

Ash struggled back to her feet, tasting bile. Her knees almost buckled right away. The Santa had his back to her and was tugging furiously on the ax, still stuck deep in Spencer's body. Crimson blood pooled around his polished black boots.

He's dead, Ash thought dully. *He's dead and it's my fault.*

Fresh movement at the coffee place entrance. Lincoln was there on his crutches, staring open-mouthed at the scene unfolding before him. The Santa saw him, paused, then went back to working the ax out of Spencer's torso.

He's dead and we're going to die too.

With a sickening *thwuck*, the ax pulled free from Spencer's chest. The effort actually made the Santa stagger back a step and his boot splatted into the spreading blood. The ax head came up by his shoulder, dripping scarlet death.

Lincoln's open mouth finally produced sound and he barked "What the *fuck*?", wavering on his crutches on *The Coffee Place* threshold like a gangly ear of wheat ready for reaping. The Santa saw him, adjusted the ax in his gloved hands, and started forward.

Spencer's dead and now Linc's going to die.

Ash sucked in a breath.

"HEY YOU FAT FUCK!"

The Santa stopped and turned slowly in her direction. Between the mussed, red-soaked top of its beard and the fluffy white rim of its hat, its skin was gray and flaking off the flesh beneath. Its eyes bulged from their sockets, weeping blood.

"Oh shit," Ash said.

"Ash, *run!*" Taryn screamed from below.

Ash spun on her heel and ran.

When the enormous man in red - the *Santa Claus* - went for Ash, Taryn, somehow, had the presence of mind to swivel away from the scene, taking Em with her. She didn't want the little girl seeing what was about to happen. She didn't want to see it herself.

"No, Santa!" Em yelled. "I want Santa!"

Taryn squeezed her eyes shut.

There was a cry from the second floor, brief and agonizing. Taryn's stomach lurched; she buried her face in Em's hair. Jeremy uttered a choked gasp to her left.

"Oh, oh no," Taryn heard him say. "Mr Bloom."

She opened her eyes and swung back around. Stars danced in her vision. For a single moment, she forgot Em was in her arms.

On the second floor of the mall concourse, Spencer Bloom had an ax in his chest. His hands were up in a defensive posture, palms facing his attacker, as though he was trying to surrender. If that'd been the case, his submission had gone unheeded. The man dressed as Santa still clutched the handle of the ax; he was dragged forward a step as Spencer fell until he straddled the other man, one shiny black boot on either side of his victim's body. Spencer clutched weakly at the ax handle for a second before his arms fell away, limp and lifeless.

Taryn couldn't contain the scream any longer and it rocketed out of her, ringing the air with terror.

She saw Ash then. Her friend was a few yards behind the Santa, picking herself up off the floor. Spencer must have shoved her aside at the last second, saving her from the killing swing of the ax. He'd paid for it with his life.

The Santa was trying to yank the ax from Spencer's torso, jerking the handle up and down like it was jammed in a tree stump rather than a person. The head came out with a wet sucking sound and Lincoln, who had appeared at the door of the coffee place, cried "What the fuck?"

The Santa looked up, saw him, and stepped forward.

"Oh no," Jeremy breathed.

"HEY YOU FAT FUCK!"

Ash's left hand was balled into a fist; the bolt cutters were still in her right hand, as though she intended to use them as a weapon. She couldn't have been more than three yards away.

The Santa swung in her direction.

"Run," Jeremy said in stunned monotone.

"Ash," Taryn screamed, "*run!*"

They watched, horror-struck and rooted to the floor, as Ash dashed away from the coffee place above them. The Santa lumbered after her, holding the bloodied ax high over his head.

"Not the escalator!" Jeremy yelled as Ash neared it. "Keep going!"

"Hide!" Taryn cried. Em wriggled in her arms, trying to see what was happening.

Ash didn't stop. She sprinted past the top of the escalator and carried on along the second level concourse without looking down at them or back at what was pursuing her. The Santa thudded after her, huge and cumbersome but keeping pace.

"Oh shit, oh shit," Jeremy said.

This isn't happening, Taryn thought. *This can't be happening. I'm in a dream.*

Ash was almost at the far end of the concourse. The Santa was still right behind her.

"The stairs!" Jeremy cried suddenly, grabbing Taryn's arm. "She can get down the stairs. Come on!"

He started running and Taryn followed. Em was a dead weight in her arms but she couldn't put her down. She'd never be able to keep up.

They sped down the concourse between the empty benches and abandoned shopping bags and blinking Christmas trees, straining to keep Ash and the man dressed as Santa Claus in their line of sight. Taryn's arms ached from carrying Em; to make matters worse, the kid's knees kept digging into her abdomen, winding her a little more with every stride.

They neared the fountain. Even from distance, Taryn could still see the ear lying on its rim in a puddle of red. Beyond it was Santa's Grotto and then *The Play Emporium*, where the elf was. Or had been a few minutes ago, at least.

"Jeremy, wait," Taryn panted, slowing next to the fountain. "Wait, please."

"We can't wait," he said, craning his neck to peer past the grotto. "Shit, I can't see them anymore."

"What're we going to do when we get there?" Taryn said, still breathing hard as she adjusted Em in her arms. "We don't have any, like, weapons or anything. And I'm holding a toddler."

Jeremy turned to her. His face was sheened with sweat.

"Let's just find her first and then we can work it out," he said.

"Hey, you guys!"

They looked back. Lincoln was standing by the second floor rail at the other end of the concourse. He jabbed a finger at Spencer's body and yelled, "What am I supposed to do here?"

Christmas music reached Taryn's ear, so faint it was barely audible. Above, snowflakes pirouetted down from the ragged hole in the ceiling.

"Just stay there," Jeremy called back. "Don't go anywhere."

"I think he's dead, man."

"Just... just stay there."

The music swelled. It was coming from the grotto.

"Wait, who's that?" said Jeremy.

Taryn saw the man come up behind Lincoln at *The Coffee Place* entrance. He wore a dark blue shirt and jeans, and his left arm was in a bandage.

Suddenly, Jeremy let out a cry that sounded like "Whoa-hey!" and fell back. Em momentarily blocked Taryn's view of him, and by the time she got herself turned, Jeremy was flat on his back on the floor.

And the elf had him by the shoulders.

"Jeremy!" Taryn shrieked.

Jeremy, winded from the fall, had no time to react. The elf was already dragging him backwards across the floor at speed.

"Hey!" Taryn yelled, running after him. "Let him go. Let him go!"

"Elf!" cried Em.

Jeremy kicked and thrashed but the elf had a firm grip on his baggy coat and the sweater beneath it, and he couldn't break free. He managed to get his fingers round the elf's wrist; it batted his hand away and grabbed his hair, dragging him by it and the coat. Jeremy screamed in pain.

"Stop it you little fucker!" Taryn shouted. "Let go of him!"

The elf hauled Jeremy, kicking and screaming, alongside the grotto. It grinned maniacally down at him, blood flowing freely from its eyes. Jeremy grabbed at the white picket fence surrounding the grotto's garden but his fingers failed to find purchase.

"Stop!" Taryn yelled.

"Taryn!" Jeremy cried. The elf got him through the gate in the fence. "*Taryn!*"

"Elf, come back!" shouted Em.

Taryn reached the gate just as the elf pulled Jeremy up to the grotto's entrance. Multi-colored fairy lights twinkled merrily around it. The music grew louder, more distinct.

Then the grotto's faux-wooden door swung open and someone stepped out.

She was dressed in red from head to toe. White fur lined her sleeve cuffs and collar, and a white apron was tied round her waist. She wore a red hat with white fur lining and a sprig of holly tied to the end; crescent-shaped spectacles perched on the end of a plump, piggish nose, through which she regarded first Jeremy and then Taryn with horribly swollen, bloodshot eyes. Like the elf, the skin of her face was gray and peeling off the muscle beneath.

"Mrs Claus!" cried Em.

The woman in red grinned toothily and stepped out of the grotto.

She had a hammer in one hand.

TEN

"**I**t's really coming down here, like a blizzard. We're snowed in."

Sue Peterson adjusted the earpiece on her headset again. She frowned at the monitor.

"Sir," she said, uncertainly. "Can I clarify once more that you're calling from *The Movie House* theater at the *Outlet Complex*?"

"That's right."

Sue had been on shift at the dispatch center since seven that morning. It was three days before Christmas and she was more than ready for a break; it didn't even matter that it would only be forty-eight hours spent at her parents' house on the other side of town, feigning delight and surprise at the same old gifts and dodging questions about "why she didn't have a boyfriend yet at her age" while her younger, married sister grinned smugly across the table. She was weary, and she really didn't have time for this sort of thing.

She double-checked the weather report displayed on one of the six screens above her desk, checked the call source on another screen, and said, "Sir, there's no snow in that area today."

Silence on the other end of the line.

Sue glanced over her shoulder at her colleague John Baker, seated at another dispatcher station across the room. He was on call with someone else, running through a CPR checklist on one of his monitors.

"What d'you mean?" said the guy on her line.

Sue checked her on-screen call notes: *Spencer Bloom. Wife, Mary, missing. Movie theater empty.*

"We're just a few miles away from your location," she said, "and I'm looking at a weather report, too. There's no snowfall in your area today."

There was movement behind her and she half-turned. John had finished his call and was going on a bathroom break. He made a "T" sign with his hands as he passed her desk and she shook her head.

Spencer Bloom's voice in her ear: "But you'll still send someone?"

He sounds dazed, she thought, *like he's in shock. Need to keep him on the line a little longer.*

"Yes," she replied calmly, "officers will be on the way shortly, Mr Bloom."

Another voice spoke in the background. She couldn't quite make it out.

"Oh shit," Spencer said.

"Sir?" said Sue.

There was a *click* as the receiver dropped back into the cradle, and the line went dead.

"Sir?" Sue repeated unnecessarily. She sighed and closed off the call.

What was the guy talking about, anyway? She'd brought up three different weather reports during the call and they all confirmed the same thing: there was no snowfall in the entire county that day.

They could be wrong, of course. Weather reports were often wrong.

Still, the guy'd sounded pretty spooked by whatever was going on there. *I'm calling because my wife's missing. Everyone in the movie theater is missing.*

Sue's fingers danced across her keyboard, tapping shortkeys. The list of available units closest to the *Outlet Complex* populated on one of the screens to her left. A car could be there in less than five minutes.

The nape of her neck bristled. She glanced behind her again; John's station was still empty - it was his first break of the day so he'd be gone for at least a few minutes. The third station - normally occupied by Cassie, who was attending a funeral - was shut down. The dispatch center was small, heavily scented with coffee and mustiness, and rarely visited by the county sheriff, even though his office was in the same building. As a largely rural police department, they wouldn't usually receive more calls than two dispatchers could handle at one time, so they never came close to being overwhelmed. There was no need for external input from the sheriff or anyone else in the department.

A two-foot-tall Christmas tree in the corner, one of those plastic-looking ones with integrated fiber-optic lights, silently transitioned from red to yellow to purple. Outside the window above Sue's desk, the last of the day's light was fading from the sky.

Her neck bristled again and she reached back to touch it. Gooseflesh had risen on her skin.

Everyone in the movie theater is missing.

She turned back to her screens, adjusting her headset. She shifted her mouse cursor towards the available units display.

The screen flickered, just once, then went black.

"The hell?" Sue muttered.

The screen displaying the weather report blacked out, followed by the call log. The remaining three flickered, settled again, then winked out simultaneously.

"What the hell?" Sue exclaimed.

She pushed back in her chair and bent down to look under the desk. Her belly bulged out from beneath her sweater and she groaned a little with the effort. All the cables under her desk were still connected and blinking green to show they were active. It wasn't a power cut.

Sue straightened up again. All six monitors were still blank. She saw her reflection in the central screen, saw the round, fuschia-colored frames perched on her round, pink nose and the untidy bangs draped above them like blonde curtains; she only saw herself there for a moment, and later wondered why she hadn't immediately seen the man standing directly behind her chair, a man in a black trench coat with a black trilby hat on his head, whose face was masked in shadow and whose black-gloved hand was reaching for her.

She saw rather than felt the hand come to rest on her shoulder. The man's face was still distorted on the screen but Sue thought she could make out the suggestion of a chin and mouth beneath the trilby. The mouth remained closed when the words whispered in her ear.

"*What did you hear?*"

Sue's reply was calm, serene: "Nothing."

"*Who were you talking to?*"

"No-one."

"*What will you do now?*"

"Nothing."

The corners of the mouth, barely visible in shadow, curled into a grin.

"*Would you like some tea?*"

Sue nodded. Yes, yes she would like some tea, come to think of it.

The gloved hand retreated from her shoulder. Behind her, the man in the black trench coat turned away from her station.

Sue blinked. All six of her monitors were lit and active.

She smacked her lips. Suddenly, she was gagging for a drink.

"Nothing happening?" said John, coming back into the room with a steaming mug in one hand.

Sue swiveled towards him and slipped off her headset. "Nothing at all," she replied. "Quiet as a mouse."

"Huh," said John, lowering himself back into his chair. "Thought I heard you on a call a few minutes ago."

"Nope." Sue stood up, tugging the hem of her sweater down again. "You've made me want tea now. I'll take a quick break if you don't mind."

"No sweat," said John, replacing his headset.

Sue Peterson left her station and headed for the break room. She didn't remember her call with Spencer Bloom, and she didn't remember deleting it from the log. She didn't remember the man in the black trench coat either (though she would occasionally see him in her dreams for years afterwards and would wake up in a cold sweat, clutching at her duvet) and no car was dispatched to the *Outlet Complex* that day. One did drive by it later, however; one of the officers inside remarked that the place was starting to look a little run-down, and the other one agreed. They drove on and rejoined the highway a mile down the road.

ELEVEN

Taryn saw Jeremy go through the door of the grotto, screaming and clawing at the makeshift threshold while the elf, grinning and bleeding from the eyes, tugged at his ankles. He was there, glasses barely clinging to his face, her friend of over half her life, and then he was gone, and Mrs Claus was coming at her with a hammer in her hand.

"Mrs Claus helps make toys," cried Em cheerily.

Clutching the little girl to her body, Taryn staggered back to the grotto gate. Mrs Claus - or whoever she'd been before - advanced towards them, head cocked to one side, bulging eyes ready to pop right out of their sockets. Taryn stumbled, managed to keep her balance, reached the gate.

"I want to go in," Em said, arms stretched towards the grotto and the thing that'd just walked out of it. "I want *toys!*"

"Not right now, Em," Taryn replied breathlessly.

"Please!" Em insisted, wriggling in her arms.

Doesn't she see? Taryn thought, as her All Stars squeaked onto the tiles again. *Doesn't she see what's happening? Holy shit, it took Jeremy!*

Mrs Claus was almost at the gate. She gripped the hammer loosely, letting it swing in her hand as though she might drop it. Or throw it. Taryn could see the dried blood on the hammer's head.

What the hell do I do?

She only had seconds. To her right were the escalators and the coffee place on the second floor, but they were at the far end of the concourse and she'd have to carry Em all the way; to her left, beneath the food court and much closer, was the mall arcade.

"Mrs Claus!" Em cried again.

Taryn bolted to her left, just as the hulking, disfigured woman reached the white picket gate and raised the hammer. Her sneakers smacked on the tiles as she ran towards the *Star-Cade*, Em bouncing in her tired and aching arms. She didn't look back, didn't slow.

She had to hide. Fast.

"Oh shit, oh shit!" Ash panted, sprinting along the mall's second floor.

She stole a glance back and immediately wished she hadn't - the Santa was closer than she'd thought. The ax, still wet with Spencer's blood, glinted evilly under the ceiling lights as the man in red pounded after her.

"Fuck me!" Ash cried.

She passed *Big Al's Hardware*, leaping over the pool of dried blood by the entrance where she and Spencer had helped Steve out from under the shutter not so long ago. Below and to her right, she could see Taryn and Jeremy hurrying along the ground floor of the concourse, trying to keep pace with her. The bolt cutters clacked open and shut in her hand.

Who's the little girl?

The food court was just up ahead, signposted with glowing tangerine letters hanging just below the ceiling. The second 'o' in *Food* flickered off and on.

Ash had spent plenty of time in the mall food court, especially since she entered high school and her parents' stranglehold on her whereabouts began to wane. In days gone by she'd have taken the bus to the *Outlet Complex* with Molly Eberly and Lauren Wekstein - once her best friends from kindergarten and elementary - and the three of them would've spent hours roaming from store to store, trying on clothes they had no intention of purchasing and sniggering cruelly at anyone foolish enough to make eye contact with them.

But after a point Ash became bored with that unchanging, predictable pattern, and when Molly and Lauren didn't, she quickly drifted away from them. During one endless summer after Seventh Grade she was friendless and terribly lonely; for two months she rarely left home, an experience that hardened and embittered her heart, and she would've remained that way if Taryn Meyer hadn't come along that fateful September day in the locker rooms after gym class. Later, Taryn introduced her to horror movies and graphic novels (and to Jeremy, who she disliked intensely at first), and then trips to the *Outlet Complex* began to include viewings of really bad films in *The Movie House*, and comic book store perusals, and of course, frozen yogurt in the mall food court.

Such happiness was a vaporous mirage as she entered the food court that afternoon. It was an enormous, semi-circular space at the back end of the mall packed with tables and chairs and lined with a plethora of fast food counters; most of the tables still contained trays of half-eaten food, abandoned by patrons when the mall had been evacuated earlier, and if Ash hadn't been quite literally running for her life, she might've snagged some fries along the way as she passed. Like the others, she was starving.

Food would have to wait.

Her breath came in ragged gasps with each juddering beat of her heart as she sprinted round the outside of the seating area. The takeout counters, with their signs still lit and their ovens still warm, flashed by in a polychromatic blur in her left-side peripheral vision.

The Santa's heavy boots thumped rhythmically on the floor not far behind her.

"Oh shit," she gasped, thinking *This psychopath's gonna kill me with a fucking ax! He's killed Spencer and now he's gonna kill me!*

She had two options at this point, and she had to pick one real fast.

The door exiting to the elevators and rear stairwell was coming up on her left. She could go out that way and take the stairs down to the ground floor, and then run like hell until she found Taryn and Jeremy. They'd work the rest out from there.

That was option one. Option two was simply keep on running and loop back round to the opposite side of the second floor concourse where, presumably, Linc and Steve were waiting. They wouldn't have left Spencer's body there, would they? Maybe he wasn't even dead at all. Had she actually *seen* him die?

He's fucking dead, you goober. He got a massive fucking ax right in the heart. He's dead as a shitting dodo.

She wasn't running all the way back there. She'd never make it.

The big guy was almost on her.

She saw the door, wedged right between *Choppy Chopsticks Noodle Bar* and *Mama Maisy's Fried Chicken Basket*. The red-lettered *Exit* sign above the door glowed like a beacon in the shadows.

Through the door, down the stairs, back to the others.

She was at the exit. She reached for the door handle.

Through the door, down -

"What the fuck!" she squealed.

Her hand had almost been on the door handle before she saw what was already gripping it and jerked away at the last second.

That recoil of repulsion saved her life - just as she pulled back, the ax skimmed the top of her head and *thunked* into the door, driving deep into the wood. The door shuddered violently on its hinges, but the ax head stayed lodged in it.

Ash staggered backwards, her boots squeaking on the tiles as she fought to stay on her feet. The bolt cutters dropped from her hand and clattered on the floor. The Santa yanked furiously on the ax handle but, just as it had stuck in Spencer's torso outside the coffee place, it remained stuck fast in the wood of the door. Just below where it was embedded, the severed hand continued clinging lifelessly to the door handle.

Ash spun away from the man in red. A shot of acid vomit leapt into her mouth and she swallowed it back down. She knew if she threw up now, there was every chance she might faint afterwards. She had to keep moving, had to get away.

A low brick wall bordered the food court seating area. She vaulted over it and crashed into the nearest table, sending a tray of untouched milkshakes tumbling to the floor. Strawberry and banana goop splashed across the tiles at her feet; she skidded on it, almost slipped, then kept going, bashing her way through the maze of tables and chairs until she was somewhere near the center of the court. Finally, breathless and nauseated, she dropped to her hands and knees and crawled under one of the tables.

What now, Ash? she thought, panting hard and trying to quiet it. *What the fuck now?*

She could hear the Santa over by the exit, still struggling to detach the ax head from the door. Even from halfway across the food court, she could hear him grunting as he tugged on the handle of the weapon.

"What now?" she breathed.

She looked down at her hands, at her fingers splayed out on the sticky tiles beneath the table. Her violet fingernails, painted so meticulously that morning, were now chipped and flecked with blood. She took her hands off the floor and saw they were trembling.

There was a *snap-crack* of breaking wood from across the food court, then silence.

Ash squinted under the tables and chairs, but she couldn't see the door from her position. Her view of it was blocked off by the low border wall. *At least that means he can't see me*, she thought.

She blew out a puff of air, forcing her heart rate to slow a little. She couldn't stop her hands from trembling, it seemed, but she *could* get her breathing under control, and that was something.

I really wish Taryn and Jeremy were here right now.

Shimmying back a few inches, she got herself up onto her haunches, brushed an untidy spill of black hair from her eyes, and peered over the top of the table.

Her heart bungeed inside her.

The Santa was *inside* the seating area, over by the wall. He gripped the ax in two red-gloved hands, turning slowly on the spot as he scanned the court. He wasn't looking directly at her but he would be in a few seconds. She had just enough time to make out the gray, peeling skin of his cheeks, nose and forehead above the filthy fake beard, and the eyes that were now fully laced in a thin film of blood, before she had to duck down again. Her heart rate had notched right back up and she had to blow out a few silent puffs to slow it again.

What's wrong with him? she thought desperately. *Is he sick? Poisoned? Crazy? Yes, Ash, he's clearly fucking crazy. He's a crazy guy dressed as Santa Claus and he wants to chop you up like logs for the fire.*

The whole situation was totally insane, wasn't it? Not so long ago, she'd been slouched in an almost-empty movie theater auditorium with her two best friends, her Doc Martens propped up on the seat in front of her, watching a crappy horror film and shoveling popcorn into her mouth. Christmas, and the brief, glorious respite from school that came with it, were just around the corner. That's what she should be thinking about right now: friends, family, food. Presents under the tree at Mom's, hot cocoa by the fireplace at Dad's.

Not this slasher movie shit.

And what exactly happened to her back in that hardware store, right before they'd heard Steve on the other side of the door? It felt like she'd fallen backwards into a dream; she was aware of the strangeness of it, of the words coming from her mouth and of Spencer trying to snap her back, but she couldn't control what she was saying, and she couldn't fully distinguish between reality and the images augmenting themselves over it. What was that called again? Lucid dreaming, or something?

She'd seen a woman, then, and somehow she'd known - known for *sure* - that the woman was Mary Bloom, Spencer's disappeared wife. And that wasn't all. She'd known something *about* Mary, too, hadn't she? Something about her being sick, about her having poisoned blood. That's what she'd asked, right? *Mary's blood is tainted, isn't it?*

In truth, it'd scared her shitless, more than finding the ear on the fountain or seeing the blood trail in the store. Those things happened externally, outside of her control. But what she'd seen and *felt* in her own mind, things that'd been so clear and visceral, things she could practically taste... that had frightened her badly. Worst of all, it wasn't the first time it'd happened to her, either. She crammed it right back down, of course, pretended like it was nothing. Just like before. And then their focus had shifted to Steve and she thought Spencer had forgotten about her, at least for the moment. There'd been more pressing matters to attend to than a fifteen-year-old's psychotic episode in an abandoned hardware store. Matters of survival and escape. Well, not for Spencer. Not anymore.

And what about the other thing? She'd seen it in the shadows of her dream, way beyond Mary Bloom and the other people whose names she didn't know. The thing in the darkness, searching for her, reaching out. *Hum... hum... hum...*

The food court had fallen silent.

Ash tugged at her lower lip. Then, clutching the rim of the table with sweat-slicked hands, she craned her neck and looked over the top of it again.

And met the Santa's gaze.

"Oh hell," she said.

He came at her faster than she'd have believed possible, a hulking mass of red and white, knocking tables and chairs out of his path like a wrecking ball. Trays went flying, plates shattered on the floor. The ax head shone.

Ash went to her right, scrambling across the tiles on all fours. Her shoulders bounced off metal table legs and her knees smacked on the floor, but she didn't feel it. There was only the Fear, and the incontrovertible need to stay alive.

That need, and the fact that she was small (she'd hated being short but *boy* was she grateful for it now), got her halfway across the food court by the time the Santa reached her original hiding place. She'd gone straight as an arrow and stayed beneath the tables, and he hadn't spotted her.

When he stopped, she did too. She was underneath another table, trembling uncontrollably but still hidden. She stayed as still as possible and listened hard; she didn't dare move.

For a moment or two, nothing happened. Above, the December wind continued caressing the roof of the mall, making the beams shudder and groan. Ash realized she was holding her breath and let it out in another silent puff.

Where the hell is he?

Then she heard him, and she knew right away where he was: exactly where she'd been just a few seconds ago, in the center of the food court. He'd gotten there and found she was gone, and now he was waiting, listening, biding his time until she moved again.

He was hunting her like an animal.

Ash stayed perfectly still. She had both palms flat on the cold tile floor; her left knee throbbed where she'd bashed it off a table leg. A dark strand of hair dangled between her eyes and she let it hang.

The Santa didn't move.

Shit a brick, now what do I do?

A droplet of salt sweat rolled onto her upper lip and she licked it off. She closed her eyes.

Now what do I do?

She tried to picture Taryn and Jeremy and the little girl standing in the lower concourse, but instead, she saw Lincoln and Steve. They were outside *The Coffee Place*, not far from Spencer's body. They were talking. Lincoln was shaking his head, back and forth like a pendulum. Steve was pointing across the concourse, jabbing a finger towards something. As Ash watched in her mind's eye, vaguely wondering *how* she was watching it at all, Steve grabbed a fistful of Lincoln's polo shirt and shouted something, right in his face. Distantly, Ash imagined she heard it.

The Lincoln in her vision stopped shaking his head and nodded instead. Steve released him. He pointed across the concourse again, and Lincoln nodded again.

Ash thought she heard the Santa move somewhere behind her, but suddenly that didn't seem so important. Suddenly, seeing Lincoln and Steve - and where they were going - seemed critical.

She squeezed her purple eyelids tighter and gritted her teeth, willing herself to see them. But the vision, or whatever it was, was already beginning to fade, becoming less distinct. Lincoln's face blurred and dissolved. The sign above the coffee place entrance evaporated. There was only Steve, turning away from Lincoln, turning in the direction he'd been pointing.

Then he looked right at her.

Ash's breath caught. Her eyes met Steve's in the black recess of her mind and he *saw* her. He was at the other end of the mall, completely out of her line of sight, and he *saw* her. His eyes were that blue-green color Ash couldn't remember the name of, and they locked onto hers with absolute precision.

And suddenly, just like in the hardware store, Ash felt as though she was falling backwards into a dream. The world melted away and darkness drew around her like a curtain.

She managed to lower her forehead to the tiles before it took her.

TWELVE

S teve saw the black kid with the glasses get dragged into Santa's Grotto, and then the big woman in red was coming out of it, and she had something in her hand - a hammer, maybe - it was hard to tell from where they were. The skinny girl had been running after the black kid, yelling her lungs out, barely keeping hold of the squirming toddler in her arms, but she'd stopped dead in her tracks when the woman in red appeared. And then the woman was going at her with the hammer, or whatever it was, and the skinny girl was running. In seconds, they'd disappeared somewhere beyond the Grotto and the concourse became silent again.

There was a muffled whimper from behind him. Steve turned and saw that the kid with the long, greasy hair was crying.

"What's wrong?" he said.

The kid, Linc, wiped the back of his hand across his nose - it came away with a string of mucus attached to it. His eyes were wet.

"What d'you mean, "what's wrong"?" he blubbered. "He's dead, man. The guy in the Santa getup, like, totally *killed* him."

Steve dropped his gaze to the lifeless corpse that had once been Spencer Bloom, husband of Mary Bloom, almost thirty years married. Spencer's body lay in an expanding pool of his own blood; Steve thought he looked like an island, and his belly was the mountain on which the native people sacrificed to their gods.

"He sure did," he replied to Linc. "He's sure as hell dead, all right."

Linc sniffed and brushed tears from his face, smearing more snot on his cheeks. Steve stared at the ragged hole the ax had made in Spencer's chest. His severed arteries were visible between the folds of his shirt.

"What do we do?" Linc said.

"Huh?"

"I said what do we do? About all this?"

Steve turned back to the concourse. He couldn't see where the shorter girl in the skirt and boots had gone. The guy in the Santa suit had been right on her tail.

"Steve?"

Had she made it as far as the food court? There were stairs at the back of it, weren't there? She could make it to the ground floor...

"Steve."

"My name's not Steve," he said, still surveying the vast, near-soundless interior of the mall. Wisps of snow tumbled from the hole in the ceiling, settling on the roof of Santa's Grotto below. *Peaceful. That's what it is. It's peaceful.* "I don't remember my real name right now, but I'll tell you when I do."

He faced the kid again, looking him up and down. "How's the foot?"

"What? Oh, um... it's ok, I guess."

"Think you can do some walking?"

Linc frowned dubiously. His eyes started to go back to Spencer then quickly jerked away.

"Guess it depends how far. I can make it to the main exit if we use the escalator. But - "

"We're not going to the exit," said Steve, "not yet."

"Why not?"

Steve scrambled briefly for the answer, found it. "Because it's too dangerous right now. You saw what happened to Spence here. And to those other kids down there."

"Jeremy," said Linc, "and Taryn. And - "

"Yeah," Steve cut in. "They're in big trouble, Linc, and so are we. Those people in the costumes, they're killers. They've murdered Spencer - " He gestured to the body, like a college professor presenting an equation on the board, " - and they'll do the same to us, if they get the chance. One of the bastards got me in the arm with a knife. And there're at least three of them and only two of us left."

"Left?" said Linc in a small voice.

"Yeah," replied Steve solemnly. "We have to assume the worst. They're just kids, after all. And so are you."

"I'm almost twenty-four."

"Well you *look* younger," Steve said, thinking *And you were blubbering like a baby two seconds ago*. "What we need right now, Linc, are weapons. Or *a* weapon, at least. Something we can use to defend ourselves. Ideally a gun, if possible."

Linc stared back, not really comprehending. "Why can't we just leave? I mean, the cops will be here any minute. Spencer called them from the movie theater,"

"We *could* try to leave," said Steve. "We could head down to the main exit and have a go at that shutter. But - " He pointed to his bandaged hand with his good one, " - I won't be much use with those bolt cutters right now - wherever they even are -

and judging by those tooth picks hanging out of your sleeves, I doubt you'd be either."

Linc looked down at his bony arms.

"So, before we get ourselves bottle-necked down there, let's find something to protect ourselves with. We don't even have to use it. It'd be more of a deterrent, really. We - "

He stopped, listening. There'd been a sound from the far end of the mall, on their level. A smashing, crashing sound. Wood and metal.

"But where do we get one?" Linc said. "There's no gun store in here."

"Security guards," Steve replied smoothly. "They carry handguns, right? That'd be enough. We just need to find where they keep them. There'll be a security office somewhere in the building. It's been a while since I was here, but maybe you know where it is, huh? I'll bet you've been here a lot, you

fucking stoner

know your way around this place, yeah? Have you seen a security office somewhere?"

Linc shook his head. "No, no I haven't."

"Come on, man." Steve stepped forward and the kid flinched. He was starting to lose patience with him now. "It's around here somewhere, isn't it? It's on this floor, right?"

Linc continued shaking his head, faster and faster. He wasn't just responding to Steve's questions anymore. He was slipping into shock.

"It's up here, isn't it?" Steve pointed behind him. "Linc."

The kid shook his head harder, almost overbalancing on his crutches.

"Hey," Steve said. "Hey!" His patience finally snapped and he grabbed Linc by the shirt. "Listen to me! We're going to go find a gun so we can defend ourselves, ok? So we can shoot these motherfuckers if they come at us with axes or knives or hammers. Alright?"

Linc slowly stopped shaking his head.

"You want to get outta here, right?"

The kid nodded, gradually at first, then vigorously.

"Good. Me too." Steve pointed across the mall again. "Can you help me find the security room? Or would you rather stay here by yourself?"

"I... I'll help you," said Linc, still nodding.

"Damn right you will." Steve released Linc's shirt and patted him on the shoulder, just once. "Let's go. You're leading the way."

Linc ducked his head and swiveled away from *The Coffee Place* entrance and Spencer's body; his blood, still running along the tiles, had almost reached the edge of the balcony. Soon, Steve thought, it would begin to drip down to the floor below.

He cast a glance back across the expanse of the mall, then followed Lincoln.

When Taryn was five, she attended her first major event: the wedding of her Aunt Jane up in Peoria. Second wedding, actually. Jane had been married before to Taryn's then-uncle Travis, the kind of guy who enjoyed playing the drums real loud in his garage and smoking pot with his friends on the weekend; as it turned out, ol' Trav also let Samantha from the local 7-Eleven puff *his* magic dragon on occasion, whether he was high or not, and when Jane found out about it, that was the end of marriage number one. Jane met Barry less than a year later, and because Barry had no penchant for pot or full-lipped checkout girls, and for a variety of other reasons, she gladly accepted his proposal when it arrived.

Jane and Barry's wedding ceremony took place on a warm day in June and Taryn hated every second of it. She hated her dress, she hated her shoes, and most of all, she hated her hair, which her mother had spent half an hour braiding that morning, followed by another half an hour after Taryn purposefully unraveled it. She'd never been to a wedding before and had never made it all the way through a church service at Easter or Christmas (the two annual occasions when her parents flirted with religion), so after almost an hour of just *sitting* while her Aunt Jane, soon-to-be-Uncle Barry, and a man in a white dress did a bunch of talking at the front of the church, she was ready to go.

Her mother, six months pregnant at the time with her eventual little brother, did her best to keep her quiet, but it was no use. Little Taryn Meyer, normally shy and contemplative at five years old, wedged between her parents in a stuffy Methodist church on a warm summer's day, couldn't be contained.

Just as the words "Do you, Jane, take Barry..." left the minister's mouth, Taryn stood up right in the middle of the congregation and, with all the gusto she could muster, yelled "I do!"; her mother, aghast, wrenched her back down to the pew as a ripple of good-natured laughter spread around the church. Even Jane and Barry chuckled. It was one of those times when you just couldn't help it, no matter how reserved you were.

Taryn's mother went beetroot-red and didn't look at her daughter again until the ceremony was over (though she did grip her little hand so hard it started to hurt after a while). Her father also avoided eye contact, but for a very different reason: each time he glanced down at Taryn and caught her looking back, his diaphragm would start bouncing and his breath would escape in little whistles through each nostril, and she would see it on his face and grin in her mischievous way that got him every time, and he knew he would simply dissolve into laughter right there and then if he didn't keep his eyes fixed on the front of the church.

Taryn hadn't understood why her parents were so tense that afternoon in the over-warm Methodist church, or why her mother had stormed straight to the car once the ceremony was over. As far as she was concerned, she'd made people laugh, and laughter was a good thing. But now, as she pressed her sweaty palm against little Emma Price's mouth and leaned back between two machines in the mall arcade, she understood the fear. She understood it, and she felt it.

She had to keep Em quiet.

The *Star-Cade* sat directly below the second-floor food court and filled an area about the same size. Like most arcades, it was packed with noisy, flashing machines, some relatively new, and some very old, survivors of a by-gone, pre-console era; a thin, space-themed carpet depicting stars and planets covered the entire floor, and the low ceiling was lit with fluorescent purple rings, creating an almost claustrophobic atmosphere that was worlds away from the bright, spacious mall concourse. The arcade was big, and there were plenty of places to hide.

Taryn whispered in Em's ear: "Don't make a sound, ok?" She felt the little girl nod and slowly took her hand away. Em rubbed her mouth with her free hand; in the other, she still held the toy cat.

They'd lost the Mrs Claus fairly quickly once they were inside. Taryn knew the arcade well and it wasn't the first time she'd played hide and seek in the place - she and Ash once spent a solid thirty minutes eluding Jeremy in the mall, giggling while he searched fruitlessly and complained via text that it "wasn't funny anymore" and told them they were "being royal douchebags". The more annoyed he became, the funnier they found it. Eventually, just when he was about to leave, they jumped out from behind an antique Pac-Man machine and scared him half to death.

Poor Jeremy, Taryn thought, remembering that afternoon. Then, the gravity of their current situation hit her afresh and she started trembling where she was, crouched between two machines in a shadowy corner of the mall arcade.

poor Jeremy poor Jeremy poor Jeremy

Em twisted round to look at her. Taryn met her gaze and the surge of panic subsided, at least temporarily.

We have to get out of here, she thought. *We have to get back to the others.*

But what others? Who was left? Jeremy had been dragged screaming into Santa's Grotto by someone dressed as an elf (*what was wrong with its eyes?*) and Ash was somewhere above them, chased by a big man in a Santa costume wielding an ax. And Spencer was... was...

Maybe they were the only ones left. Maybe Lincoln and that other guy were gone, too.

We have to get out of this building.

Taryn swallowed hard and pressed a finger to her lips; again, Em copied the gesture, indicating she understood. Dropping her arm from around Em's torso but keeping one hand on the girl's shoulder, Taryn stood and peered around the side of the machine on her left. Beyond it, a row of similar machines blinked and jingled, and the fluorescents hummed on the ceiling above. There was no sign of the Mrs Claus.

"Come on," Taryn whispered.

She took Em's hand and slipped out from between the machines, keeping her head ducked as they moved along the row.

Most of the units were tall enough to shield her from view, but some were below head-height and there were often gaps between them. If the thing in the Mrs Claus outfit happened to look their way at just the right time...

Em reached for the steering wheel of a racing game and Taryn pulled her away. They were almost at the end of the row. She imagined she could smell popcorn and chili dogs.

When we get out, Taryn thought, *we'll go straight to the other end and up the escalator. Even if it's just to the coffee place. Lincoln should be around there somewhere, and he's technically an adult. And there's that other guy. Maybe we'll be able to see the police from the windows. They've gotta be here by now. And then we'll get Jeremy and Ash, assuming they're not...*

She couldn't finish the final thought. *Wouldn't* finish it. They were her best friends and she knew they were still alive. They had to be. She'd make sure Em was safe, and then she'd get them back, even if she had to do it herself.

They reached the end of the row, where an enormous *Jurassic Park*-themed machine shunted them to the right. Here, next to an older unit displaying the words "Insert coins to continue" on its screen, Taryn paused, keeping her hand tight on Em's shoulder. It was so small beneath her purple puffer coat.

Holding her breath, she looked round the edge of the unit. The way was clear. At the far end was a crane machine in the style of a red British telephone box; inside, colorful plush toys stared at her helplessly with their plastic goggle eyes. Still no sign of the Mrs Claus.

Taryn looked down at Em and nodded. They started out from behind the machine.

Almost simultaneously, Mrs Claus crossed the end of the aisle. The hammer swung casually in her hand and her boots thumped on the carpet. She glanced through the glass of the phone box crane machine and didn't see them. Then she was gone.

Taryn had stopped dead at the sight of her and her heart had locked, just for a second. When it beat again, it felt like someone was playing a snare drum in her chest cavity.

Holy shit, that was close.

Swallowing against a desert-dry throat, she began moving forward again, ushering Em along by her side. Each step felt painfully slow, like her sneakers were filled with concrete. A cacophony of slightly diluted electronic sounds filled the air, as though someone had eased the arcade's volume dial down a notch. Every few seconds, an enthusiastic virtual character would exclaim something like "Great job!" or "You're dead!" from somewhere in the room as the games continued their endless, pre-recorded loop, unaware that no living patrons were there to play them.

Taryn strained to hear footsteps over the arcade's jarring chorus but it was impossible, even without the usual babbling of gamers hopped up on sugary energy drinks underpinning it all. The person in the Mrs Claus costume, whoever she was, prowled the room with the predatory stealth of a jungle cat. For all they knew...

Taryn whipped around, but she wasn't there. At the end of the aisle, a pixelated T-rex bore down on the back seat of a red-striped Wrangler, its frothing jaws lunging towards the screen.

Who was she anyway, that enormous woman in the festive outfit wielding the blood-stained hammer? Why was her skin gray and peeling off the flesh beneath? Why were those beady eyes behind the crescent-shaped spectacles bright red with pulsing, ready-to-burst veins?

What in the hell's going on in this place? Taryn internalized shrilly. Some part of her realized then that, like Jeremy, she was barreling towards a panic attack.

She couldn't surrender to it, though. Not with Em here. She had to stay calm, for her.

They came to the end of the aisle. Em immediately veered towards the crane machine and Taryn, anticipating it, pinned her to her side. By some miracle, the little girl remained quiet.

Taking a breath, Taryn leaned around the last machine in the row and looked.

The *Star-cade* entrance was right there, just beyond a huge, four-sided coin-pusher machine. Tinny music blasted from the machine's speakers as the coin trays, filled with dimes and nickels and pennies, slid relentlessly back and forth.

We can make it if we run, Taryn thought.

She was about to go when Em squeezed her hand and pointed.

Em Price liked the tall girl with the brown hair. She was nice. She'd given her the cat toy, which she also liked, and that made her like the girl even more. Maybe she was a friend of Mommy or Daddy, or maybe she was another cousin who Em didn't remember meeting. Either way, she'd given her a toy, and that was nice.

She didn't like the boy with the glasses as much. He'd yelled at her back in the toy store, and that wasn't nice. But he was gone now. He'd gone with the Elf into Santa's house, down to the secret place where everyone else went. Gone to see the Humbug. He'd probably stay there for a while, like the other people.

Mrs Claus was still here, though. Em wasn't sure how much she liked her. Her face was scary and there was something wrong with her eyes. But she *looked* like Mrs Claus and she was married to Santa, so she must be nice, too.

Em could see her now, standing on the other side of the big glass machine. She was mostly hidden, but her arm and shoulder and part of her gray face were visible. She was standing perfectly still.

Was she playing the game? Em wanted to play it too. She liked games, especially the kind with lights and music and moving parts. It made her think of Daddy and his work. He'd taken her there to show her what he did - she hadn't understood, but she'd liked being there with Daddy. She missed him now. And Mommy, too.

She knew the tall girl (she'd given her name but Em hadn't been paying much attention at the time) hadn't seen Mrs Claus and she thought she should know. Em suspected the tall girl was trying to find her. Maybe Mrs Claus would give each of them a new toy. She knew Santa, after all, and she obviously made toys herself. That's what the hammer was for.

Em grabbed the tall girl's hand and pointed towards the coin-pusher. The tall girl looked, frowning. Then her eyes went wide. She gripped Em's hand and edged back behind the nearest machine again.

The tall girl pressed her finger to her lips, and once again, Em mirrored the gesture. She liked this game, and the tall girl always seemed pleased when she copied her. It was an easy game, the kind Em liked best.

Then they were moving again, away from the arcade entrance. As they went, Em looked back and saw Mrs Claus slip out from behind the coin-pusher machine. She saw her coming in their direction, and then the tall girl led her round a corner and Mrs Claus disappeared.

They went deeper into the arcade, weaving quickly through a maze of machines with flashing screens and loud music. Em tried her best to see what was on each screen, but the tall girl kept them moving and she rarely got more than a glimpse. Sometimes they'd stop briefly and the tall girl would check back the way they'd come, and then turn in a circle, her head whipping left and right like a meerkat; in those moments, Em would gravitate towards the nearest machine (unless it had guns - she didn't like guns) and often get within touching distance of the console or joystick before the tall girl snatched her away again.

Em started to tire of the game - her short legs weren't made for such relentless, stop-start movement - but the tall girl didn't. She kept playing and playing, hiding behind machines or pillars or ATMs or air hockey tables, sometimes pausing to look, some-times doubling back the way they'd come, but always, always moving. Once, the girl lobbed a half-empty soda can across the room and Em heard footsteps thumping off in its direction, but still the game continued. And the longer they kept going, the more they ducked and dodged and looped back towards the entrance before veering away again when Mrs Claus appeared, the faster the tall girl's breathing became, and the sweatier her hand got as it gripped Em's.

Finally, Em had enough. She didn't want to play anymore.

They started moving again and she planted her light-up sneakers on the carpet. The tall girl turned back and hissed "Come one!", and Em shook her head.

The tall girl crouched down and took her by the shoulders, but Em knew what was coming and shook her head. "No," she said, not lowering her voice now. "No more."

She saw the tall girl's eyes widen with alarm and felt her fingers dig into her shoulders. Next to them, a spiky-haired anime character hurled a fireball across the screen and yelled "Yaahh!".

"Please," the tall girl whispered urgently. "Please, Em - "

"No," Em replied. Then, louder: "No more running. I don't like this game anymore."

"Em - "

"No. I want to go! Let's gooooo!"

The tall girl's hand went for Em's mouth but it was already too late. Mrs Claus thumped around the corner just two machines away, the sprig of holly on her hat catching purple light from the fluorescents above. Her eyes, now full-red, locked onto Em's and she rushed at them.

The hammer went up; the tall girl cried out.

Em saw the hammer arc through the air towards the tall girl's head, and for a fraction of a second she saw the Humbug, felt its eyes roving over them, felt it *reaching* for them. It took her away from the moment and she was floating, indistinct, not really there anymore; she was above herself, looking down in wonder at the top of her own head and the tall girl's scalp as Mrs Claus's hammer skimmed just above it, breezing through her tawny brown hair; had she been older, she might have called it an out-of-body experience, a dissociative episode, but little Emma Price didn't know those words yet, and when the hammer smashed through the glass screen of the spiky-haired anime character's arcade machine and blue-white sparks exploded over them, she was snapped back into her body and tumbled to the floor.

The cat toy spilled from her hand, and for the time being, everything stopped.

Part III:
Underground

THIRTEEN

He was in a dream.

He knew it was a dream because his parents were in it, too, and he was sure they'd been nowhere near the mall when the elf took him. Reasonably sure, anyway.

There was his dad, Christopher Lewis, shaking his head in wordless disapproval. Wordless, but still Jeremy *heard* the words, loud and clear: *How could you let that thing just take you like that, boy? That would never have happened if you got outdoors every once in a while, you know.*

His mom was there too, but as usual, she said nothing.

Christopher Lewis continued shaking his head, but he was already pulling away, fading into the black. Jeremy had the impression he was reaching out to his father, stretching his arms towards him like a toddler might reach for reassurance. He reached, straining, suddenly desperate for their help, because as he reached he gradually became aware his arms were *behind* him rather than in front, and something was pinning them down, something hard and cold digging into his skinny wrists.

With a muffled gasp, Jeremy snapped out of the dream into a new, tangible darkness. There was something smooth against his face, something that crinkled when he moved. A bag, maybe? Yes. A firm paper shopping bag, pulled down over his head.

He was on his keister, slumped to his right. He straightened up and tried leaning forward again, and felt the same tug on his wrists. They were bound with something made from metal.

Handcuffs.

Where the hell was he?

He shifted his head, trying to see through the gap at the bottom of the bag. And suddenly, he realized something else: *I'm not wearing my glasses.*

As any short-sighted glasses-wearer will tell you - and Jeremy was firmly in that category - losing your spectacles can be enough to send you into a mild panic. Jeremy had already flirted with having a panic attack twice that day, and this time, he knew it was coming for real.

My glasses are gone. They must have fallen off when it dragged me down that hole.

His breath started to come in short, sharp bursts.

They fell off and probably smashed and now I've got a bag over my head and I'm totally fucking screwed.

He could feel his jugular pulsating against his collar. His rapid breathing was heating up the inside of the bag. He was going to suffocate and die in the dark.

"Help!" he yelled suddenly, surprising himself. "Someone help! HELP!"

"Kid, shut up."

He didn't hear the voice right away over the bag's rustling.

"Someone HELP!"

"Shut up! You'll bring it back. You - ah, shit."

Footsteps, thudding towards him. The bag crunched just above his scalp as a hand gripped it, then yanked it off.

Jeremy blinked as the darkness of the bag interior was replaced with a gray blur of fuzzy, indeterminate shapes. He smelled vehicle oil and damp.

"Fuck me," came the voice again, whispered, but clear and distinct with the bag gone. Jeremy looked to his left, saw a vague shape resembling a man, then looked straight ahead again.

He jerked back with a cry as the elf's face swam into view. They were almost nose to nose. This close, it was truly horrific, all shredded dying skin and crusted blood. It grinned, stretching the loosened folds of its face further; Jeremy imagined its skin would *schlop* right off its skull if he grabbed it.

And it was wearing his glasses.

The man on Jeremy's left uttered a shuddering whimper. The elf turned towards him and giggled (like a child, Jeremy thought with a fresh surge of electric fear); it stared at him for a moment, as if deciding whether or not it wanted to do something to him, then returned its bloody gaze to Jeremy. He tried not to meet those bleeding red eyes but found he couldn't look away. They held him, locked in terror, slumped in the shadows with his hands bound behind his back. As the elf's eyes grew wider, bulging from their sockets, so did its maniacal grin. Jeremy knew he was right on the verge of pissing his pants.

Then, with unsettlingly-delicate movements, the elf took off his glasses, turned them over in its hands, and slipped them back onto his face, tucking the feet in behind his ears. It did all of this with the sort of reposeful care a parent might use when changing a baby's diaper; it lasted just a few seconds, but to Jeremy, it felt like an age. Finally, as he sat there paralyzed with fright, the elf gingerly pushed his glasses back up to the bridge of his nose with one cold, bony finger and sighed, satisfied.

The lenses were smudged and they sat a little crooked now, but with his glasses back on, Jeremy could see every inch of the elf's face. He had no idea what had happened to it - why its skin was broken and flaking, why its eyes were oozing blood - but one thing was now finally clear, something he'd suspected ever since it first appeared at *The Play Emporium* entrance.

The elf was a child. Or at least, it had been.

He wasn't sure it was human anymore.

"Shit," said the man on Jeremy's left.

The elf laughed then, and the sound of it made the hair on Jeremy's neck stand on end. It stood up and spun away from them, tittering, then darted off into the shadows. It was gone.

Jeremy realized he'd been holding in a breath and let it out. When he inhaled again, the smell of engine oil was stronger.

He took in his surroundings as quickly as his muddled mind would allow, momentarily ignoring the man on his left, who was talking to himself in hushed, hurried whispers. They were in a large, low-ceilinged space, lit sporadically with humming yellow lights. The floor looked to be concrete and was dotted with puddles. Directly ahead of them was a rust-colored van, stationed just beneath a ragged hole in the ceiling.

They were in the mall's underground parking lot.

Jeremy saw he had been leaning against a pillar on his right, also made from concrete, and there was a dark green car just beyond the man on his left. They were sitting in a parking bay with their backs to the wall. Jeremy looked down and saw the man's hands were latched to a pipe with (as he'd thought) handcuffs.

He also saw that both of the man's hands were red with blood.

"Holy shit," Jeremy said. It came out in weary monotone and the man looked at him. "You're the guy from the movie theater."

The man stared at him for a moment. The flesh around his eyes was red and puffy, as though he'd been weeping, or he'd recently been beaten and the bruises were yet to set. He ran his tongue over his teeth, which were stained red.

"You're one of those kids," he croaked, "from inside." His demeanor darkened. "You wouldn't open the doors."

"No," Jeremy said, remembering how it'd been. Memories from hours ago that seemed much older. "We didn't. But we tried."

"The fuck you did," the man snarled suddenly. He jerked towards Jeremy, baring those blood-stained teeth, and he would have reached him if the cuffs clamped on his wrists hadn't caught on one of the brackets supporting the pipe. "You little shit, leaving me out there. I could've fucking died."

"But you didn't," Jeremy said quickly. Somehow, he hadn't budged an inch when the guy came at him. "We would've let you in if we'd known how."

He knew that was a lie. Even if Spencer had been there at the time, they would more than likely have left the guy outside in the snow. For all they knew at that point, he could've been the one who caused the movie theater's evacuation. Maybe he did.

"I'm sorry," said Jeremy, breaking from the man's toadish stare to look down at his handcuffs. The pipe clanked and trembled as the guy continued straining towards him. "I'm sorry we didn't let you in."

"... little son of bitch..."

"Would you, if you'd been on the inside? Your hands were covered in blood, man - they still are! We thought you'd killed someone!"

The guy stopped then, his jaw working as the next expletive bounced around inside his mouth. Then, just as abruptly as the rage arrived, it left him. He slumped back against the wall.

And for the first time, Jeremy realized there was someone else chained to their pipe. He couldn't see them clearly past the guy with bloody hands, but he *could* see they had a paper shopping bag pulled over their head, one with an upside-down *JeanScene* logo on the side.

Bloody Hands Man uttered a long, despondent sigh. He smelled of stale sweat and - Jeremy noted with disgust - urine.

Why's he down here? Jeremy wondered. *He should've been long gone by now.*

As though he'd spoken aloud, the guy looked at him. His pupils were ice-blue; one was barely visible through his slitted eye.

He's definitely been beaten.

"Who are you, kid?" he said. His voice was coarse, like his throat was laced with sand.

Jeremy found he actually had to think about it for a moment. "My name's Jeremy. Jeremy Lewis. I'm... from Rockmount." When the guy didn't respond, he added, "We were in the movie theater when it happened."

That was a gamble, he knew it. The guy might clam up and that'd be the end of it. Suddenly, Jeremy badly wanted to know what happened at the *Outlet Complex* earlier that day. He *needed* to know, more than he'd needed to know anything in his entire life.

He licked his lip and added, "Where were you?"

The guy dropped his gaze to his knees. His belly was a bulging mound under his gray coveralls. Jeremy shifted against the wall and winced when the cuffs dug into his skin.

He waited. After a moment, the guy cleared his throat and said, "I was at the gas station."

Jeremy waited again. Somewhere in the parking lot, water dripped into a puddle.

"I work there," Bloody Hands Man continued, "in the garage, round the side. Maintenance, you know? Been there for years."

Jeremy nodded and his glasses slipped down his nose a little. He wondered absently where the elf had gone.

"Happened about, um... two or three, I guess. Can't remember exactly. Not even sure what time it is now." He sniffed, then swallowed. "Had my head under a hood so I didn't see it come down, but I sure as shit *heard* it. Sounded like a bomb went off in the mall. Then people started screaming and that's what we thought happened. A bomb, or a shooter, or something."

"What was it?" Jeremy said. "What came down?"

The guy swallowed again, like he had something lodged in his throat. "Can't say for sure. It came from the sky. Went right through the roof of the mall, like a missile."

Jeremy pictured the hole high above the concourse, with thick white snowflakes filtering through, floating down and down to settle on...

"The grotto," he said. "Santa's Grotto. That's where it went, right?"

"Must've." The guy nodded towards the van ahead of them. "Right above there. They moved it under the hole afterwards, but you can see where the thing came down."

Jeremy squinted. It was difficult to make out, but the guy was right - the van had been positioned directly under the ragged hole in the parking lot ceiling and directly over a shallow crater in the floor, where some object had landed. Whatever it was, it was gone now.

"So," Jeremy said slowly, piecing it together, "something came through the roof of the mall, went through Santa"s Grotto, and then all the way through the floor to this parking lot?"

"Yup."

"And now it's gone?"

"Not exactly."

Jeremy looked at him again, but he was staring into the shadows beyond the van. It was cold in the lot, but beads of sweat trickled down the guy's face anyway, negotiating the swollen lesions now rising in the places where he'd been hit. "Did the elf do that to you?" he asked.

"No," said the guy. "It was the other one. The woman."

Jeremy opened his mouth.

Before he could speak, the elf burst into view again. Jeremy jumped; Bloody Hands Man stiffened next to him.

They watched as the creature that had once been a child sidled up to them, still grinning in that horrifically disturbing way, suppressing more tittering laughter behind its broken, bleeding lips. It had something in its hands.

"Don't move," the guy muttered.

The elf stopped. Its red eyes went from the guy to Jeremy, back and forth, expectant.

What the hell does it want? Jeremy thought. His heartbeat boomed in his ears.

The elf continued staring at them, rocking a little on its curled boots. When neither of them reacted, its grin faded. Then it held up the thing it was holding, shaking it at them. For a second, Jeremy couldn't make out what it was in the dim light of the parking lot. It was small and floppy, slapping wetly against the elf's hand as it dangled it. Then Jeremy understood, and his breath caught in his windpipe.

"Oh shit," he said.

It was a tongue.

"Fuck me," breathed Bloody Hands Man.

The elf giggled, pleased at their reaction. Jeremy felt his stomach churn but he couldn't look away. The elf waggled the tongue at them, hopping from foot to foot.

The ear on the fountain, Jeremy thought. *It put it there.*

"Fuck," the guy said again.

The elf laughed aloud and tucked the tongue in its pocket. Jeremy heard it squelch as it went in. Then, without another look their way, the creature turned and scrambled up onto the roof of the van and through the hole in the ceiling. It was gone again, properly this time.

Bloody Hands Man moaned, dipping his head towards his knees.

Please don't throw up, Jeremy thought. *I can't sit here next to a puddle of vomit.* "Keep talking," he said. "Tell me what happened."

The guy sucked in a breath and let it out slowly.

"What's your name?" Jeremy said, anxious to get him talking again. "I told you mine. Tell me yours."

The guy took another controlled breath and raised his head. "It's Pete," he said. "Pete Zampetti."

"Pete," said Jeremy, "what happened after the thing went through the roof?"

Pete Zampetti sighed. He closed his eyes for a moment, like he was weighing up whether or not to keep talking. Then he opened them and said, "I don't remember everything exactly like it was. I might be remembering it wrong."

"That's ok," said Jeremy. An image of the flopping tongue swam into his mind and he batted it away quickly. "Just tell me what you *do* remember."

"Ok," said Pete. "Like I said, when the thing came out of the sky and hit the roof, it sounded like a bomb'd gone off. Everyone who was in the gas station and outside in the parking lot started panicking, going for their cars, but it only lasted a few seconds. I think that's all it was, anyway. Then everyone just stopped. Including me."

"Stopped?"

"Yeah. I was at the garage entrance. Had my phone out to call my girlfriend, and then I just... stopped. Everyone did, all the ones I could see, at least. People just dropped their keys and shopping bags." He shook his head slowly. "And the snow! Holy shit, that stuff came out of nowhere. There'd been a little earlier, nothing to write home about. Just a dustin'. But the second that thing went through the mall roof, it was like we were all inside a snow globe and someone'd given it a good shake. The stuff just emptied on us. Never seen anything like it."

"Then what happened?"

Pete sniffed and swallowed, and now Jeremy was sure it was blood from his nasal cavity. His nose must be broken.

"Everyone dropped what they had and just started walking towards the mall. No-one said anything, no-one told us to do it. We all just walked to the main entrance in silence, like a bunch of fucking zombies. I remember doing it, but I also don't, if you get me?"

"Sort of. Like it was a dream?"

"Yeah, I guess. Maybe it was. Wish it was all a dream, really. Anyway, we all went into the mall, everyone who was in the parking lot outside and the few from the gas station. All covered in snow, like we'd been out for hours, but it must've been just a few minutes. Think the movie theater folks were there, too."

But why not us? Jeremy thought.

"I remember walking down the entrance corridor, bumping into people like we were a herd of cows on our way to the slaughterhouse. I knew I was doing it - walking, I mean - but I couldn't stop myself. Didn't *want* to stop. It was like I had to go and that's all there was to it. Something was pulling us all in.

"We came into the main part of the mall and it was all lit up for Christmas n' shit. Music playing, you know. I'm agnostic myself. Don't even have a tree."

An agnostic mechanic, Jeremy thought, *cuffed to a pipe, with blood all over his hands.*

"The place was real busy, like you'd expect. Families, kids." He swallowed again. "Lots of kids. And like the folks outside, everyone was just walking, hands by their sides, like they were dreaming."

"Walking where?"

Pete looked towards the hole in the ceiling and sniffed.

"The grotto?" Jeremy said. "That's where everyone went?"

"Far as I know," said Pete, lowering his head again. "Everyone in the whole bastard complex went there. Walked right through the door. Kids following their parents but not *led* by them. We all went there of our own accord."

"So they all went into the grotto," Jeremy said, staring at the ragged hole above the van, "and down into the underground lot? Where is everyone now?"

Pete didn't hear - or ignored - the question. "I was nearly there myself, about where the fountain is. Would've just gone down too. But I didn't."

"Why not?"

"Got knocked out."

"Huh?"

Pete chuckled then; it came out as a dry wheeze.

"Like I said, I got knocked out. Was walking through the mall in a daze, just like everyone else. Then I tripped on something - a bag, or someone else's foot, or whatever - and I fell. Cracked my damn head on the tiles and went right out."

In the weak light, Jeremy could just make out a deep cut above Pete's right eye. It hadn't stood out immediately among the general damage to the guy's face.

"When I came-to," Pete continued, "most everyone was gone. Have no idea how long I was out for, but I saw a few stragglers go into the grotto. Other than that the place was empty, cleared out. And I didn't want to go after them anymore, neither. Think the whack on the head broke the spell, you know?"

Jeremy nodded, thinking *I don't know at all, but you need to keep talking*.

"So I got up and I thought I was all alone. That was the worst bit, those few seconds after I came-to, thinking I was alone in the place. Didn't know what to do.

"I was fixin' myself to get the hell out of there - just run away like a fucking coward - when this other guy appears. He came out of one of the stores. Think he might have been out back when it happened and didn't get sucked into the trance like everyone else. He just stared around him with these big bugged-out eyes at all the shopping bags and phones and shit lying on the floor, probably wondering where everyone'd gone.

"Then he sees me, and he takes a step my way and starts to ask a question with his finger raised, real polite. Think he said something like "Excuse me, sir", and I remember thinking no-one had ever called me "sir" in my whole life - not seriously, anyway - but he never got any farther than that, because the big guy in the Santa suit came walking out from behind the grotto, and he had an ax in his hands, and he took that fella's head clean off with one swing. It actually bounced when it hit the floor, like a basketball."

Pete wheezed out another chuckle. Jeremy smiled grimly, and swallowed hard.

"My brain was working just enough to tell me to get out of sight, so I got myself down behind one of the benches while the Santa had his back to me. He stood over the headless fella with the ax in his hands for about a minute, just staring down at him. Making sure he was really dead, maybe. Kinda funny when you think about it. Fella had no fucking head, you know?

"Anyway, he must've eventually decided the guy was actually dead, because he slung the ax over his shoulder and grabbed the corpse by the leg, and dragged it off somewhere. The elf came along about two seconds later and took the head."

Pete sniffed. Jeremy waited. He'd gone cold all over.

"I didn't hang around much longer after that. Soon as I could, I turned tail and ran for the doors, though I was still muddled from before and couldn't go in a straight line. Thought I heard them coming back and had to duck into one of the stores near the escalator. That's when I tripped over another person on the floor - a woman this time - and her throat'd been cut, right across from ear to ear. Think it must've been the elf. She was lying in a big puddle of her own blood between those machines that set off the alarm when you leave the store with tags still on. Those machines must've gone off when she tried sneaking out and they brought the elf right to her."

"That's how you got the blood on your hands?" said Jeremy.

"That's how. I fell right over her and landed in it. Both hands. You wouldn't believe how *sticky* the stuff gets, neither. It was like hot paint."

Jeremy shuddered. His stomach was churning faster than ever.

"The elf and the guy in the Santa costume didn't come back, so I got the hell out of there. Couldn't believe how much snow was outside. For some reason, I didn't want to go back to the gas station. Had this feeling something would be there, waiting for me. I saw the lights on in the movie theater and went there instead."

"And that's when you found us."

"Yep. And you didn't open the fucking door."

"No."

Pete stopped talking then and Jeremy didn't push him anymore. They sat in silence for a minute or two, Pete wheezing through his mashed nose, Jeremy fighting to keep his stomach under control. Blood and guts story aside, Pete really stank. He was a cloud of body odor zipped up tight in coveralls, and every so often, a wisp of that cloud managed to puff out. The smell reminded Jeremy of the boys' locker room after gym class on a hot day.

Finally, he asked, "Where did you go?"

"Hmm?"

"After we... couldn't open the doors. You ran off. Where?"

"Oh, right. Not far."

"Did you get into the movie theater some other way?" Jeremy recalled, all too clearly, how a door had slammed somewhere else in the building as they'd discussed what to do next, and that had settled the matter. "I think one of the emergency exits was open."

"The movie theater?" said Pete. "No, not there. I never went in there. I just, you know... ran, as fast as I could. Away from the mall. Wouldn't have cared if I had to run all night with snow up to my waist. I just wanted *away* from this place."

Jeremy looked at him. "So how'd you end up down here?"

Pete met his gaze as best he could and said, "Well, like I said, all that happened after I ran from the movie theater. And that's about the time things started getting strange."

"In there."

Lincoln, balancing on his crutches, nodded at the door marked 'Staff Only' and Steve tried the handle. The door swung inwards.

"And you're sure it's down here?" said Steve, holding the door open. Lincoln passed through.

"I'm not *sure*, but I think so. I know a guy who works at the mall and he told me the security office was on the second floor. Gotta be here."

Steve allowed Lincoln to lead him down the narrow hallway, staying a couple of feet back to avoid tripping him. The kid had found the staff corridor fairly quickly - it was tucked away between a clothing place and the mall drug store, partially hidden behind a full-size cardboard cutout of a grinning pharmacist reminding shoppers it was "Time to get the jab!" while holding up a liquid-spewing syringe. And, much like the ground floor staff corridor Taryn and Jeremy had found (though of course, neither Lincoln nor Steve knew about that), the door was unlocked.

About halfway down the corridor, Lincoln stopped and said, "Here."

The sign on the door simply read 'Security'. Steve tried the handle and it opened easily.

"Pretty secure, alright," he muttered.

The mall's security office wasn't much more than a broom closet with a panel of screens mounted along one wall. The cobweb-covered light mounted on the ceiling hummed like a cicada. A plain, uncluttered desk and chair were positioned below the screens and the aging computer unit they were hooked into; a full mug of coffee, untouched, sat next to the computer keyboard. The only other item in the room was a tall metal cabinet set against the wall to the right. There were no windows and the place smelled of must.

Lincoln crutched his way to the desk and flopped down in the chair. Steve noticed sweat on the back of the kid's neck, in spite of the cold.

Those bony arms weren't made to work crutches, he thought.

"How'd you break your foot?" he asked, glancing at the screens above Lincoln's head. Each of them cycled through camera feeds in different parts of the mall. He caught a glimpse of the interior of *The Coffee Place* - Spencer's body was just visible at the entrance.

"My foot?" said Lincoln, propping his crutches against the desk. "Oh, yeah. I, um... fell."

"You fell?"

"Yeah."

"And broke your foot doing it?"

"It was a bad fall." Lincoln sniffed, drawing the keyboard towards him. "I was high at the time."

"Ah." Steve tried the cabinet door - locked. *Shit*. He took hold of the padlock attached to the locking mechanism and tilted it towards the light.

"This thing needs a combination," he said, running his thumb over the four scrolling dials on the side of the padlock. "Any idea what it might be?"

"Huh?"

Lincoln wasn't listening. He was peering at the screens, his fingers hovering above the keyboard.

"Hey." Steve banged the padlock against the cabinet door and Lincoln jumped, looking round. "Guns are in here. We need four numbers. Any ideas?"

"Umm... hang on."

Lincoln leant to his left and started pulling open drawers below the desk, rifling through them. Steve glanced at the screens again. This time, he got a good look at the food court and the Santa plowing through the tables and chairs after the short girl. He said nothing; seconds later, the screen changed to show the empty concourse again.

"Might be in this."

Lincoln straightened up with a notebook in his hand.

"You think they'd write it down?" Steve said doubtfully.

"I would," said Lincoln, thumbing through the pages. "I have to write down all my passwords and stuff. Can't remember anything."

Shocking. "How'd you get here today, anyway?"

"I drove."

"With a broken foot?"

Lincoln sighed, as though he'd already explained it. "Yeah. I had to come in. No choice, we were short-staffed. But the boss let me park at the back entrance so I didn't have to walk far. Think he felt bad."

"I'll bet. We could use that car now, too. Once we get out of here."

"Yeah, that's what..." Lincoln trailed off. "Shit."

"What?" Steve's eyes jumped to the screens again.

"My keys," said Lincoln. "I don't have them on me."

"Right. Where'd you leave them?"

"They're in my coat, in the staff office. Over in the movie theater."

"No sweat, buddy. We have to go that direction anyway, right? We can swing by the office and grab 'em, and then get the hell outta here."

"Ok. Yeah, ok." Lincoln nodded and went back to the notebook. Steve watched the screens, waiting for the one in the top right corner to cycle back to the food court. He squeezed the padlock between his fingers, urging the feed to change faster. He needed to see it. He had to see it before -

"Hey, I got it!" Lincoln announced. He held up the notebook but Steve wasn't really looking. "It's right here."

"Yeah? Let's hear it."

"You're not gonna believe this."

"Just tell me, kid."

"It's one-two-three-four."

"Of course it is."

Steve dialed in the code and the padlock released. He un-hooked it and pulled the door open. There were three compart-ments inside the cabinet: a smaller one at the top and bottom, with a larger one in the middle.

The bottom compartment contained a pair of heavy-looking work boots, the kind someone might switch to before heading out into snow. Backup boots, really. Not a bad idea. Next to them was a clear plastic lunch box filled with candy bar wrap-pers and sandwich crusts.

The guard locked his lunch in the gun cabinet.

The taller middle compartment, which Steve had hoped would hold a rifle or shotgun, contained the guard's outdoor coat, hung neatly on a hook. Steve pulled it out and, seeing there was no long gun behind it, tossed it aside.

"Top shelf," said Lincoln, swiveling to face him in the chair.

Steve looked. Sure enough, there was a two-slot gun rack in the top compartment, with several boxes of ammunition stacked next to it. Next to the boxes was a hook with the word 'Cuffs' written above it in Magic Marker. It was empty.

There were two handguns in the rack; Steve lifted one down with his free hand, inspected it, and held it out to Lincoln.

"What?" Lincoln said, bemused.

"I need you to check if it's loaded," said Steve.

"Why can't you do it?"

"Because my left arm's no good, and I'd rather not shoot myself in the face checking it. So I need you to do it. Here."

Lincoln hesitated, then took the gun from Steve. He turned it over, holding it gingerly with his skinny fingers, like it might explode at any second.

"Really? You haven't fired one before?" said Steve.

"No."

"Ok, but you've shot people in video games before, right?"

"Oh yeah, sure," Lincoln replied brightly, "all the time."

"Good. Just think of this as a game, then, if it helps." Steve explained how to check the chamber, then watched with some trepidation as Lincoln pushed back the slide and peered inside. "Can you see a bullet?"

"Yeah."

"Ok, good. Let the slide go. Now, put your left hand palm-up below the gun - you're right-handed, yeah? - then push the mag release with your thumb. Don't let the magazine hit the floor."

The mag dropped into Lincoln's hand. Steve saw the bullets glint under the ceiling light.

"Great, now slap it back in there and hand it to me."

Lincoln obeyed. Steve took the gun, flicked on the safety with his thumb, and tucked it behind his belt at his lower back. He grabbed a box of ammo from the top shelf and stuffed it in his pocket, then pushed the cabinet door shut.

"Alright, we're good to go," he said.

"Back to the main entrance?"

"Soon. First, I think we should check the underground parking lot."

The bright look on Lincoln's face faded. "The underground? Why?"

"Because it's the one place we haven't been to yet, and I want to see if anyone's down there. You know, folks who didn't make it out during the evacuation earlier. They might be trapped down there and need our help. Besides, there's an external door, right? For the cars?"

"Um, yeah. But - "

"So we leave that way. Check the lot, go out the external door, get help. We might even find your friends along the way."

"They're not... my friends," Lincoln said slowly, grappling for articulation. "I just met them today. They're... I don't know what, actually. Spencer was alright, but he's dead now. And I'm pretty sure Ash hates me. But - "

"Either way," Steve cut in impatiently, "we stand a better chance of finding them heading for the underground than the main entrance. Save as many people as we can, right? Get home in time for Christmas?"

Lincoln nodded.

"Good. Then grab those crutches and let's get going."

"Sure." Lincoln swiveled back to face the desk, reaching for his crutches. Steve went to the door and brought his ear close to it, listening for indications of movement in the staff corridor. The last thing he wanted was to get cornered in there by the elf or the guy with the ax.

"Hey, what's that?"

Steve turned back. Lincoln was staring at the screen in the bottom left corner.

Shit.

"Never mind, kid," Steve said smoothly. "We've got to go."

"Look," said Lincoln, pointing. "You were right - there's someone in the underground lot."

Jeremy listened to Pete"s story the way you might listen to a child explain, with great earnestness, how their "friend" had smashed the pane in the greenhouse earlier that day, and how they'd fled the scene straight after, all the while holding under one arm the football that had done the damage. He didn't believe the story at first, not one bit. His sharp, rational mind - dulled as it was by the numbing caress of shock and terror - wouldn't allow for it. And yet, the longer Pete spoke, slouched forward in the underground parking lot with his wrists cuffed behind his back and snot running freely from his right nostril (the left one was mashed shut), the less able Jeremy was to deny two obvious points: at this stage, Pete had no reason to lie, and the truth was no less believable than anything else that'd happened to them already that day.

He just didn't *want* to believe it.

"When you didn't open the doors, I just started running," Pete began, gazing at his work boots as though Jeremy wasn't even there. "I was sure those... things... were coming after me. Even thought I saw them coming out've the mall. It was snowing by then, real heavy. Couldn't tell for sure. But it got me running and I didn't look back for a long time.

"Got out past the movie theater building and started for the road. Or at least, where I thought the road should be - like I said, it was snowing real heavy and the light was going fast. I just followed the drive that ringed the outdoor parking lot until I was somewhere near the exit lane. There was no point going into the lot itself - the cars in there were buried deep in snow, like they were homes for eskimos at the North Pole. You'd never have known it was a parking lot at all, if you'd just come across it. Made me wonder if anyone had been inside those cars when the snow came down. They'd still be there now, I reckon, frozen solid. Wouldn't be able to get their doors open."

He cleared his throat and went on.

"You ever tried running in deep snow, son? I mean, *really* running, for your life? It feels like your legs have been dipped in cement, or like you're going through quicksand that's trying to suck your boots off with every step. After a while, your lungs start burning in your chest with the effort and you feel like you're gonna collapse. But you know if you do, there's no way in hell you're getting back up again. You'll just lie there, facedown, until you're buried in it, and that's how they'd find you the next day. Frozen like a popsicle."

Pete chuckled at that. It quickly transformed into a volley of dry, hacking coughs. Jeremy didn't say a word. He just waited until the other man was done.

"Popsicle," Pete repeated sardonically. "Probably would've served me right if that's how I'd ended up. Might've been better than this. But I didn't stop. Fell a few times, sure, but I didn't stop. Kept truckin' my way through that snow until I was on the road. Knew I'd reached it because I passed the bus stop, mostly buried too, apart from the street light above it. That was the last light, right on the perimeter of the complex, and once I was past it, I was in the dark.

"There was still some light in the sky but not much, and not enough to see for sure where I was going. I thought there'd be cars on the road, or that the road itself wouldn't be buried as deep as the complex had been, but it was no different. I was still up to my knees and it was coming down just as hard.

"I looked back then for the first time. I could see the trail I'd plowed from the edge of the parking lot to where I was now, but it seemed like I hadn't gotten that far in the end. The mall, the gas station, the movie theater - they all looked close enough and well lit-up. If you'd been driving by at that point, you wouldn't have known anything was wrong.

"Could really feel my heart by then, too, banging around inside my chest like a rat trapped in a cage. Really thought I was about to have an attack, right then and there. Might've been a mercy, now that I think about it. All my troubles would've been over."

"Did you try your phone?" Jeremy asked.

"Huh?"

"Your phone. Did you have any signal, once you were away from the mall?"

"Oh. No, I never tried it. Probably dropped out've my pocket when I fell one of those times. My mind wasn't working right, anyway. If I'd had the damn thing in my hand, I wouldn't have thought to use it."

"So what happened?" said Jeremy. The beginnings of goose-flesh had started on his lower back as Pete talked and was working its way up his spine. "How'd you end up back here?"

Pete hesitated, still staring fixedly at his boots, before continuing.

"Wish I could say I tried my best," he said, slower now, "but I really thought I was gonna drop. My heart was going so hard I thought I'd pass out. Stood that way for a long time, just looking back at the mall, wondering if I should go back and find help. Maybe try the gas station, or find you guys again. But I knew I must be on the road, and if I just kept following it straight ahead, it'd take me back to the highway. There'd be cars there. People. I could flag someone down and get them to call the cops. And I could get the hell away from there for good.

"I started walking, keeping my head down. It was hard to see with the snow in my face - that shit really stings your eyes if you're not careful. I just kept looking at my feet, kept putting one in front of the other. I only looked back once, and by then I was on the far side of the movie theater and couldn't see the lights in the parking lot anymore. That was the only time I looked back at the *Outlet*.

"I kept walking and walking. Tried keeping my hands in my pockets, but then I fell and my face hit the snow, so I kept them tucked under my armpits after that. Didn't have any gloves or a coat. I could feel myself starting to freeze and I couldn't stop shivering. Thought to myself, "This is it, Pete, you chicken-shit bastard. You jumped out've the frying pan and ran straight into the fire, and now you're gonna get hypothermia and die out here in the middle of nowhere." Won't that be a great story, someday? Pete the Popsicle Man.

"I didn't notice it'd stopped snowing until my foot landed on asphalt."

He sniffed, spat a globule of blood on the ground between his legs.

"What d'you mean?" Jeremy said. "The snow was gone?"

"That's right," said Pete. "Just like that. One minute I was wading through it up to my shins, the next it was completely gone. No more under me, no more falling from above. Like I said, it was like I'd been inside a snow globe, and now I'd found the exit door. Never seen anything like it in my life."

That can't be true, Jeremy thought. *He'd gone mad. I'm chained to a pipe next to a madman.*

"No more snow," Pete continued, "except what was on my head and shoulders. The sun was set by then but the moon had come out, big and fat, and I could see the road stretching ahead of me in the light of it. All asphalt, no snow."

Mad, Jeremy thought.

Pete said, "I took a look back behind me, half-expecting to see there'd been no snow at all and I'd been imagining it the whole time, but there it was, just a few yards back, nice and bright in the moonlight. I could see my tracks in it, could see exactly how deep it'd been, how it'd only become more shallow right at the end. And I swear on my mother's grave, and on her mother's grave too - and I don't mind being struck down right here if I'm lying, because it's the God's honest truth - that it was *still snowing* back there, just beyond where I stood, real heavy like it'd been before. It was like I was looking out at it through a window from inside my house. And if I'd walked back just a few yards, it would've been falling on me again."

Jeremy could see Pete was shaking now, and he knew that whether he'd lost his mind or not, the memory was vividly real to him. The gooseflesh on his back slithered up to his shoulders.

"I started laughing then," said Pete, his cuffs clinking on the pipe as he shook. "I laughed because it was so ridiculous, so completely insane and impossible. Laughed because I still had some stranger's blood all over my hands, because I'd seen some fella in a Santa costume commit murder right before my eyes, because everyone in the mall and the movie theater and the gas station had gone into a trance and crawled into a little wooden house and disappeared. I laughed until I was howling, right there in the road with no snow on it. Howling at the moon. And when I looked round again, they were there."

It came out of Jeremy's mouth as a weak whisper: "Who?"

Pete looked at him for the first time since starting his story and said, "The men in the black coats. Two of them, a little ways up the road. They wore black trench coats that came down to their knees, the kind you'd see detectives wear in old movies; they had black hats on - fedoras, I think they're called, or trilbys - and I couldn't see their faces. They wore black leather gloves and their arms were by their sides, and they just stood there, right in the middle of the road, watching me. They didn't speak, they didn't move. They just... stood there."

Pete swallowed and Jeremy actually heard the *gulp* sound he made.

"Let me tell you, kid. I'd seen someone get decapitated not long before then, and I'd run for my very life until I thought my heart might explode inside me, but I'd never felt fear like I did in that moment. It was pure, like ice-water at the top of a mountain. It turned my blood stone cold. When I saw those two men in the road, dressed in black and not saying a word, it felt like the devil himself had come for me."

"W-who were they?" Jeremy said.

"I don't know," said Pete, staring at his boots again. "I only saw them for a few seconds - though it felt like a lot longer - because then *she* came. The woman dressed as Mrs Claus. I hadn't realized it at the time, but I'd taken a few steps back when I saw the men in the coats, and there was white under my feet again. I only heard her at the last second, crunching through the snow behind me, and before I could turn all the way around she got me in the back of the head with that hammer. Don't know how it didn't kill me at the time, but it didn't.

"I came-to as she was dragging me back to the mall. Think it was just outside the gas station, of all places. She had me by the arm and I started struggling - actually managed to knock the hammer out of her hand - but I was still dizzy from the blow to the head and didn't stand a chance. She pounded on me pretty good for about a minute, broke my fucking nose and everything. And then I passed out again, and when I woke up, she was cuffing me to this pipe. I hope that's the closest I ever get to her."

Jeremy thought of the elf's horribly disfigured face again and swallowed down the lump rising in his throat. *I want to go home. Oh please, let me go home.*

"I don't know who the men in the black coats were," said Pete, "and I don't know why that woman dragged me all the way back here when it would've been easier to let me go. Or at least, I didn't know *then*. I think I do now."

"Why?" Jeremy said. "Why'd she bring you here? Why *did she bring me here* are we down here? What's going to happen to us?"

Pete shook his head slowly. "It's better if I don't tell you, kid. You'll find out soon enough."

"Fuck that shit!" Jeremy cried, suddenly shrill. "I'm not sitting round here in the dark waiting for some psychopath to kill me. My friends are still up there."

"They're probably dead, son," Pete said, still shaking his head.

"No, they're not. I know they're not. And there's a little girl with them."

The person on the other side of Pete stirred. Pete looked at Jeremy - his face was a garbled mess of shock and despair.

"It's better not to hope," said Pete, so low Jeremy almost couldn't hear him. "It's better that way."

"Screw that, man!"

"Stop, kid," Pete said. "We're not the only ones they brought down here. There were others, when I woke up. You're not the first one to wear those handcuffs."

Jeremy stared at him. His mouth had run dry. "What others?"

"The others they found in the mall," said Pete. "The ones they didn't kill. Don't you get it? They've kept us alive for a reason, just like they did with the others. We're fresh meat.

"They're going to *feed* us to it."

"Who *is* that?"

Lincoln leaned over the desk to get a better look at the monitor. Standing behind him, Steve flexed the fingers of his injured arm restlessly.

"I think... is one of them that Jeremy kid?" said Lincoln.

On the screen, Steve could see three people, sitting with their backs to the wall in one of the underground parking bays. One of them had a bag over their head.

"Is it him?" Lincoln said.

"I don't know, Linc," said Steve, working to keep his voice steady. "I've never met him, remember?"

"Oh, that's right. Well, it looks... hey!"

The image on the monitor changed to a different angle of the underground, showing a badly-parked station wagon in one corner. The door to the stairwell was just visible near the edge of the screen.

"It's cycling through the camera feeds down there," Steve said, "it'll take a while to - "

"Maybe I can make it go back," said Lincoln. He started tapping at the keyboard, slowly at first, then more hurriedly. Text options began flashing up on the screen.

"Just leave it, kid," Steve said. His arm was starting to ache again; the bandage was already beginning to redden. *Fucking moron, Spencer.* "It'll take a while and we don't have time. We need to get down there and help them."

"Yeah, I know," said Lincoln. Suddenly, he sat up straight in the chair. "Hey, look at this."

"Look at what?"

Lincoln pointed at one of the other monitors. "I brought this up by accident. I think it's a feed from earlier today, in the main part of the mall."

Steve leaned over Lincoln's head and stared at the screen. The time in the bottom corner read two-thirty-six.

"What're they doing?" said Lincoln distantly.

Steve watched from the perspective of a ceiling-mounted camera as hundreds of shoppers trudged along the mall concourse, arms by their sides, like they were sleep-walking. Men, women, children. No-one carried anything. They just walked, almost in lines, towards the center of the concourse, streaming down the escalator and out from the stores, staring straight ahead.

"Seriously," murmured Lincoln, "what the hell?"

As the entranced mall shoppers reached the center of the concourse, they passed through the white picket gate around Santa's Grotto and disappeared through the door, one after the other, like lemmings in that very old video game. Steve saw, as well as Lincoln did, that the faux-wooden door of the grotto was being held open by none other than Santa himself.

There he is, Steve thought. *Doing his duty. Such a good boy.*

As the silent feed rolled, they saw one man catch his foot on something. He stumbled briefly then went down hard, smacked his head on the floor, and lay still. Other shoppers simply stepped over him on their way to the grotto.

"I don't get it," said Lincoln, and Steve heard the edge in his voice. "Everyone went into the little house? The Santa house? How'd they all fit in there?"

"Beats me," said Steve. He'd involuntarily begun to grind his teeth.

"But," Lincoln went on, still staring at the screen, "didn't you say everyone got... evacuated, or whatever? Like, because there was a terrorist attack, or a shooter, or something? That's what you said, right?"

"Did I say that? I don't remember now."

Lincoln swiveled in the chair. "Yeah, you did. You said there was an evacuation, and that's where everyone went. You said everyone left."

Steve met his gaze. For a moment, neither of them spoke. Then Steve grinned that easy grin of his and shrugged. "Guess I was wrong, huh? I lost a lot of blood, kid. Maybe I wasn't remembering clearly, you know?"

Lincoln stared at him, his eyes darting rapidly left and right between Steve's, as though he was trying to catch the lie in motion. Then he turned back to the monitors.

"I don't think we should go down to the underground," Lincoln said, tapping at the keyboard again.

"No?"

"No. I want to look inside the Santa house. I... need to know where they all went."

"We can do that."

Steve slipped the gun out slowly from behind his belt. He thumbed the safety off.

"They can't all still be inside," Lincoln said, looking from screen to screen, searching for a new feed. "Maybe we missed something."

"Maybe we did."

Steve took a step back and leveled the gun at Lincoln's head. In the same moment, one of the middle screens changed to an almost pitch-black view of the underground; Lincoln looked, saw Steve reflected clearly on the monitor, and cried, "Hey - !"

He started to turn. Steve pulled the trigger.

The gun went off with a deafening *bang* in the tiny room. The central monitor exploded, showering white sparks across the desk. Bright red blood sprayed evenly across the other monitors. Lincoln slumped to his right, slid off the chair and crumpled to the floor, clattering one of his crutches into the wall. The chair spun lazily, its mechanism squeaking.

Steve rocked on his feet, breathing hard. The report from the gunshot rang painfully in his ears. "Sorry, kid," he said, flicking the safety on again with trembling fingers.

That's it then, he thought. *It's done. No turning back now, buddy.*

He stepped forward, slipped the gun back under his belt, and knelt by Lincoln's body. Leaning his wounded arm on the chair, he stuffed his good hand in the kid's pockets, fishing around. Lighter. Gum. Candy wrappers.

Keys.

He tugged them out. They were on a keychain shaped like a marijuana leaf. Two door keys. One was for the movie theater staff office, where the car keys were. He straightened up, wincing, and dropped them in his pocket.

Thank you, stoner-boy.

What was next?

He had a weapon now. It wasn't much, and he may not even need it. But it put his mind at ease. A little insurance, just in case something happened. In case *they* arrived before he was finished.

Who was left?

The kids, two of them. Just the girls now. The boy was in the underground lot. He'd be no trouble, and he doubted the girls would be, either. *They* didn't have a gun, after all. They wouldn't know where to get one, either.

There'd been a little girl too, hadn't there? The little girl in the purple coat with the flashing sneakers on her feet. And there was the woman as well. They were both important, weren't they?

"Not anymore," he said aloud, shaking his head.

No, not anymore. They'd been important to Adam, the Former One, but not now. Not to him. Not to Steve, or whatever the hell they'd decided to name him. They were just obstacles, problems requiring some fixin', if it came to it. It'd be easy, too, if he bumped into them. They'd see him as he was before, as Adam, and they'd run right up to him with open arms and big smiles, and he'd drop them then and there. Pow! Right in the kisser. He had no more time for games, for *pretending*. That'd been a necessity before, when Spencer and the short girl found him in the storage room and he had to come up with something fast. But not now. Now, he had himself a GUN.

Maybe he'd go back to being Adam. Why not? He'd never really been Steve, anyway. He wouldn't even mind running into the wife again, come to think of it. That might be amusing. He could have some fun with that.

He watched Lincoln's blood run through the keyboard for a moment; below the desk, more of it soaked into the thin gray carpet, turning it black.

He smiled. "Come and find me, Liv-baby," he said.

Adam turned, opened the door, and left the security office.

FOURTEEN

Outside the mall, the temperature had dropped close to twenty degrees. It was colder than when Pete Zampetti made his ill-fated attempt to reach the highway, colder than when Spencer Bloom led three teenagers and *The Movie House* Assistant Manager to the mall, where he died shortly afterwards. Snow was still coming down on the *Outlet Complex* and showed no signs of letting up.

If you'd been there that evening, perhaps huddled in your car in the outdoor lot - and God help you if you were - you'd have seen them coming, and the sight of them might have stopped your heart dead in your chest. Certainly, if Sue Peterson (who was still on shift several miles away in the dispatcher center) had been looking directly at them through her fuschia-colored frames rather than reflected in the blank screen in front of her, she might have keeled over, right there at her desk, and her old colleague John Baker would've been too stunned to do anything meaningful about it.

There were three of them now. Sue Peterson had felt the ice-cold touch of one, standing right behind her in her office, and Pete Zampetti had very nearly run right into two more on the road to the highway. It was likely by now that more were on the way.

They drifted silently into the humming glow of the bus stop's overhead light, the same bus stop Taryn, Jeremy and Ash might have waited at earlier, had things gone differently that day. They paused there for a moment, surveying the *Outlet Complex* parking lot up ahead, three black shadows in the flurrying snow. Then, wordlessly, they started forward.

If you'd still been in the parking lot that evening and saw the men in trench coats approaching - and by now your teeth would have been clacking together faster than a pneumatic drill - you'd have noticed the strangeness of their movements, how they walked with their backs held entirely straight and their arms pinned by their sides, and yet kept their heads dipped so their immaculately-clean trilby hats shielded their faces from view. If you'd been looking closely, you may also have noticed how their polished black shoes barely touched the ground, and if you'd *really* been paying attention (though no-one would have blamed you if you'd already slipped into a dead faint by now), you might have realized that the snow behind these three black-coated fellows remained untouched, without footprints.

They didn't speak as they drifted by the gas station, where the Price family car rested at a slight angle beneath the canopy, slouched onto its two flat tires. They paused just long enough to gaze at the still-lit store interior, then carried on towards the mall. What they'd come for wasn't inside the gas station. They knew that. What they'd come for was calling to them, drawing them inexorably to its hiding place in the shadows, whether it knew it or not.

Had Lincoln Ward still been at *The Coffee Place* windows overlooking the parking lot, he might have seen them, standing there in the snowy glow of the mall entrance, staring up at him; had Spencer and the others been at the shutter, working at the padlock with the bolt cutters, they *would* have seen them, and the whole story may have ended right then and there. But no-one was at the front end of the mall by then - they were scattered inside, whether by chance or by design, and none of them saw the three men in trench coats.

No-one saw them glide to the left, passing along the brightly-illuminated front of the mall, shoulder to shoulder in a perfect line; no-one saw them heading for the east side of the building, where the exterior door of the underground lot was still down, half-buried in snow. The door wouldn't be a problem to these three, though. Doors rarely were.

They'd wait until the time was right.

No-one saw the men in trench coats that evening, no-one at all, except for Ash Buckley, who was still under a table in the mall food court, passed out cold. She saw them in her mind's eye, turning the corner of the building, quickening their spectral pace as the downward-sloping ramp of the underground lot came into view.

She'd been dreaming of Taryn in the arcade, watching as her friend ran from the thing dressed as Mrs Claus, and when the Trench Coat men stepped into her dreamscape, she bit deep into the muscular flesh of her tongue.

FIFTEEN

She heard it, clear as day. Ash's voice.

They're COMING

She snapped awake.

"Ash!" she gasped. The arcade ceiling; the flickering lights. Then: "Em!"

Taryn sat up. Her head swam and she almost swooned right back down again. She put out a hand to steady herself. Her palm pressed against warm plastic.

The arcade machine.

The woman with the hammer.

Taryn pushed hair from her eyes, blinking away the white stars dancing in her vision. The interior of the *Star-cade* materialized again, all glowing screens, multicolored carpets and looped electronic music.

There she was.

Taryn struggled to her feet. The Mrs Claus was just a few feet away, face down on the floor. Folds of back fat bulged beneath her costume. The hammer was still in her hand.

Electrocuted, Taryn thought. *The bitch deserved it.*

She looked at the machine she'd been leaning on. The screen was smashed and singed around the edges. Even now, blue-white sparks fizzled intermittently in the space the hammer had made.

Got what was coming to her.

Something warm touched Taryn's hand and she cried out, almost leaping into the machine. Em was there, gazing up at her groggily.

"I was sleeping," she said.

Taryn dropped to her knees with a relieved gasp, brushing hair from Em's face now instead. The little girl was dazed but unhurt. She continued to clutch the cat toy they'd given her in *The Play Emporium*, like it was a talisman warding off evil.

Maybe it was.

"Are you ok?" Taryn said.

Em nodded and said, "I want to go home."

Tears welled in Taryn's eyes. She pulled Em into a hug and said, "Me too, sweetie. Me too." She released her and stood again. Her head was still light but the stars had faded from behind her eyes. "Let's go."

Em looked at the Mrs Claus. "Is she sleeping, too?"

"I hope not," said Taryn.

She took Em's hand and they started through the arcade in the direction of the entrance. Taryn felt strangely at ease, as though the danger had now passed and they were heading for safety, but she knew it was a false feeling, an untrue one. They weren't safe at all.

Taryn! They're coming!

Ash's voice had been so clear, like she'd been speaking right in her ear. And what was she talking about? Who *else* was coming? Taryn shook her head as she walked, clutching Em's hand tight in her own. Had Ash spoken those words earlier that day, and now they were simply echoing back in her subconscious?

Or was it like the other time, from long ago?

Who's coming?

"We need to get the hell out've here," she muttered aloud, rounding one of the crane machines.

"You said a swear," said Em.

"I know."

The exit was just ahead. They'd leave the arcade and go straight for the main entrance, shutter or no shutter. Who knows: maybe Linc was there now and he'd gotten the padlock off? There'd been another guy with him too, right? Between them they could do it. And maybe the police were just outside, waiting to get in and rescue them. They'd take Em, and they'd go in and get Ash and Jeremy, and then they could all go home.

Taryn hesitated briefly at the *Star-cade* exit, scanning the concourse for signs of movement. She cleared her throat to call for Ash, then immediately quashed the idea. That'd lead the elf right to them. Or the Santa, wherever he was now.

Holy shit, we've gotta get out of this place.

Em pointed down the concourse towards *The Play Emporium*, and that got Taryn moving again. She couldn't have her shouting anything out in this huge, echoey space, where snowflakes still drifted down from the hole in the ceiling and wind moaned around the walls outside. They had to leave, and quietly.

Taryn led them along the edge of the concourse, just beneath the second floor balcony. Fairy lights chased up and down the pillars on their right as they passed them; to their left, the mall stores remained welcomingly bright and eerily empty.

Suddenly, Taryn stopped.

Footsteps.

She wheeled around, expecting to see Mrs Claus running at her again with the hammer held aloft, but there was no-one behind them. She turned in a circle, breathing hard, dragging Em with her.

The concourse was empty. There was no-one there but them.

The footsteps grew louder, more pronounced. A steady, confident stride.

Above them.

"I hear someone," said Em, loud and clear.

Taryn hissed at her to be quiet and the footsteps stopped.

Directly above them.

Shuddering, clinging to her latest breath, Taryn stepped just beyond the nearest pillar. *Just one look, and if it's one of them, we run.* She looked up.

A man was staring down at them, one hand on the railing. He was handsome, with wavy brown hair and turquoise eyes. Those eyes scrutinized them, boring right *into* them. Taryn felt herself shrink away from his gaze. The man saw it and grinned.

It was the man who'd been with Lincoln at the coffee place.

Em's cry of delight sliced through the thudding beat in Taryn's ears: "Daddy!"

Taryn looked at her, amazed, and then back up at the man on the second floor. He continued staring down at them, unblinking, not reacting at all to his daughter's exclamation.

"Daddy, Daddy!" Em cried again, tugging on Taryn's hand.

Her father, Taryn thought. Some of the fear melted away. *Her dad's here. We have help!*

As if reading her thoughts, Em's father's grin broke wider and became an easy chuckle. He slapped the railing once, making it ring, and said, "I think you better run."

Huh?

"What?" Taryn said.

Then she heard the footsteps, thumping heavily across the tiles behind her. She spun round, instinctively shoving Em away. It was all she had time to do.

The Mrs Claus grabbed her - one hand on the side of her sweater, the other on her upper arm - and dug her nails into her skin. Taryn gasped, more in fright and surprise than in pain. The woman's eyes were nothing but quivering blobs of acrid blood.

Then she tossed her, like she was nothing, straight at the *JeanScene* store window.

Taryn heard Em's father laughing as she crashed through the glass.

Sixteen

Olivia had only been half-listening while Pete told his story. It was hard to breathe with the bag over her head, and she was tired. So tired. Her back and shoulders ached from sitting at an angle, hands cuffed at the base of her spine, one leg bent under her; that leg had fallen asleep long ago, and she knew if she tried standing now, she'd simply keel over. She was disoriented from the darkness and the lack of oxygen inside the bag.

But when the boy said, "I know they're not, and there's a little girl with them", she came out of her muddled stupor instantly, as though someone had splashed ice-cold water in her face, and then slapped it for good measure. She was wide awake - dazed but alert - and suddenly listening closely to what the two people on her right said next.

"There were others, when I woke up," the man was saying. "You're not the first one to wear those handcuffs."

"What others?" the boy replied.

Emma, Olivia thought, shifting her weight off her dead leg. *Emma. Adam.*

"The others they found in the mall," said the man. "The ones they didn't kill."

Oh shit, oh shit. Emma. My girl.

"Don't you get it? They've kept us alive for a reason, just like they did with the others."

She strained forward. The cuffs dug into her wrists.

"We're fresh meat," said the man. His voice was rising in pitch, simmering with hysteria. "They're going to *feed* us to it."

"What?" cried the boy, abandoning all pretense of keeping his voice down. "Feed us to what? What the *fuck* are you talking about?"

Yes, what the actual fuck?

Then the hysteria boiled over and the guy began to laugh. Slowly at first, a deep baritone guffaw, chugging along like a steam train, then faster and louder, until his laughter boomed around the parking lot, reverberating off the cold concrete walls and pillars. The pipe they were cuffed to trembled and clanked as his body convulsed. The boy kept talking but the man wasn't listening anymore.

I have to get out of here.

"Hey," she called. Her voice was cracked and weak inside the bag. "Hey. Hey!"

"Pete, stop," the boy said, barely audible over the guy's manic laughter. "What's wrong with you? Stop!"

There was a metallic *bang* from somewhere nearby, muffled by the bag. The boy swore but the guy - Pete - laughed harder than ever, until what was coming out of his mouth was almost a shriek. Olivia flinched away from him, and away from the pipe bouncing on its brackets at her lower back. She was beginning to hyperventilate - the inside of the bag was moistening and constricting tighter to her face.

I'm going to suffocate, she thought wildly.

She was just about to join Pete in a scream of terror when something happened. Just as suddenly as his screeching laughter had begun, it stopped; a new sound accompanied its abrupt ending - a sharp, wet, ripping noise - like someone tearing a sheet of paper in half with one quick jerk of the wrist. Olivia heard that sound right by her ear, and at almost exactly the same moment, a thin trail of hot liquid lit neatly on the side of her neck, splattering against the bag like raindrops on a tent canvas.

The pipe shuddered one last time, then went still.

The boy moaned.

Olivia felt the warm liquid roll down her neck and slide under the collar of her sweater. Repulsed, she wrenched her head away from it and clanged her forehead off the car she'd been leaning against. A hot flash of pain burst inside her skull.

The elf giggled. So close.

Olivia gasped as the bag was snatched off her head. The parking lot was poorly lit but the sudden change in brightness still made her eyes screw shut. She sucked in a breath of gasoline-scented air (still preferable to what little had been inside the shopping bag) and let it out slowly, trying to placate her thundering heartbeat and nauseated stomach. Then she opened her eyes.

As she'd expected, the elf was right there, crouched a couple of feet away; it grinned toothily when it saw her eyes open, still giggling softly. In its right hand was the bag that'd been over her head for the last hour; in its left was a six-inch long serrated bread knife, dripping red with blood.

Olivia looked to her right.

Pete, the guy who'd been cuffed to the pipe shortly after her - just before the elf yanked the bag down over her head - was slumped forward against his knees, unmoving. A roll of belly fat bulged between his chest and thighs like a gray coverall pillow. His eyes were wide and blank.

Just beyond Pete was the boy Olivia hadn't seen yet. He was pressed tight to the pillar on the other side of their parking bay, eyes averted, breathing too quickly. Just a teenager, couldn't be more than sixteen. His thick-framed glasses had slipped to the end of his nose.

The elf, suppressing more giggles behind its yellowing teeth, tossed Olivia's bag to one side and shimmied closer to Pete. As Olivia watched and the boy tried not to, the thing that had once been a child grabbed a fistful of Pete's frizzy dark hair and tilted his head back. Pete's jaw dropped open. Then Olivia saw the ragged, gaping hole running under his chin, the opening created by the elf's sandwich knife, and she saw the dark blood flowing freely down Pete's throat and over his chest, and she vomited explosively against the gas station mechanic's dangling left arm.

At that, the elf threw back its head and laughed, and Olivia wretched a second time because it wasn't the cruel, evil cackle of a demented adult killer, but the happy, carefree laugh of a child, a boy who might have been in middle school, laughing heartily at the good joke in his favorite TV show, or at a friend who he'd just bumped into the swimming pool.

It wasn't laughing to torture them further - it laughed because it was having *fun*.

The boy moaned again. Olivia forced herself to sit up straight again and spat residual vomit on the concrete floor of the parking lot. There was more on her chin but she couldn't reach it.

Still laughing happily, the elf took Pete's jaw in its other hand and started working it open and closed, like the corpse was a toy. Olivia thought of King Kong toying with the stop-motion T-Rex and wondered how she hadn't lost her mind already. The boy - was it Jeremy, he'd said? - watched it too, wide-eyed and on the verge of passing out.

Emma, Olivia thought again, distantly this time.

Finally, the elf's laughter petered back to a chuckle and it let go of Pete, who slumped forward again with a soft *splat*. The insane child-creature, blood streaming from below its eyeballs, stuck the bread knife in its left pocket and produced a small key from the other one. It reached behind Pete's bulky corpse and, after a few seconds of fiddling with the lock, released him from the cuffs. Olivia watched it return the key to its pocket. Then it grabbed Pete by the shoulders and dragged him forward, away from the wall. He flopped limply to the floor with a thud, and the elf began dragging him out of the parking bay. His body left a shiny trail of blood in his wake.

Like a snail. Olivia let out a single, gasping laugh. The boy - Jeremy, she'd decided - looked at her fearfully. *He thinks I've gone mad too*, she thought.

The elf, straining, dragged Pete's body towards the van in the center of the lot. The mechanic was heavy and the elf didn't look especially strong; even in the dim light, Olivia could see veins bulging on its neck.

"W-what's it doing?"

She looked at the boy. He was staring at the elf. A rivulet of sweat trickled down from his temple.

"Just... close your eyes," said Olivia dryly. The sound of her own voice seemed alien to her now, like she wasn't the one using it. "It's best if you don't see it."

Jeremy turned his head towards her. "What? Why?"

Olivia didn't respond. There was no need. He'd see in a few seconds, or he wouldn't.

She watched as the elf finished hauling Pete's body to the back of the van, where they were both briefly illuminated by the light pouring through the hole in the ceiling. Panting with exertion, the elf pulled open the van's rear double doors and threw them wide. Then it stepped back.

In her peripheral vision, Olivia saw Jeremy lean forward, squinting at the van's shadowy interior. The vehicle's battery had died and the automated internal lights hadn't come on, so it was difficult to tell what was inside. Well, if you didn't already know, that is.

The elf had started giggling again, soft and muffled behind its hands.

"What is it?" said Jeremy. His voice was weak now and tinged with a sort of resignation. "What's in there?"

Olivia said, "Just close your eyes."

She didn't know if Jeremy listened, or if he'd even heard her. She could have spoken the words entirely in her own head, for all she knew in that moment.

She watched, as she'd watched twice before, as something slithered out from the darkness inside the van and snaked into the light. It was long and winding, pinkish-gray in color and thick as a firehose, covered evenly in a translucent membrane of mucousy slime.

A tentacle.

Olivia heard Jeremy's breathing rate notch up.

The tentacle slopped onto the parking lot floor at the van's bumper. It found Pete's head, seemed to investigate it for a moment, then coiled itself around his neck. The slime oozed down over his shoulders and into his hair. Then, gradually but with almost mechanical ease, it began to drag his body up into the van.

Now Jeremy was whispering, and it took Olivia a few seconds to pick it up. He was saying, "Oh hell oh hell oh hell" over and over, just under his breath. The pipe rattled behind her again.

Pete Zampetti went up into the van. The vehicle sagged under the new added weight and next to the doors, the elf started to dance on the spot. Pete slid into the darkness, dragged effortlessly by the pink-gray tentacle, until he was almost gone. Olivia wouldn't have minded if he'd simply vanished and that'd been the end of it. But she knew it wasn't. Pete had known too after watching that old woman go up into the van earlier, and if he hadn't been dead, he'd have been screaming his lungs out in abject terror at what was coming next.

As it had twice before, the light flickered, then bloomed, bathing the interior of the van in a harsh, purplish glow. The source of the light was a round orb about the size of a basketball, suspended near the van's ceiling; the orb was on the end of another tentacle, shorter and stiffer than the one wrapped tight to Pete's face, and this tentacle was attached to the head of the Creature.

When Jeremy saw it, illuminated in the purple light, he started to scream. Olivia had done the same the first time.

The Creature filled most of the van's cargo area. Its skin was the same color as its tentacles, pinkish-gray and translucent in places, displaying a network of tangled blue and red veins and arteries just below the surface. Its body was entirely round, shaped just like the glowing orb; it balanced on an array of shorter, thinner tentacles with which it gripped the van's interior, locking it firmly in place. An enormous, gaping mouth ringed with dozens of foot-long, spearhead-like teeth encompassed one entire side of its body. Four bulbous, white eyes, two on each side of its head, swiveled endlessly, seeing nothing at all. The thing was completely blind. Olivia had figured that much out, watching it eat the old woman and the pleading, shrieking Chinese man before her.

It didn't need to see, though - it had its tentacles. And the elf.

She wasn't entirely sure how it was doing it, but the Creature had been communicating with the elf the whole time she'd been in the underground lot, sometimes sending it away, often calling it back, possibly for protection. Telepathy, maybe, if there was such a thing. Either way, it made no audible sounds beyond the wet slopping of its tentacles on the concrete floor and metal interior of the van, and yet the elf would periodically spill back into the lot through the hole in the ceiling, often carrying with it another body part trophy from some poor victim elsewhere in the mall. The Creature was inside the elf's head, and it had driven it completely insane.

It wasn't just the elf, either. There was a woman, too, dressed in a Mrs Claus costume. She was the one who brought Pete down, apparently after pummeling his face to smithereens. Olivia suspected there was a third one as well but she hadn't seen it yet.

Next to her, Jeremy was trembling and moaning again. The elf heard it and giggled harder against its palms, dancing spasmodically near the van. Only Pete's calves were still outside the vehicle.

"Shut your eyes," Olivia said to the boy. "Do it now."

He obeyed, just in time. Olivia kept hers open.

The Creature's lower jaw extended, leaving a black hole of nothingness between the double rows of razor-sharp teeth. The tentacle hoisted Pete up, higher and higher, pulling his body fully inside the van. He was briefly airborne, dangling just above the Creature's mouth, blood still gushing from his open throat. Then it dropped him, and Olivia squeezed her eyes shut.

Hearing it was enough: the tearing, ripping, crunching sounds of Pete's fresh corpse being consumed by the Creature. Olivia had made the mistake of watching it once before and that'd been enough. The elf danced and giggled throughout it all. The sickening noise seemed to go on forever, but Olivia knew it could only have lasted for a few seconds. Then silence fell again.

She opened her eyes, just as the Creature's blood-soaked tentacle drew back from its mouth. The interior of the van was splattered with Pete's blood, painting the already-dried blood of its previous victims. The tentacle rose up above the Creature's mouth, contracted, and dropped something into its black maw, something round and crushed that vanished instantly: Pete Zampetti's head.

The tentacle slithered back under its body and the orb's light faded out. The Creature disappeared into darkness again. The elf danced up to the rear of the van, peered inside, then skipped off into the shadows, leaving the doors open.

That hadn't happened before.

Why?

"It's over," Olivia whispered, straining to see where the elf had gone. "Jeremy. It's finished."

She looked.

Jeremy was passed out cold against the pillar.

SEVENTEEN

Taryn frowned.

There was something in her mouth. It was a hard something, and it was sharp. Right against the inside of her left cheek.

She ran her tongue over it. Was it a tooth? Did she have a tooth there?

No, no tooth. It was too far up from her gum. And... and...

Her eyelids shot open.

It wasn't *against* her cheek. It was *in it*.

She sat up and the pain came, molten waves of it, stabbing hard into the left side of her face. She was on her front; when she moved her hand to touch her head, it sent tiny fragments of glass tinkling across the floor. The pain was dizzying.

But... there was no time.

"Em," she mumbled, tasting blood.

She pushed up to her knees, wincing as her palms pressed into more glass fragments beneath her. Every part of her body ached, but none more so than her face.

Footsteps, thumping in her direction.

She spat blood on the floor and got shakily to her feet. The dizziness almost took her but she resisted. In the corner of her eye, she saw the Mrs Claus coming her way.

"Em," she said again.

No time.

Hide.

She turned left - no, *swung* left, drunkenly, like she was on the deck of a wave-tossed ship - away from the smashed store window, and collided with a clothing rack, knocking dozens of pairs of bootcut jeans to the floor. She knew where she was then, at least. That was something.

She could hear the Mrs Claus wheezing as she came through the entrance.

Without looking back, Taryn started deeper into the *Jean-Scene* store, weaving between racks of clothing as fast as her jellied legs would allow. She didn't know why she was going that way (the store was long and narrow, and the Mrs Claus was now between her and the way out), but she had to get away. She'd just been thrown through a window and was in no state to do anything but run.

The pain in her face intensified with every step.

She'd been in *JeanScene* plenty of times. It was one of those stores you'd browse your way through slowly without buying anything, always under the watchful gaze of the customer assistants, most of whom knew the difference between those who'd go on to make a purchase and those who were just killing time. Even Ash rarely left the place with anything, and she had money to burn.

Where am I going? Taryn thought. She darted to her right, then cut left. Somewhere behind her, she heard the Mrs Claus crunch across the glass-littered store foyer. The woman - or whatever she was - had slowed down since her coming-together with the arcade game machine. Still, she was in the store, which meant Taryn's escape route was cut off.

Unless I can lose her.

She reached the checkout counter near the back of the store and dropped to her haunches. At least twenty pairs of skinny jeans were stacked there next to an electronic pricing gun. A gaudy line of silvery tinsel had been tacked along the edge of the counter.

Taryn considered ducking behind the counter, then turned right again, keeping out of sight below the clothing racks. She could hear the Mrs Claus bundling her way through the store, knocking jeans and shirts and jackets aside, no longer pursuing her prey with stealth.

If she's after me, at least she's not chasing Em, Taryn thought. And then, immediately: *unless she's already killed her.*

Swiping the thought away, she slipped into the fitting room area of the store. It ran along the back on the other side of the checkout counter wall. There were five fitting rooms on each side and a door marked 'Staff Only' at the far end.

Stepping as lightly as she could, Taryn hurried to the door and tried the handle. Locked.

Cursing under her breath, she turned back. The Mrs Claus couldn't be far from the checkout counter by now.

No time. Hide.

Most of the fitting room curtains were still pulled closed. Taryn went a few paces back and slipped into the third one down. There was a narrow wooden bench on one side and a wall-length mirror on the other. She eased herself up onto the bench so her feet wouldn't be visible below the curtain; glancing down, she was amazed to see a pair of boots and slacks discarded on the fitting room floor next to a pile of store-tagged jeans.

Whoever had been in here before her had left with no pants on, in late December.

She looked up at the mirror opposite her and clapped a hand to her mouth, suppressing a gasp of shock.

Her face was still throbbing and her mouth continuously filled with blood, and now she could see why: there was a thick shard of broken glass buried in her left cheek. That's what she could feel with her tongue - it'd pierced all the way through to the inside of her mouth.

She touched the glass gingerly and grimaced as fresh pain jolted through her face. The Mrs Claus was rustling around behind the checkout counter, searching for her.

Gritting her teeth, Taryn pulled on the shard as gently as possible. She could actually feel it slide through the flesh of her cheek. The sensation was nauseating and she had to swallow hard against the bile coming up her throat. The glass pulled her cheek out like the skin of a balloon before finally coming free. Blood immediately started running down the side of her face and she pressed her palm against it, holding the shard up to the light in her other hand. It was a good two inches long, dagger-like and red at one end.

How did I not know that was there? she thought.

Then the Mrs Claus stomped into the fitting room area and the shard of glass became a weapon in Taryn's hand. She squeezed it tight, ignoring the pain. She could only use about an inch of it, but it might be enough to take out the thing's bloody eye, or stab it in the temple.

It might buy her enough time to escape.

She held her breath as the Mrs Claus came down the aisle between the fitting rooms. She was wheezing harder than ever. *Maybe she's dying*, Taryn thought hopefully. *Maybe she'll just fall down and die before she finds me.*

She pressed herself tight to the wall, tensed and ready, as the Mrs Claus approached. She didn't pause at any of the curtains, didn't check the booths. She just carried on down the aisle, straight for the 'Staff Only' door.

This is it, the voice in Taryn's head screamed. *Go, you idiot. Go now!*

She tried, but her feet wouldn't move. Part of her knew if she tried stepping off the bench, she'd simply topple to the floor. Or she might, anyway. And the thing was too close. She'd hear her and be at her booth before she had a chance to get out.

You're a moron and you're going to die, the voice informed her.

Blood seeped between her fingers. On the other side of her cheek, it flowed freely into her mouth. She desperately wanted to spit some of it out.

She heard the Mrs Claus try the door handle. She jiggled it a few times, then stopped. For a moment, the only sounds Taryn heard were the thing's dry wheezes and her own heartbeat in her ears.

Then, to her horror, she heard the first curtain whip open.

Oh hell, she thought.

***

Oh hell.

Ash heard the words and opened her eyes. A split packet of mayonnaise was right next to her face.

Screwing her nose, she sat up and banged her head on the underside of the table.

"Shit!" she said, then froze. Elsewhere in the food court, the Santa also stopped moving. He'd heard her, just barely. Now he was listening, waiting for her to sound her location again.

Ash rubbed her scalp, then shifted silently onto all fours. Her foot almost knocked into a chair leg in doing so, and that would've been enough. The fat fucker in red would've barrelled straight in her direction at the sound of it.

What's wrong with my tongue? she thought.

As Taryn had tentatively touched her cheek in the *JeanScene* store, unaware there was a chunk of glass embedded in it, Ash didn't remember biting into her own tongue when the men in trench coats appeared in her dream. So when she ran it back along her front teeth and they caught on the freshly-hewn flap she'd just created, it was all she could do to stop herself screaming in agonized revulsion.

She inadvertently swallowed the blood that'd built up in her mouth, spitting the rest onto the floor between her hands. She shut her eyes, fighting nausea.

The moment her eyelids closed again, she saw them. They stood in the snow outside the mall, staring up at the glowing letters above the entrance, their faces mercifully hidden in shadow. Three of them, side-by-side in their black trench coats and hats, on which no snow gathered.

The Trench Coat Men.

She forced her eyes open again before the Fear took her. She'd never felt anything like it before, and something in her knew she never would again.

Why was she seeing them? Why was she seeing *any* of this?

Somehow, it didn't matter. Not right now, not here. That thing dressed as Santa Claus wasn't far away.

Cautiously, Ash placed her fingers on the rim of the table and looked over it, back in the direction she'd come. She saw the doors to the stairwell and elevators. Even from the other side of the room, she could see the severed hand still clutching the door handle.

Fucking nightmare, she thought.

Then she saw him, off to her left this time, about halfway down the food court. The ax was still in his hands, still moist with Spencer Bloom's blood and peppered with splinters where it'd bit into the stairwell door. His back was to her, but his head was slowly turning in her direction; the bauble on the end of his hat bounced merrily along the nape of his neck. She lowered herself back down again, just before the thing's red eyes settled on her.

She'd seen Taryn too, hadn't she? That had been the last image, just before she woke up. Taryn, hiding behind a curtain. She had something in her hand. Something sharp and shiny.

I have to find her, Ash thought. *And Jeremy. And Lincoln… I suppose.*

Across the food court, she heard the Santa start to move again. He bashed tables and chairs aside with the bulk of his belly, searching restlessly for her. Ash thought he sounded like he was moving away from her, back towards the stairwell door.

The bolt cutters, she thought, spitting more blood from her mouth. *They're still there, by the door. I'll get them, and then find the others, and we'll get out through the main exit. And then we'll run like our asses are on fucking fire.*

The Santa continued crashing away in the other direction. He was moving faster than before.

Wait a minute…

Gripping the table rim again, Ash peered over the top.

The Santa was indeed moving away from her, crashing noisily through the food court towards the stairwell. And someone else was coming from Ash's right, striding quickly around the perimeter of the seating area. Someone with a bandage on his left forearm. Someone who, after a moment's muddled hesitation, she recognized.

It was the guy from the store room. Steve.

Steve! she yelled internally. *What the fuck are you doing?*

The Santa reached the low brick wall at the edge of the seating area and swung one leg over it. He held the ax ready in both hands, his inhuman gaze fixed on Steve, who continued towards the stairwell door without slowing.

How does he not see it? Ash thought desperately. *He's walking right towards it and it's going to FUCKING CHOP HIS HEAD OFF.*

She had to warn him. She had to try.

The Santa stomped directly towards him. Ash started to straighten up.

Then Steve pulled something from behind his back, something that flashed under the food court lights. Ash froze, her head and shoulders above the rim of the table. Steve had a gun.

He's going to shoot it, she thought excitedly. And then, unbidden and seemingly from outside of her own mind: *Pow! Right in the kisser.*

Steve took the gun out from under his belt, just as the enormous man in red reached him. They both stopped, no more than six feet away from one another, the Santa Claus balancing the blood-stained ax in his gloved hands, Steve holding the gun almost nonchalantly down by his hip. Between them, the *Exit* sign above the stairwell door glowed hot; beyond the mall roof, wind howled like a banshee and whipped snow through the evening air.

Ash's legs burned from holding her position but she dared not move. Both Steve and the Santa were side-on to her and would surely catch anything she did now. She doubted the latter would be able to get to where she was if it spotted her now, but she might distract Steve, and that could prove fatal. If it hadn't been for Spencer when she was distracted earlier, her head may no longer have been attached to her neck.

Shoot it, she thought urgently. *It killed Spencer. Fucking shoot it!*

As though he'd heard her, Steve began to raise the gun. But instead of aiming it at the Santa, he used it to motion past him, towards the food court entrance Ash had sprinted through not so long ago. He did it with a casual flick of his wrist, as though he was giving directions to a tourist on the street: *Patsy's? That way, good sir. Best fries in town.*

Ash, her head and shoulders still clearly visible above the table and her weary legs trembling with exertion beneath, watched in silent, gawking confusion as the Santa slowly lowered his ax. Steve did say something then, but it was lost in a particularly loud bluster of wind. Ash thought he couldn't have spoken more than five or six words. And to her horror, the hulking man in red - the *thing* in the fake beard that murdered Spencer - turned on his shiny black boot heels and marched away from Steve in the direction of the food court entrance and the second level of the concourse, back towards the place where Spencer Bloom's corpse still cooled. He didn't hesitate and he didn't look back. Ash watched him all the way, her mouth hanging stupidly ajar, and then she looked back at Steve.

Steve - who had, until quite recently, been Adam Price of Madison, Wisconsin, husband to Olivia Price and father to little Emma in her light-up sneakers - had also been watching the Santa retreat across the food court. He still held the gun loosely by his hip; its barrel was still speckled with Lincoln Ward's blood. And somehow, he hadn't spotted the girl with the jet black hair and purple eyeshadow, half-concealed behind a cluttered table just a short distance away, goggling at the scene unfolding before her.

Adam didn't lay eyes on Ash Buckley, but he had some idea she was there. He didn't see her, but he could most assuredly *feel* her - somehow, some way - just as he had earlier before she passed out, and just as Ash had felt Taryn's presence in the fitting area of the store below. Both Adam and Ash were connected now, though neither knew it for sure, or knew how; they were hooked into some invisible, telepathic network, tangled up in one another's thoughts and in the primal desires of the creature still digesting Pete Zampetti in the underground parking lot. And that creature was calling out to Adam now.

Ash watched, no longer aware of the throbbing pain in her tongue, as Adam reached for the door handle. He paused when he saw the severed hand still clutching it, but only for a second. The sight of it had almost made Ash throw up, but Adam felt nothing. Not anymore. There was no time to *feel* things now.

Those were the old ways for Adam. The ways of Man.

He switched the gun to his bandaged hand, grabbed the dead gray thing attached to the door handle (just a cold, hard chunk of flesh now, eternally locked in position by rigor mortis), ripped it free and tossed it away. It bounced and skidded across the tiled floor, and was gone. Adam stepped through to the stairwell landing, letting the door swing shut behind him.

Ash stared at the closed door for a moment longer. When it didn't re-open, and when the Santa didn't stomp back into the food court off to her left, she folded limply into the nearest chair and said, "What the fuck was that?"

Taryn pressed herself to the back of the fitting room booth. She listened, holding in the breath desperate to escape her lungs. Her mouth slowly filled afresh with blood.

Heavy footsteps, then *swish*. The next curtain was thrown open.

She couldn't tell which side of the aisle the Mrs Claus was on. If it was her side, the next curtain would be the one covering her booth. If it was the other, she had a few vital seconds to decide -

More footfalls. A shadow fell below her curtain.

Every muscle in her body pulled taunt. She raised the glass shard that had been in her cheek, a tiny, pathetic weapon protruding from her fist. The curtain rippled.

Go for the eye. Throw yourself at her and stick it in her eye.

She waited, breath bated, her lungs now screaming for fresh air. Her legs burned, straining to keep her steady on the bench. The shadow remained below the curtain.

Come on, she yelled internally. *Just do it!*

Another second passed. Then another.

And then the shadow moved away. Footsteps clumped down the aisle towards the fitting area exit.

It was gone.

Taryn let out a breath, long and slow, then sucked in another. She lowered her arm, listening. She couldn't hear her anymore. Had she left?

No, no way.

She knew what happened next. This was the point in the movie when the dumbass female protagonist came skipping out from her hiding place, ready to run for freedom, only to be gored through the chest by the killer's rusty machete. She'd seen enough eighties slashers to know that much.

She lowered one foot to the floor, then the other. Taking her blood-stained hand away from her face, she stuck her tongue in the hole made by the glass shard, plugging it as best she could. The pain was intense and her eyes watered, but at least now she knew what was causing the blood flow. She'd deal with it properly when she got the chance.

I could just stay here, she thought. Just wait it out until help arrives. *The police'll be here soon. Someone will come.*

But Em. She was still out there somewhere. The Mrs Claus could be on her way to get her right now.

I can't stay here.

Drawing in another breath to steady herself, Taryn pushed back the closest edge of the curtain and peered down the aisle towards the fitting area exit. Nothing. She could see where she'd left a trail of blood droplets on the floor, and where the Mrs Claus had tramped through them, leaving her own bloodied boot prints. The same prints went back down the aisle and out into the main store again.

Taryn slipped out of the fitting room booth and started back towards the exit. She took a step, listened, took another one. Listened again. Nothing. Just the faint static buzz of wall-mounted speakers that should be playing Christmas music.

No heavy footsteps or wheezing.

She came to the fitting room exit and looked round the corner. Just beyond the nearest rack, she could see the store entrance between two display windows, one smashed through by her wiry frame not so long ago. It looked like it was a mile away, but she could make it if she ran. She knew the layout of the store better than the thing in the Mrs Claus costume.

I can make it there. I'm smarter than she is. And I'm faster.

The checkout counter was on her right, open at both ends. Better to get away from the fitting rooms as soon as possible.

She slipped around the corner and crossed along the back of the store, keeping her head below the rim of the counter. It wasn't easy: the counter was low and she was tall. She also had to move on her haunches rather than on all fours in order to keep a firm grip on the glass shard, which was now digging steadily into her hand.

Ash wouldn't have a problem with this, Taryn thought. *She could practically walk behind here and not get seen.*

She ran her free hand along the shelf behind the counter to keep her balance. It was packed with neatly-folded jeans, bags and hangers. Her fingers trailed over a rock-hard wad of gum and she flinched.

Imagine being disgusted at that now, she thought absently, *after all this.*

She still couldn't hear the Mrs Claus. Was she still in the store? Distantly, the December wind whooshed and moaned around the mall, making the building rattle and creak like a tired old man. Taryn desperately wished she'd hear a siren cut through that wind, or the voices of police officers calling "Is anybody in here?" while they fanned out across the concourse, guns poised and radios crackling. She'd take any sound right now. Anything other than this deathly near-silence that threatened to expose her position at any second.

She reached the other end of the checkout counter and stole a glance around it. There was the right-hand wall of the store, hidden behind stacks of jeans; there was the display mannequin halfway along it, its featureless face turned towards the center of the store. No movement. No Mrs Claus.

She's gone, Taryn thought. *She's gone after Em.*

She took a breath and came around the end of the counter, and let out a yelp of surprise when someone screamed out in the concourse.

In the underground parking lot of the *Outlet Complex* mall, something was happening to the Creature that had eaten Pete Zampetti.

Olivia thought she knew what that something might be.

She'd been watching the Creature since the elf dragged her down into the lot. She'd watched it greedily eat two people in the purple glow of its forehead orb. And after the bag went over her head, she'd listened.

They never found Adam earlier that day, her and Em. They barely even made it out of the mall concourse.

Olivia remembered Adam saying something about the security office being near the back of the building, so when she saw the elf scuttle along the second floor railing above the Christmas trees, its blood-red eyes practically glowing with fiendish malevolence, she snatched Em up and ran in the direction her husband had gone. That led her to the ground floor stairwell door, which opened out at the mall's single elevator. Here, Olivia Price made her second mistake of the day (her first being not keeping an eye on the car when Adam took Em to the gas station restroom): instead of going straight for the stairs, she called the elevator and waited.

Looking back now, she wasn't quite sure what was going through her head at the time. Sure, all the lights were on in the mall and the elevator was clearly working. Adam must have come this way because, unless he'd made an insane life choice and gone for a quick game of Space Invaders in the *Star-cade* instead, there simply wasn't anywhere else to go. She hadn't seen a security office, and Adam hadn't met them coming back. He *had* to have gone for the stairwell, and following him there wasn't the wrong thing to do. But in hindsight, her decision to hang around in the stairwell lobby waiting for America's

Slowest Elevator to trundle its way down from the second floor was suicide.

The stairs were right there. Why didn't she take them?

Because elevators were familiar. She rode them all the time, and not once had she been stabbed inside one by some psychopath in an elf costume. That's the kind of thing that happened in the shadows of a mall's rear stairwell.

The elevator *had* actually reached the ground floor, signaling its arrival with a carefree *ping*. Elevators didn't give a rat's ass whether you were being chased by someone who liked to slash tires in the snow, someone who might equally enjoy hurting your only daughter; elevators had one job to do, and caring wasn't part of it.

The doors had slid open and Olivia had bundled Em inside, putting on her best "everything's going to be A-OK, sweetie" voice, beaming smile n' all.

And that was when the elf burst through the stairwell door and bundled itself in after them, shrieking with laughter and waving the knife it'd stolen from the sandwich place. Olivia screamed and did the only thing she could think of in the moment, probably the only thing any mother would do in the same situation when her child was under threat: she threw herself at the elf, knocking it bodily against the side of the elevator car, and yelled, "EMMA, RUN!"

Emma Price did run, though she wasn't quite sure why Mommy was shouting like that. After all, the Elf was happy, wasn't he? Only happy people laughed the way he was laughing right now. He and Mommy were playing a game, like wrestling. She'd walked into Mommy and Daddy's bedroom once when they were wrestling, but neither of them had been wearing any clothes and Mommy's face had been in the pillow; Daddy looked like he was winning so Em had cheered "Go, Daddy, go!" and he'd been *so mad*.

So she ran, leaving Olivia to wrestle the elf. The doors closed and the elevator descended, and Olivia Price fought for her very life every second she was inside that elevator car. It was the most terrifying and bizarre physical tussle she'd ever engaged in, something akin to fending off a spindly pre-teenager, but one who was hopped up on LSD and swinging a blade. How Olivia didn't get disemboweled in that cramped space, she'd never know; how she actually managed to knock the knife out of the elf's gloved hand, she wouldn't know either. But just as the elevator reached the underground level and *pinged* jovially (still not caring what was going on inside it), one of the child-thing's flailing elbows caught Olivia in the chin and snapped her head back against the doors. She rebounded off it and took one dazed step forward, and the elf sucker-punched her in the face. There was a dull crack as her right cheekbone split. Then the doors opened and she toppled backwards through the gap, hitting the concrete floor of the underground parking lot hard. The air went out of her lungs with a gasp that sounded theatrical but was very much real; in the same moment, her phone wriggled free from her pocket and smashed on the concrete by her hip. Later, she decided if she'd tried getting back to her feet right away, the elf would have been on top of her in a flash and her intestines would have been piled on the floor next to her. The shock of the sudden fall saved her life.

Instead of cutting her open, the elf coiled its fingers round her hair and started dragging her backwards across the floor. She would have screamed but she had no breath with which to do it. She batted feebly at the thing's hands, wheezing wordlessly as her back scraped across the damp concrete.

Run, Em, was the only coherent thing going through her mind then. *Run, run. Daddy will find you.*

The elf dragged her into the parking bay opposite the van, where the Chinese man was already cuffed to the pipe. He immediately launched into a frenzied, pleading babble the moment they appeared, sobbing and rocking against the wall. Olivia realized after a few seconds that his wild begging was directed at her, but she had no idea what he was saying. Adam knew some Mandarin but she was no good when it came to foreign languages. Beyond a little High School Spanish, she'd never learned.

The Chinese man kept up his incessant pleas for mercy while the elf cuffed her to the pipe and didn't stop until it ran the knife across his bare forearm. Then he was screaming, and Olivia could still hear him now, long after the elf had got him across to the van and the Creature had snagged his ankle with one of its slithering tentacles; he'd shrieked all the way into its mouth, and finally stopped.

The old woman had been next. She'd arrived shortly before Pete and she hadn't said a word. In fact, the elf had been almost gentle with her when it drew her arms behind her back and bound her bony wrists to the pipe. Olivia tried talking to her, asking what had happened, had she seen a little girl in a purple coat up there, but the old lady just stared straight ahead through her bifocals and didn't respond. She didn't speak when the Mrs Claus dumped the bruised and bleeding Pete Zampetti down beside her; she didn't speak when the elf uncuffed her, helped her to her feet and led her across the lot to the van. She still didn't speak when the Creature's tentacle snaked around her skinny waist and hoisted her high above its gaping maw. Olivia had shut her eyes that time but, just like the Chinese man's screams, she'd never forget how the old woman's brittle bones had crunched and snapped between the Creature's jaws.

It ate everyone, Olivia realized at that point. *Everyone in the entire mall. They were all brought down here and it* consumed *them, one by one.*

She hadn't seen the camera footage in the security office, but she knew it was true nonetheless. The footprints in the snow at the mall entrance, the abandoned personal items in the concourse. Just the *sense* of it she got from being in the Creature's vicinity, like it was reaching into her skull and caressing her brain, influencing her through the same means by which it was controlling the elf, though far less potently. She knew for sure without having to know at all.

The Creature had eaten everyone.

She thought she knew something else about it, too. How it'd gotten into the underground parking lot, maybe.

The brief streak she'd spotted in the sky earlier that day as they were driving along the freeway. That'd been it, hadn't it? She hadn't been wrong about what it was.

The Creature had come down in a meteorite. It crashed through the roof of the *Outlet Complex* mall and ended up in the underground lot, probably right in front of their parking bay. The elf or the woman dressed as Mrs Claus must have moved the van below the hole in the ceiling created by the meteorite's impact and put the damn thing inside it (to protect it?), and now the elf was using that same hole to move quickly between the underground and the concourse above. In the time Olivia had been cuffed to the pipe, the thing had dropped through the hole several times and brought them a "trophy", which was usually a random body part it'd hacked off a corpse somewhere else in the mall: an ear, a finger; on one particularly horrific occasion, something round and spongy that may have been a woman's breast. Each time, it would waggle it in front of them, grinning from ear to ear, and then skip off into the shadows again.

Of course, after the old woman was gone and the elf dragged the boy down through the hole in the ceiling, most of Olivia's suspicions were confirmed. She'd sat listening with the shopping bag over her head (she didn't know why the elf had decided to do that but it'd lost its mind long ago, so predicting its next move was impossible) as Pete and Jeremy Lewis talked; Pete - who hadn't spoken to her since the elf bagged her head - described how everyone in the *Outlet Complex* had slipped into the same trance, drifted into the mall and clambered down through the hole to where the Creature was waiting. It had grown fat and round on those people. The elf and the Mrs Claus, who it was also undoubtedly controlling, now took it in turns to search the rest of the mall for any "scraps" that'd been missed the first time round while the other stayed nearby.

Pete Zampetti had been one of those scraps, and he was gone now. Only Olivia and Jeremy were left, and only she was still conscious and watching the new thing that was happening to the Creature.

The elf had left the doors of the van open for a reason. Maybe it wanted them to see.

Less than five minutes after Jeremy passed out (Olivia had no way of knowing what time it was in the underground lot so she could only guess at its passage), the Creature started trembling all over. Its bulk now seemed to fill the entirety of the van's interior, and as it trembled, the van did too, creaking from side to side on its deflated tires. Perversely, it reminded Olivia of how vehicles looked in TV shows when two people were having rampant sex inside them

when the van's a-rockin', don't come knockin'

and she had to physically shake her head to dispel the image. The Creature's trembling became more and more pronounced - violent, even - and Olivia thought it was swelling up further, filling every last inch of space inside the van with its gruesome, membranous form. The orb on its forehead flickered intermittently, spilling purple light across its hideous, distorted face, illuminating the twin rows of vicious, gore-speckled teeth over-stuffing its jaws. Two, then three of its tentacles wormed out from under its body and coiled around sections of the van's exterior for support. Its lower jaw began to extend again, just like it'd done before Pete, the old woman and the Chinese man went inside, and Olivia imagined how a scream erupting from that gaping maw would reverberate around the underground lot and up to the concourse above, and that sound would be utterly horrifying to anyone who heard it, a hideous, wailing, agonized shriek from another world.

In the food court two levels above where Olivia sat, Ash Buckley collapsed to the floor with her palms pressed to her temples, and screamed.

Olivia thought the Creature was actually going to explode - was almost sure of it, in fact - when it abruptly ceased shuddering. The van stopped creaking. To Olivia's right, Jeremy began to stir. Somewhere elsewhere in the mall, she thought she heard someone scream.

Suddenly, the orb on the Creature's forehead filled with violet light, washing the dank parking lot in a blaze of brightness. Olivia flinched away, unable to shield her eyes with her cuffed hands. Through slitted eyelids, she caught a glimpse of the Creature's lower jaw contracting; the tentacles released their grip on the van's rear doors and bumper and slithered back under the Creature's body, which itself had begun to shrink again, like a basketball deflating slowly. If it *had* been screaming, it wasn't doing it anymore.

"Wha... what's going on?" mumbled Jeremy.

Olivia didn't reply, or look at him. She was watching the Creature. It had adjusted its position slightly inside the van, shifting its bulk a little to the left, where it sagged against the vehicle's metal body.

Yes, she was certain now.

"What's going on?" Jeremy repeated. This time she did glance at him and saw he was staring wide-eyed at the Creature. The light from its forehead orb flashed in the lenses of his glasses, even as it faded out again. "Did it... did it eat someone else?"

"No," Olivia said. She realized she still had some vomit on her chin and rubbed it against her sweater. "Something else."

"What else?"

With a bang, the elf dropped through the hole in the ceiling and landed on the roof of the van. It leapt down to the floor, bounced nimbly on its youthful legs, and scurried round to the rear of the vehicle. The handle of the bread knife stuck out of its pocket.

"What's wrong with it?" Jeremy said, whispering now that the elf had returned. "Is it dead?"

"No."

"Dying?" he suggested, hopefully.

"I don't know. Maybe."

The elf peering into the van for a moment. Then, flinging its arms in the air, it began dancing on the spot, jigging from foot to foot, giggling maniacally. Inside the van, the Creature was now completely still and flopped to one side, although a little purple light still pulsed on and off in the now-drooping orb.

"Hey, lady," Jeremy said. Olivia looked at him again, slightly taken aback. Then she remembered: *he doesn't know my name.* He met her gaze over the top of his glasses. "What's happened to it?"

She stared back at him for a moment, computing the words. She looked towards the van and the Creature, and the elf. Still dancing. Celebrating.

"I think it just gave birth," she said.

***

Taryn thought, *was that Ash?*

The scream had come from somewhere above her, maybe in the food court. Ash had been going that way.

"Shit, Ashley, you better not be dead," she whispered.

Dead. Did I actually just think that?

Why not - Spencer's dead, isn't he? And maybe Jeremy, too. And Em.

A shudder ran through her entire body, starting at her scalp, working its way down to her toes. She waited for it to pass, listening to the rhythmic in-out-in-out of her own breathing. She knew her cheek was on fire with pain, but right now she couldn't feel it. She *could* feel the glass shard, though - it was warm in her hand.

Up ahead, she could see a sliver of the *JeanScene* store entrance beyond the mannequin. It wasn't far. She could make it. The Mrs Claus could be somewhere in the midst of the standing display racks, just waiting to grab her. But she was slow, wasn't she? Big and slow.

Go fast, Taryn thought, gripping the hanging leg of a pair of jeans with her free hand. *Stay low*.

She took in a breath. Held it. Listened.

Nothing.

Go now!

She went, hurrying along the right-hand side of the store as quietly as she could manage. Her legs and back burned with the effort of keeping her body angled down below the line of the standing clothing racks. She was sure the top of her head must be visible.

She got as far as the mannequin when there was movement to her left. A momentary flash of red. Suppressing a gasp, she dropped to all fours, clutching the glass shard in her fist. Her grip was too tight - dimly, she felt warm blood seeping between her fingers.

Silence again.

Forcing herself to breathe in through her nose ("It slows your heart rate, ladies," Coach Sadler had said, "you'll be glad of it on the court") she lowered her head down further and looked to her left, under the clothing racks. There was only a three-inch gap below the bottom of the display jeans and she had to bring her face almost level with the floor to peer through it. But she could see all the way to the far side of the store, where a wall of denim shirts and jackets were packed tightly together on the rail.

No movement. No red.

Then the boots moved and her breath caught in her windpipe. She hadn't immediately spotted them, partially concealed behind the feet of one of the standing racks. They stepped, across the floor, catlike and silent, no longer clumping heavily.

It was moving towards the rear of the store. Away from the entrance.

Steeling herself, Taryn shifted carefully back into a crouch position. To her right, the mannequin stood sentinel over her, gazing blindly across the store.

Get the hell out of here, she thought.

She started forward again. Blood roared in her ears but she imagined she could hear the Mrs Claus stepping on the tiles now, just off to the left and behind her, placing one foot cautiously in front of the other, drawing closer to the checkout counter where she thought her prey was still hiding. Ready to pounce with her hammer.

The entrance was just ahead. Just a few yards away.

I'll run, Taryn thought, adrenaline coursing through her system. *I'll run for the main entrance or the escalators. I'll get the hell away from her.*

She reached the entrance. There was broken glass on the floor but it was over to the left, below the window the Mrs Claus had thrown her through. The area around the doors was clear. The mall concourse spread out before her, wide and bright and empty.

Run, she thought, staring crazily about the open space up ahead. *Run and don't -*

Then she saw her.

She was most of the way down the concourse, well beyond the fountain, heading for the exit. It was just a glimpse, a flash of light-up sneakers and a purple puffer jacket, but it was enough to make Taryn forget herself. Her mouth moved before her brain could stop it.

"Em!" she shouted. "Em, wait!"

Emma Price didn't hear her - she was too far away and only interested in her dinosaur-patterned backpack, which she'd spotted on the bench. That was *her* backpack and she had to get it. And then Mommy and Daddy would come.

Em didn't hear Taryn, but the thing wearing human skin and dressed as Mrs Claus did. She crossed the *JeanScene* store in seconds, crashing through the clothing racks. In her mechanical, unthinking desire to get to the girl, to kill her (*PROTECT ME FEED ME FEED MEEEE*), she dropped her hammer somewhere along the way, and ironically, that was probably what helped Taryn Meyer avoid a swift and excruciating death.

She reached her before she knew what was happening and knocked her to the floor. Taryn gasped breathlessly, winded, just as Olivia had been in the underground parking lot. She managed to crawl a couple of feet before one of Mrs Claus's powerful hands clamped onto her shoulder and flipped her onto her back.

She fell on her, crushing her beneath her considerable weight. Taryn felt her lungs depress inside her. She saw the thing's eyes - quivering, blood-filled sacks - and jammed the glass shard into one of them. It burst like an overcooked tomato, splashing her with hot liquid. The shard came out, taking what remained of the eye with it.

For a second, the Mrs Claus didn't seem to notice. The part of her brain formerly tasked with responding to pain signals was no longer active. The organism now controlling her mind wasn't concerned with the pain of its hosts. Only its own.

Then, very slowly, the former-woman's head fell limp on the end of her neck. Her body settled on top of Taryn's like a bouncy castle deflating, pinning her to the floor beneath its bulk.

Taryn released the glass shard and it tinkled away on the tiles. She tried to take in another breath and found she couldn't - the thing was squashing her lungs flat.

"Oh," she said, and couldn't manage another word.

Eighteen

Jeremy Lewis decided he now knew two things for sure.

First of all: if one more shit-scary thing went down in front of him - if one more person got chewed up and swallowed whole by that octopus-looking monster in the back of the van, or if one more bloody, hacked-off body part got flapped in his face by that psychopathic elf - he was liable to wet his pants. Not just a little bit, either, like you might do if you laughed too hard and just couldn't hold it in any more. If he got scared shitless just one more time that day, he was going to piss his pants like a baby.

And secondly, if he didn't find a way to get himself out of these handcuffs soon - really, really soon - he was dead meat.

Jeremy Lewis, medium-rare with a side of mashed potatoes.

He knew for sure the elf would grab him next and haul him to the back of the van, and that veiny pink blob with the glowing thing on its head would wrap one of its slimy tentacles around his neck, and that'd be that.

Well, either him or the lady on his left.

He looked at her again. She was watching the blob thing closely, black hair falling across her face as she leaned forward, straining against the cuffs for a better view. She was beautiful, Jeremy noted, even with flecks of cream-colored vomit on her chin; he thought she might be around the same age as some of his teachers, maybe in her thirties. She wore an expensive-looking wool sweater and fancy boots with high heels that'd been soaked through after, he assumed, trudging through the snow outside. Ahead of them, the elf still danced in that creepy-as-hell way, like it'd forgotten they were there.

I think it just gave birth.

She'd said that, and he'd asked her what she meant, and she hadn't replied. Now, she only had eyes for the thing in the van.

The veiny blob shuddered once, rocking the vehicle on its overworked suspension, then went still again. The orb on its forehead flared again briefly and faded out.

Jeremy tried again: "What do you mean, it gave birth? To what?"

The woman didn't answer. She just kept staring straight ahead. A few yards beyond their parking bay, the elf finally burned itself out and slumped against one of the van's open doors, panting for breath like a spent dog.

Maybe it'll fall asleep. Maybe the blob'll eat it, too. That'd serve-it-the-fuck right.

"What did it give birth to?" Jeremy asked again. "I don't see -
"

"Shhh." The woman motioned towards the van with her head. "Bottom right. In front of the biggest tentacle."

Jeremy followed her gaze, squinting. The underground lot was only half-lit and his glasses were smudged. Even in *good* light with clean lenses, he might have struggled to see exactly what she was talking about. What was it, anyway? Some pinkish bulge near the blob's lower body, barely visible from where they sat. The thickest of the Creature's tentacles was curled around it, pinning it to the rest of its disgusting body, almost like a chicken might cover her newly-hatched chicks with her wing, or -

"Wait," said Jeremy softly, also leaning forward now. "Is it... an egg?"

The woman said, "I think so. It just appeared."

And then two things happened at once.

A door opened off to the right beyond the van, just within their field of vision, briefly flooding the parking lot with harsh yellow light. Jeremy saw someone silhouetted there for a second before the door swung shut again with a metallic bang. The silhouette had almost certainly been that of a man, and Jeremy's first, irrational thought was *it's Mr Bloom! He didn't die after all*, before the cold fingers of logic stole in to nip it in the bud.

In the same instant the door opened, the orb on the end of the Creature's forehead tentacle began glowing again. It was dim at first, but as footsteps started across the concrete in their direction, it pulsed steadily brighter. Pulse, pulse, pulse, correlating directly with each footfall.

It's not Mr Bloom, thought Jeremy, his heartbeat quickening. *It's the thing that killed him. The thing dressed like Santa Claus. It got Ash and now it's coming for us.*

The elf straightened up and side-stepped away from the van, facing in the direction of the approaching person, who still remained in shadow. It moved differently now, Jeremy noticed. The dancing, the celebrating - all that was over. It was cautious. Uncertain, even.

It's someone new, Jeremy thought, and right then the blob's forehead orb flared bright, illuminating the entire underground parking lot, and the woman on Jeremy's left took in a sudden, sharp breath.

The man walked into the pool of violet light and stopped by the back of the van. He looked at the elf, then into the van. Then he looked at them, and the woman next to Jeremy shrieked "ADAM!" so loudly that the elf actually flinched at the sound.

"Adam!" she cried again. She jerked against the cuffs. "Shoot it, Adam! Fucking SHOOT IT!"

That was when Jeremy saw the gun in the man's right hand. His left forearm and hand were wrapped in a dark pink bandage that might once have been white.

"Adam," the woman said, her voice cracking. "W-what're you doing? You have to kill it before... before..."

She trailed off. The man - Adam - turned to face them and smiled, and suddenly Jeremy recognized him: the tousled brown hair, the blue shirt. He'd been at *The Coffee Place* with Spencer, Lincoln and Ash earlier, just before the Santa had come up the escalator. He'd been with them when Spencer had been killed and Ash had run for her life.

So if he's here, Jeremy thought, *where's Lincoln?*

Adam's grin widened. "Olivia," he said breezily, as though he'd just bumped into an acquaintance on the street. "What're you doing here, babe?"

Olivia's response came in a dry whisper: "Where's Emma?"

A puzzled look settled into Adam's brow. Exaggerated, Jeremy decided. An act.

"Emma?" Adam said. "I've no idea. Isn't she with you?"

Jeremy looked at the woman, at Olivia. Her mouth was open, working at words that weren't coming.

"And what're you doing down on the floor, with four-eyes here?" Adam said, nodding at Jeremy. "You're gonna ruin that nice sweater, babe."

The elf stifled a giggle. Adam shot it a look and it ducked away from his gaze.

Jeremy thought: *What the fuck is going on?*

Adam turned back and said, "I'm just passing through, Liv-baby. Don't mind me. You hang tight down here, ok? You and four-eyes, there."

Jeremy could feel the pipe trembling behind him. Olivia was shivering like she'd just been dunked in ice-cold water.

"Adam," she managed, her eyes glistening, "just tell me she's alright. Just tell me you haven't... hurt her, or..."

Adam's expression went from puzzled to incredulous in an instant. "*Hurt* her? Our baby? Never. I'd never hurt our dear, sweet girl. Not in a million years. But" - he motioned towards the elf - "I can't speak for this guy. Or the others."

Olivia made a little choking noise.

"Let's just hope she stays out of their way," Adam added solemnly, "if she's still up there. That's her best chance."

Olivia exploded. "What the *FUCK*, Adam! What the fucking hell are you talking about?" She rocked against the car parked next to her, tears flowing freely down her cheeks. "What's happened to you? Get us the fuck out of here! Please, Adam! PLEASE GET US OUT!"

Adam smirked and waggled the gun at her.

"Sorry, babe," he said. "No time. Gotta run. They'll be here in just a minute, you know, and I need to be long gone when that happens."

"ADAM!" Olivia's scream was long and shrill.

But the conversation was over. As Jeremy watched, dumbstruck with fear and confusion, Adam turned towards the van and became a black silhouette against the pulsing purple light. He motioned with the gun; in response, the elf immediately hopped inside the van and crouched down next to the creature; when it turned back again, the egg was in its arms. It was about the size of a basketball and covered in the same membranous slime that clung to the Creature's body.

It handed the egg to Adam. He cradled it in the crook of his left arm, holding it loosely with his bandaged hand. The gun was still in his right.

"Geez, that's gross," Jeremy heard him mutter. He turned back to them again and a blob of slime splattered on the concrete by his foot. "Well, guess I got what I came for. You two hang tight, ok? It won't be long now."

He started to walk away, heading for the stairwell. Olivia shifted against the car and said, "Wait."

Adam stopped and looked back over his shoulder. He smiled toothily. "Yes, dear?"

Each of Olivia's words dropped heavily from her mouth and sent cold dread worming under Jeremy's skin: "Is my husband gone?"

Adam's smile never wavered. If anything, Jeremy thought it grew wider in the violet light.

"He's not gone, Olivia," Adam said. "He's right here. He's been... repurposed. Just in time for the holidays. It's a Christmas miracle!"

At that, he tossed back his head and laughed. The sound of it boomed around the underground lot - gales and gales of hearty laughter - as he walked towards the stairwell door, slipping out of the Creature's pool of light and into the shadows.

"They're coming!" he called back, and laughed at his own words. "They'll be here soon. So very soon. God bless us, every one!"

He opened the stairwell door. Jeremy saw him silhouetted briefly in the frame, still chuckling, the slimy pink egg hooked under one arm. Then he stepped through and the door slammed shut, and on Jeremy's left, Olivia Price began sobbing softly.

Giggling, the elf moved to close the rear doors of the van.

It stopped dead when a high screech of grinding metal came out of the darkness at the far end of the lot. Jeremy felt a chill breeze whip round his ankles and instantly knew what it was.

The parking lot's external access door was opening.

Taryn couldn't breathe.

The woman - or whatever she was now - weighed a ton, and she had her pinned. It was all she could do to keep from passing out. Far above her, the icy December breeze whispered through the hole in the mall ceiling.

I have to get her off me. I'm not dying here under a big fat woman.

Clenching her teeth, she shrugged one arm free and tried to twist sideways. The Mrs Claus was enormously heavy and the stench coming off her was nauseating this close. Stale body odor and congealed blood. And more blood was still flowing steadily from the fresh hole in her face where her eyeball had once been, seeping into the shoulder of Taryn's sweater. One of her favorite sweaters.

Merry shitting Christmas to me, she thought angrily.

She worked both hands free and grabbed the thing's horribly flabby arm. Then, straining every muscle in her skinny frame, she pulled as hard as she could. Inch by inch, she felt her body slide out from under the Mrs Claus: first her shoulders, then down as far as her abdomen. Finally, her whole upper torso was free, and she was able to drag her legs out from under the thing's stinking bulk. She yanked her right foot clear of the body and lay flat on the concourse tiles, panting, one hand on her belly. She barely felt the steady thrum of pain in her cheek where the glass had once been embedded.

Ok, she thought after a moment. *What now?*

She swallowed and recited their names aloud: "Em. Ash. Jeremy." *Police*.

Taryn sat up, leaning on one elbow. She looked at the Mrs Claus, a mountain of sweat-soaked red and white costume, face-down on the floor. Not moving, not breathing. Dead.

Wincing, Taryn got to her feet. Beyond where the body lay now pooling in its own blood, the mall concourse was still. No light-up sneakers anywhere in sight.

Taryn looked down at the Mrs Claus and sniffed. Her back ached where she'd hit the *JeanScene* floor after the woman threw her through the window.

"One down," Taryn said, "two to go." She aimed a kick at the thing's side and turned in the direction of the escalators.

She didn't see it move.

The hand shot out from its body and closed around her ankle. Thick, gloved fingers buried themselves in her flesh.

"No!" Taryn started to cry, and then her leg was jerked from under her and she went down. Her back slapped onto the tiles. Her lungs instantly emptied of air.

The Mrs Claus was on her again, half-blind, fully deranged. Her hands settled around Taryn's throat again, meaning to kill this time.

End the girl, take her life. Bring her below, to the nesting place.

FEED ME FEED ME

It still called to her. She still heard its voice.

This time she would obey.

She began to squeeze.

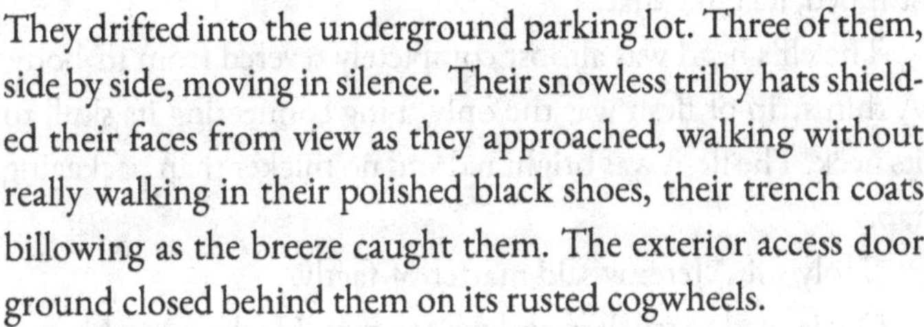

They drifted into the underground parking lot. Three of them, side by side, moving in silence. Their snowless trilby hats shielded their faces from view as they approached, walking without really walking in their polished black shoes, their trench coats billowing as the breeze caught them. The exterior access door ground closed behind them on its rusted cogwheels.

Olivia couldn't see them from her position next to the car - and even if she'd had a clear view, she was weeping too much to notice - but Jeremy saw them. He saw them duck under the exterior shutter door and disappear into the shadows when the door closed. And when they floated into view again at the fringes of the Creature's purplish glow, his heart contracted in his chest.

Fear.

The elf came around the van's open rear door and saw them too. It froze. Its hand went to the knife in its pocket.

The men in trench coats didn't stop. They kept coming. Gliding.

Jeremy heard the elf drag in a breath, and then it ran at them, screaming, the knife held aloft. It reached them at the perimeter of the Creature's glow, where the violet light met the shadows. Jeremy saw the knife flash. The elf screamed, shrill and horribly childish. There was a flurry of movement, a struggle. A flapping of material. Then the scream abruptly cut off.

For a moment, nothing happened. Jeremy saw them there at the edge of the glow, three spectres in black. He glimpsed the green of the elf's costume. The creature in the van continued to pulse its bright purple light. Pulsing, pulsing.

Jeremy gasped as the elf's body hit the ground just a yard from his boots. Black blood streaked across the concrete and up his shin. Some of it splattered on Olivia's jeans and her weeping stopped, just like that.

The elf's head was almost completely severed from its body. A thin strip of flesh was the only thing connecting its skull to its neck. The flesh was bright red and no thicker than packaging tape.

"Holy shit," Jeremy said matter-of-factly.

Olivia made a small sound next to him. He detached his eyes from the elf and looked up, and then pressed his back hard to the wall.

Fear. Like never before.

The three men in trench coats were right there, between where he and Olivia sat and the open back of the van. They stood by the twitching body of the elf, the thing that had once been a child - blood gushed from the stump of its neck, ran to the shoes of the Trench Coat Men, and flowed neatly around them. It would reach Jeremy's feet soon.

Don't move. The words whispered in the far recesses of Jeremy's mind in a voice that wasn't his. *Don't speak.*

Olivia heard that voice too and squeezed her lips together, choking back a rising scream of terror.

If the men in black coats and trilby hats were looking at them, Jeremy couldn't see their eyes. In truth, he couldn't see their faces. No eyes, no noses. No mouths. Even this close, their features were masked in shadow. Did they even have features? Were their faces below the brims of those hats?

Don't move. Don't speak.

The musty air in the underground lot was crackling with static now. A sound Jeremy thought he'd been imagining was building steadily, bearing down on his eardrums, making them throb: a dull but constant whine, piercing right into his brain. He was in an airplane again, dipping towards the runway at O'Hare. He was six years old and he was crying while his father told him to keep quiet, it was almost over.

Don't MOVE. Don't SPEAK. KEEP QUIET.

The Trench Coat Men turned, slowly and in perfect unison, to face the van. The creature inside it disappeared from Jeremy's view but the glow from its forehead orb began to burn brighter. Jeremy's eyes ached behind his glasses; he longed to shut them but something was willing him to look, to watch. The dark figures by the van's open doors became shimmering shadows, bleeding into one black mass. It was, Jeremy thought in a strange, absent sort of way, like looking directly into an eclipse.

It's almost over.

The figures moved as one and climbed into the back of the van.

The doors swung closed of their own volition.

I'm going to die, Taryn thought.

The hands fastened around her neck, the thumbs pushing into her throat. They weren't those of a person. They weren't human anymore.

It's almost Christmas and I'm going to die. I'll never see my family again.

The Mrs Claus pressed harder, squeezing tighter. Taryn could actually feel her windpipe being sealed shut, cutting off her air supply. She'd never experienced anything like it before.

How strange.

Mr Krighton's voice, from the front of the biology classroom: "When we inhale, we take in oxygen. That oxygen diffuses from the alveoli in our lungs into our bloodstream, where it's picked up by hemoglobin in our red blood cells. At the same time, carbon dioxide passes the other way from our blood into our lungs, and we exhale it as a waste gas. That's what *breathing* is, ladies and gentlemen."

So strange.

Her hands spasmed by her sides. She was blacking out, she could feel it coming. The thing choking her was grinning, just like the elf had been earlier. It was a fixed smile, molded into a once-human mask. Its remaining eye rolled wildly, entirely red now and weeping blood from the socket.

I wonder who she was, Taryn thought, looking past the Mrs Claus at the hole in the mall ceiling, far above them. Snow wasn't drifting through it anymore. Darkness pushed in around the edges of her vision. *I wonder if she knows she's killing me.*

The thing's belly bounced against her torso as it worked at her throat. Taryn imagined she could hear Christmas crackers being pulled somewhere and just barely understood that it was really the bones in her neck starting to crunch together.

I'm going to die, she thought again. A gradual dawning realization. Nothing she could do about it.

The mall ceiling was eaten by the darkness.

* * *

The handcuffs bit into Jeremy's already-bruised wrists. His boots scraped and scuffed on the concrete as he thrashed his feet, scrambling for purchase with his heels. If he could get his legs under him - maybe even behind him - he might be able to slide one hand free. And then he could get the other one out, too.

He hadn't really tried, after all, had he? Anything to get out.

Anything, if it meant he could put his hands over his ears and block out the *sound*.

It started the moment the van doors closed. Banging, thumping. Muffled metallic clanging. The sound of things slamming into other things in a small, enclosed space. A struggle.

The purple light continued pulsing from inside, brighter and brighter, seeping through every paper-thin gap in the body of the vehicle. There were no windows in the rear doors but it was coming out around their edges, and between them. It was coming from under the van, through the front windshield, through the driver and passenger side windows. With each sudden, violent movement, the light blazed brighter, sending crazy shadows leaping around the underground parking lot.

And now the van was rocking from side to side, suspension groaning, the remaining air hissing from its mostly-deflated tires. Something hit its interior panel with enormous force, causing a huge dent to bubble outward.

The sound. The sound he desperately wanted to stop, to escape from any way he could.

The sound of savage, frenzied murder.

The van rocked towards its front wheels and the windshield blew out, showering glass over another vehicle in the next bay. Jeremy got one leg under him. He finally had some leverage and started pulling with every ounce of his strength against the pipe, straining until his wrists were screaming and sweat stung his eyes.

Anything to make it stop.

Next to him, Olivia's head was down and her hair masked her face, but Jeremy could see her shoulders heaving rhythmically. She was either hyperventilating or sobbing, or both.

"Lady," he stammered, panic taking over. "Hey! Olivia."

She shook her head; she heard him and she wasn't going to look up.

"Olivia!" Jeremy spat. The cuffs bit into his skin, splitting it. His eyes blurred with tears. "We have to get out. Right now. Please!"

She started to raise her head.

And suddenly, it all stopped. The van rocked one last time and settled onto its spent tires. The parking lot was once again illuminated solely by the sickly yellow fixtures spaced too far apart around the walls, and by the shaft of light spilling down through the hole in the ceiling. The purple light was gone.

Jeremy slumped back against the wall. His wrists were cut and bleeding, but he couldn't feel them. It was over - their chance was gone. The whole thing had lasted less than a minute. They were next.

Just beyond their parking bay, the van doors creaked open and the Trench Coat Men stepped back out.

***

Taryn had been in darkness, right on the cusp of passing out, when the hands gripping her neck abruptly released.

Her eyes went wide and the mall concourse flooded back. She gasped air back into her body. Just a little. Not enough. The Mrs Claus was still on her, straddling her on the mall tiles, crushing her beneath her bulk as blood trickled from her gored eye socket. But those powerful, murderous fingers weren't wrapped around her throat anymore.

Taryn gaped up at her, bewildered and agonized. The Mrs Claus wasn't looking at her now; she was staring straight ahead, her hands poised in midair like she was waiting for something and might still return to killing at any moment. The grin, still fixed on her face, flickered.

Suddenly, her teeth parted and a horrible, animal moan escaped her mouth. It started low, like a cat mewing, and then shot to a high keening shriek. It was the first time Taryn had heard her make any sound at all and it turned her insides to ice.

The Mrs Claus stood up. Taryn's lungs expanded gratefully and air rushed into them, and she exploded into a fit of painful coughing, rolling onto her side. She clutched at her throat; she could still feel the fingers there, digging in.

Flailing drunkenly, the Mrs Claus stepped over her, narrowly missing her arm with one of her heavy boots. She staggered away, still screeching like a wounded animal. Taryn watched her through hot tears, coughing so hard she feared her throat might come out of her mouth. But she could breathe again - that's all that mattered.

What's wrong with it? she thought, wheezing air into her burning lungs.

Something was definitely happening to the Mrs Claus. With each step, her body seemed to crumple a little more, as though her bones had turned to jelly inside her. Taryn saw her sideways from her position on the floor, thumping heavily across the concourse, leaving smatterings of blood in her wake; her knees were beginning to buckle and her costume was darkening all over as more blood soaked through from beneath.

She's going to collapse, Taryn thought, propping herself up on one shaky elbow. *She's trying to escape but she won't make it.*

She glanced back towards the *JeanScene* store, half expecting to see the Santa lumbering towards her to finish the job - "I'll get her, dear, don't worry" - but the place was just as empty as before. Bright, welcoming, abandoned.

Taryn's eyes fell on the hammer, resting beneath one of the free-standing display carousels. Its handle was dark red with dried blood.

Sensing another coughing fit on the way, she forced herself to sit up and looked back down the mall concourse.

Mrs Claus was gone.

NINETEEN

E mma Price hadn't found Daddy.

She *had* found the candy machine, however, and that'd do just fine for now.

Daddy would be along soon, anyway.

She'd retrieved her dinosaur backpack from the bench - the one she and Mommy had been sitting on when they'd first seen the ELF - and that'd been the first good thing. She liked dinosaurs and so she liked her backpack, just as she liked her dinosaur-patterned bedroom curtains and the plush dinosaur toys lined neatly on the shelf above her bed. She also liked the cat toy the tall girl let her take from the store and she stuffed it into her backpack for safe keeping - she'd introduce it to her dinosaurs once they were home from visiting Grandma and Grandpa after Christmas.

Em had been slipping the pack on when the candy machine caught her eye. It was just beyond the entrance to the concourse, in the corridor that led to the exit, and it was the second good thing. They'd used the corridor earlier, after they'd been out in the snow. Maybe it was still there. She could build a snowman.

That'd be the *third* good thing. One, two, three.

Em walked to the candy machines, her sneakers flashing pink across the tiles on either side of her. Somewhere further back in the concourse, she thought she heard noises. Someone shouting, maybe. But the noises were brief and far away, and the candy machine was right there.

There were three machines, all lined up right next to the concourse entrance: one for sodas, one for chips, and one for candy. Em went to the third and put her palm against the glass, gazing up at the colorful candy bars stacked uniformly in their spirals. There were plenty she liked - KitKats, Skittles, M&Ms, Reece's Pieces - and looking at them made her stomach gurgle. Mommy wouldn't want her having candy before dinner, but she wasn't here. She'd gone away with the elf, down below in the elevator.

Em stretched for the vending machine keypad but couldn't quite reach it, even on her tiptoes. Even if she could have pushed the buttons, she had no money. The concept of exchanging currency for goods hadn't quite landed with her just yet.

She settled back on her soles. There was a lady's handbag on the floor next to the machine and she thought *Mommy has a bag. She could reach the buttons. Or Daddy.*

"I want Mommy," she said.

Suddenly, a great bubble of sadness and fear surged up from deep inside her. The numbing effects of shock she'd experienced since entering the mall were beginning to fade; what she felt now was panic, or the beginnings of it, and that new sensation - one she was so unfamiliar with - manifested itself in hot, welling tears and a trembling in her throat.

I want Mommy, she thought, *and Daddy. I want them here.*

Em opened her mouth to say it again, and this time it would have tailed off into a desperate wail of despair that brought the things prowling the mall straight to her, but before she could speak, a new sound carried her way. A nearby sound.

Something metal.

Em turned to her right, her keen ears zeroing in on the new noise. It was close. Just round the corner, maybe.

Two warm tears broke free and rolled down her cheeks, but her panic abated for the time being. The new sound called to her and she started walking towards it distractedly. Maybe the sound was Daddy. Maybe he was coming back for her and Mommy, and they could go home.

The sound again. Metal on metal.

Em came to the corner of the corridor. The ATMs were on her right, glowing silently, watching what was about to happen. She turned the corner and looked.

First, she saw the shutter. A metal barrier blocking off the mall exit, the way they'd come in. It hadn't been there before, had it? Cold wintery wind blustered through it and danced up the corridor, nipping at her bare hands. Beyond, she could see the roofs of some cars in the parking lot, glinting under starlight.

Next, she saw Santa. He was crouched by the base of the shutter, fiddling with something. His big shoulders jiggled under his red coat and the bobble on his hat bounced against his ear. There was an ax on the floor next to him.

Em drew in a shuddering breath and was about to yell "SANTA!" when something stopped her. A prickling on the back of her neck, like lightning had struck somewhere nearby. It pushed the cry of delight back down her throat and held it there.

Something had changed in that moment, in that exact second. Something that had been was now gone.

Santa jerked something away from the base of the shutter with a grunt and straightened up, pushing the barrier up in the same movement. The shutter rolled open, exposing the mall entrance again. Santa stooped to grab his ax, and froze.

Em took a step backwards. She didn't know what made her do it.

Humbug.

She saw it, then. Felt it.

Humbug.

It was going away, or had already gone. That thing, that "Bad! Humbug!" creature down below, where Mommy had gone, where the Elf had taken the boy with glasses. Em hadn't seen it with her own eyes but she knew it was there. She'd known the moment they walked into the mall. It was *there*, and now it wasn't.

The bad humbug.

At the other end of the entrance corridor, Santa spluttered out a series of nonsense words and spun clumsily on his heel. Em turned the corner in the same movement. She pressed herself to the wall and closed her eyes.

Thud, thud, thud. Santa was coming, rushing up the corridor towards her. He was moaning now, like a deer that's been nicked by a hunter's bullet. A wounded, panic-stricken animal.

Em squeezed her eyes tighter, just like she did last Christmas when she was trying to make herself fall asleep before Santa came.

He was coming now.

Thud, thud, thud.

"Mommy," Em whispered. "Daddy."

The Santa Claus came around the corner, ax in both hands, and thundered right past Emma Price. The hem of his coat brushed her backpack but his blood-laced eyes didn't see her, and even if they had, his melting brain wouldn't have allowed him to stop. He had to get back, to protect it, to *PROTECT IT AND FEED IT AND SAVE IT*.

Em stayed where she was, eyes closed, long after the Santa's heavy, erratic footfalls had faded. She didn't see where he went, didn't see how he staggered and bled and coughed bile into his artificial beard. She stayed right where she was, whispering "Mommy, Daddy" over and over.

When she opened her eyes, she was alone again.

TWENTY

T he three stood between them and the van, wraiths in shadow, featureless and silent. The mall creaked and groaned above them; in some far corner of the underground lot, water dripped melodiously into a puddle.

Plop. Plop.

Olivia watched them through the sweat-soaked strands of her hair. Her ears felt stuffed, like she'd just gotten off a plane. Her own, rasping breaths sounded far away.

The three didn't move from where they stood, but their presence reached for her anyway, invisible fingers tracing her skin, chilling her to the bone.

She knew the kid, Jeremy, felt it too. He was quaking next to her, his cuffs rattling against the pipe.

Behind them, the van doors were wide open. The Creature was gone - completely gone - but the van interior was still painted with its remains: globules of pink flesh clung to the metalwork, dropping off the ceiling and slipping down the walls in liquidy chunks that splatted on the floor; a strip of frayed muscle tissue hung down over the rear bumper, swinging gently.

There wasn't a spot on *them*, however - their black coats and gloves and hats were impeccable, unstained and blemish free, as though they hadn't just dismembered and killed

eaten

another living thing in its entirety. It'd sounded like a ferocious fight to the death was underway just a few moments ago, but here they were. Spick and span.

As if to emphasize the point, the one on the left reached into its coat and drew out a black handkerchief. Olivia watched, unblinking, as it leaned across and dabbed at the chin (or where the chin must be) of the one in the middle - three or four light touches - then replaced the handkerchief in its coat. The one in the middle nodded once to indicate its gratitude.

And then it started towards them.

On Olivia's right, Jeremy's teeth started chattering like they were in a Bugs Bunny cartoon.

She watched it coming. She didn't - couldn't - take her eyes off it.

The man in the trench coat stepped into their parking bay and stopped. Olivia tilted her head back, staring up into his face, trying to discern something under the trilby hat, though no part of her truly wanted to see what was under the brim. In the weak light of the underground lot, she could make out the suggestion of a chin, and perhaps a mouth, but nothing more. The rest was lost in shadow, black as treacle.

When he spoke, she heard the words in her mind; she knew the kid did, too.

"Where is it?"

No lips, no mouth. But she heard it all the same.

"Where?"

Her own lips parted. She forced them together and clenched her teeth. Even so, something tugged at the edges of her mouth, insistent, eager.

Jeremy cleared his throat next to her. "I... I don't - "

"Shut up!" Olivia spat. "Stop talking."

The kid's head didn't turn, but his eyes rolled towards her behind his glasses. They bulged white with terror.

A coarse, rasping chuckle by her ear. She gasped and whipped her head, almost smacking it off the parked car again.

The man in the trench coat remained where he was, only now, the others had joined him. Olivia was dully aware of her heartbeat, knocking hard and fast against her sternum.

"Do you know where it is, my dear?"

A wave of nausea started at the crown of her head, filtering downwards.

Excruciating.

"Do tell, dear."

He stepped soundlessly towards her. His polished shoes glinted.

"No," Olivia moaned, ducking away as his black gloved hand extended in her direction. "No. Please. I don't know what..."

The hand rested lightly on her head and her resistance evaporated: she saw Adam next to her in the car, back on the highway, laughing in that easy, infectious way of his; she saw him leading Em through the gas station towards the restroom, tilted to one side so she could comfortably hold his hand; she saw him striding away from them down the mall concourse and her heart cracked in two.

Finally, she saw the elf handing him the thing it had taken from the Creature, and the hand withdrew from her head.

"Thank you, Olivia Price."

The man in the trench coat reached up and tipped his hat. She heard the chuckle in her ear again, distant now, echoing in the black. Then, as one, the three men turned on their heels and walked away, making no sound. Olivia managed to raise her head long enough to see them pass the van, briefly disappear into the parking lot shadows, and then reappear again in the far corner below the red EXIT sign. The stairwell door swung open for a second, and then they were gone.

And suddenly, Jeremy's tongue was loosened.

"Who... what..." he stammered. He shook his head, as if trying to defog it, and his glasses slipped off the end of his sweat-saturated nose. "Ah shit. Shit!"

"They're gone," Olivia breathed.

"Who's they?" Jeremy cried. "Who *were* they? Holy shit, I - "

"I don't know," Olivia cut in. Her own mind was beginning to clear. *Adam*, she thought, *they're going after Adam*. "I don't know what they were."

Jeremy took a breath, shuddered it back out.

"It's the egg," he said, "the one the guy took. That's what they want."

The guy. Olivia bit back whatever murky thought her mouth was about to articulate.

"I heard them," Jeremy went on, talking faster. "They said "where is it?", and they meant the egg, didn't they? I heard their voices in my head. And holy shit, did they *eat* that thing in the van?"

Olivia nodded, realized he couldn't see her, and said, "I think so."

Jeremy moaned, leaning against the pillar. "That's messed up, man. That's fucking sick. It ate Pete, and then they ate *it*."

"Not just Pete," Olivia said. She knew it all now for sure, knew from the moment it touched her head. There'd been a connection, one that was cold and clear. *They're going after Adam.* "It... ate everyone... who was in the mall earlier. Everyone. And now it's gone, and those three want the egg. It's all that's left of it and they want to eat it as well. And it's with..."

She felt Jeremy's eyes shift to her. "That guy," he said. "You knew him."

"Yes."

"He's your... husband?"

Olivia looked up at the gore-strewn van. "He was."

"But what - "

The stairwell door swung open. Olivia caught a fleeting glimpse of someone stepping through, and then it slammed shut again with a bang.

"Oh shit, what now?" Jeremy said.

Footsteps coming their way. Slow at first, then quickening.

"It's her, isn't it?" Jeremy said, panic rising. "It's Mrs-fuck-ing-Claus. Oh man, I can't take much more of this. All I wanted to do was watch that shitting movie and go home."

The figure materialized by the van, stepping into the muted light from the hole in the ceiling. A girl, with something in her hand.

"Jeremy?"

"ASH!" Jeremy exclaimed.

The girl grinned and held up the bolt cutters.

"What's happening, dork?" she said.

TWENTY-ONE

A dam almost dropped the egg when the creature died.

He'd been in the stairwell, almost at the door leading to the mall concourse, when he felt *them* enter the building down below. Their presence, so close, drained the power from his legs and he dropped to his knees on the steps. He had to use his gun hand to keep from toppling over - if the safety hadn't been on, it might have gone off right there and then.

"Hell," he muttered.

The egg was slippery (*what* is *all this goop on it?*) and he didn't have a firm grip with his injured hand. He had to pin it tight to his torso, and even then he felt like it might squirm free at any moment.

Why couldn't the elf have done this, anyway? Or the Santa? Why'd it have to be him?

Because they're dying, and you're not.

His heartbeat quickened. It answered in his voice, as if it was his own conscience. It was in him now, wasn't it? It *was* him.

They'd never make it. They're too far gone.

It had to be him. He was fresh and strong. Adam - the Former One - hadn't been there when the thing from space crashed through the mall roof and landed in the grotto, bristling with radiation, spewing toxicity. They'd been in there, waiting for the next child to come and sit on Santa's lap and rhyme off all the things they wanted for Christmas, and the extra-terrestrial energy pulsing from the space rock had killed them instantly and then brought them right back again, brains blown like overworked fuses and then rewired, now consumed with its will alone. *FEED, PROTECT, FEED*. Their new purpose in life.

Well, afterlife.

They protected it, and then they helped feed it after it'd pulled everyone else in the *Outlet Complex* down to the underground lot, all those poor saps who'd been shopping in the mall or had been ushered outside when the movie theater was evacuated. The Grotto trio got the thing into the van after it hatched and then scoured the mall for stragglers, folks like Pete Zampetti and the group that came from *The Movie House*, and they kept it fat and full until it was ready to lay. They were the grunts, the footsoldiers, the workhorses. But they'd been exposed and it was too much. They were burning from the inside out, melting, like they'd been upwind of a nuclear blast, and it needed someone new. Someone *alive*.

He hadn't realized it was drawing him until it was too late. He'd taken the stairs down to the underground - the same stairs he was slumped on now - as though the security office might be down there, and he'd gone straight to the van, and that was the last thing he remembered before waking up in the hardware store with a deep cut on his arm. He thought the creature might have done that (had he tried to fight it off at first?), but he couldn't be sure. He'd trailed a piss-load of blood into the store, though; he'd been in there looking for something - a weapon, maybe, to help defend his new master - when Spencer and the girl came, and he had to lock himself in the back storeroom. The Creature hadn't accounted for them, and so *he* hadn't accounted for them either. He had to think fast, but that was ok. Adam had been good at that and now he was, too.

He felt the Trench Coat Men enter the underground lot, and he knew when they'd killed the elf. He knew what would happen next. The Creature put those images in his head, pictures of things he didn't understand from faraway places he'd never lay eyes on - that no human would ever see - but the story was clear enough: when the Creature arrived, they followed soon after. They came to eat, to consume, to destroy. It was their only reason for being. The Creature was the Christmas goose, succulent and juicy, fattened up on the living things it'd landed amongst, and they were the guests of honor. They'd come a long way and they'd waited a long time for their feast, and they were *starving*.

They ate greedily and the Creature was gone, and Adam almost let the egg slip from his grasp when its parental lifeforce winked out. Now, it was all that remained of the thing, and he was its only chance of survival. It was now his sole purpose in life. He had to get it far away from here, had to give it a chance to birth and consume and grow fat, and then lay again. And again, and again.

Until there was nothing left to eat.

With a grunt, he got back to his feet, pressing the egg against his body. He could feel it moving inside, squirming, ready to hatch. He didn't have long. They'd come for him next.

Clenching his jaw, he compelled his legs to move, mounting the few remaining steps to the stairwell exit. He just about got the door open with his gun-wielding hand and went through, blinking in the bright light of the mall concourse.

"The car," he said, forcing his brain to work. "Keys. Movie theater. Office."

He'd take Lincoln's car and drive until the tank was empty, or until he hit the next town. It didn't matter which it was, as long as there were plenty of people there - and there would be, wouldn't there? They'd gather for the holidays and they'd exchange gifts and eat turkey, and they'd grow fat. And once the egg hatched, it'd pull them all to it and they'd step right into its open maw, and it'd grow fat too. The faster it ate, the faster it'd reproduce. And then he wouldn't be the only one to help spread its seed. It'd have more soldiers next time, plenty more, and there'd be more eggs.

But not if *they* got to him first. He had to hurry.

He started up the concourse. His head was pounding now and the twinkling, multicolored lights weren't helping one bit. If only Spencer had managed to get him those painkillers from the drug store. But no, Santa had gotten him first, of course. That brainless, lumbering idiot with the ax. And then he'd needed a weapon himself.

Santa's Grotto was up ahead. He noticed the smashed glass front of the *JeanScene* store on the left, a little closer. Mrs Claus had tossed the girl through it, hadn't she? A smile tugged at the corner of his mouth. He wondered what happened to her after that. She was most likely dead by now. Come to think of it, what happened to...

He stopped.

The girl was there, directly ahead of him. He hadn't seen her right away. She was standing still, blood running down her cheek, staring at him and the egg cradled in his bandaged arm.

She had a hammer in her hand.

Adam squeezed the handgun grip tighter. Then, in his cheeriest voice, he called out, "Hello again, miss. What've you got there?"

TWENTY-TWO

A sh was three years old when she had her first premonition.

It was a Thursday night. Her mom was tucking her into bed and her dad was downstairs watching TV. It was drizzling outside.

"Mom," she said, as Laura Buckley leaned down to kiss her forehead.

"Yes, sweetie?"

"Where's Fuzzles?"

"I put her out. She's probably in bed by now, just like you."

Little Ash frowned. "But, why's she with Mail Man?"

Laura also frowned, puzzled. "The mailman?"

"Yeah."

"I, um... I'm not sure what you mean, honey." Laura tugged the duvet a little closer to her daughter's chin. "Did you see a mailman on TV?"

"No. He's outside. With Fuzzles."

"Oh." Laura hesitated, then stood up. "I'm sure your kitty cat's fine. You just go to sleep now, ok?"

Ash rubbed her eye with the back of her hand. "Ok."

Laura flicked off the bedside lamp and left the room, keeping the door cracked open. She didn't mention anything to her husband, and she'd largely dismissed it by the time they went to bed. Kids said strange things all the time, didn't they? Her little Ashley was certainly no exception.

The next morning, Laura was pouring herself a coffee and thinking about the long day ahead when someone knocked on the front door. Setting her mug down, she went through to the hall. She saw him through the frosted glass, and her brief, strange conversation with Ash from the night before came back with crystal clarity. A heavy boulder of dread settled into the pit of her stomach as she opened the door.

"Mrs Buckley?"

"Yes?"

"I, um..." The mailman, one she recognized but had never really spoken to before, shifted uncomfortably. "You have a pet cat, right?"

"Yes."

He's outside, with Fuzzles.

"A little black one, with white paws?"

"Yes."

"Um... I'm afraid I just found him in the street, a couple of houses down."

Laura swallowed. The boulder in her stomach threatened to pull her to the floor.

"Dead?"

The mailman nodded. "Yes, ma'am. Sorry to be the one to tell you."

Laura thanked him and closed the door. Her fingertips lingered on the handle for a moment and she didn't hear Ashley straight away.

"Mommy?" she said again.

Laura turned and saw her at the top of the stairs, clutching her raggedy teddy bear in one hand. She tugged at her lower lip with the other.

"Did Mail Man find Fuzzles?" she said.

Ash's second premonition, the one she remembered vividly (the first was quickly lost in the fog of early childhood), happened four years later at her seventh birthday party.

By then, she'd experienced several episodic flashes of what she called Other People's Bad Dreams, strange instances when she saw things in her mind's eye that were deeply confusing and often upsetting, usually involving people she didn't know: a grown man sobbing in a white room while a doctor gripped his hand; a little boy following an old woman into the woods at night; a hunter lining up a magnificent stag in the crosshairs of his rifle. Most of the things she saw were about someone or something dying, as the first premonition about Fuzzles had been, and almost all of them happened in daytime.

Her parents and family were gathered around her in the garden when she leaned over to blow out her candles. She was standing on a chair (Daddy had offered to lift her up but she refused, she was *seven* now) and had both palms flat on the checkered tablecloth on either side of her *Moana* cake when she saw it, right behind her seeing eyes, scrolling like a movie. It lasted no more than three seconds, and then she puffed out her candles. Those gathered whooped and cheered and asked what she'd wished for, having taken her brief hesitation to be the moment of decision. Laura Buckley, however, who'd witnessed more than one of her daughter's "flashes" first hand since the cat's untimely death, had also seen it, and knew better.

Later, she asked Ash what she'd seen. Ash simply shook her head and replied, "Nothing, Mom."

"You didn't see anything?" Laura probed. "No people? Animals?"

"No, Mom."

Five days later, there was an electrical fire at a textile factory on the edge of town. The place was a major employer in the area - almost two hundred people had been in the building when the fire broke out, and though most of them got out safely, several dozen had been trapped in the factory warehouse. Twenty-three people died of smoke inhalation and a further thirty-six ended up in hospital in critical condition. It was the worst disaster the town had ever experienced.

That night, as the local news anchor grimly delivered his report over images of the smoldering, blackened husk of the factory and Fred Buckley shook his head, muttering "no safety measures in that place, been saying it for years", Laura caught her daughter's eye across the room: little Ashley, seven years old and cradling an iPad, held her gaze for a moment with huge, watery eyes, and Laura knew for sure. She never asked her about it, never made her rehash what she'd seen as she'd prepared to blow out her birthday candles. Laura never asked about her premonitions ever again.

After that, Ash actively tried to suppress the Other People's Bad Dreams, and by and large, she succeeded. There were always warning signs when one was about to come on: a peculiar throbbing at the back of her skull; a hazy vignette at the fringes of her vision; a sense of "otherness" that migraine-sufferers might describe as an aura. When these signs started coming - and they always came one after the other, like clockwork - she'd jam in her earphones and blast the heaviest music she had on hand. She didn't care what it was. As long as it blocked out the visions, it didn't matter.

Silence and solitude became her enemies. As her childhood years rolled by and the premonitions continued to threaten at the edges of her mind, patiently prowling like big cats sussing out a herd of wildebeest, she surrounded herself with the most extroverted people she could find, the sort who thrived on constant interaction, who drew energy from it and expelled it back into the world just as quickly. Ceaseless talking, perennial *doing*. Anything that distracted her from the waking nightmares that always, always came true.

She didn't see everything, however. When she was nine, Fred Buckley suffered a mild heart attack when driving home from work, crashed his Buick into a tree, and died instantly. Laura Buckley didn't ask Ash about it (she'd have known if she'd seen it) and they quietly drifted through the grief that followed. Two years later, Laura married Rodney the bank teller and Ash gained three step-siblings, one of whom she liked - the other two were in their twenties and wanted nothing to do with her, the short, spoiled girl with the potty mouth and colors in her hair.

Then, just as suddenly as they'd started, her premonitions stopped. Or at least, their looming presence diminished so much she barely felt them anymore. The "friends" she'd hitched her wagon to quickly became tiresome, and once they sensed her pulling away, their allegiance shifted like the tide. It was as if a target had appeared on her forehead. Looking back, she knew things could've gotten bad, turned ugly. She'd been on the other side of it and knew exactly what those girls said about people in private, what they giggled about in the hallways and cafeteria, what they purposefully filtered throughout the rest of the school. But then she became friends with Taryn, and then Jeremy, and everything fell into place. What those girls said or did no longer mattered in the slightest. She had *real* friends now.

The premonitions weakened and faded, and she allowed herself to believe it was finally over.

Then the thing in the underground parking lot had reached into her brain and given it a twist, and some internal valve that'd rusted shut long ago was unsealed again. She felt it clawing at her mind, trying to pull her in. It knew she sensed its presence and it wanted her, needed her. COME TO ME PROTECT ME FEED ME. She pushed back, fought it, resisted. It almost had her in *Big Al's*, when she saw Mary Bloom and the cancer in her veins. If Spencer hadn't been there to shake her out of it, the creature might have taken her, and Adam Price would've had a partner in his maniacal guardian duties.

But it was gone now. They'd come. They'd removed it, purged it from existence. They were fat and sleek and full to bursting. The Trench Coat Men. The cosmic balancers, who always came.

Ash knew about them now, more than anyone else ever had or likely ever would. She knew (as well as her fifteen-year-old mind could comprehend, which was far from the entirety of it) what they were, and where they'd come from. She knew it as well as she was able, because no-one could truly have understood the things Ash saw that day in her mind's eye while she helped Spencer walk Steve to *The Coffee Place*, or while she pretended to rifle around behind the counter for the First Aid kit. She saw places that weren't on Earth, places far beyond where humans would ever walk or even imagine, and in every place, the men cloaked in black shadow carried the Fear while they sought out the Creatures to satisfy their relentless hunger. The more Ash tried to force the scenes from her mind, the harder they pressed in. She'd grown weak, sloppy, having not exercised that muscle in years. The images came, playing faster and clearer all the time, and she couldn't stop them. Not when the Trench Coat Men were so close.

They had to get out of the mall.

She'd waited as long as she could, and then she'd gone to the stairwell door. Steve, or whatever his real name was, hadn't taken the bolt cutters when he passed. She picked them up, opened the door the dead hand had once clung to, and went through to the stairwell itself. She put one hand on the stair banister, withdrew it, and called the elevator instead.

Two levels below, Adam started up the stairs with the Creature's egg under one arm.

The elevator *pinged* just as the Trench Coat Men climbed into the back of the van. The elevator doors slid open and Ash stepped inside. The doors closed again but she didn't press the button marked "UG" right away. Instead, she waited, clutching the bolt cutters in one hand. Halfway up the stairs, Adam dropped to his knees as the Creature was ripped apart in the rocking van. Ash felt it just as keenly, but she'd known it was coming. She stood where she was, eyes closed, focusing instead on the throbbing pain in her tongue where she'd bitten into it earlier. It'd mostly stopped bleeding but it still hurt like hell.

The Creature was gone. In the underground lot, the van doors swung open; in the stairwell, Adam regained his strength and started for the door leading to the concourse.

Ash waited. She counted to ten... no, twenty... and pushed the "UG" button.

The elevator descended.

It reached the underground section of the stairwell just as the Trench Coat Men started up the stairs, their black-gloved hands trailing lightly on the banister. They heard the elevator *ping* and the doors slide open, but it was of no consequence to them. They knew where their prey was now.

Ash took a breath and stepped out. She could hear them ascending the stairs, but just barely. Their footfalls were almost inaudible.

She pushed open the door to the underground parking lot and went through. She saw them right away, over by the far wall between a pillar and a parked car. The van was right in front of them, just below the hole in the ceiling.

"Oh man, I can't take much more of this," she heard him say, his voice high with fright. "All I wanted to do was watch that shitting movie and go home."

She came up beside the van and saw him there, hands behind his back and glasses askew, next to a dark-haired woman with vomit on her sweater.

"Jeremy?" she said.

"Ash!" he exclaimed.

She grinned despite herself and said, "what's happening, dork?"

"Where the *hell* have you been?" Jeremy cried.

"Oh, you know," she said, glancing at the van. *I can still feel it here*. "Just farting around up there, trying not to die."

Jeremy gaped up at her like a goldfish in a bowl. Ash smirked - she might have found it funny if he didn't have blood splattered down one side of him.

"What're those?" Jeremy said.

"Bolt cutters. Spencer and I found them in the hardware store. Well, *I* found them. They're pretty heavy actually - "

"Ash!"

"Yeah, coming."

She went to him, throwing a quick look at the woman. Her head was against the car, not far from the rear tire, and her hair had fallen over her face. Ash couldn't tell if she was looking their way or staring at the ground.

"Behind me," Jeremy said, leaning forwards. "Hurry up."

"Keep your pants on."

It was difficult to see the cuffs, or Jeremy's hands for that matter. Ash maneuvered the bolt cutter blades to where she assumed the handcuff chain was, steadying herself against the cold concrete wall with one shoulder.

"Lean forward."

"I *am* leaning forward."

"No, I mean, put your head down. I need some light here."

Jeremy did so, and Ash saw the chain. She also saw how the cuffs had burrowed deep into Jeremy's wrists and grimaced.

"That pipe's pretty thin," she said, angling the bolt cutters around the handcuff chain. "You couldn't have, you know, just broken it, or - "

"Just cut the cuffs, Ash!"

She pushed the bolt cutter arms together and the blades closed around the chain. There was some resistance, then a *clang* as the cutters bit through the cuffs and the blades bounced off the pipe. Jeremy toppled forward and slumped to the floor. His glasses finally dropped off the end of his nose and folded neatly by his face.

"My arms," he gasped, dragging them from behind his back, "I... can barely feel them."

"Are you ok?" said Ash, standing awkwardly by him.

"Yeah," he replied, replacing his glasses. "I think all the blood had... holy shit, my wrists! Look what those things did to my wrists."

"Hey."

Ash jumped and turned around. The woman was looking up at her, head tilted to one side.

"Little help?"

"Oh, yeah. Sorry," said Ash. "Can you lean forward please... um, ma'am?"

"Olivia." The woman coughed, bending forward to expose her wrists; out of the corner of her eye, Ash saw Jeremy wobble to his feet. "It's Olivia. Get me the hell out of these things."

"Sure thing." Ash brought the bolt cutter blades down to Olivia's wrists, angling for the chain. "Just hold still for - "

With a crash, Mrs Claus dropped down through the hole in the ceiling and landed on the roof of the van. The vehicle's one remaining inflated tire exploded with a bang and the glass in both rear doors shattered, spraying the parking bay.

"Oh fuck a duck," said Ash.

Mrs Claus rolled off the van roof and landed face-down on the concrete with a heavy, wet thud. She didn't move. Next to her, the van's suspension creaked wearily.

Ash remained where she was, statuesque with the bolt cutters in her hands, staring at the mound of costumed human flesh a few yards away. It still wasn't moving.

Is she dead?

"I think she's dead," said Jeremy, failing to mask the quiver in his voice. "I think the fall must have - "

Mrs Claus shrieked and Ash dropped the bolt cutters. The thing heaved herself to her feet, groping at the van for support. She raised her head with some effort and Ash swore again, because one of her eyes was missing, and the other looked like an overripe tomato just waiting to burst.

"Kids," said Olivia, "get out of here now."

Ignoring her, Ash snatched up the bolt cutters again. In response, Mrs Claus lumbered forward, howling like a wounded animal, but instead of coming straight for them, she staggered to the back of the van, pivoting around one of the open doors, her boots crunching on broken glass. She looked inside at where the

Creature had been, the Creature Ash had never seen with her own eyes but knew intimately in the dark recesses of her brain, and when the Mrs Claus saw it was gone, her howl became an ear-piercing scream.

"Run," Olivia said. "Fucking run!"

Ash went back to the cuffs. She saw the chain and tried to close the bolt cutter blades around it.

Then she came at them, stumbling drunkenly towards the parking bay. Her face was a horrorshow of gray skin pulled taut over bone, splitting in places, weeping coppery blood, her red jelly eye and the obsidian hole next to it fixed on them, her mouth contorted into a grin-snarl of bloodlust. She stepped indifferently over the elf's corpse and crossed the painted white line into the parking bay.

Jeremy darted to the right and cried "Hey, this way! Hey!", desperately waving his arms, but she kept coming. With each step, her knees buckled a little more and the liquid patches under her costume darkened further. She was collapsing into herself, and Ash knew it was because the Creature was gone and it'd been keeping her alive all this time. But she kept coming.

"Shit!" Ash said. She got the bolt cutter blades around the handcuff chain and drove the handles together, but it was too late.

She saw the blood-soaked gloves reaching for her, saw the maniacal grin push wider. She saw the skin at the corners of the thing's mouth split apart.

Oh no, Ash thought. It was all she could manage.

Then the Mrs Claus stopped. Her whole body went rigid. The grasping gloved hands locked in mid-air, inches from Ash's head.

The bolt cutter blades bit through the handcuff chain and Olivia's arms flopped limply at her sides.

Mrs Claus uttered a choked gasp as Jeremy drove the knife deeper into the back of her neck. His biceps trembled with exertion; his clenched teeth flashed.

"Jer," Ash blurted. She dropped the bolt cutters with a clatter.

Grunting, Jeremy wrenched the elf's knife out and staggered backwards. Mrs Claus gawked wildly, her mouth opening and shutting, producing no sound. She clutched at her neck and took an unsteady step back. Oily black blood gushed over her lower lip and down her front.

Then her heel snagged on the elf's corpse and she toppled, slamming hard onto the glass-strewn parking lot floor. Blood spurted out of her mouth. Her body spasmed once, twice, then went still. A pungent stench of rot and loosened bowels immediately filled the air.

"Yeah," Jeremy panted, dropping the knife, "that'll do it." Then he turned away, bent over and wretched.

"Is she dead this time?" said Ash over the sound of it.

"Who cares," Olivia groaned, using the car to haul herself up. "It's time to go."

Jeremy turned back to them, shakily wiping his mouth. He nodded. "Ok. The stairs will be quicker than - "

"No," Olivia said, shaking her head. "There's no time for that." She pushed her hair back from her face and pointed. "We're going that way."

"Up there?" Ash said dubiously, looking towards the hole in the ceiling above the van. "Can we even get through it?"

"If that psycho bitch can, so can we," Olivia said. "It's the fastest way back into the mall. I have to find my daughter. Now come on."

Taryn looked from the gun to the slimy pink sphere under his arm, and back to the gun again, and she guessed there might be forty feet of mall concourse between them. He wouldn't miss from that range.

She tightened her sweaty grip on the hammer and thought *what're you going to do, throw it at him?*

His grin was warm, inviting. "Everything ok, miss? Looks like you've got a cut on your face, there. Was it them? The ones in costume? I can help get you out of here, if you like?"

He was talking fast. She hadn't realized he'd taken a few steps forward until he shrugged and she noticed the gun again.

"Stop," she said, alarmed.

He did stop. But the gun remained raised, pointed towards the stores on his right. Somewhere nearby (below, maybe), Taryn thought she heard a metallic crash.

"I can't wait around," he said, still smiling, but she could see it was fixed now. "Got somewhere I need to be, if you'll excuse me."

He started to step to her left. She mirrored the movement, blocking his path.

"I... can't let you leave."

What're you doing? He's going to shoot you.

"Why's that?"

I think you better run. That's what he'd said. He didn't care. He was going to let them die.

He was going to let her *die.*

Taryn swallowed and set her feet. "I just can't."

He sighed and leveled the gun at her. She saw the unsteady waver in his arm and held up a palm. "Wait!"

He cocked the hammer. The click it made echoed around the concourse. "Move."

Keep him here.

"She's your daughter, isn't she?" Taryn said breathlessly.

"Move, or I'll kill you too."

Too?

"Emma," Taryn said, her hand shaking. "Em's your daughter, isn't she? I found her. I saved her from... from that thing. The woman. But she ran away, she's by herself now. Don't you want to find her? Don't you care if she's safe? You're her father!"

She saw his turquoise eyes flicker, just for a second. Something in them.

When he spoke again, his voice was completely different and Taryn's bladder almost let go inside her.

"Child," he said, deep and rasping now. His eyes burned, cutting right through her. "I am no father. I have no daughter. Adam was the Former One - I'm what remains now. I'm the guardian, the protector. I *must* protect. I'm the only one left who can. And you're in my way."

She saw his arm stiffen.

Keep him here.

"Adam!" she cried, latching onto what he'd said. "You don't have to do this." In the crook of his bandaged arm, the fleshy pink ball was visibly throbbing. "It's... it's controlling you, isn't it? Just put it down. We'll go find Em together, ok? We'll find her and you can take her home, and she'll be safe."

The flicker of doubt in his eyes again. His finger was on the trigger. A high-pitched whine screamed somewhere in Taryn's head.

"Please," she said.

"Move," he said again in his old voice.

"I can't let you," she said.

There was a sharp *crack* as the gun went off. Taryn felt the bullet part the air by her left ear, heard it thunk into something behind her. She let out a small gasp, but that was all. She didn't move, and she didn't drop the hammer.

Adam's arm swayed. His teeth were clenched tight now.

"Stupid girl," he hissed. "Fucking move."

That wasn't a warning shot. He missed.

"No," she said.

Spit ran down his chin. "Little bitch," he snarled.

Taryn saw the stairwell door open behind him. He didn't hear it.

"When I'm done," he said, eyes bulging, "I'll come back for the others. The boy with the glasses, down below. I'll kill them all."

They were in the concourse now. Three of them. Drifting silently towards him.

"You hear me? I'll shoot them all..."

Her eyes widened. She couldn't help it.

He saw it, frowned. Turned.

They went for him, black shadows, hands outstretched. Adam screamed and started shooting. The mall filled with noise.

Taryn threw herself to the floor.

TWENTY-THREE

"What the hell?" Ash said.

She was halfway through the hole, one hand on the ragged edge, the other clutching Jeremy's wrist. Olivia was below, boosting her feet.

"Gunshot," said Jeremy quickly. "Hurry up!"

He dragged her up through the hole. It was angled slightly and easy to find purchase, but her knee caught on the edge as she went through.

"Ow!" She scrambled to the side and held it, grimacing.

"Help me," Jeremy said urgently. "There's someone out there."

Together, they leaned into the hole and grabbed Olivia's extended hands.

"Pull," Jeremy said.

They heaved her upper torso through the hole. Olivia's sweater snagged on the crumbling concrete edge and tore.

"Let go," she gasped.

They did. She got both hands on the floor of the grotto and began pushing herself up.

Someone screamed, and a gun started firing.

"Get down!" Jeremy cried.

He and Ash threw themselves to the floor, covering their heads. Olivia pulled her hips through the hole and flopped onto her side, breathing hard.

The gunshots were deafening, ringing around the mall outside the fake wooden walls of the grotto. Jeremy pressed his hands to his ears; the handcuffs, still bound to his wrists, brushed his cheeks.

Another scream. A man's voice.

Then it stopped. The sound continued to reverberate through the concourse.

Jeremy took his hands away. Ash was curled into a ball next to him. She opened her eyes, met his. Olivia shifted onto all fours and started to get up.

Just then, footsteps went by the grotto. Someone running, panting. They clapped on the tiles, fading quickly.

Jeremy glanced at Olivia. Her hair hung loose around her face again. The handcuffs glinted on her wrists, too.

He changed position, getting onto his haunches, listening. Ash did the same.

Inside, the grotto was all tinsel and fairy lights and fake gifts wrapped in red and silver paper. There was a large red satin chair in one corner and an upended camera tripod in the other. At least a quarter of the ceiling was gone, and there were chunks of wood and plasterboard strewn over the floor.

They were in here when it happened, Jeremy thought. A take-out cup emblazoned with *The Coffee Place* logo still stood next to the red chair. *There were probably kids in line outside.*

Olivia stood up and Jeremy did the same.

"Let's go," she said.

"Wait!" Ash hissed, holding up a hand. There was something in her eyes, some far-off look.

"Why?" Jeremy started, and then froze. Cold tendrils of fear skittered up his spine and into his skull. He knew the others felt it, too.

Three shadows went by the grotto door, drifting from right to left. There were no voices, no footfalls. They floated past, one by one, and then they were gone. Jeremy let out the breath he hadn't realized he'd been holding.

Ash got unsteadily to her feet. Jeremy took her by the arm. She was trembling.

"It's ok," he said, "they're gone."

Ash's smile was weak. "I know."

Olivia brushed her hair back with both hands. Jeremy noticed she wasn't much taller than him, maybe a couple of inches. Her right cheek was bruised and swollen, and there was blood on her neck.

Pete's blood, he thought dully.

"Safe now?" she said, directing the question at Ash.

Ash blinked, then nodded. "Safe."

Olivia pushed open the grotto door and stepped out. Jeremy motioned for Ash to go next, then followed.

Outside the little building, the mall concourse was blindingly bright. Jeremy raised an arm to shield his face from the light. His eyes struggled to adjust after being in the underground lot for so long.

Olivia crossed to the white picket gate and pulled it open. Ash followed, her Doc Martens tramping on the fake snow in the grotto's garden. Jeremy peered down the concourse towards the escalators and main entrance. That's where they'd been going, those three things. That's where the person with the gun had gone.

Olivia's husband. Adam.

Jeremy's eyes strayed up to the second floor, to the entrance to *The Coffee Place*. Spencer's body was still there, the top of his belly just visible above the balcony. Jeremy quickly looked away.

Olivia started in the direction of the mall entrance.

"Wait," said Jeremy, following Ash through the grotto gate. "What're we going to do?"

Olivia stopped, turning back to them. "I'm going to find my daughter."

"But, those things - "

"The Trench Coat Men," said Ash, as though they discussed them regularly.

"Yeah," said Jeremy. "Them. And, you know..."

"Adam," Olivia said without expression. "My husband."

"Yeah."

She stared back at him for a moment. Above, a chill breeze whispered through the hole in the mall roof.

"I'll... deal with him," Olivia said, "when the time comes. But I have to find Emma. I know she's here somewhere. She's still alive."

"She is," said Ash.

Olivia looked at her. "You've seen her? Do you know where she is?"

"No," Ash said slowly. "I just... know she's alive. I know it doesn't make sense."

"I've seen her."

Jeremy spun on his heel as a figure came round from the other side of the grotto. She had a hammer in her hand and blood on one side of her face.

"Taryn!" Ash squealed.

She launched herself at the other girl, throwing her arms around her. Taryn hugged her back, burying her face in Ash's hair. Their shoulders bobbed up and down and Jeremy thought they were sobbing, but when they pulled apart their faces were bright with laughter.

Taryn grabbed his collar and yanked him into the embrace. After a second, laughter started bubbling up inside him too. Relief. Disbelief.

They came apart, red-faced and still laughing. Taryn wiped her eyes and Jeremy did the same.

"What's on your wrist?" Taryn said, sniffing.

"Handcuffs," he said. "Don't ask."

"I saved him," Ash announced.

"Yeah, but I killed Mrs Claus," said Jeremy.

"You did *what*?" Taryn said. "Did you kill the elf, too?"

"No, that was them."

"There was an elf?" said Ash.

"Yeah, didn't you see it on the floor when - "

"Kids!" Olivia cried.

They stopped, turned to her. "Sorry," Ash said sheepishly.

"We can all catch up later," said Olivia, "when there's time. Right now, I... I need you three to help me. If you can."

Jeremy studied her then for the first time. Her brown eyes, wide and desperate, flitting from him to Ash to Taryn. Her clothes, surely once pristine, now stained and torn in places, her sweater splattered with sweetly-pungent dried barf. She'd been through the ringer, like they all had. But unlike them, she'd lost people she cared deeply about: her daughter, and now her husband, who'd clearly lost his mind.

And yet, here she was, still standing. Fists balled and jaw set.

Ash got there first. "We'll help you."

"Yeah," Jeremy agreed, glancing at Taryn. "We found her in the toy store earlier, we know what she looks like."

"She was heading for the main entrance, last time I saw her," Taryn added. Jeremy heard the tremble in her voice.

Olivia's eyes shone with tears. She blinked them away and said, "Ok, then that's where we'll go. Follow me."

She turned and started in the direction of the escalators. They hurried after her.

"Where'd you get the hammer?" said Ash.

Taryn - Jeremy noticed she was limping a little - looked at it as though she'd forgotten it was in her hand. "It was hers, the woman dressed as Mrs Claus. She almost killed me with it."

"That bitch!"

"Well, she's dead now," said Jeremy. They were passing the fountain; he glanced down and saw the severed ear was still lying on the rim. "I got her in the neck."

"That was pretty cool," Ash said breathlessly.

Ahead of them, Jeremy saw Olivia throw a look over her shoulder.

"I... had to do it, you know?" he said, remembering how the knife felt in his hand as the blade went into her flesh. Far too easily. "Just wish I'd kept the damn thing."

"You dweeb," said Ash. "It's ok though, we have Taryn's hammer. She's the Mighty Thor now. She'll protect us."

A grin flickered across Taryn's mouth, and was gone.

They passed the Christmas trees lining the concourse, then the escalators, then the vending machines. Olivia was a few paces ahead of them, striding purposefully, her boots clocking on the tiles. She rounded the corner and stopped suddenly; Ash, who'd been looking at the ATM, walked into her.

"Shit! Sorry," she said.

"Hey," Taryn said. "The shutter."

Jeremy looked past Olivia. The metal shutter had been rolled back up, exposing the sliding glass doors. They could get out.

"Who opened it?" said Taryn.

"Does it matter?" Ash replied. "Let's get the fuck - "

"Wait," said Jeremy, frowning. Something wasn't right about what he was seeing, and for a moment, he simply couldn't connect the dots. This time, Taryn beat him to it.

"The snow!" she cried. "The snow's gone."

"Ho-lee shit," said Ash.

Taryn was right: the snow was completely gone. Even from their end of the corridor, they could clearly see the outdoor parking lot, completely devoid of the white blanketing it earlier that day. Every buried vehicle was now visible again, glinting in the moonlight. No snow was falling, and there was no snow on the ground.

"How?" Olivia said softly.

"There was so much," said Taryn.

"It went away when the creature did," said Ash in monotone. She was staring at the entrance, arms by her side. "It was... all part of it."

"What do you mean, part of it?" said Taryn.

Jeremy heard it at the last second. *Clump, clump, clump*. He turned, saw it coming, and with a cry, shoved Ash and Taryn to one side.

The ax sliced through the air, missed, and thunked into the wall. The Santa roared in fury, tugging on the handle.

"OH FUCK!" Ash yelled.

Jeremy saw Olivia stagger forwards, almost losing her balance. She spun round and her eyes widened at the sight of the thing in the red costume.

The words left Jeremy's mouth before he could stop them. "Go!" he shouted. "Go find Em! We'll distract him."

"We'll *what*?" cried Ash.

The Santa heaved on the ax handle, jimmying the blade out of the wall. He almost had it.

"Go!" Jeremy repeated.

"Run!" Taryn echoed. Jeremy felt her hand close on his arm, yank him backwards. He saw Olivia hesitate a second longer. Then she turned and bolted for the doors.

With a crack of plasterboard, the ax came free from the wall. The Santa turned. He was now between them and the entrance, a hulking red monster whose only purpose was to kill.

Jeremy grabbed for Ash's hand, found it, and then they were running.

Back towards the mall concourse.

TWENTY-FOUR

You can't leave them, Olivia thought, even as her legs propelled her towards the entrance. *They're kids. You can't just leave them.*

The doors slid apart. Cool air blasted into her face, whipping back her hair, and she realized for the first time just how warm the inside of the mall had been. Even the parking lot, where sweat had gathered under her armpits, and trickled down her back. It hadn't just been from fear. The whole building was fucking *warm*.

Her boots skidded as she turned to look back. The corridor was empty. Voices echoed from around the corner. Shouting, yelling.

They're just kids and you left them behind.

"Emma," she said aloud, turning away again with some effort.

She scanned the parking lot, still amazed at the complete lack of snow. There'd been curtains of it coming down when she was last here, walking from the gas station just behind Adam as he carried Em, her little legs kicking happily in mid-air. They were just looking for some help with their car, and they'd walked right into a horror show, like lambs to the slaughter. And now, Em was missing, and Adam was...

What the hell was he? Under that thing's control? Had he lost his mind?

Tears stung her eyes and she immediately fought them back.

"Later," she said, her voice lilting through the night air. The parking lot, full of snow-free cars, listened to her in silence. "Not now."

Where did Em go?

She looked across the lot to where their Volvo was still parked beneath the gas station canopy, glinting in the store's glow. Even from distance, she could see the two flat tires on the passenger side.

Bastard elf, she thought.

No sign of Em. But she could be in the store, couldn't she? She'd tried to snag candy earlier, she'd remember it was there. Even the sight of the car, something familiar, might draw her.

Olivia took a step towards the gas station and stopped. Something else caught her eye, off to the left. Another warm glow in the December darkness.

The movie theater.

Like the gas station, it was still brightly illuminated inside, spilling light onto the paved sidewalk by its entrance. Under any other circumstances, it might have been inviting.

It *would* be inviting to a little girl.

Is she in there? Olivia thought, staring hard across the parking lot at the movie theater entrance. The glass doors were wide open; the lobby walls were a gaudy red inside. *Is* he *in there?*

He. *He* was Adam. Her husband.

And were *they* in there, too? Those things in the black coats? She watched them kill the elf, and then the Creature in the van. Brutally, mercilessly. And with ruthless efficiency.

Not killed - eaten.

Devoured.

"Adam," she whispered.

Then something clicked in her head, came together like a circuit. It was something she'd seen earlier, something that hadn't been important at the time. She'd dismissed it as strange and then promptly forgotten about it.

But she remembered now.

"I'm coming, Em," she said. "Hold on."

With a final glance towards the movie theater entrance, Olivia started for the gas station.

As they turned the corner back onto the mall concourse, Jeremy thought *we're going the wrong damn way.*

He could hear the thing in the Santa costume pounding along the corridor after them but he didn't dare look back. Its dry, rasping breaths seemed far too close.

"Shit!" Ash cried, the heavy soles of her boots slapping on the tiles. The concourse stretched out ahead of them again, its twin rows of Christmas trees extended like open arms, as if to say, *Welcome back, kids - finally ready to die?* "Now where do we go?"

"I don't know," Taryn replied. Her limp was more pronounced now and she winced with every step. "Somewhere."

"There's *literally* nowhere to go - "

"Ash..."

"Wait, look!" Jeremy said.

They looked back, still moving. The Santa had entered the concourse and was lumbering after them, the blood-stained ax still gripped firmly in his gloved hands. But as he drew alongside the escalators, passing under the second-floor balcony where Spencer still lay, they saw he was already slowing: his legs wobbled unsteadily as he came closer and his left foot was beginning to drag; damp patches had appeared all over his suit and were spreading quickly, and more blood cascaded out from under his beard and down his front, turning the white faux-fur trim a dark pink. His wheezing had become a liquid gurgle.

"He's falling apart," said Ash, still backing away.

"The same thing happened to Mrs Claus," said Taryn.

"The Creature was keeping them alive," Jeremy said, his eyes fixed on the staggering figure. "It's gone, and now they're dying as well."

"Good fucking riddance," Ash spat. She stooped, snatched up one of the fake gifts at the foot of the nearest Christmas tree, and hurled it at the Santa with a theatrical cry of, "Take that!"

The wrapped cardboard box bounced harmlessly off the hulking man's shoulder; he stopped, looked down at the box as it tumbled lightly to the floor, and back at them.

"You thought there was something inside that, didn't you?" said Taryn.

"Yes," said Ash.

With a muffled roar, the Santa stumbled towards them, raising the ax. Ash screamed.

"Watch out!" Jeremy cried.

They scattered. He darted to the right and his boots squeaked over the floor, struggling for purchase. He heard the squeal of the ax head glancing off the tiles behind him.

"Jer!" Ash yelled.

He looked back and saw the huge costumed man coming after him, dragging the ax along the floor. The shriek of the metal blade ricocheted around the concourse. With a gasp, he grabbed hold of the nearest Christmas tree and yanked it down behind him, blocking the Santa's path. Baubles came loose from the artificial fir branches and bounced away across the floor.

The Santa stepped over the fallen tree, caught one of his boots and almost went down. The stumble bought Jeremy precious seconds. He regained his own balance, backing hurriedly away along the inside of the pillars. The escalators were coming up behind him; on his right, he glimpsed a bench, then an up-turned trash bin. The one Lincoln had knocked over, long ago.

"Hey!" he heard Ash shout. "Over here, douchebag!"

A half-full soda can thunked into the Santa's face, splashing his beard with cola. His head swiveled robotically towards the source and he abruptly changed direction, instantly forgetting about Jeremy. He stepped between the pillars and briefly disappeared.

"Oh shit!" Jeremy heard Ash cry. "Taryn!"

"Keep moving," came Taryn's out-of-breath reply, "he's almost down."

Jeremy passed another Christmas tree, knocking more baubles to the floor. He saw Taryn across the concourse, saw the blood caked to her cheek, and wondered distractedly what had happened to her while he'd been in the underground lot. The hammer in her hand looked pathetic compared to the enormous ax the Santa was wielding.

The ax that killed Spencer.

Ash was a few yards away from him, feet planted in the pile of trash from the overturned bin. She bent to pick up another soda can. Just beyond her, the Santa lurched towards Taryn, leaving a trail of blood in his wake.

Then Jeremy spotted it, a sliver of glinting red under the bench.

"Taryn," Ash shouted, then screamed: "TARYN!"

Jeremy saw her fall. She landed hard on the floor with an "Oomph!" and the hammer slipped from her grasp, clattering across the tiles. The Santa bore down on her, hoisting the ax above his head. His sagging arms wouldn't hold out much longer, but there was enough strength in them for one more swing. One downward arc to cut Taryn Meyer in two.

Ash screamed and hurled the soda can.

Jeremy ran for the bench.

Olivia tried the door of the sedan and was only mildly surprised when it opened easily.

Driver was probably about to refuel, she thought, *and then the meteorite came down, and he ended up in the mall with everyone else.*

Inside, the car smelled of stale sweat and cigarettes. She reached across the back seat and swept the sleeping bag aside, fully exposing the shotgun beneath. She grabbed it by the stock and pulled it out of the car; it was double-barreled and huge, heavier than she'd expected. The gunmetal was cold in her hands.

"Ok," she muttered, dipping the barrels towards the ground, "what's inside you?"

Adam's father was a keen shooter. When she'd first met the Prices - the very day she'd been introduced, in fact - Victor had taken them out for a shooting lesson at the local range. Olivia still remembered the acrid gunpowder smell, could still feel the butt thumping into her skinny shoulder. Adam, who'd handled guns most of his life, had been good; she'd done enough to get by without embarrassing herself, and Victor had graciously allowed her to bow out after her fourth wayward shot. A trial by fire, Missouri-style.

She snapped the breach lever and opened the break-action. Two clean, intact brass casings stared back at her. Fully loaded.

"Ok," she said again, and closed it. *Click.*

Leaning the gun against the car, she reached inside and fished around the back seat. The interior ceiling light was weak and it took her longer than she'd have liked to find them. She came out with the box and popped it open. It was at least half full of shells.

She studied them for a moment, listening to the breeze whisper across the gas station forecourt, feeling it pluck at her hair. Then she pulled four shells out and tossed the box back into the car. She slipped two shells into each side pocket of her jeans, cursing herself for choosing a pair of skinnies that morning.

But you didn't think you'd be here, *did you?*

The breeze changed course and she caught a whiff of the sickly-sweet vomit on her sweater, now dried into the wool. Nauseated, she stepped back from the car and worked the sweater over her head, gritting her teeth as the fabric brushed over her cracked cheekbone. The black vest top she wore underneath was soaked through with sweat and her bare arms and neckline - now exposed to the December night - were instantly chilled.

Her mother's voice in her ear, clear as day: *You'll catch your death, Olivia.*

She dropped the ruined sweater at her feet and snatched up the shotgun.

Then she headed for the movie theater.

The ax hit the tiles by Taryn's arm, cracking one in half. She gasped and rolled away. There was the hammer. She scrambled towards it.

"Taryn!" Ash squealed again.

Her fingers brushed the hammer's wooden handle and the ax came down again, biting into the tiles. She felt the blade part the air by her shoulder, just as Adam's wayward bullet had done, and her heart missed a beat.

"Hey! HEY!"

Taryn grabbed the hammer and rolled onto her back, expecting to see the ax head hurtling towards her face, steeling herself for the blow. But the Santa wasn't looking at her now; he was looking at Ash, still standing by the toppled trash can, her black hair wildly askew. She had a full water bottle in one hand, and as Taryn hurriedly crab-scrambled backwards, she heaved it at the Santa's head.

Once again, the walking costumed corpse made no attempt to dodge the oncoming object, and the bottle bounced off his forehead, causing it to rock on the spot. The red and white Santa hat slipped off, revealing a completely bald, liver-spotted scalp; Taryn could see the elasticated loops pinning the fake beard to his ears.

He started towards Ash.

We can't keep this up forever, Taryn thought, getting to her feet. Had they bought Olivia enough time by now? Had she found Em?

Ash staggered backwards. Her eyes were huge green orbs, full of terror. Out of ideas.

The Santa bore down on her, stomping heavily across the concourse floor, easily eating up the short distance with his long strides.

She's freezing up. It's going to get her.

"Oh no," Taryn breathed.

"Over here!"

She followed the voice and saw Jeremy rise to his feet a few yards to Ash's left. He had something red in his hands. Taryn didn't compute exactly what it was until he yelled, "Ash, get down!" and yanked out the safety pin, and then the Santa changed course and headed straight for him, preparing to swing the ax.

Ash dived to one side and Jeremy squeezed the fire extinguisher's handle, and a jet of white shot from the nozzle gripped in his other hand. For the second time that day, his aim was uncharacteristically true, and the Santa's face was instantly coated with foam. This time, he did stop; he swayed on the spot, blinded by the foam, his feet planted stupidly while Jeremy continued spraying. He lowered the ax, reaching for his face.

"Kill it!" Ash screamed; Taryn couldn't see her past the Santa's foam-splattered bulk. "The hammer! *Kill it now!*"

Taryn looked down at the hammer in her hand. She'd forgotten it was there; it felt too light, like a toy. *It's not enough*, she thought.

"TARYN!" Ash and Jeremy howled in perfect unison.

Her legs got going before her brain did. She charged, lifting the hammer high. Jeremy released the extinguisher's handle and the foam cut off.

Go for the head, a voice inside her skull shrieked. *Smash its brain!*

She got within a foot of it and actually managed to swing the hammer at the Santa's temple (*go for the head THE HEAD*) when the bulging red arm came at her, crane-like, and caught her square in the chin. Her head flicked back, taking her neck and the rest of her with it, and she hit the floor hard. Her teeth clacked together; effervescent stars popped and fizzed behind her eyes. Once again, the hammer slipped from her grip and bounced away across the tiles.

Breath rushed out of her lungs and she simultaneously thought, *here it comes* and *I'm not ready*.

But he didn't come. In fact, the Santa barely noticed he'd knocked her aside. He had new prey now, prey that'd actually managed to stop him in his tracks. Nothing else had been able to do that; not the security guard who'd been in the bathroom cubicle, wondering why his phone service had cut out; not the family trying to hide in their minivan in the underground lot. Not the bearded man outside the coffee place, the one who'd saved the girl. Nothing else had slowed him down all day.

Until this *boy*.

The Santa swiped a gloved hand across his face, slopping blood and foam onto the floor. Then he dropped the ax; Taryn cringed as the metal head clanged onto the floor. Jeremy shrunk back from the sound, clinging uselessly to the empty fire extinguisher canister, the lenses of his glasses fogging over.

The Santa stepped towards him, huge and looming and dripping with murderous hunger. He reached for him, ready to grasp his throat, to break his neck in one swift movement. Taryn saw Jeremy prepare to throw the extinguisher. She knew it would do no good.

"Jeremy!" she cried weakly.

His name hadn't completely left her mouth when a sharp bang, amplified and elongated in the cavernous mall concourse, sliced through the air. The Santa stopped just short of grasping Jeremy's throat. The left side of his body jerked back as though an invisible cord had snagged on his arm and given it a vigorous tug. Taryn saw a plume of red erupt from his shoulder, spraying the floor behind it.

"What - " she heard Jeremy say.

Then there was a second *bang*, louder than the first, and the Santa's head snapped backwards. Blood and pink stuff blew out through a freshly-opened hole near the base of his skull. He took a step back, swayed for a moment, then fell. Taryn watched him go down as though it was happening in slow motion; when his body hit the floor, she felt the tremor at her feet. The Santa's limbs twitched once, twice, and went still.

"What?" Jeremy repeated, lowering the fire extinguisher.

Ash, who'd just picked herself off the floor, said, "Who... who shot it?"

"That'd be me!"

They all turned; Taryn's jaw dropped open.

Someone was coming down the escalator, brandishing a handgun. Someone in a black polo shirt with dark, blood-matted hair, leaning awkwardly on a single crutch, grinning happily.

"Linc?" Jeremy cried.

"Trash-tipper!" Ash exclaimed.

"That's Mr Ward to you kids," Lincoln replied, beaming. He waved the gun in the air. "Looks like I saved the day after a-"

He reached the bottom of the escalator. The step he'd been on disappeared into the floor; he tripped on the landing plate and sprawled face-down on the concourse tiles, dropping the loaded gun in the process. His crutch clattered down next to him and Ash gave a laughing whoop of delight.

PART IV: EMMA

TWENTY-FIVE

A dam looked around the movie theater lobby and said, "Shit."

Where's the fucking staff door? he thought.

He'd been in the *Outlet Complex* mall plenty of times as a kid (the place was damn well ancient, after all), but back then the "complex" had just been the mall, the gas station and a crappy diner that closed long ago. Now, *The Movie House* sat where the diner had been, and Adam had never been inside it.

"Shit," he repeated through gritted teeth.

The lobby doors, frozen in place by the snow and yet to fully unthaw, were halfway open when he arrived. There'd been just enough space for him to walk inside with the quivering pink-gray egg pinned to his side, and that'd been a welcome positive, because he wasn't sure he could have prized the doors apart with his injured arm and didn't want to waste the precious few bullets he had left shooting the glass. But that'd been the *only* positive thing that happened since he left the underground parking lot: first - and though he'd anticipated it, it'd still been a shock to his system - the Creature had been destroyed, and the seemingly-limitless supply of strength and energy he'd enjoyed for hours had cut off in an instant; next, the girl in the concourse got in his way and slowed him down, just long enough for those things to drift right up behind him and shitting-well nearly get their skeletal fingers round his throat. He'd put at least four rounds in the closest one and it'd gone down, and the other two had drawn back; he'd run then, as fast as his energy-sapped legs would carry him, without looking back. He was certain the one he'd shot had gotten right back up again and all three were in slow but steady pursuit, but he hadn't paused to check.

The entrance shutter had been raised, just as he'd ordered, and he went straight for the movie theater. The snow was gone but the ground was still slippery, and he hadn't been able to go as fast as he'd have liked for fear of dropping the egg. He had the feeling it'd survive the fall, but he couldn't take any chances - not now, with those things so close behind him. He knew what would happen if they got a hold of it, and that'd be the end of the Creature entirely. And by extension, the end of him, too.

Lincoln's keys had jingled in his jeans pocket as he hurried towards the movie theater. Why the hell hadn't the kid just attached his car keys to the same keychain, like a normal person? He could have bypassed the staff room entirely and just skirted around the outside of the building to the rear entrance, where Lincoln's car was parked, ready to whisk him far away from the complex and the things floating silently after him. Put some miles between them. It'd buy just enough time for the egg to hatch, and then it'd be over - the next Creature would birth, grow, consume, and reproduce. More eggs next time, more Creatures. More servants like him to spread them out wherever they could, planting them like seeds in densely-populated places. And the cycles would start again. On and on and on, until there was no-one left. Merry Christmas, folks.

But here he was, standing in the movie theater lobby with absolutely no idea where the staff room was.

And his arm was fucking *aching*.

Cursing, he limped past the lobby Christmas tree towards the concession stand, gripping the gun hard in his right hand. Below it, his right leg was starting to give, even though he'd done nothing to injure it. There was no wound, no tweaked muscle. He knew his body was starting to disintegrate, now that the Creature was gone. Maybe the egg was the only thing keeping him alive.

What a way to go, Adam-boy.

The thought made him stop, a yard from the concession stand Spencer Bloom had leaned over not so long ago while searching for his wife, as though she might be hiding in the popcorn trough. *You're going, aren't you?* the thought went on in a thin voice, barely audible behind the muddled, garbling noise now occupying his skull. *This is it. No going back. You're not Adam anymore.*

But he was... wasn't he? The Creature was gone, after all. Maybe. Maybe, if he just -

PROTECT ME PROTECT ME FEED ME

He winced as white-hot pain lanced through his arm, as if the egg had suddenly become radioactive. The image of Olivia and Em that'd begun to materialize in his mind evaporated in an instant and the voice screamed louder: PROTECT ME PROTECT ME PROTECT MEEEEE

"Fuck!" Adam snarled. His head was suddenly pounding.

I have to put this thing down before my arm falls off.

He took a step towards the concession counter, clean and white under the lights, then stopped. *Can't leave it there.* He strained to arrange his thoughts. *Too visible. They're coming, They'll be here soon.*

Hide it.

He turned, scanning the lobby. Concession stand. Ticket podium. Trash bin. Giant fucking Christmas tree.

The tree.

He went to it, stooped, and stuffed the egg inside. The inhuman voices in his head shrieked in protest but he shunted them aside. The tree shook as he pushed the egg in between the firs; a couple of baubles dropped off and bounced away. He pulled a ream of silver tinsel down over it and stepped back. It was far from invisible, but someone passing by probably wouldn't notice at first glance, unless they crouched down to look. He didn't have long, though - those things were drawn to the Creature like it was a homing beacon, and the egg may not be much different. He could only hope whatever signal it gave out was weaker, harder to pinpoint.

Unless they were tracking *him* now.

The bandage around his arm was completely red, soaked through with blood. The clear, mucus goop from the egg was all over the left side of his body, clinging to his sweater.

"Staff door," he said hoarsely, and was surprised to hear how dry and gravelly his own voice now sounded. "Hurry."

His headache, which had been a dull throb when he left the mall, was now banging. It had jumped in intensity the moment he let go of the egg; it stung the back of his eyes as he looked around the lobby, searching for the staff door.

Maybe it's not here, at the entrance, he managed to think. Squinting down the hall (were his eyeballs actually *burning* now?), he read the signs above the auditorium double-doors: Screen Three, Screen Two, Screen One. All on the left. On the right, a handful of seating booths, an out-of-order water fountain, and a pop-up cardboard display featuring a blue-eyed husky pulling a sleigh, with the tagine "Santa Paws is coming to town - December 15, at a theater near you!". And right between the display and the fountain, a single door marked with the word 'Private'.

"Bingo," he said.

He cast a quick glance at the open entrance doors, gave the gun grip a squeeze, and started down the lobby.

Em watched Daddy from her position at the end of the concession stand counter, right beside the penny candy station. He walked quickly down the lobby, dragging his right leg a little. He hadn't seen her, hadn't thought to look. She watched him arrive at the 'Private' door, throw it open and disappear inside.

She hadn't called out to him when he came puffing into the movie theater, cradling the slimy pink thing under his arm. Before, she'd have run to him without a second thought, arms outstretched and beaming, but not now. Something had warned her to stay right where she was, hunkered down at the end of the counter, thumbs looped under the straps of her dinosaur backpack: a whispering voice, gentle but urgent, drifting through an open window at the back of her mind. It was a girl's voice, one she didn't know. But she knew she should listen and so she stayed put, even when Daddy said the Bad Word he wasn't supposed to say around her. She didn't see him put the pink egg into the Christmas tree, but she *did* hear the branches rustle and the baubles drop to the floor (one rolled right to her feet and she almost reach for it), and when she heard him stomp off down the lobby and peered around the counter, her eyes went to the tree.

As soon as Daddy was gone, Em stood up and walked to where the tree stood. Her toe caught one of the baubles and sent it flying across the thin lobby carpet. The door Daddy had gone through remained closed.

Run.

She heard the girl's voice again, right in her ear. She liked her voice, even though she didn't know it. And she would run, in a minute.

Em wiped the back of her hand under her nose (it'd started running when she crossed from the mall to *The Movie House*), rubbed it on her coat, and reached into the tree. The egg was spongy and moist under her small palms. She pulled it out from among the firs; it was heavier than she thought it'd be, and when it came loose from the tree she almost fell over. More baubles dropped to the floor and rolled away.

Something was moving inside the egg. She could feel it shifting around, probing at the fleshy shell encasing it. The egg itself was warm, growing warmer.

Run.

Run where? Back outside, back to the mall? No, not there. Mommy might be there, but so were the men. The tall men in the black coats and hats. They were coming. They'd be here very soon.

Em turned in a circle. She saw the tree and the colorful lights strewn inexpertly over its branches; she saw the concession stand and *smelled* the now-burned popcorn, and she saw the unmarked door next to it that led to the staff room, the one Adam had completely missed in his madness-induced tunnel vision. She saw the movie posters on the walls and the bill-stuffed wallet someone dropped earlier when the meteorite first came down, and she saw the stairs leading to the second floor.

The stairs.

Run!

Clutching the egg to her chest, Em waddled over to them and started up the steps, not knowing why, but knowing she should. She turned the corner just as three dark shapes arrived soundlessly at the movie theater entrance and slid, one by one, through the gap in the doors.

TWENTY-SIX

Ash opened her eyes and said, "She's in the movie theater."

Jeremy, easing Lincoln down onto the bench, replied, "Who?"

"The little girl. Olivia's daughter."

"Em?" said Taryn. She moved closer to Ash, studying her face. "Does she have curly hair? And a purple coat?"

"I... I think so."

"And light-up sneakers?"

"It's not a fucking camera feed!"

"Who's Em?" said Lincoln, pressing a hand to the bloodied side of his head where Adam's bullet had grazed him. "And how do you know where she is?"

"Yeah," Jeremy said, frowning. "How?"

Ash met Taryn's gaze. She hesitated, started to speak.

"It's... it's hard to - "

"It doesn't matter," Taryn cut in, rescuing her. She saw a flicker of gratitude in Ash's eyes and turned to the others. "If Em's there, we have to help her."

"Who's Em?" Lincoln asked again.

"She's a little girl," Jeremy said, his eyes darting between Taryn and Ash, trying to read them. "We found her earlier. Olivia's gone after her, but she might not know where she is."

"Who's Olivia - "

"Shut up, trash-tipper!" Ash exclaimed.

"What do we do, though?" Jeremy continued. "Even if we find her, how can we protect her? Or get away from here?"

"We don't have weapons," said Ash, softer now.

"Yeah, we're not cops."

"Cops," Taryn echoed slowly. Then: "Cops!"

Ash's eyes widened. "The snow! It went away when the creature did, so maybe..."

Jeremy already had his phone in his hand. "I have service again!"

Taryn pulled hers out. The screen was badly cracked, but it lit up anyway when she touched it. There were three bars in the top corner.

"Me too," she said.

"Me three," Ash added. "Holy shit, I've never forgotten about my phone before!"

Taryn heard herself laugh. Notifications were populating on her screen in rapid succession: social media updates, a text from her Mom, an excerpt from a breaking news story: *Possible atmospheric debris sighted over highway.*

"My phone's blowing up here," said Jeremy.

"Mine too," said Ash. "Did you see - "

"Guys!"

They stopped and looked at Lincoln, slumped on the bench. Blood trickled down the inside of his arm from the palm pressed to his head.

"Someone want to, yunno, call for help?"

"Oh, yeah," said Jeremy. "I'll do it." He started to turn away, paused, and said, "Who do I ask for? The police, or an ambulance?"

"Both," said Taryn. "Ask for everything."

"The army, too," said Ash. "And the FBI. And maybe a priest."

Taryn smiled. Ash returned it grimly and Taryn felt a lump push up from the back of her throat. *What the hell kind've a day has this been?*

"You ok, princess?"

"I'm ok, Tar-tar Sauce."

Taryn held Ash's gaze, reading it. Jeremy had the phone to his ear and wasn't listening. She lowered her voice. "Was it like before?"

Ash nodded. "Mostly. More intense."

"You wanna talk about it?"

The other girl shook her head. "Not right now. Maybe later."

"Ok."

Jeremy was talking to the dispatcher now, stumbling through the conversation. Lincoln was listening to him, leaning forward.

"Geez," said Taryn, gingerly touching the cut in her cheek, "I wish I had superpowers, too."

"Superpowers," Ash scoffed, "piss off." Taryn saw the flush of red in her cheeks, however, and the suggestion of a smile tug at her mouth.

Jeremy turned back to them, lowering the phone. "They're on their way," he said. "I... don't know if they believed me."

"What'd you say?" said Taryn.

"Did you tell them an alien ate everyone and Santa tried to kill us with an ax?" said Ash.

"What?" spluttered Lincoln.

"I told them I thought it was terrorists," said Jeremy. "That's all. They said they'd send police, paramedics, everything. She wanted me to stay on the line but I said we had to go."

"We do," Taryn said. To Lincoln: "Can you walk?"

He grimaced. "I think so. Maybe. Depends where."

"We're going back to the movie theater," said Ash. "For Em."

"Um, I dunno if that's - "

"Ok, you can stay here," said Jeremy.

"No wait!" Lincoln cried, groping for his crutch. "Dude, I'm not staying here by myself. Help me up."

"He'll slow us down," said Ash.

"Hey - "

"Well, you will!"

Taryn watched as Lincoln threw an arm over Jeremy's shoulders, almost knocking his glasses off. "Jer, can you help get him out of here?"

"Yeah. Wait, why?"

"We're going to go get Em," said Taryn. "To help Olivia. She'll need us."

"No, you can't just - "

"We can - it's happening," said Taryn firmly, in the most adult voice she could muster. Ash nodded next to her. "Take Linc outside. Anywhere other than the mall. Maybe the gas station. Wait for the cops and tell them where we are when they get here. Ok?"

"Ok," said Jeremy sullenly. "But you better not die. Not after all this."

"No promises," Ash said.

Taryn turned to her. "You know where she is, right?"

"Yes."

"And you know where *they* are?"

A shadow of apprehension passed over Ash's face. "Yes."

"Ok," said Taryn, shifting the hammer to her other hand. "Then let's go."

TWENTY-SEVEN

Adam spent a solid minute in the room with the door marked 'Private' before realizing it was nothing more than a storage space.

The door had swung shut behind him the moment he stepped inside, and his eyes, which were beginning to bleed, hadn't registered the industrial-style shelving untidily stacked with cleaning supplies, concession snacks in cardboard boxes and shrink-wrapped bundles of toilet paper. The door slammed behind him and he was plunged into darkness.

"Are you shitting me?" he muttered, feeling around for a light switch. The Adam Price of several hours ago would have gone for his phone without a second thought and flicked on the flashlight, but that Adam was almost gone, and the entity now occupying his crumbling brain had just one thing on its mind: *find the keys, drive far, start again. Protect the unborn.*

Adam banged his shoulder off the shelves, knocking a row of bleach bottles to the floor. He spluttered a jumble of nonsense words in the voice Taryn heard him use earlier, hands flailing around where he thought the light switch must be. Finally, his fingers brushed over the familiar shape and he flicked it.

A bare, dust-covered bulb hummed to life above his head, swinging gently. Adam got one look around the storage room through slitted eyes, spat a series of expletives and turned back to the door.

No fucking staff office, he thought.

He yanked the door open and staggered back into the movie theater lobby. The abrupt changes in light were making his eyes sting. He rubbed them with the back of his fist and heard his right eyeball squelch. Warm blood seeped over his lower eyelid and trickled down his face. The stabbing jolt in his eye socket might have shocked him if the pain in his head hadn't been so much more intense.

Dying, he thought dully, turning back to the center of the lobby. *Don't have long. Hurry*.

His boots - expensive little numbers he'd bought for himself only a few weeks ago - now felt like they were packed with lead. His feet barely lifted off the floor as he dragged each one across the movie theater carpet, slouching his way towards the Christmas tree and its precious hidden cargo.

Just keep it with you. He squinted at the tree and discovered he couldn't see through his right eye anymore, and couldn't quite remember why. *Just carry it. Shouldn't have left it. Staff room can't be far*.

Was he going to be able to drive the car?

He approached the tree, accidentally kicking one of the fallen baubles. It skittered across the carpet and came to a stop at the base of a door by the concession stand, one Adam hadn't noticed before. One leading somewhere not intended for the public.

The staff room.

"Ah, fuck," he mumbled, and his lower lip detached from his face. Hot blood spilled down his chin and under his shirt. His lip dropped silently to the carpet.

Adam turned to the tree, bending to part the artificial fir branches. More baubles dropped to the floor. The branches where the egg had been were still sticky from its goopy mucus coating. Where the egg *had* been.

It was gone.

"Oh fuck me," Adam said, but it came out as something different with no bottom lip to make the "F" sound. He said it again anyway. "Fuck me!"

PROTECT ME, it shrieked in his head, distant now. SAVE ME. PROTECT ME. PROTECT, PROTECT...

He straightened up, dizzied with pain. His entire body felt like it was about to crumple; he was sure his brain would soon explode inside his skull.

It's gone, he thought, stumbling away from the tree, back the way he'd come. *How? Where the hell is it? I left it right there, and I was only gone for...*

A finger of ice traced down his spine. His hand, still gripping the gun, went numb.

He turned and saw them enter the lobby, filing soundlessly between the jammed-open doors. All three of them, including the one he'd shot back in the mall. It hadn't died, after all.

His feet were glued to the lobby carpet. They'd followed him to the movie theater, drawn by the egg's calling - maybe even by the smell of the thing, or whatever scent *he* was giving off - and now they were passing the ticket booth, shoulder to shoulder with their faces shrouded, walking towards the tree.

Adam watched, planted in plain sight like a decomposing statue, barely keeping hold of the gun in his good hand. He wasn't sure he'd have the strength to pull the trigger anyway.

Would there be any point? He waited, unbreathing. Waited for them to break formation and rush at him. He waited for it all to end.

But it didn't. Instead of charging at him, they stopped, just a few feet from the tree. They stood completely still, arms by their sides, trilby hats dipped to cover their faces. Only their heads moved, angling towards the tree, studying it.

Looking for the egg.

For one endless moment they just stood there, side by side, facing the tree. The breeze from the open entrance tugged at the hems of their coats and rustled the branches of the tree. Another bauble dropped, bounced, and rolled away.

What the hell? Adam thought. *Do they even see me here?*

The one nearest him shifted, flexing its gloved hand. Then its head moved again, swiveling in his direction, and his good arm became limp. The gun slipped from his hand and dropped onto the carpet.

"Shit," he blurted.

The men in the black trench coats started towards him, knocking the Christmas tree aside.

"Oh shit!" Adam cried in a high, thin voice.

He stumbled backwards, forgetting the gun. He knew if he stooped down to pick it up, his legs would finally give way and he'd collapse to the floor. And then they'd be on him instantly.

He spun in a half circle, saw the sign for Screen Three, and staggered for the double doors.

TWENTY-EIGHT

Taryn tilted her head back to look at the sky. It was clear and cloudless, blanketed with stars. The red and green navigation lights of an airplane winked in and out directly above them.

Can you see us? she thought.

Ash shivered next to her. "It's cold as fuck out here."

"No it isn't," said Taryn. "It's warmer than before. And there's no snow."

"Yeah, but you're not wearing a skirt."

"Whose fault is that?"

Ash scowled but said nothing. Taryn peered across the snowless parking lot at the movie theater entrance. It didn't look that far from the mall, or at least, not as far as it'd seemed earlier when they'd had to tramp through the white on their way between the buildings. The mall's sliding doors started to close, then opened again. They were still within their sensor range.

"What're we waiting for?" said Ash, crossing her arms.

Taryn looked over at the gas station, still lit up in the December night. "I... I'm not sure. I just wanted to check, in case they're out here. If we run into them before we find Em or Olivia..."

"We won't," Ash said, "They're in the movie theater."

"You're sure?"

Ash nodded. "Pretty sure. Come on."

She started towards the theater. Taryn hurried to join her; behind them, the mall doors slid closed.

"Why d'you think this is happening now, again?" Taryn said. "After all this time? It's been, like, two years. Right?"

"Something like that, yeah."

Taryn shook her head. "I remember that night. It was freaky."

"Funny, I remember it too," Ash replied sardonically. "Think I scared the shit out of Becky Magill."

"Well, you *did* say a bunch of real weird stuff." Taryn stared at the ground as she walked, still marveling at the complete disappearance of the snow. "Stuff you couldn't possibly have known. And stuff that hadn't happened yet. Stuff that *did* happen after - "

"I know, Tar."

"I'm just saying. It's bizarre that it started happening again today, after so long."

"It's because of the Creature," Ash said, stepping onto the sidewalk that ran by the front of *The Movie House*. "I think it... unlocked something in me... or woke it up. I've been seeing weird shit all day. Hell, I even *said* some of it to Spencer earlier, back when we split up - "

" - which was a totally dumb thing to do, by the way."

"*So* dumb. Fucking Spencer."

They stopped talking then. Ash's boots clocked on the sidewalk as they approached the movie theater entrance.

"Shit," said Ash, "I forgot about the blood."

Taryn grimaced, remembering how the man with bloody hands had smeared it over the glass while he screamed at them to let him inside.

"Whatever happened to that guy?" she said, walking tentatively towards the doors. They seemed to be stuck part of the way open.

"Beats me," said Ash. "Maybe he got away?"

"You mean you can't tell, Super-Buckley?"

"Shut up. Let's find them and get out've here fast."

"Yes," Taryn said. "Fast."

They went inside.

Olivia had entered the movie theater barely two minutes before Taryn and Ash. She'd glimpsed the Trench Coat Men go in ahead of her and hadn't slowed down.

The shotgun was heavy - her left arm was already beginning to tire from propping up the barrel by the time she passed between the last of the parking lot cars and arrived at *The Movie House* entrance. She knew it was going to kick hard into her shoulder when she fired it.

Fire at who, though? The question wafted through her conscience, cold and numbing, like stale air released from a coffin. *At those things? At Adam?*

My husband, *Adam?*

The glass doors were ajar, frozen in place by some earlier malfunction and, Olivia noticed, smeared with blood. She side-stepped between them into the movie theater lobby.

It was warmer inside - she imagined the boiler was still chugging away somewhere out back, unperturbed by the seismic events of the day - and the skin on her bare arms and neck tingled. On her right, computer monitors glowed on the other side of the ticket booth's plexiglass screen. An artificial Christmas tree lay toppled on the floor up ahead. The air was scented with burned popcorn.

Em's somewhere in here, Olivia thought, thumbing the safety off the shotgun.

But she didn't move right away. There was something else in the air, something more than a smell: a tangible just-missed-it sensation, like something had happened mere seconds ago and she'd caught the tail end of it.

A door banged shut. The sound came from the right, around the corner.

Olivia's feet carried her forward before her brain engaged. She passed the fallen Christmas tree, didn't notice the scattering of baubles on the floor or the translucent goop dripping from the lower branches. The right wing of the lobby was empty.

She faced the concession stand with its trough of slowly-smoldering popcorn, half-expecting Em to appear on the other side of the counter with a bag of Skittles in her hand and that imploring look on her face. *Pleeease, Mommy!* But there was no Em, and no Adam. Just the dull heartbeat pulse in her ears and the dead metal weight in her hands.

Movement to her left. She swiveled mechanically towards it and said, "Emma."

Nothing. Just the silent, empty left wing of the lobby.

"Shit, Olivia," she breathed.

Em could be anywhere in the building, couldn't she? The auditoriums, the bathrooms. She could've been here and left already. Walking off into the night, sneakers flashing in the dark.

Olivia shook the image away. No, she was here. She had to be.

She turned in a full circle, trying to decide which way to go. Again, she felt the weight of the gun in her hands. A hunk of cold, unliving metal.

Who're you planning to shoot, Olivia?

Then she saw the handgun. It was on the floor not far from a door by the concession stand, its grip smeared with blood.

It had to be Adam's.

Olivia's heart started pumping harder, faster. *He's definitely here*, she thought, scanning the lobby, looking for him now. *He can't be far away.*

But why'd he drop the gun?

Her eyes swept her surroundings again, taking in the ticket booths, the concession stand, the toppled tree and now the scattering of Christmas baubles. Several had been stepped-on, the others knocked every which way.

She traced them across the floor and found herself staring at the foot of the stairs.

He might be up there, hiding. He could have Em.

She took a step towards them, and someone screamed.

The strength drained from her arms and the shotgun almost slithered from her grasp. It'd come from the right wing of the lobby. A man's voice, muffled. Agonized.

Olivia started towards it automatically, passing the stairs. Sweat ran down from her temple and trickled into her split cheek. She didn't notice the stinging salt-pain anymore.

I've never heard Adam scream before, she realized. *I've never heard him in real pain.*

Maybe it wasn't him.

Then it happened again, louder and longer this time. It came from behind the doors of Screen Three.

Olivia reached for the handle.

"Did you hear that?" said Ash.

"Hear what?" Taryn said.

"A door, I think."

"I didn't hear it."

They passed the ticket booth. The coffee mug was still inside, no longer steaming.

"It was definitely a door," said Ash, staring wide-eyed around the lobby entrance. "I think."

They stopped a few feet from the fallen tree. Beyond it, the concession stand was as bright and empty as before. An image of Spencer Bloom bent over the counter, searching in vain for his wife, came back to Taryn with precipitous clarity. She could smell burnt popcorn.

"I actually can't believe we're back here," Ash said, gazing at the crushed baubles on the carpet lobby.

"Me neither," Taryn replied.

"It's still... creepy."

"I know, right?"

Ash's dark bangs swished across her forehead as she looked up and down the lobby. "What do we do now? Should we call them?" She drew in a breath.

"No!" Taryn cried, clapping a hand over Ash's mouth. There was a muffled "What the fuck?" against her palm and she took it away slowly. "Don't shout. They're here somewhere, but so's he, right? And those things might be here, too."

Ash touched her fingers gingerly to her lips, wincing. "Fine. But you didn't have to do that."

"I'm sorry."

"I bit through my lip earlier, you know."

"Did you get glass in your face?" Taryn pointed at the ragged gash in her cheek and Ash recoiled.

"Shit."

"Yeah."

"How'd that happen?"

"I'll tell you later." Taryn glanced down the lobby towards Screen Four, where just hours ago they'd watched a crappy Christmas horror movie and talked about teenager things. It seemed like a week had passed since then. The question spilled out of her before she could properly articulate it: "How did we dodge it?"

"Huh? Dodge what?"

"Yunno. The creature, or whatever it was. It sucked everyone down to the underground, everyone in the complex, right?"

"Right."

"So why not us?"

Ash frowned. "Maybe they just... forgot we were in there? It was just the three of us, and Spencer, and Mary. And look - " She pointed at the Screen Four sign above the double doors. " - it normally shows the movie title on the little screen, right? Ours wasn't on."

Taryn nodded. "You're right. It must've been broken."

"So they didn't check on us when they evacuated the building," Ash said. "They took everyone else outside..."

"... and the creature pulled them into the mall," finished Taryn. She shook her head. "Geez, that could have been us. What are the chances?"

"All thanks to a shitty movie," Ash said, "that Jeremy made us go see."

Taryn laughed humorlessly. *I hope it was all for a reason*, she thought, *and not just dumb luck*. She pointed down the lobby. "We should check the auditoriums, see if they're inside."

"No," said Ash.

Taryn heard the change in her voice and looked back. Ash's eyes were glazed and far-away again.

"You know where she is?" Taryn said.

"Yes."

"Em or Olivia?"

A pause. "Emma. She's... above."

Taryn looked up at the ceiling. Her eyes trailed along it until they found the stairs.

"Come on," she said, grabbing Ash by the hand.

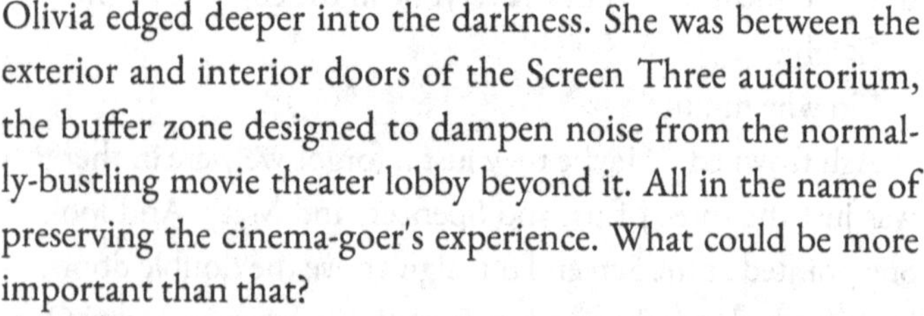

Olivia edged deeper into the darkness. She was between the exterior and interior doors of the Screen Three auditorium, the buffer zone designed to dampen noise from the normally-bustling movie theater lobby beyond it. All in the name of preserving the cinema-goer's experience. What could be more important than that?

The moment the exterior door closed, she heard Adam scream again.

Pain. Agony. The words bubbled up inside her, solidifying near the surface of her sanity. *Dying. Death screams.*

Her breath came in sharp, ragged bursts now, as though she'd just crossed the finish line of the hundred-meter sprint. She thought *I sound like a scared child*, and leaned her shoulder against the interior door. She cracked it an inch and paused, listening. Waiting.

Voices.

No. One voice, jittering and garbled. Close.

Olivia eased the door open and slipped inside the auditorium, the gun pinned to her body. She moved forward a few paces, keeping her head ducked below the divider on her right that separated the entrance area from the rows of seating. The door closed quietly behind her.

Whatever movie had been playing in Screen Three earlier in the day had finished long ago. The projector, however, was still on, and continued to beam a blank digital image onto the screen; Olivia could hear the machine whirring up in the projection booth above the last row of seats. *It's bound to overheat at some point*, she thought in a detached sort of way, creeping closer to the end of the divider. *Projectors still running in every auditorium, all overheating. This place will burn to the ground by morning.*

She noticed an empty trash bin up ahead (*empty because they were all still eating and drinking their concession snacks when it happened*), and then the voice came again, distorted and liquidy, and she froze. It was somewhere behind and above her, further back in the rows of seating. She had some idea what it was without having to see.

She looked up and the shadow fell across the screen, and her knees nearly buckled.

It was a man, right in the center. He rose from the bottom of the screen - unfurled, rather - as though he was a patron simply going to the bathroom or back to the concession stand for more popcorn. She used to hate that, when someone stood up during the movie and blocked the projection, their stupid silhouette shuffling to the end of the row, their whispered "Sorry, sorry!" drifting down the auditorium. A heavyset man had once stepped on her toe as he passed; it'd hurt like hell but she hadn't told Adam until he noticed her limping across the parking lot afterwards. He would only have done something at the time.

She knew it was his shadow on the screen now. She knew what she'd see when she turned the corner, and she didn't want to see it, but she had no choice. She was compelled to see it.

Three more steps brought her to the end of the divider. She brought the shotgun up, drew in another ragged breath, and came around the end.

First, she saw the rows of empty seats, and what had been left behind: half-empty boxes of popcorn and soft drink cups with straws still angled towards where their owners had been sitting; coats, jackets, scarves and hats draped over unused adjacent seats or bunched on the floor; cell phones and handbags had been abandoned as well, but there were fewer of them. Folks didn't like leaving their phones behind, even when they were rushing from a building that was potentially on fire or under attack.

Then she saw Adam.

He was almost exactly halfway up the auditorium, right in the middle of the row. Some might call it "the best seat in the house", the sweet spot where speaker sounds converge most effectively and movie-goers have the optimum view of the screen. They were always the first seats to go when tickets went on sale. And Adam was there now, standing tall with his head thrown back, the beam from the projector fanning incandescent light around him like an aura. Olivia stood there, staring and gaping, thinking *He looks like an angel* but not quite comprehending; for a few seconds, she simply couldn't reconcile the image - the way Adam's arms spasmed by his sides, the unnatural twist in his midsection - and she didn't see the man in the trench coat standing next to him.

When she did, she tried to scream, but managed only a whisper: "Adam."

The thing in the black coat heard her anyway. His head slowly turned in her direction, regarding her from the shadows beneath the brim of his hat. A dark, faceless wraith with one gloved hand clamped around her husband's throat.

For a never-ending moment, Olivia's world locked in place. The man in black (*the Trench Coat Men - is that what she'd heard Ash call them?*) didn't move. He stood perfectly still, facing her from further up the auditorium, trilby hat dipped low while Adam jerked sporadically in his grasp. There was no indication he was breathing, that he was really even there. And just before the dry, rasping voice whispered in her ear, Olivia realized something else, something that hadn't been apparent in the gloom of the underground parking lot: he cast no shadow. Adam's was the only one on the screen.

"Hello again, my dear."

As before, it spoke directly into her mind, though it may as well have been right by her left ear. She could practically feel its breath brush lightly over her earlobe and it was all she could do not to scream.

"How delightful to see you again."

Olivia tried to swallow, found her mouth had run dry. "Let him go."

The thing's head cocked almost imperceptibly to one side. Adam emitted a choked gurgle and Olivia tightened her grip on the shotgun.

"Will you help us, dear?" the Trench Coat Man said, ignoring her demand. *"Will you help us again?"*

"Get your fucking hands off him," Olivia said, fighting to keep her voice steady.

"Will you tell us where it is, dear?"

Olivia gritted her teeth. She could feel the thing's invisible tendrils caressing her brain, even from the other end of the auditorium. His head was still tilted to one side. He held Adam aloft with no visible effort.

"I don't know where it is." She forced the words. "And even if I did -"

The other one flew at her. All her focus had been on Adam and she hadn't seen it approaching along the front row. She screamed and squeezed the trigger.

The shotgun *boomed* and punched into her bicep; her right hand came off the grip and she almost dropped the gun entirely. The second Trench Coat Man jerked to one side, as though an invisible line had hooked him by the shoulder and yanked hard. He stopped, but he didn't go down. The acrid smell of gunpowder immediately filled the auditorium.

Olivia got the gun up again, jammed the butt into her shoulder. Her ears still rang painfully from the first shot. She raised the barrel.

The Trench Coat Man swung back towards her, his right arm smoking. Olivia aimed, exhaled and squeezed the trigger.

The second barrel erupted and the butt slammed into her shoulder, but she was ready for it now. She let the force of it knock her back against the divider, used it to stay standing. Her aim was true this time, hitting the second Trench Coat man square in the chest. He sailed backwards, fully airborne, and tumbled into the lower seating area. She saw his hat fly off but didn't glimpse his head. There was no blood.

The shotgun had knocked the wind out of her, but she was still on her feet. Panting through her teeth, she looked up the auditorium again and saw that the first Trench Coat Man hadn't moved. He was still watching her, dangling Adam an inch above the floor.

The voice came again, sharper this time: "*That was rude of you, dear.*"

"Put him down," Olivia said breathlessly. She took a purposeful step up the aisle; the spare shells in her pocket pressed against her hip and she stopped. *It's empty,* she thought, *and I won't have time to load it again.* "Put him down," she repeated.

Instead, the Trench Coat Man bent Adam's head back further. The tendons in his neck cracked. He tried to cry out but could only produce a weak moan.

"Stop!" Olivia said. She took another step. "Please!"

"*Tell me where it is, Olivia Price,*" the thing said.

"I don't fucking know!"

"*Are you lying, Olivia? That would be most unwise.*"

"Please, just let him go and - "

"Livia."

It was all Adam could manage. He was looking at her now, side-on. His sweat-soaked chestnut hair was flat against his scalp and the one eye she could see was almost fully red with bulging blood vessels, but he met her gaze and held it; below the Trench Coat Man's hand, her husband's wasted body had gone completely limp.

But he was Adam again, at the last.

"Liv," he said, straining it out. Olivia's heart dropped into her stomach. The auditorium melted away around her. The gloved hand around Adam's throat tightened further and something in his neck popped. His eye widened; Olivia saw a flash of turquoise within the red.

Adam Price grinned his easy grin and said, "Save Em", and the Trench Coat Man closed his hand into a fist. Olivia watched as her husband's neck crumpled like wrapping paper, the muscles and bones disintegrating, blood unloading in a red torrent from the bottom of his skull. The Trench Coat Man released his grip and Adam's body folded; his head rolled off the top of the bloodied glove, bounced once on the seat below, and hit the floor with a wet thud.

Olivia turned and ran.

TWENTY-NINE

"What was that?"

Taryn glanced back. "What?"

"I don't know," said Ash. "Might've been a gun."

Taryn didn't respond. They were almost at the top of the stairs.

"He had a gun, right?" Ash continued. "Her husband?"

"Yeah. Are you sure she's up here?"

"Who?"

"Em."

"The little girl?"

"Yes!"

They came to the top of the stairs. The second-floor auditoriums were directly ahead: Screens Seven, Eight and Nine. To the left of the stairs and facing the auditoriums was the Santa movie cardboard cutout. The sight of it sickened Taryn now.

"Alright," said Ash, "what now?"

"We check them," said Taryn.

But neither of them moved right away. They faced the double doors, side by side. *It's only been a few hours since we last checked these*, Taryn thought, squeezing the handle of the hammer. *We'd been looking for Spencer's wife then...*

"Which one?" she said.

"Huh?"

"Do you know which one she's in?"

"No. How would I know that?"

"You knew she was in the movie theater, and that she's somewhere up here. Use your... powers, or whatever."

"My powers? I'm not a motherfucking Jedi master."

"Well, then we check them, like I said." Taryn pointed at Screen Eight. "You take that one, and I'll take - "

"Whoa, whoa," said Ash, holding up her hands. "No fucking way. We are *not* splitting up again. Not now."

"You can't be serious," said Taryn, fixing her with a look. "After all this, you're *still* scared to go in there alone?"

"I'm not scared, I just don't want to get murdered. For all we know, there's some psycho with bleeding eyes and a chainsaw behind one of those doors."

"So what? I hit him with this?" Taryn held up the hammer.

"Better than nothing, Tar."

"Ash," Taryn sighed, exasperated, "we don't have time for this. Em could be - "

"Hi."

Ash screamed and propelled herself into Taryn's arms, almost knocking her over. With considerable effort, Taryn turned both of them around. She knew the voice.

"Em?" she exclaimed.

Emma Price sat in a chair by the second floor windows with her small hands folded in her lap, as though she'd been expecting them. Her sneakers dangled well above the floor.

"Hi," she said again, grinning.

"Taryn," said Ash, releasing her. "Look. On the table."

The gooey pink sphere Olivia's husband had been holding earlier was now perched on the table in front of Em. Thick, translucent mucus trailed down its fleshy body, pooling around its base. And it was quivering.

"Where did you get that?" Taryn said, zig-zagging between the other tables and chairs as she hurried across the room. Ash was right behind her.

"It's the bad humbug," said Em.

"The bad what?"

"Humbug."

"Where did you get it?" Taryn repeated, at Em's side now. The egg looked bigger than before. *How did she carry it up here by herself?* "Where, Em?"

The little girl blinked up at her. "I found it."

"Where?" Taryn said. She was getting frustrated and set the hammer down too hard on the table. "Did... did your dad give it to you?"

Em shook her head, her dark curls bobbing.

"I found it. I took it up here." She pointed. "It's doing stuff."

"No shit," muttered Ash, leaning over it. "It looks like it's about to blow."

"Don't do that," said Taryn, tugging Ash's sleeve. "Don't look at it from above. Something might pop out and grab your face."

"Ok, Ripley," said Ash, rolling her eyes. But she took a step back anyway.

Taryn crouched next to Em. "Do you know where your dad is?"

"No."

"Did you see him?"

"Yes."

"Did you see your mom?"

A crinkle appeared on Em's brow. "No. Just Daddy. He went away."

Taryn opened her mouth, changed her mind and closed it again. She stood and turned to Ash. "So what now?"

"Huh?" Ash had been staring glazedly at the egg.

"What do we do now? Do we just leave?"

"I... umm - "

"I want Mommy," said Em.

Suddenly, there were footsteps on the stairs. Pounding up the steps. *It's him!* Taryn thought. *He's coming back for it.*

"Shit," said Ash.

Taryn instinctively reached for Em's hand. "Em, we have to go. Right now."

"But I want Mommy."

"Em, please," Taryn insisted, trying to grab her hand. She squirmed away. "Em, come on!"

The footsteps grew louder, faster. Almost at the top.

"I want *Mommy*!" Em whined, kicking her feet. The lights on her sneakers flashing.

"Tar," Ash said dully.

"Em, we have to hide," Taryn cried desperately, snatching Em's hand, pulling her off the chair. "We have to hide."

"Mommy..."

"Em - "

"Mommy!"

Taryn heard the change in her voice. She released Em's hand and turned.

Olivia stood by the top of the stairs, panting hard. She stared at them with wild, tear-blurred eyes. She had a shotgun in her hands.

Her daughter's name came out in a disbelieving gasp: "Emma?"

"Mommy!"

Em slid off the chair, pushed past Taryn and ran towards her mother. Olivia staggered across the second-floor lobby, tears rolling freely down her face. She sent the gun clattering to one side, spread her arms and scooped Em into a frantic hug, burying her face in her hair.

"Oh my baby," she sobbed. "My baby."

Taryn and Ash watched as Olivia sank to her knees, weeping, smothering her daughter in kisses. Em giggled and let her do it.

Finally, Taryn thought, with an odd mixture of relief and sadness. She smiled, blinking through her own tears, and wondered aloud, "Where'd she get the gun?"

When there was no reply, she looked at Ash, and her heart skipped a beat.

Ash's eyes were still glazed and she was staring at the floor, arms by her sides. Her mouth worked, producing no words.

"Ash?" said Taryn. She reached for her shoulder. "Ash, what is it?"

"They know," Ash said in a voice that Taryn barely recognized. "They're coming."

Something rose and then dropped hard in Taryn's stomach. Cold sweat broke at the base of her neck, sending an ice shiver racing down her spine. Her fingers dug into Ash's shoulder.

"Ashley," she said.

Ash shuddered and closed her eyes. She swayed on the spot while Olivia spoke softly and hurriedly to Em, and for a moment, Taryn feared her best friend was going to pass out. Her hand slipped from Ash's shoulder to the small of her back, preparing to support her when she went down.

Then Ash opened her eyes again, blinked rapidly for five seconds, leveled her gaze at Taryn, and said, "We have to kill it."

"What?"

Ash pointed at the egg. Alarmed, Taryn saw it was now throbbing, causing the table to tremble.

"It's going to open," said Ash, "to hatch. When it does, it'll be like before. Like the first one that came down from the sky. It'll call all of us and we'll go to it, and it'll eat us: you, me, Olivia and Em. Jeremy and Linc, too, and anyone else who's still out there. We won't be able to stop it. And then it'll grow, like its parent did, and it'll lay more eggs, and it'll find more hosts to protect them and spread them around. And that'll be the end of everyone."

Taryn gawked at her. Ash hadn't paused to take a breath.

"It's going to hatch, Taryn," Ash said. "You have to use the hammer to kill whatever's inside before it has a chance to do what the first one did. Do you get it? Do you hear me?"

Taryn broke away from Ash's penetrating gaze and looked at the hammer shuddering across the surface of the table. The blood-stained hammer she'd almost been killed with herself.

"You said they're coming," she heard herself say. "Why don't we just give it to them? Let them take it and destroy it, like the first one? It's what they want, right?"

Olivia was approaching them now with Em in her arms. Taryn could see them out of the corner of her eye.

Ash shook her head. "No, we can't do that. We're... *supposed* to kill it. I think *they* have to consume all of it - the monster and its offspring - to stay here, in this world. It's how they stayed after the last one. It gives them power, and there's more power in *this* thing than the first one. So much more. It's what they're really after, what they've wanted all along. If we destroy it - if we kill it - they have to leave. For good."

Taryn looked at the egg, then back at Ash. "I hope you're right."

"So do I." Olivia was at their side now, wearied and haggard but fiercely holding onto her daughter nonetheless. She'd heard everything Ash had said. "And we better do it soon, because we'll never get far enough away to escape it now. Em, go sit over there."

She lowered her to the floor. Em looked pleadingly up at her; Olivia cupped her face in one hand. "Please, baby."

Em stared up at her a moment longer, then walked towards the corner of the seating area. As she climbed into another chair by the window, Olivia turned to Taryn. "Can you do this?"

I don't know.

"I... I think so."

"Do you want me to do it?" Olivia said.

Maybe.

"No," Taryn said. "No, I'll do it. Ash, can you hold it steady?"

Ash winced but nodded.

"Good," said Olivia, smoothing her hair back with both hands. "I'll hold them off as long as I can. They could be here any second." She turned and started towards the gun, lying discarded on the lobby carpet.

"Olivia," Taryn said softly, already knowing the answer to her question, "did you find him?"

Olivia paused. Without looking back, she said, "Yes." Then she went for the gun. Taryn watched her go, then swallowed down the firm lump in her throat and picked up the hammer. She and Ash stepped closer to the egg.

"Ugh," Ash muttered, "gross."

She placed both hands on the trembling pink sphere; her hands squelched into the mucus and she swore. For the first time, Taryn saw the dividing line in the egg's outer body, like a crack in a shell; more mucus glooped out of it and ran over Ash's hands, slopping onto the table.

"Oh hell, it's really hot now," said Ash. "This thing is *disgusting*."

"This was your idea!" Taryn said, leaning over the egg, just as she'd warned Ash not to do.

"Can we swap?" Ash said, grimacing.

"No," Taryn replied, raising the hammer.

"Hurry up, you two," Olivia called. Taryn glanced over her shoulder and saw her halfway between the seating area and the stairs; the shotgun was cracked and she was pulling a shell from her jeans pocket.

"Jeremy should be doing this," said Ash. "How'd that dweeb weasel his way out of - "

Suddenly, the egg stopped trembling and went still on the table. Taryn saw Ash loosen her grip; in the corner of the room, Em kicked her feet and gazed out the window.

"What's happening?" Olivia said, snapping the shotgun closed. Then: "Shit, they're coming up the stairs. Shit!"

"Ash," Taryn said softly. "Is it..."

"Stop there!" Olivia demanded, not to them. "Stop! I'll shoot!"

Then the egg cracked open. Taryn saw something inside, something round and purple and full of teeth. Ash screamed her name.

The shotgun unloaded with a *boom* and Taryn brought the hammer down.

***

It was Christmas Eve.

She was in her bedroom, back among the tacked-on movie posters and dog-eared books and rumpled clothes piled near, but not quite in, the laundry basket. She smelled cinnamon, and beyond the frosted window above her desk, she heard leafless tree branches rustle in the wind. The glow from her lamp threw familiar shadows over the walls.

Taryn swung her legs off her bed. She was in her pajamas, the ones she always wore - all faded polka-dots and little tears that were becoming holes - and her feet were bare. Her soles nestled into the thick carpet and she scrunched her toes, listening to the swaying tree branches, smelling the cinnamon from down the hall.

She brushed a loose strand of hair from her face and frowned. It *was* Christmas Eve, wasn't it? She couldn't quite remember much of the run-up to it, but the last days of school before the holidays were always like that, weren't they? Class parties, exchanging silly gifts with friends. Movies.

She stood. It was nighttime, her parents must be in the house somewhere. Neal would be here, too. He was probably waiting to ambush her in the hall, jumping out from the bathroom to scare her. Somehow, he always succeeded.

Her door was ajar; warm light spilled through the gap. She padded across to it and pulled it open, bracing herself for Neal. When he didn't appear, she went out to the hall. The doors to her parents' and Neal's room were also ajar, but there was only darkness within. A night-light glowed softly near the top of the stairs.

Taryn started down them and the smell of cinnamon grew stronger. It was the smell of Christmas, a nostalgia-inducing scent she loved, but something felt off about it right now. Something was different.

Her palm slid along the wooden handrail. Framed photos of her and Neal hung on the wall above it, along with a couple of her parents: there they were, all together on their last family vacation to Yellowstone, sun-burned but smiling; there was Neal on his tricycle, rosy-faced and laughing while their father chased after him among the Fall leaves in the Amber Hill woods; there she was in her Girl Scouts uniform, eight years old, freckled and happy. How often had she passed those photos without really looking at them? There just never seemed to be any time.

Her palm felt damp. She stopped, halfway down the stairs now, and looked at it. For a bizarre moment, her skin appeared to glisten red, like it was slick with blood. She blinked, and it was gone.

Just then, the sound reached her from the family room. A dry, crunching sound.

She cleared her throat. "Mom?"

The crunching went on.

"Dad? Neal, is that you?"

Still it went on, as though she hadn't spoken.

As she descended, she dipped her head to peer between the tinsel-wrapped staircase balusters. The family room was just off the ground floor hall through an open archway; her mother had draped more silver and gold tinsel above the opening, mostly for Neal's benefit. Taryn wasn't a fan of it, and right now, it was stopping her from getting a clear view of the family room, and the source of the crunching. She saw the back of the couch and the Christmas tree in the corner, but that was it.

Crunch, crunch, crunch.

The carpeted stairs ended and her feet set down on the cool wood of the hall floor. It creaked beneath her weight, as it always did, under even the lightest foot. Ahead was the front door - the narrow panes of glass on either side of it were even frostier than her bedroom window - and the rack, where their heavy winter coats hung drying in the warmth of the hall. She'd helped Neal build a snowman in the front yard that afternoon; their hands felt like blocks of ice afterwards, and the roaring after-dinner fire was very welcome indeed. Taryn had curled up on the end of the couch with a steaming mug of hot chocolate and half-watched *Elf* while messaging Ash and Jeremy, but she knew all the best lines anyway and recited them before her parents did, every time. Neal had been worried the fire might deter Santa from coming down the chimney that night, but they'd all assured him it'd be fine. Santa had come through worse, they'd said.

All of these thoughts, these *memories*, came to her as if they - or she - were emerging from a fog. They materialized too slowly; she had to strain to see them, to make them clear and real.

I just woke up, she thought, and the words echoed. *My brain isn't working properly yet*.

Then she found herself in the family room, standing behind the couch, and she didn't quite remember walking to that spot. The door to the dining room and kitchen were on her right, and the fireplace was directly ahead of her, and now she saw where the crunching sound was coming from, and when she said "Oh", it came out far, far too loud.

The crunching stopped. Taryn's palm was damp again, and her left cheek was throbbing.

She wasn't aware the couch had vanished until the hulking man in the red costume turned and she realized there was nothing between them. She could hear her pulse, louder and slower than she'd like it to be; suddenly, she was small and weedy, Taryn "Tar-Tar Sauce" Meyer, alone in her house with Father Christmas.

His eyes were on her now, two blazing purple lights beneath the white fur trim of his hat, and if he had skin, she couldn't see it. His beard was a wild tangle running as far down as his crotch, matted in places with globules of dried blood and ragged chunks of flesh. There was more blood around where his mouth must be, and Taryn could see his cheeks working, chewing on something. The crunching started again. As he straightened up and turned his jiggling bulk towards her, she saw a tumbler of milk in his left hand, stained red on one side by blood-soaked lips.

She didn't want to look. She tried to hold his gaze, to lock on to the bulging purple orbs quivering in his eye sockets, but she couldn't stop herself. She thought she knew what she might see, but she looked anyway.

There was no plate of cookies on the hearth. Four Christmas stockings hung from the mantel, each embroidered in gold thread with the names of the Meyer family, each one stuffed with chocolates and fruit and silly little gifts no-one really wanted; on top of the mantel, festive figurines had been carefully arranged around the clock, which ticked and tocked blindly, and showed no time at all. There were warm embers in the fireplace and leftover logs in the basket next to it. But there was no plate on the hearth.

Taryn looked until her eyes hurt. She knew the bloody-splattered, dismembered mess on the hearth was Jeremy only by his glasses, which still hung askew from what was left of his face. His mouth gaped in shock and his eyes stared back at her without seeing. Little remained of his torso other than one twisted arm and the ripped fabric of his sweater - the rest had been torn apart and hastily eaten, including everything that should have been inside him. Taryn could see one of his ribs jutting from the fleshy red mass and understood what the crunching sounds had been: Jeremy's bones. It'd even eaten his bones.

Her knees threatened to buckle. The thing dressed as Santa drew itself up to its full height and swallowed another piece of Jeremy Lewis. It gulped it down and belched, and the smell was like cinnamon.

Suddenly, there were more people around them. Dozens, hundreds, impossibly packed into the small family room of the Meyer house. All watching her.

She felt a weight in her hand and looked down. She was holding an ax.

When she looked up again, the Santa-thing's head was tipped back and it was draining the tumbler, slurping noisily from the glass. Milk spilled down its chin and trickled through its beard, making the dried blood run pink; it lowered its head again and smacked its lips, displaying the empty tumbler like a trophy, and suddenly it wasn't just some featureless monster anymore. There was another face in there, muddled in amongst the scraggly artificial hair and pulsing purple eyes, a face Taryn knew, if not well.

It was Spencer Bloom.

She gasped and he grinned, bearing sharply pointed teeth through the beard. In a voice that barely resembled Spencer's, he said, "*Have you seen my darling wife?*"

Taryn took a step back and Spencer began to chuckle, a low, guttural sound, animal-like and brimming with menace. "*Have you seen my Mary?*"

She took another step back and felt them close behind her, the people in the room, the great crowd of watchers.

And she knew who they were: the men, the women, the children. All faceless but staring, silent but whispering her name anyway. Packed shoulder to shoulder into the family room of her house, waiting for what was inevitably going to happen. She looked back at them, meeting their eyeless gaze, the people from the movie theater and the mall, the people the Creature (*the Bad Humbug*) had consumed in the underground parking lot, one by one. She remembered it all - the empty, cavernous building, the child dressed like an elf, the woman with the hammer. It was all real, and what was happening now... wasn't. She was in a dream, and if she didn't break free of it, something terrible was going to happen.

"*Taryn.*"

She looked, and Spencer was gone.

Ash stared back at her, arms by her sides, dark bangs framing her face. She appeared young and small in the soft glow from the Christmas tree in the corner. Her irises were purple.

"*You'd never hurt me, Tar,*" she said. "*You know I'd never hurt you.*"

Taryn felt the fog creeping under her skull again. She fought it, struggling to get the words out: "You're not really here."

"*I know you'd never hurt me, Taryn.*" Ash smiled, tilting her head to one side. "*You couldn't hurt me if you wanted to.*"

Taryn felt the weight of the ax again. She looked down at it and understood.

"*Hi.*"

She squeezed her eyes shut. *No, not her. Please.*

"*I want my Mommy.*"

Taryn sighed and opened her eyes again. Em stood in Ash's place, dressed in her purple coat, clutching her dinosaur backpack by the strap. She shuffled forward a step and her sneakers flashed. The people in the room inched closer.

"*I want Mommy,*" she whined. "*Take me to Mommy.*"

"I can't do this," Taryn whispered. "Please don't make me."

The thing wearing Em's face held out its arms pleadingly. It took another step forward. Taryn felt the room grow hot. There was no air.

"*I want Mommy,*" Em said again, louder now.

"No," Taryn moaned, shifting the ax in her hands. "No, no, Em - "

"*Mommy*," said Em, reaching for her, grasping at her. There was almost no space between them now. Somewhere, Taryn heard high, faint laughter. She gripped the ax handle hard.

"I can't," she said, salt tears stinging her eyes. "Please don't make me."

Em moved to grab hold of her. Taryn looked down, met her gaze, saw the purple in her eyes. Saw it burn. The laughter swelled.

Spencer, Jeremy, Ash. All of them.

"*MOMMY!*" Em shrieked. Her mouth was full of fangs.

With a yell, Taryn heaved the ax downwards. Em's scream pierced the room as the blade connected with her scalp and drove through it. The people around them dissolved and Taryn felt her body catapult backwards, away from Em and the fireplace and the family room. Back, back, into the darkness.

The laughter became a howl of agony, and abruptly stopped.

"Taryn! Taryn! *Stop!*"

Ash was there, grabbing her arm with both hands. Digging her fingers into her skin, shaking her.

"It's over," she said, "it's done. Stop."

Taryn's breaths were sharp and labored, and her vision swam. She squeezed her eyes shut and hot tears rolled down her face, stinging the cut in her cheek. They were the same tears she'd shed in the dream. She opened her eyes again and looked at what she'd done.

The egg was gone. In its place was a sludgy mess of crushed flesh and gore, spread over the table; parts of the shell still remained intact, but whatever had been inside it had been beaten to a pulp. Splatterings of purple blood and pinkish muscle membrane dripped from the hammer still clutched in Taryn's trembling hand. She dropped it onto the cracked and splintered table with a *clunk* she barely heard.

It's gone, she thought, still breathing hard.

Ash released her arm. Taryn looked at her, saw she was staring behind them, and turned.

The Trench Coat Men were there. All three of them, just a few yards away. Tables and chairs were upending to their left and right where they'd plowed through the seating area - there were no more between them. Olivia was crouched in the corner with her arms around Em, her eyes wild with fury and fear; Em saw Taryn looking and waved. The shotgun had been returned to the lobby floor, its barrels still smoking.

"That was most unwise."

The voice floated venomously into her mind. She knew Ash and Olivia heard it, too.

"It doesn't matter," Taryn said, fighting to keep her voice steady, to stay on her feet when her legs wanted so badly to fold. "It's gone now. It's over."

"It is never over."

The one in the middle took a step forward. Taryn and Ash drew back, bumping into the flesh-strewn table. *Don't run*, Taryn thought, and she wasn't entirely sure her own internal voice had spoken it.

"It is," she croaked, staring up at the shadow beneath the hat. "It is for now."

A long moment passed. No-one moved, no-one spoke. Taryn heard a high-pitched ringing sound in her right ear; it became louder and more distinct as the air grew thicker. She desperately wanted to sit, to collapse to the floor. She wanted it to be over.

Finally, the voice came again: *"For now."*

The Trench Coat Man turned silently on his heel and walked away. The other two fell into line on either side of him; they drifted across the lobby, shoulder to shoulder, stepping over the discarded shotgun as they went. At the top of the stairs, they filed into a line and descended, disappearing from view.

"Fuck me," Ash breathed. "That was too close."

Next to her, Taryn melted to the floor.

THIRTY

They returned to the ground floor lobby. Em led the way, holding tight to her mother's hand. Olivia let her set the pace; she was content to go slow. Taryn's legs were still weak and she went down the stairs with one arm slung across Ash's shoulders.

The men in black coats were gone when they reached the bottom. The Christmas tree was still on its side and the lobby was completely silent. Olivia paused here, glanced at the doors to Screen Three, then started towards the exit. They followed her without speaking. None of them wanted to be inside the movie theater anymore.

Outside, a brisk chill wind nipped at the exposed skin of their faces and hands. Taryn was glad of it after being in the oppressive, airless lobby. The dream - or vision, or whatever it'd been - was still fresh in her mind. She could still see Spencer, purple-eyed and chewing on Jeremy's internal organs.

"There's Jeremy," said Ash.

Taryn looked towards the mall. She could see Jeremy and Lincoln ambling their way; Linc had an arm slung over Jeremy's shoulders and was leaning unsteadily on his one remaining crutch, ducking his face away from the glare of the complex streetlights. Jeremy raised a hand and waved at them. Taryn waved back.

"Those dorks missed everything," Ash said. "They'll never believe us."

"They might," Taryn said.

"Mommy, look," said Em, pointing. "Look at the lights."

They all followed her little finger to the parking lot, where rows of glinting cars had been buried in snow less than an hour ago, and suddenly Taryn understood why Lincoln was turning his face away.

The bright glare wasn't coming from the complex streetlights.

The Trench Coat Men stood right in the center of the parking lot. They were in a circle, facing inwards, no more than a foot apart. The hems of their coats moved in the breeze, but other than that, they stood completely still.

"What is *that*?" said Ash.

Directly above where the trio stood in the parking lot, a harsh white light had appeared in the air; it was perhaps one hundred feet above them, pulsing brighter by the second, catching on the aluminum of the cars parked below. The light knifed into Taryn's eyes and she had to shield them with her arm. She imagined she could hear a faint but steadily-strengthening drone in the air.

Jeremy and Lincoln approached the movie theater entrance like one ungainly, blood-splattered creature. They too were staring towards the parking lot, wide-eyed in the spectacular, otherworldly glow.

The Trench Coat Men tilted their heads back and gazed up at the light, arms by their sides, their faces still somehow dark and indistinct beneath their trilby hats. The light continued to grow brighter, blazing now, filling the *Outlet Complex* with pure white luminescence, and the droning sound grew with it, rising in pitch. Taryn turned her face away and saw Em still pointing up at the light, babbling excitedly; Olivia was crouched beside her now, arms around her, smiling in agreement. Her eyes sparkled with tears.

Ash said something Taryn didn't pick up right away. She looked at her: "What?"

"Do you see them?" Ash said, raising her voice over the sound of the thing in the air. Taryn caught the weird thrill in her tone. She leaned closer. "See what?"

Ash pointed. "Taryn, look. Look!"

She looked, and she saw.

There were people in the parking lot now.

They filtered between the vehicles, dozens of them, hundreds maybe. They were shadows, barely human in form, drifting around where the Trench Coat Men still stood gazing up at the light in the sky. Spectres in a cemetery of glistening metal and sodden asphalt.

But as they watched from the movie theater entrance, the figures began to solidify: Taryn could see limbs, and heads, and even suggestions of clothing; some of them were tall, some short, and after a moment she realized the latter were children, running and skipping and jumping between the cars in the lot. She began to discern colors as their clothing became more distinct - sweaters and jeans and coats, skirts and dresses, sneakers and boots. They were the people from her dream, those who'd gathered in her family room, the silent, hopeful watchers.

They were the people from the mall.

"Ho-lee shit," Ash breathed.

They heard voices now, slowly rising as one in the still December air, a chorus of soft murmurings and whispers. The people in the lot were calling to each other. They floated between the cars with outstretched arms, coming together in grateful huddles, gathering their loved ones. Some were weeping inaudibly; others smiled - beamed - as they gently locked arms and embraced one another and said things those beyond the lot couldn't quite pick up, all the while steering clear of the three mysterious men in black coats beneath the light. The complex, which had been dead and silent mere minutes ago, now echoed with hushed, expectant voices.

Jeremy, who stood beside them now, croaked, "What the hell?"

"How?" Taryn said, echoing his tone, gazing in wonder as a man near the edge of the parking lot swept a grinning boy into his arms. "How... are they here?"

"They came back," said Ash, matching her tone. "When you destroyed it, you brought them back. All of them."

"Not all of them," Olivia said. They looked at her - she was staring straight ahead, but they could see the tears in her bloodshot eyes, and they understood. Taryn put a hand on her shoulder and said nothing more. Em had fallen silent, too.

"But even these aren't *really* back, are they?" Ash said.

"What d'you mean?" said Jeremy. Next to him, Lincoln muttered something incomprehensible.

Ash's voice was far-off again. "They're here," she said, "but they're not here. It's them, the people from the mall. But it also isn't."

"I don't understand," Jeremy said slowly.

I do, Taryn thought, watching the men and women and children move around the lot, drifting between the cars, gathering around the Trench Coat Men; there were voices on the night air, beginning to blend together into a steadily-fading chorus, but there were no footfalls on the asphalt, no ripples in the silver puddles left behind by the snow. Taryn knew, if the snow had still been there, that there'd be no footprints in it this time.

They're here. But they're not here.

Then the droning sound leapt upwards in pitch and the light flared brighter than ever, engulfing everything in its colorless glow. In the center of the parking lot, the Trench Coat Men stretched their hands towards the great invisible thing in the sky above them; their hats and coats flew off, and they melted upwards into the light, and vanished into it. The people from the mall went with them, rising as one ghostly mass, still embracing one another, their collective chorus lilting softly on the breeze, melodious, unafraid.

The light bloomed once, sunbright.

And just as suddenly as it had appeared, it was gone. Taryn caught a momentary glimpse of something rocketing upwards, then her vision became a kaleidoscope of popping colors and she had to squeeze her eyes shut.

When she opened them again, the parking lot was empty. They could all hear sirens in the distance.

No-one spoke.

After a moment, Olivia straightened up shakily. Em took her hand in both of hers.

"Mommy, can we go now?" the little girl said, gazing up at her.

Olivia smoothed her curls. "Yes, baby. We can go."

She glanced towards Jeremy and Lincoln, and then at Taryn and Ash. Her eyes were pools of moonlight.

"I think we can all go home now."

Far above, the December night was full of stars. One of them flickered, cut across the sky, and was gone.

Epilogue

Taryn reached for the bowl of popcorn and Ash slapped her hand away.

"Hey! Get your own, Meyer."

"It's my popcorn," Taryn replied. "You're in *my* house."

"Squatters rights."

Taryn grabbed a handful from the bowl, spilling some on Ash's sweater. The other girl swore profusely, batting her hand again.

"Will you two shut up?" Jeremy snapped.

"Calm down, Jer," said Taryn.

He was sitting between them on the floor with his back against the couch. Ash flicked a popcorn flake at his head and it caught in his ear. He didn't notice, and Taryn sniggered behind her hand.

"Shut *up*," Jeremy repeated.

"You're getting cranky in your old age, Lewis," Ash said. "You're not as fun as you used to be. I remember when you were *fun*."

"I haven't been fun in a long time."

"Maybe not. But you were less cranky, at least."

"I just want to hear the-"

"It's just another *Insidious*," Ash said, gesturing towards the TV. Her lime-colored fingernails glinted in the glow from the corner lamp. "We all know what's going to happen. They're all the same."

"We don't *all* know what's going to happen," Jeremy replied, still staring fixedly at the screen. "Some of us don't have superpowers."

Ash made a face behind him. "I don't have superpowers."

"Well," Taryn ventured. "You kinda do, Ash-tastic."

"Super Bucks," Jeremy said.

"Buck Rogers."

"The All-Seeing Ash Buck- OWW!"

Jeremy bent forward, clutching the back of his head where Ash's palm had connected cleanly. Taryn burst out laughing.

"Even without superpowers, you shouldn't seen that coming," Ash said.

She caught Taryn's eye, briefly tried to suppress her own laughter, then joined in. Jeremy, who was still rubbing the back of his head, couldn't help but do the same.

For a few moments, all three of them laughed, louder by the second, shoving each other and spilling popcorn over the couch and carpet. If they'd been upstairs in the family room, Taryn's mother would've been shushing them by now, or Neal would've tattled on the mess they were making. Down here in the basement, though, it really didn't matter. It was just good to be together, doing something normal.

And it was good to laugh again.

Finally, their throats grew tired and the laughter petered out. They went back to watching the movie without speaking. Taryn

took the popcorn bowl from Ash's lap and the other girl immediately turned to her phone.

Standard Ash, Taryn thought, grinning.

As the movie wore on, her mind drifted back to *The Movie House*, where they'd emerged from the auditorium with no phone signal. Ash had been pissed then, almost panicking at the thought of missing some meaningless post or video on social media, as if it would've been the end of the world. It'd seemed so important then. It'd started to feel important again, after all this time.

Maybe we're finally becoming normal.

Three months had passed since the incident at the *Outlet Complex*. The "incident" was how everyone referred to it now - all of the other words and phrases were too harsh, too visceral. Massacre. Bloodbath. Abduction. The news headlines finally settled on "incident", and that seemed to be enough.

No-one had ever been able to explain what happened that day. Almost no-one has survived it, beyond the three of them, the remaining Prices, Lincoln Ward, and one fortunate stranger who'd fallen asleep in Screen One and missed the whole damn thing. The guy had wandered out into the lobby, bleary-eyed and confused, just as a dozen police officers in tactical gear flooded the building and screamed at him to hit the dirt, assuming he was one of the terrorists who must've been holding the movie-goers hostage. The poor fellow had dropped to his knees with a cry of surprise and squelched right down on top of Adam Price's detached lower lip.

They'd taken Taryn, Jeremy and Ash in, of course. Olivia, Em and Lincoln, too. There'd been no-one else in the parking lot *to* take. Everyone - the people they'd seen gathered beneath the light with the men in trench coats - were long gone by the time the single police cruiser trundled down the slip road.

Apparently, another driver had arrived at the complex shortly after the snow stopped, noticed the slashed tires on the Price family car and the completely motionless parking lot, and rightly suspected foul play. He called 9-1-1 (the dispatcher actually logged it this time), and two officers were sent to investigate; they found the survivors sitting on the sidewalk outside the theater, didn't quite register what they were saying but observed the still-drying blood on their clothes and the gunshot wound ("just grazed him", Ash had claimed) near Lincoln's temple, and radioed for all available backup.

What followed had been nothing short of a circus. Emergency responders descended on the complex and began scouring every inch of the place for more survivors, or hostage-takers, or bodies. They found very little of anything, aside from a handful of stomach-turning remains and the bodies of Spencer Bloom and Adam Price. All traces of the Creature and its spawn had vanished, while the Santa, the Mrs Claus and the elf had all disintegrated into piles of indeterminate rotting gore and bloodied clothing. Any security footage from the cameras in the mall, movie theater or gas station had been scrambled or lost. It was practically impossible for any investigator to come up with a satisfying explanation for what had happened.

They'd tried, naturally. For weeks, the survivors had been questioned, over and over, individually and collectively, by multiple agencies. Those who knew what had *actually* occurred stuck rigidly to the story they'd hurriedly agreed on just before the first cops arrived on the scene: some projectile seemed to have crashed through the ceiling of the mall, and everyone who'd been in the complex at the time had left ("don't say they were *taken*", Olivia had warned); the five from the movie theater had gone to the mall for help, found it abandoned, and had then been attacked by three psychopaths in festive costumes.

One of them had murdered Spencer. Then the Price family had stumbled unwittingly into the midst of it and Adam had been tragically killed as well.

Honestly, it wasn't far off the truth. And fortunately, Em seemed to have forgotten the majority of what happened, beyond getting the cat toy and *not* getting Skittles, so her account held very little weight. Olivia had been relieved at that. She promised to buy her all the candy she could ever want in future.

They hadn't seen Olivia or Em since the initial round of questioning, back in January. As far as they knew, they were alright. There'd be court hearings at some stage, and they'd likely see them then. In the meantime, Taryn just hoped they'd cope with Adam's passing. Olivia later told them she'd considered him lost the moment they separated on the mall concourse. Everything that happened afterwards simply hadn't involved her husband. *That* version of Adam had been something else entirely.

And that was that.

Months of police investigations, trauma therapy, candlelit vigils and rabid national coverage hadn't really changed the facts of the matter: just shy of nine hundred people had been in the *Outlet Complex* three days before Christmas, and almost none of them had come home. A few were dead. The rest were simply gone.

Taryn didn't know where they were now. But she did know they'd never return.

The Creature had eaten them, and the Trench Coat Men had taken whatever part of them was left.

The news cycle moved on after a few weeks.

"Is something in my hair?"

Jeremy brushed the top of his head, skimming the popcorn flake. Ash glanced over at Taryn and smirked.

"No," she said. "You're imagining it."

Taryn grinned back at Ash, watching her for a moment.

She hadn't been the same since that day back in December. None of them had, of course. But something in Ash had changed the most. A part of her had been lost, replaced with something else Taryn couldn't quite put her finger on. There was some indefinable quality to her now. Some deep, lasting, irrevocable alteration. Something that-

"What the fuck are you staring at?" Ash said.

"Nothing."

Ash blinked back at her, her brow furrowing beneath her bangs. They were electric blue now. She'd changed her hair every month since Christmas.

"Don't be weird, Tar-Tar Binks."

"I'm not."

"You're both talking again," said Jeremy. The popcorn was still in his hair.

"We're *trying* to have a conversation, Jeremy," Ash replied, with mock indignation. "Maybe *you're* interrupting *us*, did you ever think about that?"

"No."

They'd told Jeremy about Ash's abilities a few days after Christmas. He hadn't fully believed - or understood - them, at first. How could anyone understand it, really, when Ash couldn't wrap her head around it herself? And she'd had most of her life to try.

But Jeremy was smart. Logical in the extreme. Taryn and Ash had watched as the cogs turned in his head, and the frown deepened on his face, until they could see he'd gotten it. Like them, he didn't understand how (or why) Ash could do what she did. But after considering everything they'd been through, and *how* they'd ultimately managed to survive at the time, he was able to accept it, and that was the main thing. When he took off his glasses and started cleaning them on his sleeve, they knew he was in.

The secret, shared for so long by two, had a third keeper.

And now, here they were. Months later, back in the Meyer family basement, with the door locked so Neal couldn't barge in halfway through their movie.

Safe.

Alive.

But not forever.

The words came floating to the forefront of Taryn's mind like a dead leaf on a river current. It wasn't the first time it'd happened. She knew they weren't *her* words.

She looked to her right. Ash was staring straight ahead, just above her phone screen but not quite at the TV. Her eyes had taken on that familiar glazed quality, the one Taryn - and now Jeremy - had come to recognize easily.

We're not safe forever.

Taryn's eyes dropped to the couch. Her lips didn't move. *Why not?*

Ash's thumb swiped mechanically on her phone screen. *Because. They're still out there. The men in the long coats.*

They'll be back?

Not sure. Maybe. Swipe, swipe, swipe. *Yes. I think so. Unfinished business.*

It's ok. We'll be ready next time.

You think so?

"Yes," Taryn said.

"What?" said Jeremy

She glanced at Ash again. The other girl didn't meet her gaze, but a small smile tugged at the corner of her mouth.

"Nothing. Just thinking out loud."

The movie shifted to black for a moment, and they saw themselves on the screen. Behind the couch, the rest of the basement was empty.

Beyond the narrow window near the ceiling, the early evening sky was a deep navy, and the waxing moon had begun to appear.

whoarethetrenchcoatmen.com

Acknowledgements

Humbug was born from a real life situation: my wife and I emerged from a movie theater auditorium (where we'd been the only viewers) to find the rest of the building seemingly abandoned. It was right in the middle of the pandemic and life was often a little strange, but that moment really stuck with me.

I remember saying to Christine at the time, "This feels like we're in a horror movie."

As always, my first and foremost thanks go to Christine (not just because she agreed that, why yes, this *does* feel like we're in a horror movie scenario), but because, as always, she was the first person to read this story, and gasped in shock at all the right moments.

I'd also like to thank the folks at MIBLART for taking my cover idea on board and running with it, and for their endless patience during revisions.

Finally, I'd like to thank you, dear reader, for spending a little quality time in my festive funhouse of horror. Your ongoing support and encouragement are always much appreciated, and I hope you stick with me for future stories.

David writes from his home in Northern Ireland, where he lives with his beautiful wife Christine and their two dogs, Lupin and Ghost. He loves books, movies, football (he's better at watching than playing), and getting his hiking boots dirty.

Lou Jennings, a high school English teacher in the quaint Illinois town of Amber Hill, is struck down with the flu shortly before Thanksgiving. She spends the next few days in bed, cared for by her attentive husband Derek and their two kids, Ben and Ruth.

Upon returning to school, Lou finds a substitute teacher called Evelyn Sparrow holding the fort - as all good substitutes should do - except now, no-one remembers who Lou is. The students, the teachers, everyone in school. As far as they're concerned, Miss Sparrow has always been the English teacher at Amber Hill High, and they've always adored her.

In the days that follow, the once-stable fabric of Lou's life begins to unravel right before her eyes. Friends forget her, family no longer recognise her. Piece by piece, Evelyn takes everything, stripping Lou of all she once held dear, driving her to the brink of madness.

But Lou isn't alone. One student at Amber Hill High - Jason Rennor - notices something about Miss Sparrow, something that's not as it should be. He starts to suspect she may not even be human. Then another student goes missing, and Jason knows for sure - Miss Sparrow is evil, and it isn't long before he finds himself in her crosshairs, fighting for his very survival.

Maurice Baxter knows exactly what Evelyn is. She's left a devastating mark on his life and he's spent months tracking her all the way to Amber Hill, fuelled by grief and vengeance, guided by his dreams. Those dreams bring him to Jason, and then to Lou. Together, they concoct a last-ditch plan to rid the world of Evelyn Sparrow and restore Lou's life before it's lost forever, or the Substitute finds them first.

Grab your copy of *The Substitute* today.

www.ingramcontent.com/pod-product-compliance
Lightning Source LLC
Chambersburg PA
CBHW010254100726
47904CB00011B/2589